The dragon's eyes caught the firelight, drank it up until it spread into a pale yellow glow. Ariel's voice came from a long way off. "It's the campfire. Dragons use their fire breathing as a mating call." She paused. "It thinks the campfire is another dragon. . . ."

I grabbed the crossbow from Ariel's pack. "Just in case," I said.

"You'll probably just make it mad," Ariel said. "I think it's wondering what happened to the dragon it thought was here. With any luck, it will forget about it and go away."

"If it came here to get laid," said Shaughnessy, "it won't forget about it that easily."

"I wouldn't know."

Shaughnessy gave Ariel a sidelong look, one eyebrow raised. "How do unicorns mate, I wonder?"

Ariel looked away from the circling dragon. "None of your goddamned business."

"Steven Boyett is a new writer and one to watch. Ariel *is a grand entree into print for a man whom I hope is already hard at work on another book, because I want to read that one too—and the next."*

—Roger Zelazny

"Anyone that can breathe new life into unicorns, manticores and dragons, couple them with martial arts and post-holocaust scenarios, and handle the whole witch's brew with so much grace and wit, is an alchemist himself. I had more fun reading Ariel *than I've had with any other first novel in living memory."*

—Janet Morris

Other titles available from
Ace Science Fictions & Fantasy:

A Lost Tale, *Dale Estey*
Murder and Magic, *Randall Garrett*
Tomoe Gozen, *Jessica Amanda Salmonson*
The Warlock in Spite of Himself, *Christopher Stasheff*
Elsewhere, *Terri Windling & Mark Alan Arnold, editors*
The Devil in the Forest, *Gene Wolfe*
Time of the Fourth Horseman, *Chelsea Quinn Yarbro*
Changeling, *Roger Zelazny*
Unicorns!, *Jack Dann & George Zebrowski, editors*
Bard, *Keith Taylor*
Daughter of Witches, *Patricia Wrede*
Harpy's Flight, *Megan Lindholm*
Jhereg, *Steven Brust*
The King in Yellow, *Robert W. Chambers*
King's Blood Four, *Sheri S. Tepper*
Koren, *Tim Lukeman*
Pavane, *Keith Roberts*
Sorcerer's Legacy, *Janny Wurts*
Annals of Klepsis, *R.A. Lafferty*
Citizen Vampire, *Les Daniels*
An Unkindness of Ravens, *Dee Morrison Meaney*
Songs From the Drowned Lands, *Eileen Kernaghan*

ARIEL

A Book of the Change

STEVEN R. BOYETT

ACE FANTASY BOOKS
NEW YORK

ARIEL: A BOOK OF THE CHANGE

An Ace Fantasy Book/published by arrangement with
the author

PRINTING HISTORY
Ace Original/December 1983

ACKNOWLEDGMENTS

The epigraph is from *For Lancelot Andrews; essays on style and order*, by T. S. Eliot, © 1928. Published by Faber and Faber Ltd. Permission to reprint granted by the publisher.

The poem on p. 32 is from SELF RELIANCE, by Duane Locke, from the anthology *A White Voice Rides a Horse*, © 1980 by Duane Locke. Published by the University of Tampa Press. Permission to reprint granted by the author, Duane Locke.

The quote on p. 40 is from *Broca's Brain*, by Carl Sagan, © 1974, 1975, 1976, 1977, 1978, 1979 by Carl Sagan. Published by Random House, Inc. Permission to reprint granted by the publisher.

The quote on p. 79 is from *Time Enough for Love*, by Robert A. Heinlein, © 1973. Published by G. P. Putnam's Sons. Permission to reprint granted by the publisher.

The quote on p. 93 is from *The Dragons of Eden*, by Carl Sagan, © 1977. Published by Ballantine Books. Permission to reprint granted by the publisher.

The quote on p. 256 is from an article by Paul J. Nahin entitled "For Your Eyes Only," which appeared in OMNI (December, 1980). © 1980 by OMNI Publications, Ltd. Permission to reprint granted by the author, Paul J. Nahin.

The quote on p. 322 is from *The Last Unicorn*, by Peter S. Beagle, © 1963. Published by the Viking Press. Permission to reprint granted by the publisher.

ISBN: 0-441-02920-5

Ace Fantasy Books are published by The Berkley Publishing Group,
200 Madison Avenue, New York, New York 10016.

PRINTED IN THE UNITED STATES OF AMERICA

To Lisa,
who helps me see things
as they are

Grateful acknowledgment is made to those people and organizations who helped out immensely in the technical speculations involved in the writing of this novel. Some of them were pestered into the wee hours of the night; others weren't aware of what they were getting into. Thanks to: Myron Tisdel and Phil Lindsey, Kerry Hudson, the team of Mullin & Delaney, Bob Marlin, Andy Solomon, the United States Hang Gliding Association, and the Society for Creative Anachronism.

A special thank you goes to Dr. David R. Colburn, who made things so much easier, and to Rose Hillardt.

. . . we fight rather to keep something alive than in the expectation that anything will triumph.

—T. S. ELIOT

one

What is your substance, whereof are you made
That millions of strange shadows on you tend?
Since every one, hath every one, one shade
And you but one, can every shadow lend. . . .

—Shakespeare,
"Sonnet LIII"

I was bathing in a lake when I saw the unicorn.

The water was cool and clear; the pollution had vanished years ago. I'm young, but I can remember the times before the Change when the filthy water would catch fire by itself. Now, though, I could leave my clothes next to my blowgun on the shore, grab a bar of Lifebuoy, and wade on in. It was clean enough to fill my drinking flask from.

I was scrubbing myself, enjoying the feel of slippery lather. It was a quiet day—as quiet as it ever gets, only the wind and the rustling of leaves, the accompanying insects. I usually sang when I bathed, to fill up the silence, but that day the silence was fitting and right, and I remained quiet.

I had just scrubbed my face, and I ducked under to wash off the soap. When I came back up, I brushed wet hair from my eyes and spat out a sparkling stream of water. I shook my head rapidly and rubbed my eyes.

There was a unicorn pawing at my clothes on the shore.

I had seen unicorns before, fleetingly. They are shy, cautious creatures that usually bolted when they sensed me; like quick flashes of sunlight on metal. In the five years since the Change I had become used to seeing fairy-tale things, living myths, but as I looked upon this creature I knew I had seen nothing to compare to it for sheer beauty. I felt as if some cold fish had slid across my belly as I marvelled in the cool water.

It is an injustice to say merely that its coat was white. Oh, it was white, all right, but it was more than that. It was a white like I remember the best vanilla ice cream, but finer and smoother. Sometimes the sun hit it just right and bright rainbow crescents fanned out like light through a fine spray of water. The hooves were mirror bright—platinum or silver, I couldn't tell. A distant lighthouse beacon on a lonely night, the spiral horn rose from the noble head: milky white, warm and welcoming.

I can't say how long I watched it. Seconds, minutes, hours. Its tail swished randomly. Its nose was pressed against my backpack, but suddenly the majestic head lifted and it regarded me with two paralyzingly black eyes. Eyes full of life and intelligence. Eyes I could fall into. Lover's eyes. . . . As it moved, the mane shimmered on its muscular neck like a road on a hot day.

We looked at each other. Why did I suddenly have the feeling that I was the one who had no place in the world, that it was more real than I was? I was afraid to move, thinking I might frighten it away. Instead, I did the only thing I could think of to do:

"Hello," I said.

The silky ears pricked up, but otherwise it just stood there, reading my soul with those eyes.

I began walking cautiously toward the shore. Fear flashed in its eyes and I spoke to it in what I hoped was a reassuring voice.

"It's all right," I said. "I won't hurt you. It's all right." I said this over and over again as I inched closer. Soon I emerged, naked and dripping, from the water.

I held out my hands: let's be friends. There was pain in the beautiful face, and my smile disappeared when I saw why. The right front leg was broken. Swollen and discolored, it was made even uglier because such a thing didn't belong on this perfect beast. No wonder it hadn't run away.

"Oh, you poor thing," I said, kneeling.

It backed away, half-dragging the broken leg.

"I want to help you," I said, and stood up.

It looked straight at me. Its eyes were level with mine. "Bwoke," it said in a little-girl voice.

"I know. Here—" I reached out slowly and stroked her shoulder. It felt like. . . . I don't know. Somewhere between cotton and silk.

It—she, rather—flinched at the touch, but I stroked her mane until she relaxed.

"Bwoke," she said again.

"Yeah, it's broken. Pretty bad, too. I've got to find something to use as a splint so I can set it, okay?"

"Kayyy," she agreed.

I put on my pants and shoes and picked up the blowgun, then slid a handful of darts into a rear pocket. "Don't go away, all right? You'll hurt your leg even worse."

"Bwoke."

"Right." I smiled and darted out to the road, followed it about fifty yards until I came to a driveway leading to an abandoned house. I entered cautiously. I wasn't worried too much about squatters or vigilantes, but it never hurts to play it safe. I took a sheet from a musty bedroom, bundled it up, and walked into the garage.

The car parked there was an old Volkswagen. The tires were flat and the windows were caked with dust. I picked up a rag from a work bench and wiped at the front windshield.

There was a corpse sitting behind the wheel. It looked as if it had been there a long time. Years. There was a bottle beside it. The label read *Potassium cyanide* in bright red, with a skull and crossbones beneath. I wondered why he—she?—had done it.

I shrugged. Suicide had never been a viable option to me. I liked life, crazy as it was.

I turned around and picked up two long, thin boards from a small pile against the wall. The eerie feeling that the corpse was watching me made me feel like a dozen mice had skittered down my back.

I hurried from the dead house and ran down the road.

The unicorn was nuzzling my backpack when I arrived.

"No, get away from there," I told her firmly. There were

a couple of weapons in the pack, knives included, and I didn't want her nosing it open and cutting herself.

"Candy," she said.

"What?"

"Candy," she repeated plainly.

"Sorry, little one. I don't have any. . . ." I trailed off and untied the pack flap to let her see. "Well, I'll be damned."

There was a small pack of peppermint candies nestled between a hunting knife and a foil packet of freeze-dried chili. I'd have sworn it hadn't been there before.

"Candy."

"Right." I fished out the packet. Brach's. Forty-nine cents. Shaking my head slowly, I tore open the plastic, untwisted one of the red and white wrappers, and held the peppermint out in my palm. She took it gently with her mouth and crunched. "Candy," she said again.

"Be good and I'll give you candy after I fix your leg."

"Bwoke."

I made a splint from strips of the sheet and the two boards. It must have hurt like hell as I bound it tight, but she never flinched or made a sound.

Thinking about Androcles and the lion, I stood up and gave her another piece of candy.

I made a fire as it grew dark. Supper had been freeze-dried beef and rice and warm instant lemonade. She wouldn't eat anything I offered except peppermint candy.

I washed my utensils after supper and leaned back against a palm tree. It was a nice night. October in Florida is always nice. It's the first lessening of the summer heat, and the first taste of winter is in your mouth. By day the sky is a big blue bowl, and by night it is as pure as crystal, stars shining and crickets humming.

I lit up a cigarette and looked up at that wonderful sky. After a minute I noticed the unicorn was standing next to me, staring. "What's the matter with you?" I asked.

"Bad," she said in that innocent-girl voice.

"Bad? What's bad?"

She lowered her head and, almost faster than I could see it, flicked the cigarette from between my fingers with her horn.

"Bad," she insisted.

I started to protest, but stopped. Maybe the smoke bothered her. I shrugged and nodded. "Okay, sure. Bad. Gotcha. Smoking—bad."

She nodded approvingly and turned away.

"Schmuck," I added.

She snorted. It sounded playful.

I stood up, stretching. My cigarette was still burning on the ground. I stamped it out and got ready for bed.

My sleeping bag was snuggly warm. I lay in it, thinking, and from time to time I raised my head and looked at the pale form a few yards from me, silent and motionless.

I smiled and rolled over onto my side. Eventually I slept.

I awoke next morning to find myself staring into lovely black eyes—snowman's eyes.

She stood over me, lover's eyes regarding me patiently. The early morning sun caused an occasional pale orange glimmer on her left side.

"Well, good morning," I said, standing. "How's the leg?"

"Bwoke."

"Yeah, right. We're going to have to teach you a few more words."

She watched me carefully as I buried last night's garbage. "Feel like walking a little?" I asked her. "We'll take it slow and easy. There's a small town about five or six miles from here. I need some stuff—food and a couple other things. Sound okay to you?"

"Kayyy."

That voice was so sweet it gave me shivers. I gave her a piece of peppermint—the last one—and stroked her luxuriant mane.

We followed the road until we got into the town.

W   OME TO ARCADIA! proclaimed the roadsign, with a hole shot through the "welcome." It must have been that way before the Change; firearms didn't work anymore.

I left her outside while I went into a pharmacy. I had to smash a window to get in; it was locked and, surprisingly, the large front windows were still intact. I was lucky; looters hadn't found this place yet.

I unslung my pack and dragged it behind me, top flap open so I could toss in anything I wanted as I walked among the aisles. Ace bandages for the unicorn's leg. Cigarettes from behind the cash register. And—I smiled when I saw them—a half-dozen small bags of Brach's peppermint candy.

The pharmacy had a lunch counter to one side. Behind it I found a few canned goods I could use. Mostly beans and franks. I was sick to death of beans and franks. Most of the cans were dented, and some had scratches on them that looked as if they might be teeth marks. Why would somebody be hungry enough to try to bite his way into a can, but pass up bags of peppermint candy?

The stockroom was mostly empty. The back door, which led to an alleyway formed by the back of the pharmacy and another store, had been pried open. So the place had been looted. Not a very thorough job, though.

I had just turned to leave when something smacked into the wall just above and behind my head. I dropped, rolled behind a stack of cardboard boxes, and snatched my blowgun from its sling. It was an Aero-mag break-down model, all aluminum with piano-wire darts.

A box just above my head thunked and slid back toward me a little. An arrowhead and half a shaft protruded upward from it.

Upward—that meant he was down low and firing high. His bow wasn't too powerful, either; the arrow hadn't gone through the box. I set the pack in front of me as protection, carefully slid two boxes a fraction of an inch apart, and risked a quick peek.

It was a kid. He wore filthy blue jeans and nothing else. His black hair was shoulder length and grimy. His ribs protruded and his belly was distended. His eyes were dull and insane. He couldn't have been more than thirteen years old. As I watched he pulled another hunting arrow from the makeshift quiver strapped onto the back of his right thigh, fitted it, and drew. He barely had the strength to bring the string back to his cheek.

I ducked quickly and an arrowhead sprang into being through a cardboard box, inches to the left of my backpack.

"Kid!" I yelled at the top of my lungs. "Kid! You can have some of my food! Christ, you can have all of it; I don't care!"

Silence. Not even the thump of arrows striking boxes. That unnerved me even more. I ventured another peek and caught motion out of the corner of my eye just in time to see him coming around the boxes at me, a feral gleam in his eyes as he drew back the bowstring.

There wasn't time to think. I grabbed the pack and threw it at him, raised the blowgun to my lips, and puffed *hard,* grunting as I launched the dart.

It hit him in the eye. He screamed and fell, and was still.

I just sat there, hands clamped aorund the aluminum shaft of the Aero-mag. I trembled. God, he'd been a kid, just a little kid, and I'd had to kill him. . . .

I drew a shaky breath and stood. Hating myself, I walked over to him and pulled the dart from his eye. I had to. I might need it again.

I found where he had lived, behind some shelving in a corner of the stockroom. It was rank. Roaches crawled everywhere. There was shit on the floor and a small pile of cleanly picked bones on one side. Among them was a human skull.

He hadn't been after my pack.

The unicorn waited patiently outside the pharmacy. How to describe what she looked like in the bright sun? Neon milk? She looked at me strangely as I came out. I was probably pale. No doubt my walk was uncertain.

"Bad," she decided.

I tried to smile. It didn't work. "Yeah," I said. "Bad."

I shouldered my backpack and slung the Aero-mag. "Come on—let's find a library."

If the pharmacy had been undisturbed, the library was a veritable temple. It was untouched and unlocked: not very big, probably twenty or thirty thousand books, but at least there were a lot of high windows and it was well lit inside. A fine layer of dust had coated everything. The electric clock on the wall had frozen at exactly four-thirty.

The unicorn looked over my shoulder as I thumbed through card catalog drawers. I couldn't find anything between UNICEF and UNIFORMS, so I looked under MYTHOLOGY. There were about a dozen books listed; I found them, sat down on the floor, leaning against a bookshelf, and began reading.

I learned some damned interesting things—for instance: Unicorns are symbols of purity. The horn is supposed to have healing properties. They are generally meek and shy, but fight ferociously when cornered. They are traditionally pictured as being cloven hooved. My unicorn (*my* unicorn!) wasn't. No illustrations showed the prism effect of the light on the coat, nor did any have silver hooves. The *Encyclopedia Britannica* said the legend had originated in Greece about the time the Greeks began trading with the Egyptian Empire, and that it probably sprang from muddled accounts of the oryx or the rhinoceros.

I laughed, and the unicorn watched curiously.

You had to be a virgin to touch a unicorn. . . .

A flush crept up my neck. Okay, so I'd touched her. Being a virgin had some advantages after all. Hooray.

I read until the light was too dim to see by, then set the book aside, rubbed my eyes, and made a small supper. The unicorn just wanted another piece of candy.

I was dying for a cigarette. Earlier in the day I had opened up the pack and found them gone.

"Hey," I'd said to the unicorn, "did you do something with my cigarettes?"

"Bad," was all she replied.

To vent the jitters I was getting from my nicotine fit, I decided to take a walk around the library. There was a browse-a-book section filled with art collections and paperbacks, and on one stand was a largish softcover which had a painting of a unicorn on the front. It was golden and quite beautiful, but nothing compared to the real thing. I picked it up and held it high, squinting in the dying light.

Ariel, proclaimed the title. *The Book of Fantasy*.

"Ariel." I said it out loud, liking the sound. It was light and sounded like silver. What the hell. I couldn't keep calling her "unicorn," and Ariel was as good a name as any and better than most.

I carried the book to the unicorn. "Ariel," I told her. "That's your name, okay?"

She snorted.

"I'll take one snort to mean yes and two for no."

One more snort.

"Ariel it is, then."

I set it atop some books on magic and witchcraft I had put aside to read while I walked the next day. Ariel seemed to know I was getting ready to go to sleep and began to pace restlessly around the library. She had tried to lie down earlier, but the splint was too uncomfortable.

I squirmed into my sleeping bag and sleep came quickly.

Just before I dozed off, I thought: *I wonder if she'll ever learn more than baby talk?*

two

How sharper than a serpent's tooth it is to have a thankless child.

—Shakespeare,
King Lear

"Hey, Pete—get your ass in gear!"

Ariel and I traveled along the abandoned Interstate. We usually didn't say much as we walked; there didn't seem to be a need to. But today I was lagging behind somewhat. I was footsore and fatigued; she was eager and almost hyper. I got the feeling she was a bit apprehensive about going into Atlanta; she was in a hurry to get there and get out again.

I walked with my head bowed, watching the pavement seem to flow beneath my feet. Every so often one of Ariel's marvelous hooves slid along the asphalt and a stream of sparks scattered. The novelty of walking on paved road never seemed to wear thin on her.

A unicorn is a rare enough thing to see; burdened ones are unheard of. But she never complained about having to carry one of my packs and whatever weapons I happened to possess at the time. Today I carried the blowgun, broken down and slung onto the magnesium frame of my backpack where I could get to it quickly. Two bags were slung across Ariel's back, and the handle of a pair of 'chuks dangled from a pocket.

Poking from the top of her pack was a crossbow, which I'd use only if all else failed. It was powerful and good for long distances, but unwieldy and time-consuming to reload.

Ariel looked at me as I caught up to her. "What's the matter?" she asked. "Tired?"

I nodded.

"How much farther?"

I reached back and dug out the map from a side pocket, unrolled it, and traced a finger down a line marked *US 23/41*. "Let's see. . . . We left Macon when?"

"Two days ago."

"Right. We've been doing a little less than thirty miles a day, and it's about fifty miles as the crow flies. We ought to be in Atlanta sometime tomorrow afternoon."

"Shit—another night on the road." She had picked up many of my speaking habits. It's strange to hear a unicorn swear. Come to think of it, it was strange to hear a unicorn talk at all. "Hey, it's not so bad," I told her. "We could be spending the night in a city." Cities are where all the rejects hang out.

"Where, no doubt, you'd get us into another test of our defense capabilities."

She wouldn't leave me alone about Jacksonville, no matter how much I insisted it wasn't my fault. I'd gone to a trading bar to look over some equipment and weapons. I was always on the lookout for new things I might need.

Trading bars are nasty places. They serve as a combination bar/whorehouse/trading post/news center, and are mainly frequented by inner-city dwellers and loners "just passing through." Some loners have "buddies"—animals held to them by loyalty spells. Occasionally you see somebody with a *Familiar*—a person with an almost symbiotic relationship with a magical animal—like Ariel and me. As Familiars will fight ferociously to protect each other, and spellbound buddies will die to protect their masters, they aren't allowed in trading bars, so I had to leave Ariel outside. I didn't like it one bit and neither did she, but those were the rules and everybody abided by them—or else. She stood in front of a furniture store across the street, well away from a buddy-lion crouched beside the entrance to the trading bar. It watched us warily.

There were a few people inside, mostly loners, it seemed, looking at the weapons display tables. Over to one side was the dark entranceway to the bar. I walked among supply aisles, looking for anything that struck my fancy. There were no prices on any items; you had to negotiate with one of the dealers. Haggling had become a fine art again.

At the end of the aisles was a guard shouldering a cocked crossbow, expressionlessly watching the customers. Nobody stole from trading bars.

At one aisle I reached for something—I think it was a small, folding camp stove—and picked it up to look it over. They'd want an arm and a leg for it, but it might be convenient sometimes. It was the only one on the shelf.

Somebody snatched it from my hand. I turned to see someone huge and hairy and looking like an almost human grizzly bear glaring down at me. "Hey, little fuck," he said, holding up the folding stove, "this mine. Saw first." His teeth were rotted. He stank. He wore a black leather vest, cut-off blue jeans, and combat boots.

"Sure, fine," I told him. "I was just looking at it. If you want it, go ahead."

"I want, I take anyhow, little fuck," he growled.

Since he already had it and I didn't really want it anyway, that should have been the end of it. But he just stood there like an oak tree, as if he expected me to say something.

I turned and walked into the bar.

It was lit by a few candles scattered here and there, and the air smelled heavy and pungent like a barn. I dropped my pack beside a barstool and sat down. The bartender came over to me.

"Yeah?" he said.

"Uh—" I hadn't wanted anything; I'd just come in to get away from that gorilla. "Do you have any Coke?"

"Coke?" He smiled a left-sided smile and I felt stupid and started to tell him never mind, but he bent down behind the bar. I heard a rattling as he unlocked something.

"It'll cost you," he said, straightening back up. "This stuff don't grow on trees." He held a small cellophane packet of white powder between thumb and forefinger.

I flushed. Cocaine! I'd wanted a Coke, you know—Coca Cola.

"Where—where do you get this?"

"Guy comes in from New York twice a year, regular. Rides a griffin."

New York! I'd heard things about what New York was like now. They were horror stories.

He put his elbows down on the bar and leaned toward me. "Just drops off these little bags and takes one of them." He nodded toward one of the three women sitting toward the rear of the bar. When she saw us looking her way she said something to her companions and stood, walking toward us.

"You still want the coke?"

"I—well, no. I doubt I could afford it." I stood to leave and felt a light tap on my shoulder. It was the girl.

"You like me?" she asked.

I started to reply but she cut me off. "A half-pound of dried meat, any kind, in advance. Or if you don't have any, we could make a deal."

"No," I said, moving away.

"What's wrong? You queer or something?"

"No, just selective." I picked up my pack and walked out of the bar just as the big gorilla type walked in. He stopped and started to say something to me, but I just kept walking through the trading area and out the door.

Ariel was across the street. She faced the buddy-lion, regarding it with what looked like tolerant amusement. She turned to me as I hurriedly approached her. "This lion is stupid. It can't communicate with me at all."

"Of course it's stupid. It's just an animal."

She blinked once and stared at me. If she could have smiled, I'm sure she would have.

"You know what I mean—it's a dumb lion under a loyalty spell."

"Wonder who it belongs to."

"I don't even care. Look, let's get out of here."

"What's the matter? Trouble inside?"

I shook my head. "Not really. I just don't like cities. Creeps everywhere. Come on." We turned to leave just as the gorilla type walked out the door, arm around the whore I'd turned down. She pointed at me. Shit.

He began walking across the street toward me, talking as he came. "Little fuck, I kill you. You and your horse, too, hah-hah-hah."

Ariel gave me a sidelong look as he lumbered toward us. "No trouble, huh?"

I shrugged out of my pack. "That's the reason I wanted to get out of here."

"Looks like a pretty good reason to me."

"Right." He had stopped in the middle of the road, expecting me to step out and meet him halfway. I had a better idea. "Let's run away," I suggested.

"Too late. Look."

The big yotz had turned to face the buddy-lion. He pulled something out of his leather vest, held it between thumb and forefinger, and pressed it. It was one of those cheap metal clackers that make an annoying noise like a cricket on speed. He clacked it three times and the lion rose.

"Come on, Rasputin," he said. The lion licked its chops, shook its mane, and blinked. We couldn't run away now; the lion would catch us before we got ten yards. Before I could get ten yards, rather; I wouldn't put it past Ariel to outrun it.

Then they were both coming toward us and everything happened fast. The lion stopped in front of Ariel and gathered itself for the pounce, relaxing and looking lazily up into her eyes.

"Come on, come on," said Ariel impatiently. "You might as well pounce now; you're going to sooner or later."

Then I could no longer pay attention to them because this huge, hairy arm swung around like a shaggy club and broke my nose. I went down onto the sidewalk, eyes blinded by sudden tears. Warm wetness flowed onto my lips. I saw the blur as he bent down to finish me off and my right foot lashed out, heel hitting his kneecap. He yowled as it snapped. I got up as fast as I could and punched him in the throat. He went down choking.

I looked toward Ariel. Blood dripped down her horn and thc lion lay in a pool of red at the curb. Her lover's eyes were black and soft. "You look awful," she said.

I tried to smile. "I thig by nothe ith broge," I said.

Remembering Jacksonville as we walked down the Interstate, I reached out and stroked Ariel's shimmering mane. She shivered. "Do you want to call it a day and set up camp, hornyhorse? Leg still hurting?"

She gave a gentle laugh like wind chimes tinkling. "No, I'm all right. We'll camp at sundown, same as always."

I agreed and we continued walking. I thought about her

slowly healing leg as we plodded on. It had been over a year, and it still bothered her. I'd asked her about it, when she'd learned enough words to answer, but she refused to talk about it.

"Sunset, Pete," she announced after a while, knowing how much I liked the sunset effect.

I looked up at the horizon. Sunsets were bright and dazzlingly beautiful since the vanished air pollution had taken with it all the dim reds and burnt cinnamons. I looked away, and melted at the sight of Ariel. The fading light sent rainbow ripples spreading everywhere on her body, sweeping prism-broken light from neck to flank. Her spiral horn caught the sunlight and her tail looked like my memory of a fiber-optics lamp. I watched until the sun disappeared and all that remained was the faint glow of her horn.

We set up camp beside the Interstate. I unslung my sleeping bag and unrolled it on the grass. Ariel struck sparks on the road and I got a fire going. I opened a can and was soon eating hot beef stew. Ariel didn't eat anything. All I'd ever seen her eat was peppermint candy, and that only because she liked it. I don't think she needed to eat. I'd asked her, once, what kept her alive.

"I'm not sure," she'd answered. "The light from the stars. The music of crickets. Clean living."

"I'm serious. A creature can't live without some kind of sustenance."

"Those are the old rules, the ones that don't work the way they used to. Magic is what works now, and I'm a magical creature. You might as well ask why guns or electricity don't work anymore. You've told me that the world doesn't work like it did before. It's magic, and that's all there is to it."

The world doesn't work like it did before. Wasn't that the truth.

I lay on my sleeping bag, staring at the night sky and remembering. *"The light from the stars. . . ."* When had there been so many stars in the sky? Before the Change the city glow pushed them back and the cities were cut off from the rest of the universe under their own domes of light. Now the Milky Way spread out above me like a band of chalk dust.

The ghostly form of Ariel stirred beside me. "Pete?"

"Yeah."

"Is there any special reason we're going into Atlanta?"

"We've gone over this before. I want to go to a library. We haven't been to one since Jacksonville."

"Oh."

"What's the matter? You don't want to go into Atlanta?"

"Cities make me nervous. But whither thou goest. . . ."

Silence for a while. Then:

"Hey, Pete?" Softly.

"Mmm."

"Sing me that song. You know, The Song."

"Sure."

Music was something I missed with a quiet pain, and I tried to make up for it by singing. The lyrics of the songs I liked had stayed with me, and I would sing them as Ariel and I walked the roads from town to town. But there was one song—I'd forgotten where I'd first heard it, or even what it was called. I just called it The Song, and I sang it whenever I was afraid of what might be waiting at the end of the road. I sang it to Ariel:

"So we'll go no more a-roving
So late into the night,
Though the heart be still as loving,
And the moon be still as bright.

"For the sword outwears its sheath,
And the soul wears out the breast,
And the heart must pause to breathe,
And love itself must rest.

"Though the night was made for loving,
And the day returns too soon,
Yet we'll go no more a-roving
By the light of the moon."

A cry came from far overhead.

"Roc," I said. "Usually don't see them around here."

But Ariel was asleep.

I rolled onto my side and soon I was asleep, too.

We reached downtown Atlanta about five o'clock the next afternoon. The gold dome of the state capitol building gleamed from between the tall skyscrapers to my right. To the left was the squat, brooding shape of the Fulton County Stadium, where the Falcons and the Braves used to play. It reminded me of pictures of the Coliseum in Rome—a deserted, dead arena. I wondered who—or what—might be there now.

"Sure feels empty," observed Ariel, glancing around.

"Yeah." I smiled. "The whole world feels empty."

"We're being watched."

I looked at her. "From where?"

"Overpass. About a mile away, straight ahead. Three people. One of them is looking at us through—what do you call them? Bulky black things, make things far away look closer."

"Binoculars."

"Right. One of them's using binoculars. There's something perched on his shoulder—some kind of bird."

"A Familiar, maybe?"

"How would I know? Looks like a regular bird from here."

"Well, we're headed that way anyhow. We'll worry about it when we get there."

In ten minutes I could see them fairly well. One wore a T-shirt and blue jeans, one was decked out in a fancy assortment of knives, and the third wore a leather jacket on which the bird—a falcon, I now saw—was perched.

As we neared, the leather-jacketed one raised something to his lips and blew. I didn't hear anything, but Ariel's ears twitched and the bird flew straight up and began circling.

"Buddy," I said.

"They keep their bases covered." This from a creature that hadn't the vaguest notion of what baseball was.

"Yeah. Let me do the talking, okay? They may not have seen a unicorn before; we don't want them knowing any more than they have to."

We stopped looking up at the three men on the overpass.

"What's your business?" asked Leatherjacket in a mild Southern accent.

We seek the Holy Grail—it was tempting. "We're trying to get to the public library," I said.

"Public library. What's there?"

"Books."

He flared. "Smart guy."

"No, really. I need to look at a road atlas and some maps."

They simply stared at me.

"I'd like to make it to the library before dark, if you don't mind," I said.

They remained silent.

"Well?" I demanded.

"That yours?" He indicated Ariel.

"We're Familiars, yes. Anything wrong with that?"

"Don't be so defensive, son. We just like to keep track of what animals come and go in our fair city, both four- and two-legged."

"Besides," broke in the one wearing knives, "unicorns are pretty rare. They're supposed to have a gift for healing. They say if you grind the horn into powder and mix it with—"

"That's enough," said Leatherjacket.

The man in the T-shirt and jeans tapped him on the shoulder and whispered into his ear. Leatherjacket's eyes widened and he seemed to want to laugh. "That right?" he asked.

T-shirt nodded.

Leatherjacket looked at me. "Does your Familiar let you touch it?"

I flushed. Damn!

"Yes," I admitted.

"You've never had a woman?"

"No."

"You'd best be careful around here, then," said T-shirt. "There's some awful mean women around, hide in dark places and grab you just like that." He snapped his fingers for emphasis. The other two snickered.

"Well, I can't see any harm in letting them go to the library," said Leatherjacket. "Long as you don't wander around the streets. It'll be dark soon. Ain't safe."

"I'll remember." I took out the city map I had obtained from an abandoned gas station and unrolled it.

"Don't bother with that," he said. "Just take this exit. Turn left at the second red light and go on down the street until you see it on the right side. About a mile."

"Thanks."

We started to walk on, but he yelled for us to stop before I had taken two steps. I halted and looked up at him.

"Don't move until I call Asmodeus," he said, pointing toward the hunting falcon circling overhead. "She'll rip your eyes out otherwise."

"Don't bother." I looked at Ariel, who nodded. She snorted, tossed her head, and looked up.

The falcon settled gently onto her back.

Leatherjacket's jaw dropped. The other two looked at him wide-eyed, almost as if they were afraid for him.

"No one—I was told nobody could order that bird but me!"

I just smiled.

Leatherjacket's eyes formed two slits. He lifted the whistle to his mouth and blew. The bird didn't move from Ariel's back.

"Let her go, Ariel," I said.

Ariel tossed her head and snorted. The bird flew off and glided to Leatherjacket's shoulder. He was still glaring at me, and the other two looked on with their mouths pressed into angry lines.

"Let's go, Ariel."

We went.

"That was a damned stupid thing to do," observed Ariel once we were out of earshot.

"Sue me."

"I'm serious. Let me do the talking, you said. We don't want them knowing anything more than they have to, you said. So what do we do? We show off! Now there'll be talk, and if word gets around that we bypassed an obedience spell—even if it was just a bird—people will get curious."

I said nothing.

"It was a childish thing to do."

I glared at her but remained silent.

"Well? Why'd you want to show off like that?"

"I was embarrassed," I muttered.

"You were what?"

"I was embarrassed, dammit!"

"Why? What was there to be embarrassed about?"

"I'm a virgin."

"So am I."

"That's different. You're not a human. You aren't a man. See, human males have this . . . this. . . . Oh, forget it."

"Pete, there is great virtue in being pure. If you weren't a virgin, you couldn't have me."

"Look, just drop it, okay?"

"All right." She fell silent, and neither of us said another word until we found the library.

The library was of ultramodern design—few windows and now useless electric glass doors. I looked around for something I could break in with.

"Don't bother," said Ariel sullenly, and she ran for the glass front door, head down and horn aimed straight ahead.

"No!"

But I was too late. She had already bolted up the steps, sparks streaming from her hooves, and leapt into the air. Her horn hit the glass and shattered it; her momentum carried her through.

"You idiot!" I ran up the steps to find her standing quietly amid the broken glass. "What are you trying to do, turn yourself into hamburger?"

"I got us in, didn't I?"

"So what? You could have waited another two minutes while I found something to bust it open with, rather than jumping through like some comic-book hero. You could have cut yourself badly. I don't have any way to treat you if you ever really hurt yourself, you know that? What if you snapped your horn?"

"It can't snap. Not while I'm alive. Besides, unicorns avert harm. We rarely get injured, and when we do, we heal fast."

"Oh? And how, may I ask, did you manage to get your leg broken nearly in two, despite all this ability to avert personal injury?"

Her nostrils flared. "I don't want to talk about it." Her coal eyes blazed.

"Why not?"

"Why don't you want to talk about your virginity?"

"Oh, go to hell."

She snorted and walked farther into the library.

three

Glendower: *I can call spirits from the vasty deep.*
Hotspur: *Why, so can I, or so can any man;*
But will they come when you do call for them?

—Shakespeare,
King Henry IV

Nobody ever thinks to use a library. Most people feel they're too busy trying to stay alive to take time to fool around with books. They're right, to some extent, but libraries have given me books on camping, food storage and preservation, backpacking, arms and armor, self-defense, magic, mythology, and mythological animals—to name but a few. Libraries have probably saved my life a dozen times. Even before I met Ariel I went to them to read books on how to survive, and after she came along I also read books on magic and mythology. I read anything that might help me understand what the world had become.

I remember the librarian at my junior high school who always reprimanded me for not being quiet. She and all the librarians in the world now had their revenge: the place was like a tomb. I smiled: a tomb for tomes.

Ariel and I checked upstairs and down to make sure the building was empty. The clocks had all stopped at four-thirty.

Before dark I looked through the card catalog and gathered together what books were new to me, piling them atop a desk in a corner of the first floor. I would read them over the next few days. Most of the books I wanted weren't there.

When darkness came I unloaded gear and set up "camp" on the second floor, beside the staircase. I couldn't light a fire for food, so I opened a packet of dried beef. I drank water from my *bota*—a kind of kidney-shaped wine flask with a nipple end. I lit two small candles, retrieved from the nether regions of my backpack.

I leaned the crossbow against the banister after cocking it and readying a bolt. It was a Barnett *Commando,* self-cocking, one hundred seventy-five pound pull; scope, three hundred yards-plus range. I won't say how I got it; it cost me dearly.

The nunchakus—two tapered, foot-long pieces of wood joined at the smaller end by a short length of rope allowing it to be used as a flail—were on my left side; the Aero-mag blowgun was on my right, a dart half-loaded.

Ariel watched me quietly, tail swishing rhythmically. She knew I was still mad at her, and damned if I didn't have good cause to be. Trying to act like some superhero just because she's a unicorn. That horn of hers must have been embedded deep into her skull, for all she—

"Talk to me," she said.

"What about?"

"Oh, come on. You're acting like a little kid."

"I am not. And besides, how would you know what a little kid acts like?"

She cocked her head curiously. "Now, isn't that odd? How would I know that?"

Despite my sullenness I was interested. "Listening to me, maybe." I took another drink of water. "Can you remember what it was like where you came from, before you came here?"

"I—I don't remember any place but this one."

"Well, what's your earliest memory? When did you first become aware of yourself?" I'd asked her this before, but it was before she'd learned to speak well and she hadn't understood.

"That's odd—I've never really thought about it before." She sounded distressed. "The earliest thing I can remember is . . . waking up one day. That's all, really. I felt warmth on one side and it was the sun, and I stood up—I remember my legs were wobbly—and I looked around. I was beside a railroad track, and even though I didn't know what it was, somehow . . . I don't know . . . it didn't seem *right;* it looked like it didn't belong. Same for the roads and roadsigns, and later for houses and buildings and cars stopped on the streets. They didn't fit." She looked at me with a strange, half-fearful look in her eyes. "You know, nothing I saw, except for the magical animals I encountered and the things that were—I don't know, natural, like forests and lakes and the sky, nothing else seemed right. Until I met you."

"Me?" I hadn't expected that.

"Yes. You were. . . ." She stopped for half a minute. "It's hard to put the feelings into words. I guess you were pure, a virgin, I mean, and you fit in with the kind of creature that I am."

"How do you know so much about being a unicorn?"

"How do you know so much about being a human? You learn about yourself as you grow. I certainly had enough other things to compare myself to."

"You were a baby, that day you woke up by the railroad track?"

"Of course. I was still pretty much a baby when I met you, wasn't I?"

"Yeah. Those were the good old days, before you knew more than about two words." She'd also grown a lot. My eyes now came to just above the level of her shoulder.

She snorted. "If I hadn't come along you'd still be talking to yourself."

I looked to my left. "You hear that?" I asked, jerking a thumb at Ariel.

"Cute." She walked to my open pack and nosed it. "Hey—no peppermint!"

"You're slipping, you horse with a horn. Why don't you just zap some into existence the way you used to, instead of making me scrounge deep, dark, and dangerous candy stores to satisfy your sweet tooth. Teeth."

"What little power I have was ill spent when I was younger. Spells shouldn't be wasted."

"Easy for you to say. You aren't dying for a cigarette."

"Suffer."

I started to make a retort but froze when a thump and a scuffling came from downstairs. I blew out the candles and whispered to Ariel. "Stay up here. He'll see your glow if you go down." Sure, she was quiet as snowfall, but a huge, ghostly white unicorn sneaking around inside a dark library is not inconspicuous. I wiped my fingers on my pants and picked up the crossbow. Listening carefully for a moment revealed nothing more. I was about to tell Ariel to come around behind me when a deep voice reverberated below.

"Hello?"

I cradled the Barnett and crept down the stairs, hugging the banister.

"Hello, is anybody here?"

I saw him now, a faint, fairly large figure in front of the card files. His back was to me. I brought the Barnett up, resting it on the banister. "Don't move," I said, knowing full well that when he heard my voice he would move anyway. Sure enough, he turned toward me.

"Don't move," I repeated, "or I'll kill you."

That stopped him. I'd figured that, too.

"I don't want any trouble," he said. "I'm looking for a kid. Came in today with a unicorn."

"Why?"

He stepped toward me. "Hey, is that a rifle you're holding? Don't you know that guns won't—"

"It's not a rifle."

"Oh."

"You were saying."

"Huh? Oh, yeah. This guy—I guess you're him; nobody else would be in here—you and your buddy—"

"She's not a buddy. She's my Familiar."

"Sorry. You and your Familiar managed to override my buddy's obedience spell. I want to find out how you did it. I never heard of it happening before; the guy who set the spell for me said it couldn't be broken."

"You were on the overpass? With the leather jacket?"

"Yeah."

Snap decision: "Hungry?"

"Since you mention it, yes."

"I've got some food upstairs. Come on over here, but keep your hands where I can see them and move slow."

He did as I said and stopped in front of me. "Oh," he said, seeing the Barnett, "a crossbow. I shoulda known. Stupid of me."

I didn't bother to contradict him.

"Name's Russ Chaffney."

I lowered the crossbow. "Pete Garey." He held out his hand. We shook.

"Food's upstairs," I said. "You'll have to go first. Ariel won't like it if I go ahead of you; she'll think you might have a weapon at my back."

He agreed and I called to Ariel that we had company and were coming up. At the top of the stairs he hesitated, seeing Ariel watching him warily. She saw me behind him with the Barnett and relaxed.

"Ariel, this is Russ Chaffney," I said. "Chaffney, my Familiar, Ariel."

He looked at me as if I were crazy, then looked at Ariel. "Um, how do you do?" he managed.

"Do what?"

He gaped. He stood there, speechless. Looking at him, I told Ariel, "It's just a figure of speech. It means, how are you?"

"Oh. I'm wonderful, except I want some peppermint candy. You wouldn't happen to have any, would you?"

"I, uh, no, I don't have any candy. Sorry."

"Don't worry about it," I said. "She eats too much of it anyway. She's getting fat. I'm going to ditch her in someone's stable if she doesn't leave the stuff alone."

She lifted her nose. "Unicorns don't get fat."

"Don't believe her," I stage-whispered. "She used to be skinny. Now look at her."

"I was not skinny!"

I shrugged. "Have it your way." To Chaffney: "She's always been fat."

"Do you two always talk like this? I mean, I didn't know unicorns could talk." He was having trouble coping.

Ariel pounced on the chance to use the old joke. "We can't talk. The hairless monkey over there is a ventriloquist."

"Who you calling a hairless monkey, conehead?"

Chaffney folded his arms and looked at her critically, trying to appear unfazed. "I also didn't know they could do magic," he said.

"Magic?" she asked innocently.

"Yeah. At the overpass this afternoon. Asmodeus—my falcon."

"Oh. I thought I recognized you from somewhere. Humans all look alike to me."

I made a rude noise.

"Come on," I said. "I'm still hungry."

I leaned against the marble balustrade, listening to Ariel and Chaffney discussing magic. He still didn't understand how she could have bypassed a loyalty spell.

"Look," she explained patiently, "a loyalty spell is nothing. You could weave one. *Pete* could weave one."

I let it pass with merely a sneer.

"All it involves is fixing the animal's attention on you," she continued. "The dumber the animal—that is, the smaller the brain size—the harder it is to get its attention, but the easier it is to keep it. It has no will to fight back."

"But the guy who set the spell told me it was impossible to break," he persisted. "That's why buddies are so loyal. Asmodeus has been with me for two years now and she's never obeyed anyone but me. Saved my ass a few times."

"And she's still loyal to you. What I did was to change her focus of attention momentarily from you to me."

"She didn't come when I called," he protested, finishing off a can of Vienna sausages and wiping his fingers on his pants.

"I hadn't released her yet."

"So, if you'd wanted to, you could have kept her as your buddy."

"As long as I could make myself her center of attention, yes."

"Who taught you all this?"

"Nobody. It comes naturally. But it'll work for anybody who uses it correctly. Ask Pete."

I shifted uncomfortably. I knew she'd bring it up. Russ was looking at me expectantly, so I told him about it. "One night I tried something stupid," I said. "I found a book of spells in a library in central Florida. It was an old book; the pages were yellowed and the cover was made out of real leather. It had a 'Special Collection' label on the bottom of the spine and on the flyleaf. The spells were in Latin, mostly, though there were some other languages I didn't recognize."

"You read Latin?"

"No, I just knew what it was. I didn't know what the words meant. Ariel read over my shoulder and stopped me on one of the pages. She told me to try one out. It had instructions, and the incantation was beneath it in boldface print.

"We went to a shopping plaza. It was a small town and I hadn't seen anybody around, though there were probably a few scavengers here and there. I'd bagged a deer that day with the crossbow because I needed food, and I used the drained blood to draw a pentagram on the concrete in the center of the plaza."

"To draw a what?"

"A pentagram," supplied Ariel. "A five-pointed star with a circle around it, used in incantations. Supernatural forces can't break into or out of one."

"Anyway, I got five candles from a looted pharmacy and placed one on each point of the star. Ariel watched while I lit the candles and picked up the book. I began reading out loud. It was Latin, I think, but the words sounded ugly. A lot of hard consonants. It hurt to pronounce them." I shrugged. "I don't know. They sounded just plain *ugly*. Once I looked back at Ariel. She was still watching. There wasn't a moon that night and she was a shadow. She didn't look real." I stared into the candle flame, remembering. It was still vivid. "I finished the conjuration and shut the book. Things started happening right away; the air was shimmering inside the circle I'd drawn in blood."

The candle flame undulated as my breath reached it. It made Chaffney's face look waxen, highlighting the seams at the corners of his eyes and mouth. Ariel was a pale, ever-changing orange and yellow.

"Something started forming inside the pentagram, like . . . like a tea bag in hot water. There was a sound like thunder rumbling. The shape in the circle was darker than the night. I watched it form."

I paused for a minute, looking at the flame. A bead of wax dripped down to the base of the candle. "I only got fleeting impressions of what it looked like. It was . . . huge. Muscular. Black. Sharp claws, and eyes like a fireplace. I could feel it hating me. It dripped hate the way a tree oozes sap. All this hit me in flashes, like it was revealed by lightning. I started to feel that I was losing control, that if I didn't stop it would break out of the pentagram and snatch me in its teeth like a cat shaking a mouse. But I couldn't move.

"Ariel bolted forward and touched her horn to the blood circle. There was a scream like tearing metal and she flinched, but she didn't draw back. The thing in the circle threw something. It wasn't a fireball, it was the opposite; it was some kind of black sponge that would drink her into it, that would absorb her light and her . . . I don't know, her soul, I guess. Her horn flared and dimmed. She dragged the tip of it along the concrete, breaking the red circle. The thing bellowed, then it faded away."

Silence for a long time in the library. I don't know how long it was before I stopped looking at the candle and saw Chaffney staring at me. "I think I want a cigarette," he said, shaking his shaggy head.

I frowned. "Ariel doesn't like to be around cigarette smoke. She won't even let me smoke. Damn horse."

"Love you, too, Pete."

Chaffney leaned forward. "That's all that thing did? It didn't hurt you?"

"It sure as hell tried. Oh, Ariel was perfectly all right, and I was okay, except for being jelly-kneed and dry-throated, and wanting very much to go to the bathroom." I looked up at Ariel. "You sure know how to pick your spells."

She said nothing.

"You ever try anything else?" he asked.

"No. I kind of stayed away from spells after that."

He smiled. "Don't blame you."

"Hey, where's your buddy, anyway?" I asked. "What's its name?"

"Asmodeus. I left her home. I didn't want to bring her after what happened this afternoon."

"It won't happen again," said Ariel.

"Tell me," he said, "what else can you do?"

Ariel shot me a warning look. "She can make peppermint appear and make cigarettes disappear," I said.

He scowled. "And she can read Latin."

"No, I already told you I can't. I read magic. There was something about the way the spell was put together that made me know what it was about. I don't understand it, I just do it."

"I've got a friend," Chaffney said carefully. "The guy who cast the loyalty spell on Asmodeus. He reads a lot about magic. He wants to know what caused the Change."

"Don't we all," I said. "You have any ideas?"

He tossed his head to the side, his version of a shrug. "Only what I've heard. A lot of people I know think we're in a place in space where old laws don't work anymore."

"Do you believe that?"

"I don't know. I wouldn't throw the idea away, but I'm not sure it holds water, either. Laws are laws."

I nodded. "'God doesn't shoot dice.' Einstein said that."

"Why don't you ask Ariel about it?" he said. "Since she knows about magic."

"I have. Tell him, you Salvador Dali version of an Appaloosa."

"Hairless monkey." She looked at Chaffney. "I haven't the slightest."

"She couldn't have been around until after the Change took place," I said. "She wouldn't remember any of it."

"God, I do." He rolled his eyes. "Everything just stopped, all at once. I was watching Dallas at L.A. It was the third quarter. Dallas was on top, twenty-one to nothing. The power cut out and the TV went dead. I waited for the electricity to come back on but there was nothing. When I picked up the phone to report a power failure after about ten minutes, the phone was dead. Nothing, not even static. Then I noticed how quiet it was. Really quiet. I could hear birds chirping, but no traffic—that wasn't right for Decatur. I walked outside with my wife and it was spooky. Cars stopped dead in the middle of the street. People stood up and down the block, seeing the same thing I did—something different." He leaned back. "Sometimes I wonder what happened to the people in airplanes or on ships in the middle of the ocean. What happened to people on cross-country car trips who were in the middle of Utah or Arizona? Christ, we even had a Shuttle up!" He shook his head and laughed. "You know the funniest thing about it? The thing that really burned me the most?" He paused, waiting for me to ask him what, but I said nothing. "I had a hundred bucks riding on the game, and I never did find out who won it. All those people stuck in elevators, everywhere, and all I could do is wonder whether or not L.A. at least beat the spread."

"What were you saying about your friend?" I prompted. "The one who reads on magic." I was afraid he'd start talking about his wife, and I wasn't sure I needed to hear about it. I doubted he needed to remember it.

"Oh, yeah. His name's Malachi. Weird name, huh? It's from the Bible."

"Last book of the Old Testament," said Ariel. "It means 'my messenger.'"

"She reads a lot," I explained to his blank look. "It's a pain in the ass—I have to turn the pages for her."

"I'll take your word for it. But he's a strange guy. Lives like he's Japanese, like one of those samurai." He mispronounced it. "Swords and all. Sometimes even one of those dress things, a kimono. He lives alone in a pretty nice house not too far from here." He frowned. "Well, not quite alone—he has a buddy, sort of. A big black chow. That's a dog."

"I know."

"Oh. It's a mean bastard. Damn near chewed my leg off once when I got too close to Malachi. That dog goes wherever he does. Malachi's real private—he leaves everybody alone, they leave him alone, mostly. You'd like him; like I said, he's really weird. You could talk to him about the Change. I know he'd want to see Ariel. He's interested in magic."

"Is he a sorcerer?" Ariel asked.

Chaffney shrugged. "He messes around. Tell you what—I'll take you to meet him tomorrow, if you want. I really think he'd be interested in both of you." He looked hopeful.

Ariel and I exchanged glances. "Why not?" she said.

I looked back to Chaffney. "Sure. I'd be interested in seeing how he defends a house by himself, anyway. That's hard enough for a group of people."

"You'll understand when you meet him."

"Oh. All right."

"Well," he said suddenly, getting up, "it's getting late. I ought to be getting back."

I stood also. "What time should we expect you tomorrow?"

"Around noon, I guess. It's about two, two and a half hours' walk from here."

"We'll be here."

He nodded. "I'll find my own way out. It was definitely a pleasure meeting you two, to say the least." He grinned at Ariel. "Good night."

"Good night."

Halfway down the stairs he paused. "Hey," he called up. "Remember the guy on the overpass with me? The one with all the knives?"

"The jerk who talked about grinding up my horn?" Ariel asked.

"He may be a jerk, but he's got friends. I'd watch out for him. I think he was serious about your horn. He'd try to take anything he thought he could get a good price for."

"I thought he was a friend of yours," I said.

He shook his head, looking up at me. "No friend of mine. I just stood a border watch with him. His name's Emilio."

"We'll keep an eye out for him. Thanks."

"Sure." He turned and walked the rest of the way down the stairs. His shoes scuffed the carpet until he reached the front door and the sound changed to the crunch of glass underfoot, then silence.

"Well," said Ariel when he was gone, "he seems nice enough."

"Yeah. I don't think he's about to go out and re-invent calculus, though." I looked away from the staircase. "So it seems there's a man after your own horn."

"It won't be the first time."

I grunted. "Do you think we should block off the entrance-way that you so delicately smashed in, so no one cuts my throat tonight?"

She snorted. "If I hadn't done it you'd have used a brick and done the same thing."

"Irrelevant and immaterial, but never mind. I'll slide a card catalog in front of it so I can hear if somebody comes in. They'll have to slide it out of the way."

"So I can hear, you mean. You sleep like a dragon."

"Whatever."

four

That night somebody stole my radio
and I had to do my own singing.

—Duane Locke,
Man's Relationship to his Self:
SELF RELIANCE, BASED ON AN ESSAY
BY EMERSON

Next day I read a *A Book of Five Rings,* a book on Japanese swordplay by Miyamoto Musashi. It wasn't easy. The thing was kind of vague, and Ariel's complaining didn't help any.

"Will you hurry up and finish that thing?" she whined. I sat on the front steps of the library while she paced restlessly. The day was bright and clear; nobody on the streets, no sound save the occasional echo of a bird cry.

"Be quiet. Besides, when I finish this I'll just start another."

"Wonderful."

"Look, you refugee from a Disney flick, some of this stuff keeps me alive."

"I can't wait until noon."

An hour later I finished the book. I frowned at the cover, opened it again, and started over.

"Oh, shit," muttered Ariel.

I finished it again two hours later. I scratched my head. Either the translation was bad or I was missing something here.

"Why do you care?" asked Ariel, irritated at my perplexity. "You don't have a sword."

"A lot of other people do. The more I know about sword tactics the better I'll be able to handle myself against one if I have to. Besides, I get the feeling there's more going on in this book than I realize."

"Okay, okay—I didn't ask for a lecture. What time is it?"

I shrugged. "How would I know? Ten-thirty, eleven. You're the one with the clock inside her head." I looked up from the book. "You're really anxious to meet this Malachi character, aren't you?"

She cocked her head to the side, looking past me. "I have a feeling about him."

"Good feeling or bad?"

"I'm not sure. He feels . . . important."

I frowned. "What's that mean?"

"Nothing more than that. I just have a hunch about him."

I'd learned to trust her hunches; they tended to pay off. I left her alone about it, though, and continued reading until Chaffney came for us at noon. He wore the same leather jacket he'd worn yesterday, with no shirt underneath. Even without a shirt it must have been hot. It was unzipped most of the way, only a few inches holding it closed about his waist. Thick, black chest hair looked as if it were trying to grow its way out through the V-shaped opening. Perched on his right shoulder was Asmodeus, wearing a black hood. The letter "A" had been embroidered on it in red; he should have named her Hester Prynne.

Chaffney gently removed the hood and waited for a reaction when she saw Ariel, but the falcon merely cocked its head quizzically, blinking.

I put on my backpack and slung the Aero-mag.

"You don't have to take that," said Chaffney.

"Sorry. I go, it goes."

He shrugged.

I set Ariel's pack on her back, dangling one end of the nunchakus from an open pocket. I cocked the crossbow across my knee and set it in its strap on the side of the pack.

"Are you always this cautious?" asked Chaffney.

"Paranoid, you mean. Yeah, I guess so."

"Pete thinks of everything in terms of survival value," Ariel interjected.

"Keeps me alive."

"See?"

"Nothing wrong with that," said Chaffney, "as long as you don't get too carried away."

"I don't think I do. I'm still here, aren't I?"

He smiled. "You're young."

We left. On the way out, Ariel passed close by Chaffney and he reached up to pat her on the neck.

"Aah, shit!" He stomped around, flapping his hand.

"What's the matter?" I demanded.

He wrung his hand for about half a minute, wincing and biting his bottom lip. Ariel stood a good distance away from him, eyes blazing. I couldn't tell if she was angry, hurt, or both.

"Shit!" repeated Chaffney. He said it another dozen times.

"What's the matter?" I asked again when he'd calmed down.

"My hand."

No shit. I waited for him to go on.

"It feels like I shoved it into a tar kettle. Christ, all I did was try to pat her on the neck!"

"You're not a virgin." I turned to Ariel. "Are you okay?"

She nodded. "I've never felt anything like that before." She sounded shaken. "So cold . . . like an icicle through my neck."

Chaffney still nursed his hand. Whatever had happened to it, it looked all right. "Keep your hands off her," I said. "You aren't pure; you aren't fit to touch her. She's *my* Familiar."

Asmodeus, sensing the threat in my voice, screeched and spread her wings.

"Ease off, Pete," said Ariel. "He didn't mean anything by it."

Chaffney reached up and stroked Asmodeus to calm her. "Look, I'm sorry. Really. All I did was try to give her a friendly pat, the way anybody would if they were standing by a horse."

"She's not a horse."

"I know that. I forgot for a minute, okay? I won't do it again." He paused. I avoided his gaze. "Okay?" he repeated.

"Sure."

Ariel pawed at the library steps, striking sparks. "Come on, let's get moving."

We walked, Chaffney leading. None of us spoke. Every so often Chaffney reached up to stroke Asmodeus reassuringly. He didn't look back at us.

Ariel, walking on my right, kept her head inclined, watching the pavement flow beneath her. I heard her hooves as they touched the asphalt. Every now and then she looked up and gave me a curious, sideways glance. I frowned and looked away.

After twenty minutes of this I'd had enough. I caught up to Chaffney. He didn't say anything as I walked beside him. I checked a sudden desire to stroke Asmodeus' feathers—I realized my urge to touch his buddy was the same as his had been to touch Ariel. "I'm sorry," I said, adjusting the waistband on the backpack frame just to have something to do with my hands.

"Don't worry about it."

"All you did was try to pet her. I shouldn't have reacted like that. I don't know why I did."

He leaned his head forward so he could squint at me past Asmodeus. "No big deal. I understand."

I tried to apologize further but he interrupted. "It's all right," he said, glancing back at Ariel. "I understand."

We reached Malachi Lee's house around two-thirty. It was a medium-sized, wooden, two-story house in the middle of a residential block. The yard was small and well-kept—unusual in an age where power mowers wouldn't work. A black iron fence surrounded the yard. The vertical bars ended in sharp pikes. On six of the pikes at the left side of the fence were six human heads.

I tried to smile. "Intimidating."

"People who tried to take the house," said Chaffney.

"Cute," said Ariel. "Makes people think twice about trying the same thing."

"Doesn't that attract buzzards?" I asked.

"Maybe he thinks the deterrent value is worth it." Ariel glanced at me, black eyes soft. "Chin up, Pete."

The first three heads had been there long enough to be nothing more than clean-picked skulls. They reminded me of those statues on Easter Island, maybe because their empty eyes looked toward something I couldn't see. The fourth and fifth skulls were eaten half away, and the sixth had been put up recently. I guessed it had been there three or four days. Most of the features were still recognizable. I swallowed a lump in my throat.

Chaffney struck a bell on a post beside the gate.

"Look, he's probably busy," I said. "We really don't need to see him, anyway. It's not that important."

"Sure it is. He'll want to meet Ariel. You can talk to him about the Change."

"But what if he doesn't want to meet *us?*" I whispered to Ariel. She looked pointedly at the skulls on the fence. Great.

Chaffney rang the bell again. The front door opened and a man walked out, followed by an enormous black chow. As they neared I saw the intelligent sparkle in the dog's eyes. It seemed to grin sloppily as its black tongue lolled.

Malachi Lee was tall and had black hair. He wore a black silk kimono. A samurai sword in a black lacquered sheath was thrust into the left side of the wide sash about his middle, blade up. It was a long, curved, two-handed sword with a dark green, twined grip. He dialed the padlock on the gate, opened it, and stepped through. The dog followed.

He stopped when he saw Ariel. I think I know some of what he felt: he was seeing her and nothing else. He walked around her, just looking her over. His face was impassive.

He stopped in front of her. "Well," he said.

I stood straighter, proud to be associated with something that took your breath away to see. And today Ariel was particularly breathtaking: her coat glowed in the bright afternoon sun with a white almost painful to look at. Her horn shimmered like a fire opal in soft but fiery colors: greens, yellows, blues, reds, and oranges buried deep within the horn, fighting furiously to escape.

"Hello," said Ariel after a while.

Chaffney shifted. Malachi didn't notice. Chaffney cleared his throat. "Malachi, this is—"

"Quiet."

Chaffney shut up. Malachi Lee drew his sword. I jumped and started toward him, but a stern look from Ariel halted me.

"I am Malachi Lee," he said, holding up the sword. It flashed in the sun. He lay it carefully on the ground before Ariel's bright mirror hooves. "And I would consider it an honor to be at your service."

She looked carefully into his eyes. I felt a pang in the pit of my stomach—jealousy?

"I am Ariel," she said after a minute, and she touched the tip of her horn to the sword. "And I thank you."

Malachi Lee nodded. He retrieved the blade and sheathed it. It found its way back into the scabbard as though it had eyes of its own. He just looked at Ariel and she gazed quietly back, tail swishing, sending rainbow dots everywhere.

I coughed into my hand. Malachi Lee seemed to break from a pleasant daydream. "She's yours?" he asked, looking me up and down. Big Man On Campus sizes up wimpy date of prom queen.

"Uh, yes. That is, we're each other's. I'm Pete—"

He bowed a short bow and stepped forward with his hand extended. I shook it. Strong grip. Calluses like leather. The expression on his face was unreadable. "You're a very lucky person."

I felt my face turning red. "Why, thank you." I felt genuinely flattered and wasn't quite sure how to handle it. I looked at Ariel. Her eyes smiled back.

The falcon screeched and spread its wings. Malachi turned to her. "I hear you, Asmodeus." He looked at Chaffney for the first time. Both men had a distant, guarded look in their eyes. "She's living up to her name, I hope?"

Chaffney folded his arms. "She is, yes."

"Name?" I asked tentatively. Why did I feel there was more going on here than I knew?

Malachi turned back to me. "Yes, Asmodeus. Demon in Christian mythology. And Jewish. Had its roots in Persia. Asmodeus was the prince of the Revengers of Evil—for what that's worth—often portrayed as a winged man."

"Malachi named her when he cast the loyalty spell," supplied Chaffney. "He . . . asked a high price for her loyalty." He studied Malachi Lee levelly. "She was worth it. I've never regretted it." He unfolded his arms, and with that the strange tension seemed to melt away. "I thought you'd like to meet them," he said.

"Yes."

"They came into the city yesterday afternoon. Me, Emilio, and Harry were standing overpass watch on the east side. I'm afraid Emilio started getting ideas about her horn."

Malachi frowned. "That's not good." He looked at me. "You don't need any trouble from him. He's no trouble by himself, but he has too many friends. Let me know if he bothers you."

"Thanks, but I think I can take care of my own problems."

"Suit yourself. But the offer still stands."

The big chow barked. Malachi bent and ruffled its thick fur. "Sorry, boy. Didn't mean to be rude. Pete, this is Faust, faithful companion and partner in hard times."

"Hi," I said, half-indulgently.

Faust barked once.

"Did you cast his loyalty spell?" I asked.

For a moment he looked angry. "No one did," he said. "We're friends." He patted the dog again. "Faust, this is Ariel. She's a unicorn, and as long as you know her I want you to treat her and guard her as you would me."

I thought that was a strange thing to say, but the dog barked once to Malachi and again to Ariel. She woofed once in return. I cast her a sidelong glance—I don't know if she really spoke dog-ese or if she was just humoring our host.

"Ariel's a good name," said Malachi. "Did you pick it?"

"Yes. I liked it."

"Shakespeare would have loved it."

I shot him a puzzled look.

His eyebrows crept up. "I thought that's where you got it. Shakespeare. *The Tempest*. Ariel was a magical character."

"Oh." I felt stupid. "I saw it on a book with a picture of a unicorn on the cover. I thought it fit her."

"Oh, it fits her, all right. Come inside." He shook his head wonderingly. "I'd like to find out what it's like to be the Familiar of a unicorn." He turned and held the gate open for us. Faust, Chaffney and Asmodeus, Ariel, and I—a dog, a leather-jacketed man with a falcon on his shoulder, a unicorn, and a twenty-year-old virgin—walked into the yard. Malachi locked the gate behind us and caught up to Russ. He extended his arm. "Do you mind?"

Russ spread his hands. "Go ahead." He shrugged his right shoulder and Asmodeus flapped onto Malachi's proffered arm. He stroked her head with a finger. "Faust—you two go play."

The bird flapped from Malachi's arm and sped across the yard, flying close to the ground. Barking, Faust ran after her.

I shook my head. What a day.

The front door was booby-trapped. It was rigged to kill anybody who walked in after it was armed. The door opened outward. Tied to the inside knob was a string which turned a corner round a pulley, went through the trigger of a loaded Wildcat crossbow, and was secured on a nail driven low into the wall. The bolt was aimed belly-level at the door. Once it was opened, the string tautened, the trigger pulled, the bolt flew, and there was a body on the front porch. There was no way you'd be able to slam the door or duck in time.

"What if somebody stays behind the door when they open it?" I asked. "The bolt'll hit it and they'll just come on in."

"Faust is my watchdog at night." He reset the string on the knob after we were inside. "He usually stays in the yard. Anybody in front of that door has to deal with him first. You can see the iron grillwork set in the windows. There's no other way in; all other doors have been bolted shut and reinforced from the inside."

"What if somebody kills Faust and comes in? It could happen, you know."

"Then they'll have me to deal with."

"What if you're asleep?"

"I'm a light sleeper."

"Oh."

five

It is an astonishing fact that there are *laws of nature, rules that summarize conveniently—not just qualitatively but quantitatively—how the world works. We might imagine a universe in which there are no such laws, in which the 10^{80} elementary particles that make up a universe like our own behave with utter and uncompromising abandon.*

—Carl Sagan,
Broca's Brain

"I'm not sure it had a cause," said Malachi. "I think it may have just . . . happened."

We sat—with the exception of Ariel, who stood—in Malachi Lee's living room. The furniture was shabby: springs broken, linings showing, chair legs wobbly, threads hanging from the upholstery which had pulled loose from the bottom of the couch. The walls were undecorated, except for one which was covered by crammed bookshelves. All kinds of books, from cheap paperbacks to leather-bound, gold-stamped hardcovers. Many had been stolen from the Atlanta Public Library; no wonder I hadn't been able to find some of the ones I'd been looking for.

"How could the Change have 'just happened'?" I countered. "Change implies cause, and cause implies source. Things don't just *happen.*"

"Then I have to ask my question again: what caused the old universe—call it the Newtonian universe. Until you can answer that I'm forced to conclude that things either do happen without cause, or that they have causes we'll never be able to understand or prove. I don't think there's anything 'supernatural' at all about the world as it is now. It just works under different laws of physics."

"'Different laws of physics,'" said Ariel, "and 'supernatural' seem synonymous to me."

He frowned. "All right, I'll grant you that. But the end result is the same. 'A difference which makes no difference is no difference.' I cast a spell and it works whether you call it supernatural or different operant physics. I conjure a demon and it appears. No matter what the cause, the result is the same. To say it can't be is to say Ariel can't exist—yet there she is."

"Thanks. I was starting to think you guys were about to tell me I couldn't be here. I'm told that's rude."

Chaffney pursed his lips. "But what about when you conjured that demon, Pete? I mean, what were you trying then? Were you trying to do magic, or—"

"I was curious," I interrupted, not wanting to be reminded of the affair. "I just wanted to see what would happen. I don't need proof that magic exists—why should I?" I hooked a thumb at Ariel.

Malachi stood. "You tried a conjuration?"

I nodded.

"Yeah, tell him about it, Pete," Chaffney said. He looked at Malachi. "He told me about it in the library last night. It's a great story. Go on, Pete. This is Malachi's thing."

Malachi rubbed his chin thoughtfully. "I would like to hear it."

I sat back in the threadbare chair. "You tell him," I told Ariel sullenly. "I'm tired of telling people about it."

She snorted, but told him the whole mess pretty much as I had related it the previous night. The story gave me the creeps; I didn't want to repeat it. Not that listening to it was much better. The more I re-lived it the more I realized I must have got off lucky.

There was silence when she finished. Malachi Lee searched my face for some reaction. "That's what happened?" he asked.

"Yeah."

He shook his head. "You're very fortunate, you know that?"

"I'm beginning to appreciate it, yes."

He went back to looking thoughtful and then walked to his bookcase, searching titles with sweeps of his index finger. It stopped in front of a black, leather-bound book. He pulled it out, opened it, and turned pages until his eyes rested on something that seemed to satisfy him. He read for a minute, nodding to himself, then handed the book to me. "Is this the conjuration you used?"

The book was a dead weight. To touch it was to hold something grimy, like the oily dust that collects in garages. The archaic print, the yellowed pages—everything was the same as that other book. Even the leather was as worn and cracking. And the conjuration—no way I would forget that spell. It didn't matter that I hadn't known the meaning of the words; they looked foul and sounded worse. "Yes, this is it."

"You're sure?" He looked as if he hoped I would deny it.

"Positive."

He took the book from me and held it open before Ariel. "Ariel?"

She barely glanced at it. "I think it is. I don't remember very well."

"Sure you do," I said. "You're the one who picked it out. You said you were curious about that one. You remember."

"I don't read Latin," she said.

"But last night you told Russ you knew what it meant." She avoided my gaze. "What's wrong?"

"You knew what this was, didn't you?" Malachi asked her.

The barest dip of her horn.

"You knew what this meant and you let him go ahead? Why?"

She turned away. "I thought I understood the risks."

"Why?"

Her head swiveled back and she looked darkly into his eyes. "I thought I could handle it!"

"You thought you. . . . You mean you didn't even tell him?"

"Tell me what?" I asked.

"He wouldn't have done it! And I couldn't have. I can't make the motions, or—"

"Do you need to test your power that much?"

She was silent, but there was something in the way her eyes flashed at him that I'd never seen before: it was almost . . . resentment. A woman scorned, perhaps. But she said nothing and the question hung thickly in the air.

Malachi turned to me with the book. "Do you know what this means?"

Ariel interrupted."You don't have to—"

"He deserves to know. Do you, Pete?"

"Judging by the results I got from using it," I said carefully, "I would assume that it's a spell for conjuring a minor demon."

"Oh, it's that, all right." His lips pressed together tightly. "This is the translation of the conjuration you used." He cleared his throat. I glanced questioningly at Ariel but she wouldn't meet my eyes.

"I summon thee,
O Dweller in the Darkness,
O Spirit of the Pit.
I command thee
To make thy
Most evil appearance.
In the name of
Our mutual benefactor,
In the name of
Lucifer the Fallen
I conjure thee
By his blood-lettered sacraments,
By Hell and by Earth
To come to me now,
In your own guise
To do your will.

"I adjure thee
In the name of
The foulest of masters
By his loins,
By his blood,
By his damned soul,
To come forth.

"I order thee
By all the unholy names:
Lucifer, Satan, Beelzebub,
Belial, Shai-tan, Mephistopheles,
Thy hair, thy heart,
Thy lungs, thy blood,
To be here
To work your will
Upon me."

He closed the book.

Ariel still wouldn't meet my eyes. "*'To work your will upon me'?*" I whispered. "Ariel, how could you?"

A ripple flowed down her flank. "I had to know. I'm sorry, but I had to know if I could beat it."

"You're sorry! That conjuration practically offers my life if a demon comes!"

She lowered her head until her horn almost touched the floor. When she raised it again there was a crystal-bright streak beneath each ebony eye. Tears stung in my own eyes at the sight. "Oh, Pete," she said softly. In her voice I heard that lost-little-girl voice from when I first met her, saying "bwoke" with such hurt pleading. "I was much younger then, and foolish. It was done from my ignorance and insecurity. I never meant to play games—stupid games—with your life, Pete. You know that."

"I thought I knew that." I was numb inside.

"Pete! You don't mean that." She looked in desperation at Malachi. "Why did you have to tell him?"

Calmly: "He deserved to know. You should have been the one to tell him."

"It was stupid; it was a stupid thing for me to do!" She stepped toward me but I held up a hand.

"No. I . . . think I'll take a walk or something. I want to be alone." I wanted so much to say that yes, it was okay, that it was no big deal and of course I loved her. But I couldn't, not the way I felt then. It wasn't so much that she'd used me, but that she'd never told me.

She was still talking, but she sounded far away. The walls closed in on me; I wanted out.

"Pete, please! It was long ago; I was still growing up. I didn't understand what any of it meant."

I paused at the door. "You still could have told me." I turned to go out the door.

Everything happened with horrifying suddenness, but with the slow motion of a dream. It felt choreographed, executed with precision timing. I grabbed the knob and turned it. Behind me Malachi yelled *"No!"* and I thought, fuck you, you can't make me stay, and I opened the door. I looked back as I did so, just in time to see a white blur as Ariel cleared the space from the living room to the front door in one leap. With a movement almost too fast to follow she twitched her head, batting at something with her horn. I started to wonder what she was trying to do. The thought never had time to complete itself because a muscular giant buried a sharpened pickaxe in the middle of my back.

I looked down at myself as I fell. Something protruded from my stomach. I wondered what it was, but was interrupted by the distant thump of my body hitting the front porch.

Gee, I thought, *it doesn't even hurt.*

A giant black heel came down from the sky and blotted out the sun.

six

Will the unicorn be willing to serve thee, or abide in thy crib?

Canst thou bind the unicorn with his band in the furrows? or will he harrow the valleys after thee?

Wilt thou trust him because his strength is great? or wilt thou leave thy labour to him?

Wilt thou believe him, that he will bring home thy seed, and gather it into thy barn?

—Job, xxxix; 9–12

It was dark out there.

That's all I remember thinking for a long time, that it was dark out there, that I was at the bottom of an ocean of black water and was fighting my way up to distant daylight. It was formless black and stagnant, no eddies or swirls.

Starless, I thought. *Starless and Bible black.*

I couldn't feel anything. Why couldn't I feel anything?

Because someone stuck a giant hypo in your back and shot you full of Novocain. Whole body. Numb. Numbnumbnumbnumb.

Oh, yeah. It's frightening to walk in the dark if you can't even feel your way around. What did that remind me of? Oh, sure: "The Pit and the Pendulum." Good old Poe.

Was there some deeper hole out there in that blackness, waiting for me to find it?

(Pete.)

Whoa. Where did that come from? I didn't say it. Did I?

(Pete.)

No, I didn't say that. Wonder who—

(Pete, I'm trying to help you. You have to want me to.)

I tried to talk. Mouth wouldn't work. Full of cotton. I turned the mental volume all the way up and shouted: GO AWAY! I LIKE IT HERE. IT'S COMFORTABLE. If only I could feel something. . . .

Instantly I regretted the thought. I could feel again, all right, and what I felt was pain, pain and nothing else, not even any room for relief at being *able* to feel pain. The pain was a white spearpoint of light, a hot poker rammed into my back and spreading as though gunpowder laced my veins, and everywhere the light touched it set the gunpowder off. It hurt and I cried. What had *I* done?

The light burned through the fuse of my veins until it had seared through my entire body, reaching my head last. The points of sewing needles were jammed against my upper bicuspid molars and I was forced to bite down hard. White heat tried to melt all the bone of my skull, and everywhere the burning white touched it left a space, an empty spot, where the blackness used to be.

(Good, Pete. Help me.)

Vise grips clamped onto my lower back and stomach. They tightened and tightened and tightened. Internal organs were pushed together, a wet, rubbery, sliding feeling, and something gave like an overfilled water balloon: *poosh!* I vomited. It fell away into that blackness without a splash.

(Closer, Pete. We're getting closer.)

Closer to what? Fuck you, anyway, I liked the dark better. It didn't hurt. That's what I get for listening to voices in the dark. Who cares if I can see the light? Who cares if I can feel it? It *hurts!* I need more than that. I need. . . .

(Tell me.)

I can't! I don't know what it is. I need something. . . . A child's thing. . . .

(Tell me what you need, Pete.)

A . . . teddy bear? No, but close. Something—something I can hold on to in the dark, something . . . silken. I need a guide. . . . Something that only I can touch because I am special. But there's no such thing; magical companions don't exist.

(Pete, listen. Please listen, Pete.)

From far away, like an old gramophone recording (those don't work anymore, I thought), came a voice, the voice of a lost child:

(For the sword outwears its sheath,
And the soul wears out the breast.)

Somewhere something stirred. A forgotten memory pricked up its soft ears. Silver . . .

(And the heart must pause to breathe,
And love itself must rest.)

Yes, silver . . . hooves, and—sparks, streams of sparks, falling like glowing red snowflakes onto asphalt. And a name—

Ariel! The name was cast to me and I seized it before I could be pulled back under. Ariel, help me, bring me back!

(Always remember that I love you, Pete.)

I was picked up and thrown into the middle of the blackness, and it shattered. The dark fragments fell away, and beyond them was light, not painful light, but the pure light from an ivory horn.

I reached out to touch it and pitched forward. Darkness reigned again.

The wait in the darkness was not as long this time, and when I woke up it was six years earlier.

seven

May you live in interesting times.

—Ancient Chinese Curse

As I swallowed the last bite of Spaghetti-o's the phone rang and a car horn blared outside. I dashed to the door, stuck my head out, and yelled, "Be there in a second, Grace!" Behind the wheel of her Falcon—on its last legs, poor thing, but we still called it the *Millennium Falcon* with affection—Grace smiled and nodded. I ran back to the phone and lifted the receiver in mid-ring. "Hello?"

"Hey there."

"Hi, Mom. I hate to cut you short, but—"

"What time is your debate tournament?"

"Four, and it's three-thirty already. Grace just pulled up."

"Things would be a lot easier for you if you'd go to work and earn enough money to get yourself a car."

"Mom—"

"All right." Her voice warmed. "Do well at your tournament, hon."

I smiled. "Don't I always?"

"I wouldn't know. You've never brought home a trophy."

"'Bye, Mom."

"I'll see you when I get home."

I hung up, put on my ugly brown and green coat, and stuffed its non-matching tie into a pocket so I could carry the briefcase and card file outside. I hoped Grace wasn't pissed off; she'd gone out of her way to pick me up as it was.

Accouterments dumped into the back seat, Grace put the car in gear and we headed out. "Where is everybody?" she asked, commenting on the empty driveway.

I ticked them off on my fingers: "My brother has a soccer game in Miami Springs. My parents—my mom, I mean—is at work. I'm going to a debate tournament. I think our dog's out on the back porch. My father's dead."

"Not funny."

"So solly."

The rest of the drive to our high school was spent in silence. Grace parked in the senior parking lot because it made her feel superior; we were both freshmen.

At the cafeteria Grace and I spotted our school's other three teams.

"Master debaters," I announced, "we are here!"

Bill Thurgood looked up to regard me blandly with his pasty-faced expression. "You'll pardon us if we don't stand up," he said.

I gave him my best diabetes-inducing smile. "I thought you *were* standing up, Bill." Bill was short.

Jim Allen, the club president, handed us a dittoed sheet still smelling faintly of alcohol. "We've got a bye in the third round." I pointed out the shadowed box to Grace.

"You've also got a round right now in two-thirty-six. You're negative team."

"Wonderful."

The team was waiting for us when we got to 236. We set up quickly, introduced ourselves, shook hands all around, and got started.

The lights went out just as I concluded my rebuttal speech. It was four-thirty. We opened the shades to brighten the room and resumed the debate.

We had an hour-long break between first and second rounds. Grace and I went out to her car, planning to grab dinner at Burger King.

The car wouldn't start.

"Did you check the tires?" I asked.

"Funny." She turned the key in the ignition once more, pumping the gas pedal with her high-heeled foot.

"Alas, poor *Falcon,*" I said mournfully. "I knew it well."

She shot me a hateful look. "Don't you know anything about cars? I thought all guys were supposed to."

"Fortunately, I am not the typical high school male. This is everything I know about cars: you put the key in and turn it. Through some mystical process I'll never understand, the engine starts. If you want to go forward you press your foot down. If something goes wrong you fix it."

"And how do you fix it?"

I shrugged. "You call a mechanic."

"Gee, thanks." She pulled the key out of the ignition. "I suppose it hasn't occurred to you that this is your way home tonight too."

"Yes, it has. Look, your engine's not even turning over. It's probably your battery. Maybe we could get a jump from somebody."

"Yeah, okay. Good idea." Her tone said that she didn't think it was such a good idea, but that she had no better one.

I got out and walked over to another car with two guys sitting in the front seat. They looked familiar; I think they were from Killian High. I explained our situation to the driver and asked if he could give us a jump. Grace had cables in her trunk.

"Sorry," he said. "I can't get mine to start, either."

I frowned. Looking over the roof of his car I saw three people trying to push-start a Volkswagen at the far end of the parking lot. "Have you looked under the hood yet?" I asked him.

"No. It's probably the same problem you've got, though. Dead battery."

"Or a missing one." I pointed at the Volkswagen. "I wouldn't put it past somebody to come by here and steal batteries out of some of the cars."

He got out and opened the hood. The battery was still there. "Well, that answers that. Let's try something." He opened his trunk and pulled out a set of jumper cables. After attaching them to the battery's terminals he held the loose ends and touched them together. "Nothing," he said. "No spark."

"Holy shit!" yelled his friend on the passenger's side. "Did you see that?"

"What?" the driver and I asked simultaneously.

He pointed. "From out of the trees by the road there. It was . . . huge. Some kind of animal. Like a lion, but bigger. Lots bigger."

"Bear, maybe?"

I made a rude noise. "Our school might be out in the boonies, but it's not that far out." The guy who'd seen the animal got out from the car. "Where'd it go?" I asked.

"It just shot out from between the trees and ran around the corner, that way." He pointed west. I looked at the intersection where he was pointing. The red light was out. Below it were unmoving cars.

Grace came up beside me. "It looks like everything's stopped at once," she said.

Grace and I tried to call home for rides. The phones weren't working. Not even a dial tone.

Nobody else could give us a ride home either. Their cars wouldn't work. Even electric watches had stopped.

"Come on," I said to Grace. "Let's go home."

"How?"

"Your legs still work, don't they?"

"It's at least a three-hour walk!"

I grabbed her arm. "Grace. Something's happened. I don't know what could have caused it, but nothing that uses electricity is working."

"Let go of my arm."

I took my hand away. "Sorry."

She rubbed her arm and looked around—taking the opportunity to back a step away from me. "Everything feels . . . different. I don't like this. It's too quiet."

I nodded. "No cars. No power hum. No planes in the sky."

She bit her lower lip, looking at the cars stopped beneath the dark traffic light. "It's like a scene from a movie I saw once. There was this flying saucer and a robot—"

"*The Day the Earth Stood Still*. The robot's name was Gort."

"Oh." She blinked. "The robot's name was Gort." She tried to smile and her lips quivered.

"Come on, let's go. It'll be dark soon and I don't want to spend most of my time on the road at night." I looked toward the trees where the huge animal had been seen.

"My debate stuff. I don't want to leave my debate stuff here. It'll get stolen."

I didn't argue. I found a janitor and explained to him that we were leaving and wanted to stow our things—could he possibly open our debate class? He could.

That accomplished, we hit the road.

We were silent most of the way, each wrapped in our own thoughts and one question underlying them all: *what had happened?*

It was completely dark before we were three-fourths of the way home. My feet were aching by the time we got there. Hers couldn't have felt any better. I walked her to her house, which was some five miles from mine. I guessed it was a little after eight o'clock when we arrived. We'd seen no people on the road, only a few useless cars stopped in the act of turning or abandoned in the street.

Her house was empty. No lights, which I'd been expecting, but no candles burning either. No telltale flickering through the windows of neighboring houses. The front door was unlocked and we entered cautiously.

"Mom?" she called out. Her voice wasn't very loud. "Dad?"

Nothing.

"Dad's probably still at work," she told me, "but Mom should be here."

"Maybe she went shopping." The nearest shopping center was Cutler Ridge—fifteen miles away.

"Maybe." She was silent a minute. "Pete, can we go outside? I don't like it in here. I can't see my hand in front of my face."

"Sure." We went outside. The neighborhood was eerily quiet, the only sound the chirping of crickets and croaking of frogs.

Grace sat down on the concrete front porch. She hugged her knees and looked at the ground. "What do I do?"

I sat wearily beside her. "You could stay here, but you don't know when your parents might be back. I'd offer to stay with you but I can't. My mother's at work in Miami—or was, at any rate—and my brother might even be home by now. It's still almost two hours' walk from here."

"I'll go with you."

"What about your parents?"

She shut her eyes. "I don't want to be alone here."

"Okay." I stood. "Let's get a move on then." I tried to smile.

"Hold on. I need to go to my room and get some socks and another pair of shoes." She started back into the house, but paused at the doorway. "Now that I think of it, I'd better bring some clothes and things, too. I doubt I'll be back before tomorrow at least."

She came back in a few minutes with a small overnight bag in hand. "I left a note. Let's go."

We left. She didn't look back.

We took back roads toward my house. The further we stayed from Krome Avenue and other main roads, the less paranoid I felt. If this thing continued people would panic, and I wanted no part of it.

Once we saw a small group of people in the distance. They carried torches and their shouts reached us clearly through the quiet. It looked like a scene from one of the old Universal horror movies: angry villagers march on Frankenstein's castle. We stayed clear.

About a mile from my house Grace saw something moving in the bushes. We stopped and I cocked my head to listen, but heard nothing except spooky wind through the trees. We resumed walking and then I heard it, too: a heavy sound, as if something that weighed an awful lot were stomping through the brush. Curiosity told me to wait and see what it was. Rationality told me to keep right on going. Rationality won.

In a little while we reached my neighborhood. It was sparsely populated and a bit spread out; everybody had built their houses at random there in the boondocks. Grace and I crossed the bridge over the dark canal and headed down the street toward my house. We were tired and our feet dragged. It was quiet except for the wind and the frogs, but there was nothing unusual about that. No lights were on in any houses, though; no cars passed us along the way. I was used to blackouts where we lived; heavy storms often brought lines down. But the thing that made it all seem wrong was the absence of the pale orange city glow of Miami to the north.

We stopped at the foot of the driveway. Wooden posts holding up a pitifully sagging fence framed the entranceway. A wooden sign, painted by my father years ago, read *The Gareys*. As I'd expected, no lights were on, no candles burned in the living room windows. Mom's car wasn't in the driveway, either.

"What now?" Grace asked.

"We wait. See if my brother makes it home. Or my mother. If not I'll leave a note and tomorrow we'll go back to your house and see if anybody showed up there."

"And after that?"

Any reply I could have made was stopped by the shattering of glass. I jerked my head toward the house. One of the living room windows was now broken. As I watched, the window to the left of it smashed as a portable television—my brother's—hurtled through to crash onto the front porch.

Grace started to say something but I motioned to her to stay quiet. The sound would carry far in the silence. I wanted to whisper to her but couldn't swallow the lump that had formed in my throat.

We squatted low by the mailbox, our voices tight hisses.

"Well?" demanded Grace. "Now what?"

I shook my head, looking at the grass at Grace's feet. It needed mowing. "I don't know."

"Could that be your brother in there? Could he be throwing things because he's mad, because he's afraid?"

"Yeah. Get serious."

"We need to find out. If it's him, we can't just leave him."

I let out a short laugh. "Sure. But who bells the cat?" I looked up at her. "I find it extremely likely that it's not my brother."

She blinked. "Well—there's one way to find out."

"Yeah, I guess so." I pulled a clump of grass from the dirt and tossed it aside. Standing, I brushed my hands against my slacks. "I'll be back in a few minutes. I hope."

"No way. I'm not standing here. I'd rather go with you than wait here." She glanced around to indicate the silent neighborhood.

"Suit yourself. But we've got to be quiet. Understand?"

"I know how to be quiet. Even girls can do it, under pressure."

I raised an eyebrow at her, then turned toward the house.

The house sat in the middle of a two-acre lot. Grace and I stayed off the U-shaped driveway; we would have been black shadows against the light gray concrete. Instead we crawled on the grass beside the driveway until we were even with the front porch, then I crawled left until I was against the garage wall. I found all this surrealistic: I felt as if I were playing Army, as if I were leading a commando raid against my own house. I waited until Grace caught up to me and put my lips to her ear. "Wait here," I breathed. "I'm going to see if I can get a good look through the window." She started to protest but I squeezed her arm hard. "One of us has less chance of being seen than both of us." I turned away from her.

I crept along the grass the length of the garage wall until I reached the front porch, where I stopped and tried to calm my breathing and slow my heart, which was trying to hammer its way out of my chest. Shards from the broken window flashed on the front porch, my brother's television in their midst. By the front door was something white and shapeless. It looked like a towel that had been tossed there and forgotten.

I inched forward on hands and knees until I was beneath the nearest window. I stopped under it and held my breath. Voices came from inside. I made out at least three, all male. I glanced behind me. Good—the road made a dark backdrop. When I looked through the window I didn't want my head showing as a black silhouette against a light background.

Placing my hands on the windowsill, I raised myself up slowly. The curtains were drawn; I couldn't see a thing. Next window, then. I went back to hands and knees and crawled four feet to the next window, our big picture window. I cut my palm on a piece of glass, but not badly. I wiped it against my pants.

As I got under the window and prepared to look in, I glanced toward the front door and was shocked to recognize the shapeless white towel. It was Snoopy. She lay on the doormat with her head bashed in. I sat there, looking at her, for a long time.

Grace's scream brought me out of it. I jumped up and turned toward her. *Fuck—if anybody was looking toward the front windows they know you're here now, idiot.*

A man was holding Grace in a bear hug. She struggled futilely, kicking his shins. As I ran for them I heard the front door open behind me, but I didn't look back.

I'm sure I looked ludicrous when I reached Grace: I stopped dead in front of her because she was between me and her attacker. I ran around them so I could hit him from behind, but they whirled as they struggled, so that she faced me again.

Her fingernails left bloody trails on his arms. I only hesitated a moment, then ran in, pushed Grace's head out of the way, and hit him full on the jaw. He let go of Grace and staggered back. I recognized him then. Mr. Hess, from up the block. What the hell was he doing here? He was a *cop*, for God's sake.

I should have moved in and finished him off while he was still dazed, but the moment of recognition had caused me to hesitate yet again. Good ol' Pistol-Packin' Pete, always quick on the draw. That hesitation probably cost me everything—I was hit hard from behind. If I'd been on concrete I'd have come away with at least a fractured skull. As it was, I got the wind knocked out of me as I pitched forward onto the grass with two of them on top of me. They turned me over and held me down. I didn't struggle; it would have been stupid. One of them bent over and punched me in the jaw. I didn't go out, but bright blue-white sheeted across my vision. One of them kicked me in the crotch. Nauseating fire spread in waves. I'd been hit there before, but not like that, never full out like that. All I remember from then on is fists blurring into one another, over and over again until I couldn't feel them anymore.

I woke up in a ditch. Sunlight lanced my eyes. My mouth was a puffy mass somebody had taken an electric sander to. A dull, heavy ache in my groin. Ribs seemed bruised but not broken. Beside me was an upside-down wheelbarrow. I recognized it; it was from our garage. They must have wheeled me out here and dumped me. Maybe they'd left me for dead. I think they came close.

I found I could move well enough to get out of the ditch, albeit painfully. I counted my blessings and dragged myself to the side of the road and lay there, eyes closed. I was tired, so tired. . . .

When I opened my eyes again the sun had just set. I got up—I won't say what it felt like. The ground kept slanting and I saw double. That went away soon but my vision was still blurry and my head rang.

Looking around, I realized I was less than two hundred yards from my house. My feet began moving automatically; I stood before the front door before I realized what I was doing. I looked down. Snoopy was still there. Two windows were shattered. The television rested in the glass. It took two hands

and all my strength to press down the latch and open the door.
I found Grace inside.

Next day: in the kitchen I stuffed the last of what food I could take into the green, magnesium-framed backpack my parents had given me one Christmas. I closed the flaps, secured the cords with tight knots, and put my arms through the shoulder straps. I fastened the waistband and walked into the living room, looking around grimly once more before going out the front door for the last time in my life. A cloud of flies buzzed away when I stepped over Snoopy. I walked down the driveway and onto the first of many long roads I would take from then on.

I stopped at the canal a half-mile away. The water was crystal clear. The weeds, or whatever the hell you call them, swayed languidly on the bottom. I set my pack down and sat on the edge of the bridge, looking into the water for a long time.

That canal used to be filthy. Neighborhood kids swam in it; I never understood how they could stand it. The water had been brown, the edges of the bank lined with dark green scum. Now it was clear. No scum, no floating beer cans. No rusted shopping cart, pushed in by Jeff Simmons a year ago. I shook my head, not understanding, and shouldered my pack. I turned to go and stopped cold.

Something stood on the road ahead of me. It was the size of a mobile home. I'd never seen anything like it, not outside a theater or an H.P. Lovecraft story. Superficially it looked like a lion; at least, it had a lion's body. It was shaggy and the hair was darker and much coarser than a lion's, almost like a Brillo pad. It had a disturbingly human face. The features were almost caricatured: practically no lip, a large, wide, and vaguely Negroid nose, bushy eyebrows, and smoldering red eyes. The face was framed by a thick, brown mane. On its rear end, where a lion's tail should have been, was the tail of a scorpion. It was long and segmented, and poised with the contained power of a cobra's neck. It ended in a needle-like stinger a foot long. The tail waved back and forth in the air.

It was motionless and silent, regarding me with hot, cherry-red eyes.

(A year later I would be in a library, leafing through a text on mythological animals, and I would stop when I came across a picture resembling this creature. I would remember the name underneath: *manticore.)*

It headed for me, slowly at first, but gradually gathering speed. There was nowhere to run, no way on earth to get away from this thing. It left the road, ran a short space on the grass by the canal bank, and jumped when it reached the bridge. It sailed over my head and landed on the other side of the canal. The force of its landing vibrated through the soles of my shoes. I almost wet my pants. The thing didn't even look at me as it hit; it just began running at terrific speed down the road. I watched until it disappeared in the distance down the long, straight road, and then for a long time watched the space where it had vanished.

Somehow the world had changed. Just looking at that space where this impossible thing had been a few minutes before, I knew that. There'd been a Change, and the world would never again be the same.

I never found my mother or my brother. I left behind me the house I'd grown up in, empty except for the stiffening corpse that had been Grace.

eight

God brought them out of Egypt; he hath as it were the strength of the unicorn.

—Numbers, xxiii; 22

I opened my eyes.

I was flat on my back in a bed, staring at a ceiling. It was covered with centerfolds, pictures of nude women in an amazing array of poses. I followed them with my eyes, across the ceiling, down a wall—

Ariel stood by the door, looking at me unblinkingly with those dark eyes.

"Hi, there," I said.

"You're back," she said.

"Back? I never. . . ." And then I remembered. I looked down at my stomach. I wasn't wearing a shirt and could see the scar tissue where the bolt had come through. "Yeah," I said, avoiding her eyes. "I'm back."

She nodded and turned away, walking silently out the door. A minute later Malachi Lee entered, wearing baggy black pants and a white T-shirt. On the front was a picture of two vultures sitting on a fence. One of them was saying, "Patience, my ass—I wanna kill something!" Malachi's sword was slung at his side. I wondered if he ever let it out of arm's reach. "It even stays at the head of my bed when I sleep," he said, watching me look at it. I smiled.

"You certainly look better," he said as he came to the head of the bed. "How do you feel?"

"Like shit. How long did it take you to collect enough magazines to wallpaper this room?"

"Not long. I went to an adult bookstore downtown and brought them back in a wheelbarrow."

"Christ." I looked around the walls. "Don't you think this stuff is degrading?"

He shrugged. "It was something to do. You haven't seen the bathroom walls—one-dollar bills."

"Toilet paper, too?"

"Show some respect. Toilet paper is large denominations only, preferably with at least two zeroes. There's a healthy stack beside the chamber pot in case you need some."

I looked away from him. "How long was I out?"

"A long time. Four days."

Four days! "Did I eat anything? I ought to be starving but I'm not."

He nodded. "Last night you came out of it long enough for us to get some food and water into you. I don't think you knew where you were; you had a fever for three days. The sheets were soaked from your sweating. It broke last night."

I looked again at the pink mass of scar on my stomach. "It couldn't have been too bad; I'm almost healed. I thought I was dead when it happened."

He opened his mouth, closed it, and opened it again. "It was pretty bad."

"Oh, I'm sure I was probably a mess. I know the bolt came through here"—I patted my stomach—"but I must have lucked out and it didn't hit any vital organs—or did it? Come on, you can tell me. Did you have to do any backwoods surgery on me? I can take it, doc, long as I can play the piano again. What'd you have to use? Sewing needles and brandy? Exacto knives?"

"We were too late for surgery. You were dead by the time I got to you."

His face yielded nothing. "Yeah, sure," I said. "That's why you're telling me about it now."

He shrugged. "Have it your way. Do you want anything to eat?"

"How about just a glass of water?"

He nodded and left. I looked at the nude women on the

ceiling. Dead? No, how could I have been? I was here now. But I remembered that darkness I'd felt, and I shivered. It must have been a dream, a fever dream—one of the strange, eidetic dreams a person can have while sleeping a recuperative sleep. Or maybe in some way I had been aware of my comatose state. Hell, I didn't know.

Malachi returned with a glass of water. Ariel followed him in. I thanked him and he left. I drank. The water was warm; nobody had a way to keep water cold in the summer anymore.

"How are you feeling, Pete?" asked Ariel.

I set the glass on the nightstand to my right. "Fine." I avoided her gaze and after a minute she began looking around at the walls. "This room is odd. So many pictures of naked women."

I said nothing.

"What are they for?"

"They're . . . pornography. Pictures intended to . . . to elicit an erotic response."

"Oh," she said, as if that explained everything. I knew it didn't; she'd stopped inquiring because she could tell I was uncomfortable.

She inclined her horn toward my stomach. "You're healing well."

I nodded.

"Talk to me, Pete. Please."

"I don't have anything to say."

"Your feelings are still hurt."

I hesitated. Why bullshit? "Yes."

"You feel I betrayed a trust between us, right? And look what I've caused you—a stab in the back. Is that it?"

Tears welled in my eyes and I didn't respond.

"Okay," she said. "I'll leave you alone." She turned and left. The room was silent and still with the feeling that she'd never really been there at all; she could have been a dream I had had while I was feverish.

I thought about getting out of bed to see if I could move around a bit, or at least stand up on my own. I thought about it until I went to sleep.

Three days dragged by. Malachi Lee came in to feed me each day and we talked. I saw nothing of Ariel. When I asked about her, Malachi shrugged and said, "I don't know. The other day, the day you came out of it, she asked if she could borrow Faust for a week or two and they both left."

"She say where she was going, or when she'd be back?"

"No." He handed me another sandwich—Spam spread on biscuit. "You ought to get your head straight about her."

I shifted uncomfortably on the bed. Ever since I'd come out of my coma I'd figured I was strong enough to walk around, but Malachi would have none of it. "What do you mean?"

"You know what I mean. You're closing her out."

I didn't say anything.

"You have something most people would give up everything for, and you're taking it for granted." He stood. "You're a spoiled child."

"What the fuck do you expect me to do? Come out of it and say, 'Hey, Ariel, you almost got me killed and cost me my soul, but no sweat'?"

"She tried to explain it to you. She was immature, even if it was only a year ago. She didn't understand what it meant."

"She was using me to test her abilities, dammit."

He cracked his knuckles absently. "Little kids play with matches, but they're not trying to burn down the house." He sat down. His sword clinked against the folding chair beside the bed. "I saw her those four days you were out of it. You didn't. You were too busy being dead."

I snorted.

"Yes, dead." He leaned forward. "Perhaps you blame Ariel for your carelessness in getting a crossbow bolt through your back. But you better realize something—she brought you back." He sat back, folded his arms, and crossed his legs. "Russ and I watched her do it. It took her all that night. For a few hours she just looked at you, never taking her eyes from your face. There was no doubt you were dead, Pete—rigor mortis had begun to set in, and so had dependent lividity, when gravity makes the blood seep to the lowest points in the body because the heart's stopped pumping. Your pupils were dilated. Your bladder and sphincter muscles—"

"Stop!"

"Sorry. But you can't deny what I saw—I was there and you weren't."

"You don't have to be so graphic about it."

The hint of a smile returned. "We'd removed the bolt, and after a while Ariel touched the wound with her horn. It started to glow. It was dim, like a flashlight with near dead batteries, to use an anachronism. She stayed that way a few minutes and your whole body twitched. Your lips moved as though you were talking, but nothing came out—you weren't breathing yet. Then you started going through convulsions. Ariel told you that was good and for you to help her." He cleared his throat. "You vomited. It was bad; there was a lot of blood in it. Ariel said you were getting closer. You kept mouthing words at her until she started singing to you. She told you to always remember that she loved you and her horn got so bright Russ and I couldn't look at it. It was like a nova. It died down and she lifted her horn from you and walked past us. Russ stayed with you and I followed Ariel into the living room. She damn near collapsed onto the floor. She was crying." He paused. "You know what it's like to see her cry."

"Yeah."

"She was completely drained; all the energy had been taken out of her. She said she thought you'd be all right. I could barely hear her voice." He shrugged. "That's most of it. You'd started breathing when her horn went bright, and after a while Russ had to leave. Your fever started and Ariel and I took turns keeping a watch on you. You didn't even move until the fourth day, when we managed to get some food into you. You know the rest."

I felt stupid. What was I supposed to say? "I didn't know."

"I know you didn't. But don't shut her out. It's obvious she loves you. You don't need me to tell you she's more than just a horse with a horn, more than a unicorn, even."

I learned enough about Malachi Lee in those three days to be fascinated by him. We swapped Where-were-you-the-day-of-the-Change stories. It had become a way to get to know someone, a conversational ice-breaker, the same way many things in the past had been: Where were you the day John Kennedy was shot? Where were you when the Japanese invaded Pearl Harbor? When Apollo Eleven landed on the Moon?

His story was simple. He'd been reading a novel in the living room of the house I was in now. About five o'clock he'd looked up from the book. Something didn't seem right; it was too quiet. After doing what just about everyone else seemed to have done—discovered the power out, the phone dead—he went outside and saw it was the same everywhere, and not just for things a power failure would account for. His mind made one big leap: he marked his place in the novel, fed Faust, took his sword from its stand, and sat on the front porch, petting Faust and waiting for looters—though he didn't get his first fence decoration until a week later, when a marine sergeant type tried to rob him with a shotgun. "No doubt he didn't realize he'd have been better off with a baseball bat," he said, remembering, "as a shotgun isn't even well-suited as a club. But a sword—" he patted the black lacquerered sheath at his hip. "A sword always works."

On the fourth day after I regained consciousness Malachi caught me wandering around the house and ordered me back to bed.

"I'm okay," I insisted. "Watch." I bent down, touched my toes with my palms, straightened up, and bent partway backwards. "No fuss, no muss." I raised my shirt. "See—nice, pink, healed scar."

"It's your funeral."

At least he stopped harassing me about staying in bed and let me have the run of the house, allowing me to work my body back into shape. He showed me a few stretching exercises to help out, but mostly left me to my own devices. I was bored silly.

Three days after I'd got out of bed he caught me thumbing through his copy of *A Book of Five Rings* and asked if I wanted to learn to use a sword. Enthusiastic in my ignorance, I said yes.

The next two weeks were a nightmare. He worked on building stamina in my arm muscles, on honing my reflexes, and on my leg and arm flexibility, which was almost nonexistent. The training served a triple purpose: not only did I want to learn, but I'd lost a lot of weight during those four black days and felt I needed to get back into shape. It also helped keep my mind off Ariel. I had trouble sleeping because I was worried about her.

"The first thing you have to learn," Malachi said, "is how to control a blade." He handed me a long piece of wood, like a baseball bat but thicker, heavier, and squared rather than rounded, and made me pick an imaginary spot three feet in front of my head. He told me to swing at it with all my strength, but to stop the bat right on the mark and not let it go past. I went past it by a good eighteen inches my first try.

"Again," he said.

I kept it up for about fifty tries and then he made me reverse direction and do the same thing. My arms ached and my hands were numb against the wood by the time I finished. I asked for a break.

"Sure," he said.

I sighed with relief, took a long drink of water, and spread out in a big X on the grass.

"Break's over," he said.

He made me swing the bat overhead and down fifty times, stopping it at chest level. I hit the ground the first three tries.

I was given a wooden sword and told to carry it at all times, never letting it out of reach. Once he rushed into my room in the middle of the night, screaming like a lunatic. I barely had time to get my hands on the wooden sword handle before his blade was at my throat.

"You're a snail," he said mildly. "You have the right idea but you're slow." He sheathed his blade without looking at it. "How can you teach swordplay to someone with no instinct for self-preservation?"

He tried to teach me accuracy by hanging sheets of notebook paper on string from the ceiling. There'd be a blur as he drew his sword and returned it to the sheath, and a neat, one-inch strip of paper would waft its way to the floor. Before it hit he'd draw again, so fast I couldn't see the blade move, and another one-inch strip would join the first.

"You try," he said, and handed me his sword.

I tried. Sometimes I even managed to hit the paper.

"Hopeless," he said. "It's hopeless."

By the end of a week's time we were dressing up in armor left over from his days in the Society for Creative Anachronism and going at it full out with the wooden swords, which were called *bokkens*. Our battles consisted mostly of him blocking everything I threw at him and knocking me on my ass with well-placed slashes and thrusts every time I did something stupid. I did something stupid a lot.

He taught me about breathing and how it must be controlled: in through the nose, out through the mouth, gradually slowing it down, using the diaphragm to expand the lungs' capacity for oxygen.

A week is time to learn a lot of things, too short a time to master any of them. Malachi even told me, "Right now you know just about enough to get yourself killed, because you have technique without expertise. You'll have to work on it on your own—it takes a long time."

"How long have you been doing it?"

"I'm thirty-three years old. I've been 'doing it,' as you say, ever since I began studying martial arts, which was when I was sixteen."

"Oh."

I learned about the sword itself—how a samurai considered it the embodiment of his soul because it kept him alive and represented his way of life. I learned never to touch a blade because oil from the skin mars it, causing rust and showing carelessness and disrespect. I found the twined handle was superior because it absorbed sweat and provided a firmer grip, and that the long, curved blade was meant more for wicked slashes than straight thrusts.

At the end of that first week Malachi gave me a sword. It was wrapped in oilcloth. I unrolled it carefully and there it was: black-twined, in a plain black lacquered sheath. I held it in my left hand and drew the blade. Its mirror finish blazed in the late afternoon sun. Reflections spread across the grass as I turned the blade.

I put it back into the sheath. It settled in with a comfortable snick. "I can't take this."

"Yes you can. Oh, sure, it's worth a fortune—the blade was forged in the sixteenth century; I saved for ten years to buy it from some idiot who didn't know how much it was worth. But I have this one now." He patted his side. The *tsuba* rattled. "I found it in an arms museum. It's worth a dozen of the one you're holding." He reached out and I handed him the sword. He put it in his belt next to his own and drew it. It whicked as it cut the air. "This blade," he said, looking at his reflection in it, "is an exceptionally good one. I expect you always to treat it with the respect it deserves. Take care of it, keep it well-oiled and clean—I'll show you how. It ought to last your lifetime." He half-smiled. "If it doesn't get used too much, that is." He returned it to me. "And give it a name."

"A name?"

He nodded. "Every good sword has a name."

"Oh. What's your sword's name?"

"Kaishaku-nin. Literally it means 'one who assists.' You know about *seppuku?"*

I nodded.

"The *kaishaku* was the one who stood behind the man committing *seppuku,"* he continued. "He waited until the proper cuts were made, then took off the head with one clean stroke of his *katana*. Usually a *kaishaku* was a close friend or relative of the man committing *seppuku*. It was a great honor."

"Does the sword have to have a Japanese name?"

"Not necessarily."

I nodded. "I'll have to think about it."

"Take your time. Work with it, get used to it, and it will name itself." He went on to tell me an improbable story about a *ronin*—a sort of unemployed samurai, a loner—who had a set of swords with the unlikely names of Pecker One and Pecker Two. The sun had set by the time he finished.

A week later as we gathered our gear and started inside after a particularly gruelling session, we heard a dog barking at the front gate. Ariel and Faust had returned.

"Where the hell have you been?" I demanded.

Malachi was out back, wrestling on the grass with Faust. The black Chow growled ferociously, play-biting his arms. Malachi had already fed him two bowls of Jim Dandy.

I'd hugged Ariel when Malachi and I had greeted them at the gate. She felt so good to touch, my arms around her dove-soft coat. I became cross when we got inside, though—I'd been *worried*. She looked indignant. "I took a sabbatical. I thought we needed a break from each other. At least it seemed like you needed a break from me."

"I didn't need a break from you, I just . . . didn't know how to feel." I paused. "Ariel—Malachi told me what you did for me. How you brought me back. Why didn't you tell me?"

"And hold it over your head? I didn't want to use it against you. No one should use somebody's gratitude as ammunition."

I shook my head. "I remember the darkness, the way you pulled me out of it. And then the day of the Change—it felt so damned real, as if I were there again."

"It was a memory, Pete. Nothing more."

"But I lived it over again, all of it. Why? Did you do it?"

She nodded. "I'm sorry, Pete. Sorrier than you could know. You tried so hard to forget all that had happened to you, and I had to bring it back."

"Why? I'm not mad at you, I just want to know."

"When you were dead—that darkness you felt—I tried to bring you back. But I couldn't unless you wanted to come back, and I couldn't make you want to; you had to do that from within yourself."

"The Song."

"Yes. It gave you strength. It broke you from death and into a coma. But that didn't mean you were going to be able to come back to me. You still could have died any time. I needed to give you something vivid, something concrete that you could hang on to. Good or bad." She lowered her head. "Those were your strongest memories, I'm afraid, and I had to make you live them over again. Please forgive me."

"Forgive *you?* I'm the one who should be saying that. I overreacted. I'm stupid sometimes."

She said nothing.

"I love you, you know."

She blinked. "I love you, Pete."

"Yeah, I know. It shows. So where the hell have you been!"

"No place in particular. Faust and I just wandered around the city. I found out some things you should know."

"Such as?"

"Well—most important: Emilio wants me. It appears he's been offered a large amount—of what, I don't know—for my horn."

"Why, that son of a bitch."

"Whatever. Faust and I went back to the library to follow up a hunch I had. Russ had told us about Emilio and I thought maybe he'd come looking for us after we had left the library."

"And?"

"It was a mess. Somebody had been there."

"Lovely."

"Faust led me to trading bars. I hung around and listened to talk. Apparently Russ Chaffney told somebody about me when he got back, either after we met him on the overpass or after leaving Malachi's, and—"

"—And they told somebody else, and so on. I get the idea."

"Yes. Someone wants me, all right. Half the city knows. We're probably among the last who don't, because Malachi keeps himself pretty separated from the rest of the goings-on here. I'd expect Emilio to show up within the next few days."

"Why would he wait that long?"

"I'm not sure. It seems as if he's waiting for someone, though—I'm sure he wouldn't come here alone."

"Simply wonderful. I'd better tell Malachi." I turned to go out the front door—the rest were still boarded shut. I looked back at Ariel. "Didn't anyone notice you poking around in trading bars?"

"I doubt it. I mostly stayed behind the buildings and listened—my hearing's better than yours. Besides, I can be pretty quiet when I want to."

"Gee, I hadn't noticed." I went outside to tell Malachi.

Next day: routine as usual. Up at six a.m., stretch out, work basic slashes, thrusts, blocks, and parries; practice drawing the blade and returning it without looking—*that* was hard as hell—break for a while, fight Malachi with *bokken* and homemade armor until I could barely lift my arms, then break for lunch.

I dragged myself inside, sweating.

"You're getting pretty good with that thing," said Ariel.

"Oh, yeah? You'd be good, too, if you had a homicidal maniac on the business end of it trying to do to you before you did to him."

"You're getting into shape. Amazing for a few weeks' time." She blinked. "You've changed, too. You seem more self-confident."

I grinned. "You, too, can fear no man! Send check or money order today to Malachi Lee's Sadistic School of Swordplay. Money back if not completely worn out in half a month." I got serious. "You've changed, too. Something I can't quite put my finger on. You act. . . . I don't know. Older."

She nodded. "I feel it. You can't bring somebody back from death and not be changed. I saw a little of what you felt in that darkness, Pete. It changed me. Innocence is in many ways ignorance. I lost some of my ignorance when I saw that."

"That's not good."

She tossed her head. "It happened." She scraped at the floor, then looked up, dismissing it. "So tell me about the new addition to your arsenal." She inclined her head at the sword at my left hip.

"My new appendage? Malachi gave it to me."

"That was very generous of him. He must have a lot of confidence in you; I doubt he'd give a sword—especially one as valuable as that one seems to be—to just anyone."

"You wouldn't know it, to hear him talk. 'Hopeless' this and 'waste of time' that. I'm just not Jedi material, I guess."

Though she couldn't have understood the reference, she laughed. It was good to hear; I hadn't realized how much I missed it until I heard it again.

"I'm supposed to give it a name," I said, smiling.

"Oh, really? What are you going to name it?"

"Nothing spectacular. Got any suggestions?"

"Lady Vivamus, maybe? *Anduril? Durandal? Stormbringer,* perhaps?"

I shook my head. "I think I'll name it Fred."

"Fred?"

"Sure. Why not?"

"Fred?"

"I like that name," I said defensively. "Tell you what—I'll make it official." I walked out the front door, making damn sure the crossbow trap wasn't connected. I'd become gun shy; every time I walked out the door now I felt this cold, prickling sensation in the small of my back.

Ariel followed me down the porch steps. I stood in the yard and drew my sword, holding it so the sunlight blazed along the length of the curved blade. I squinted up at it. "I dub thee . . . Fred!"

"Oh, shit," said Ariel, tail swishing.

I slid the blade back into the sheath without looking and with only minor fumbling. I was just beginning to get the *feel* of the blade, as if it really were an extension of my arm. "There you go," I said, walking back to Ariel. "It's done."

"Wait until Malachi finds out. He'll kill you."

I snorted. "I am luff tuff Nipponese swordsman now. Utterry invinciber."

Ariel's eyes widened and I turned to see Malachi behind me, shaking his head. Faust was close beside him, bright-eyed and panting in the heat. "Hopeless," said Malachi, and he turned away, still shaking his head and muttering something about silk purses and sow's ears. Or casting pearls before swine. Or something like that.

* * *

Someone shook me awake and I reached for my sword.

"Hold on, it's me!"

"Wha?" I shook my head. "Russ?"

He nodded. "Come on, get up. We need you."

I sat up and swung my legs over the side of the bed. I rubbed my eyes, still not completely awake. "What are you doing here?"

"Keep your voice down." Asmodeus sat on his shoulder. "I just got here," he said, stroking the falcon's neck feathers. "Emilio and four other people are on their way here to get Ariel. They're about a half hour behind me."

I hurried into the living room, clutching Fred. I'd been sleeping in my clothes in case I had to get up in a hurry. "What's up?" I asked Malachi.

"You know as much as we do. We're waiting."

Hell of a way to wake up. . . . Russ was looking at me strangely. "What's wrong?" I asked.

He blinked. "Oh—nothing. You just look a lot better than the last time I saw you. You ought to change your name to Lazarus."

I said nothing and looked out the window at the heads on the fence.

Russ saw me looking. "Sometimes he reminds me of those World War Two pilots who stencilled swastikas and bombs on the sides of their planes to mark their kills. Morbid." Asmodeus stirred on his shoulder. He stroked her with a finger. "It's okay," he said. He looked from the falcon to Ariel and Faust. "Place is turning into a goddamn Doctor Doolittle set," he muttered.

I looked at Malachi. He was perched on the edge of the couch. He stared out the window and didn't move.

"What are we going to do?" I asked no one in particular.

Russ answered. "We're going to wait and see what they do." He nodded at the sword in my hand. "Malachi tells me you're a natural with that thing. I sure hope so. I brought my baby." He hefted a thirty-inch Adirondack wooden baseball bat. He flipped it, caught the heavy end, let the other end fall against his forearm, and casually extended his arm toward me. The business end of the bat shot toward me, stopping an inch in front of my chest. Before I could move it was snapped away and the bat was twirling like a baton. He fanned it until he was holding it in a sort of batting stance, one hand on the smaller end, the other halfway up. He lowered the bat and grinned. "Nervous?"

"Yes."

Malachi stood up from the couch. I looked out the window. Motion. I counted four people. They began helping each other over the fence, which Malachi had kept padlocked.

"We ought to nail them as they come inside," said Russ.

Malachi shook his head. "They won't come in. They'll wait for us. We'll play it their way, for now." He turned from the window and looked at us. "Let's go."

We met them just inside the front gate. Malachi wore a full dress kimono of black silk with *Kaishaku-nin* secured at his side. Russ dangled the baseball bat casually. On his shoulder Asmodeus spread her wings. Faust stood quietly beside Malachi, displaying none of his usual excitement. I'd grabbed my blowgun quickly, intending to try to get off one good shot if it got down to it. Fred was slung tightly at my hip. Ariel stood behind us.

We must have looked like something out of a comically absurd Western. *The Magnificent Seven* meet *Fantasia*. I'd have been laughing if I hadn't been scared out of my wits.

One of the four men was Emilio. Another I recognized as the other man who'd been on the overpass when Ariel and I arrived in Atlanta. He carried a hatchet. The third man was tall, with long blond hair. He carried a Bear compound hunting bow with a quiver attached. The fourth swaggered with a broadsword thrust through his wide leather belt.

Emilio still wore his knives. They gleamed in the morning sun: throwing knives, trench knives, push-blades, two boot-knives. In his right hand was a black-handled and wickedly curved machete. In his left was chain coiled around his palm with about three feet dangling free. I looked nervously at Malachi, but his face registered nothing. He'd told me once during training that a good length of chain, wielded by a man who knew what he was doing, was a sword's natural enemy. "It can be thrown hard against the blade," he'd said. "It wraps around and makes the edge useless. A good tug and you're thrown off balance—and balance is everything to a swordsman. If you try to slash and hit the chain, same thing—it binds the blade."

We stopped about five yards from them. The one with the compound bow reached out, pulled out an arrow, and fitted it, but kept the bow pointed down.

Emilio and the one with the broadsword stepped forward until they were eight feet from us. "We want the horse," said Emilio.

"She's not a horse," I said. I hadn't meant to say anything but it came out before I could stop it.

Emilio laughed. His eyes flicked to my sword. "You didn't have that when you came here." He glanced at Malachi, who regarded him with absolutely no expression. "I suppose now you think you're pretty bad with it."

I tried to follow Malachi's example and said nothing.

He raised the chain, letting it swing back and forth like a pendulum. "Come on," he said to me. "Just you and me. You win and nobody bothers your pretty horse. You lose, she's mine."

"No," said Malachi. "If you want somebody, you come for me."

"Since when did you become a Boy Scout?" asked the broadsword carrier.

Malachi's face remained impassive.

"Okay," breathed Emilio, and suddenly he grinned. His teeth were even and white. "You and me, *samurai*." He laughed at the word.

"All right." Malachi separated himself from us, never taking his eyes from Emilio's. The two squared off. Emilio crouched forward, waving the chain from side to side. The machete weaved in slow circles, waiting. Malachi flowed into his stance. His feet were wide apart. He stood with knees bent, up on the balls of his bare feet and leaning forward slightly, bent at the waist. He'd pushed down on the sheath of his sword so that the handle pointed down, the tip up. His right hand gripped the twined handle firmly, just beneath the guard. His eyes were leveled at Emilio's chest, but they looked through him, as if he saw something there that I didn't, something hypnotizing.

Emilio twitched the chain, trying to draw Malachi into movement. Malachi remained still. His eyes narrowed; he was judging distance. Suddenly he moved, and if I hadn't spent long hours learning from him I would have missed it completely. As it was I only saw the blur. He drew his sword and slashed horizontally. It split Emilio's nose. Maintaining the sword's momentum, he turned his right wrist so the sword arced up, brought his left hand up to grab the bottom of the handle, and sliced straight down. The movement brought the sword vertically through Emilio's nose, quartering it.

The whole thing took less than half a second. Emilio hadn't had time to move.

Emilio put his hands to his face and screamed. Bright red blood flowed from between his fingers, down his forearms.

I had to piece together what happened after that. Emilio, blood still streaming freely, sank to his knees. The broadsword wielder drew and headed for Malachi, who leaned back, holding *Kaishaku-nin* so that the sword's tip almost touched the ground, edge upward.

Ten yards away, the one with the bow lifted it, took aim at me, and let fly. The arrow sped at me, though of course I couldn't see it, and then Ariel was in front of me, head snapping down and, just as quickly, up. The arrow broke in two.

The man looked after his shot in disbelief. He drew another hunting arrow. I brought the Aero-mag to my lips and blew. The shot was hurried, though, and the dart hit him wide of my mark. He dropped his bow and spun, clutching his shoulder. He tried to pull out the dart and couldn't; it was wedged in the socket and probably against bone. He ran away. In the confusion he must have managed to pull himself over the fence one-handed. We didn't see him again, anyhow.

Russ Chaffney, meanwhile, had engaged the hatchet-bearer. He blocked the man's powerful swings successfully with the baseball bat, holding it with both hands and catching the hatchet on the handle, just beneath the blade. He couldn't counter, though; the heavy blade didn't give him time to swing. Asmodeus had taken wing and was trying to get in at the man's eyes, but he was slashing too wildly. As Russ kept trying to get in on him the man backed out of range.

Malachi's fight with the broadsword bearer took exactly two moves. His opponent aimed a powerful stroke at Malachi's head. Malachi brought the sword straight up from its low guard position and cut through the man's wrists. The hands fell to the ground, still clutching the heavy broadsword. Without hesitating, Malachi brought the sword back, stepped in, and crosscut through the man's neck. The head rolled. Spurting blood caught Malachi across the waist as the body fell.

Russ blocked his opponent's hatchet once more, this time

pulling back on the bat as he did. Wedged under the blade, the tug brought the man off balance. Russ kicked him in the stomach as he fell forward. He let out an empty-sounding *whuff!* and lost his grip. The hatchet fell to the grass.

Asmodeus clawed and screeched. The man brought his arms up to ward off the falcon and Russ's bat at the same time. Russ raised the bat and advanced. The man backed up and the point of Malachi's sword appeared almost magically through his chest. It made a ripping sound as it came through. The sword pulled back and he fell, hands twitching randomly.

It was over. Not ten seconds had gone by. I looked at the blood and bodies and vomited.

Emilio got away.

I had to help Russ and Malachi with the bodies. I won't talk about that, if you don't mind.

Malachi put the heads on his fence.

"Getting pretty crowded up there," said Russ. There were now eight heads atop the black spikes.

"There's plenty more room," I said heavily. "Besides, the fence goes all the way around the yard."

Russ put his hands on his hips and cocked his head to one side. "What's the matter with you?"

"Nothing. I'm always this cheerful when I kill people."

Malachi looked at me. "You didn't kill anybody, Pete."

"No. You did."

"What did you expect?"

I waved him off and turned away. "I don't know."

"Was it the blood, Pete?" asked Ariel. "You didn't expect it to be like that, did you?"

I shook my head.

"Killing isn't clean," said Malachi. "You've killed before; you should know that."

"Yeah, I've killed before. When I had to. But not like that."

Malachi stood next to Russ. "Pete. Nobody said swords were bloodless. It's not lofty and chivalrous. You had this Errol Flynn movie in your head; you never stopped to think that when you cut somebody, he bleeds." He pulled out his blade and looked at it. He'd cleaned the blood off with a silk rag. "Swords aren't romantic, glorious things. They're messy."

"You like it and you know it."

"No. I love the artistry in knowing how to use a blade, in being good with one." He raised an eyebrow. "And yes, there can even be a certain artistry in killing a man with good technique. But I don't have to like it. And I don't."

"Then why do you do it?"

"Because my sword is what I know. Because I only use it in situations where it's kill or get killed. Not because I like it. Do you think it's any less right to kill a man with a sword than with a blowgun, just because one's bloody and the other isn't?"

"It makes me sick."

Russ put a strong hand on my shoulder. "Me, too. You get used to it. You have to."

I looked at him in disgust. "Get used to it? I never want to have to."

"You have to," he repeated firmly, "or you end up like that." He jerked his head toward the fence.

We made preparations to get out of Atlanta. If someone had offered a reward for Ariel's horn, staying in one place would probably get us killed—Malachi, too. So I cleaned myself up and began packing gear away in my backpack while Ariel kept me company. We went into the living room when I finished packing. Malachi had already sponged the blood off himself and shouldered a backpack of his own. He'd had it ready for years, just in case he had to get out in a hurry. "We all ready?" he asked.

"You shouldn't come with us," said Ariel. "We don't need to cause you more trouble than we already have."

"Trouble doesn't bother me. I'm sworn to your service, if you'll remember."

"I'd not ask you to endanger yourself when it can be avoided by my leaving."

"There'll still be a reward for you, for your horn. People will still look for you."

"It won't be so bad," I said, "if we keep on the move. We've never liked to stay in any one place too long; it won't make that much difference. Except maybe to make life more interesting."

Malachi's face was stony. He adjusted a shoulder strap. "Let's go," he said.

"I'll walk with you for a while," said Russ. "But I'm staying here." He shrugged. "Atlanta's my home."

"You've helped more than enough," said Ariel. "Thank you."

We shouldered our packs and went outside. It was near noon and very hot. "So," I said, "I guess we're going to just set out and—" I stopped.

Emilio stood at the front gate. There was a large, white bandage across his nose, with a large red blotch in the middle. It looked absurdly like a Japanese flag.

"What the hell?" said Russ, frowning. "You should have killed him when you had the chance." Asmodeus shrieked. "Quiet, babe." He patted her claws, gnarled as the stumps of old bonsai trees.

"I wonder what he wants," said Ariel. "You'd think he'd have learned his—"

"Malachi!" We turned as one when Emilio shouted. "Malachi Lee!"

"You don't think he wants to take you on again?" I asked.

"One way to find out." He headed toward the gate.

"No," said Russ. "Wait. Let him come to us. If he's got back-ups, so much the better. We can get them as they come through."

Malachi scratched the back of his head. "I want to know what kind of game he's playing." We stood on the front porch, watching Emilio at the gate. Malachi folded his arms, silent.

"You're dead," Emilio yelled. "You're dead." He held onto the bars of the fence and laughed.

"I don't get it," said Russ. "I don't see anyone else around."

Faust had been sitting beside Russ's leg. Now he stood, the fur on his back bristling. He growled: low, throaty, and threatening. Asmodeus spread her wings and shrieked. Both animals were looking toward the front gate. Malachi glanced back at them, then turned back to where they were looking. There was motion behind Emilio, and what I saw heading toward us made me react—funny I could still remember the sensation—as if I'd stuck my finger in a light socket.

Coming down the road toward Malachi Lee's house was a griffin.

nine

Do not confuse 'duty' with what other people expect of you; they are utterly different. Duty is a debt you owe to yourself to fulfill obligations you have assumed voluntarily. Paying that debt can entail anything from years of patient work to instant willingness to die. Difficult it may be, but the reward is self-respect.

—Robert A. Heinlein,
Time Enough for Love

My *Webster's New Collegiate Dictionary* says this about griffins: "grif·fin *n*. Also grif·fon, gry·phon. A mythical beast with the head and wings of an eagle and the body of a lion." The description doesn't do it justice.

The griffin heading down the road toward us didn't look anywhere close to mythical to me. It was the size of a tank. A *big* tank. A man rode on its back in some kind of saddle, weaving from side to side in time with the beast's odd walk.

It stopped in front of the fence. From the porch I could see the rider's face clearly; his lips were upturned just the slightest bit, like the hull of a large boat. He nodded; a knowing, calm nod.

Malachi nodded back.

At a command the griffin jumped the fence, sail-like wings flapping four or five times. Its claws dug into the earth when it landed; I imagined the sound of grass ripping. The rider remained in the dark brown saddle.

Malachi started down the porch steps, hand firm on *Kai-shaku-nin* at his hip.

"We can't let him go out there!" I told Russ.

"You're right." Muscles tightened along his jaw. He headed for the steps.

"Are you crazy?" I asked. "We don't stand a chance." I'd meant that we should stop Malachi, not join him.

Russ stopped. "What chance does he have without us?" Asmodeus spread her wings, the right one ruffling Russ's hair. He soothed her gently. "Besides—he's doing it for you, Pete." He went down the steps.

I looked at Ariel. Her face was impassive.

Baseball bat in hand, Russ caught up to Malachi. They nodded to one another. They faced the griffin and rider and began walking closer. I looked again at the hellish beast. Its eyes were molten gold. As I watched it opened its arm-long beak and snapped it shut.

"Pete." Ariel was beside me now. "Help me get this pack off. I can fight better without it."

Oh, hell—I looked at her, then back to the griffin. The thing was big enough to come bulldozing into the house if we tried to stay inside anyway. "I'm coming, too," I said, and shrugged off my pack. I untied hers and dropped it onto the porch. I felt better, once the decision was made.

Ariel's hooves made a clopping sound as she walked down the steps beside me; then we were on the grass.

Malachi and Russ stopped when they heard us coming. We caught up with them. Russ nodded and smiled, tight-lipped. Malachi's face showed something I couldn't read.

We halted twenty feet from the griffin. It snapped its beak and screeched. My nostrils flared at a smell like hot brass. Liquid gold eyes blazed at Ariel. It lashed out with a leonine claw.

The rider spoke a word softly and the beast calmed somewhat, though with an obvious effort. I kicked myself mentally: *shit—I should have brought the crossbow.* It was in Ariel's pack on the front porch. I only had Fred at my side. I gripped the handle firmly, evenly spaced ridges pressing into the calluses which had begun to form on my palm. It would have to do.

Leather creaked with a comfortable, worn sound as the rider leaned forward and patted the beast on the base of the neck—the highest he could reach. "There, there, Shai-tan," he said. "Be nice." Plain black T-shirt, black straight-legged pants, scuffed and dusty riding boots—he should have been pouring sweat, but he wasn't. The cross-shaped handle of a broadsword was on his left side, the side facing away from us. It was thrust through a dark brown leather belt at least four inches wide. There was an indentation where the belt pulled into his stomach on the right side; the sword must have been heavy.

His face was angular, vaguely Germanic. "Shai-tan doesn't like to be held back," he said. He looked at Ariel for almost a full minute, then back at us. "Who owns the unicorn?"

Beside me Ariel spoke before the rest of us could answer: "Nobody owns a unicorn."

Rider and griffin blinked in unison. "So you think."

I stepped forward. "No one owns this unicorn. Her will is her own." I hoped the shaking of my hands on my sword handle wasn't visible.

He smiled at me. "It's you, then. What do you want for her?"

Malachi spoke up. "Get out of here." He glared through slitted eyes, his impassiveness discarded.

The rider looked at him as if barely acknowledging his existence. "This is none of your business, Lee," he said mildly. "I want to settle this reasonably with this young man here."

"You're on my property."

"I'll leave when I get what I want." He turned to me. "Now, what do you want for her?"

My bottom lip worked uncontrollably. "Fuck you."

He sighed theatrically. The griffin grumbled and lowered its head at me. The feathers on the back of its neck ruffled up like the hair on the back of a snarling cat. I stepped back, as if that would do any good. "I'll have her whether you agree to it or not," said the rider. He smoothed feathers on the griffin's neck. "But this would save us both a lot of trouble. You more than me." He saw my hand clutching Fred's handle. "How about your sword?" He cocked his head speculatively. "I could make it invincible in your hands."

"You sure think he sells out cheap," commented Russ. He'd had to put a hand to Asmodeus' talons, where they clutched leather on his burly shoulder, to keep her from flying at the griffin. "Or was that just for starters?"

The rider jeered. "You idiot. This isn't your concern, either. You're going to die over something stupid."

Chaffney shrugged, looked at Malachi to his left, Ariel and me to his right. "They're my friends," he said. Asmodeus shrieked.

The rider laughed. He said a word I didn't understand and the griffin turned to face us.

"No matter what you do," said Ariel, "I won't go with you. Even if you win."

"If I win you won't have a choice."

"You can't take me alive."

"Then I'll settle for the next best thing. Unless you'd rather Shai-tan held you down while I snapped off your horn. I'm sure my power is as strong as yours."

Ariel shuddered. I remembered her saying her horn couldn't be taken while she lived. So . . . take the horn, and she dies.

"Why are you doing this?" I asked suddenly, struck with a desire to reason with him, to reach some sort of common ground on which to settle this.

"He's doing it for someone else," said Malachi. "Aren't you?" He looked up at the rider.

The sharp-featured man ignored him. "You know," he said to Ariel, "that I'll kill them if you fight me."

"I know you'll try." She blinked and looked to her left. "Malachi, Russ—I'm sorry. But I can't let him take me."

"We understand," said Russ. "Nobody expects you to give in to this motherfucker."

"Pete—" She lowered her voice. "I can't go with him."

"You won't, Ariel. I promise."

"Enough bullshit," declared the rider loudly. "Shai-tan."

The griffin shook its huge eagle's head and cleared the twenty-foot space between us in two steps. It left clods of earth and torn grass where it had landed after jumping the fence. Malachi and I drew, but the beast knocked us aside with its bulk. Ariel leaped nimbly away. Russ hit it with the bat but the griffin didn't even blink as it reached out a brown-furred claw and knocked Russ on his back. Asmodeus screamed and flew from his shoulder.

Malachi jumped up and hacked at the beast's neck. Feathers flew like an exploded pillow, but no blood, no sign of injury. It had a claw on Russ's chest but wasn't bearing down. He struggled beneath it.

Instead of hacking, Malachi thrust into the thing's neck. All his weight went into it but the sword only penetrated a few inches. Whatever the hell was beneath those feathers, it was *tough*.

I got up and began hacking at the claw that pinned Russ. As if brushing away an annoying fly, the beast casually tossed its head and sent me sprawling. Fred landed blade up on the grass just before I did. I saw it at the last moment and managed to do a shoulder roll over it. My momentum kept me going as I tried to come up from the roll and I landed on my tailbone hard enough to jar the wind from me. I picked up Fred and struggled to my feet once more.

Ariel and the rider glared at one another. I felt something was going on between those gazes and behind them, some deadlocked struggle for power.

I made it back to the griffin's huge lion's leg and began to jab and saw. Something I did made it scream. My lungs filled with hot air, a nauseating, smelting-plant odor. Malachi couldn't have been making any headway either; the thing felt like concrete beneath black and white feathers and brown fur.

I felt a change in the leg's pressure: it was bearing down harder on Russ. I looked up. The rider smiled down at Russ's struggles. "What good are your friends now?"

But Russ couldn't answer. His face had turned an odd red, dark and bright at the same time. His mouth made fish-out-of-water movements. His eyes began to film. Giant knuckles popped: Russ's ribs. Blood flowed from both corners of his mouth.

I screamed in impotence and tried thrusting upward at the underside of the leg joint where it joined the body. It turned its long neck so it could snap at me. I pressed my body against its, feeling hot, matted lion fur against me from the chest down, cool eagle feathers against my cheek. I flinched at the sharp snap at my ear as the halves of the beak slammed together. The foundry smell was strong, and so hot I was sweat-soaked in a matter of seconds. I'd have vomited if I'd had anything left to vomit.

It shrugged its shoulder and I fell onto my side, holding Fred clear. I landed at just the right angle to see what I hope no one else saw: the fierce eagle head lowered to Chaffney's bloody one. It screeched and put its beak over his face.

Snap.

I turned away. Malachi was sprawled face down on the grass ten feet from the griffin, unconscious or dead. *Kaishaku-*

nin was still in his right hand. Ariel and the rider remained locked in a kind of battle I couldn't understand. It looked on the surface like an adolescent staring contest, hard coal eyes versus bright blue ones.

A screech that was not the griffin's broke the rider's concentration. He looked up, and a tangle of blood-colored feathers plummeted onto the rider's face, flapping, tearing, raking. Flailing hands blurred with beating wings. Human screams mixed with falcon shrieks. Bright red blossomed and dripped onto the dark leather saddle. Desperate hands finally gripped the feathered wrath and threw it away. Asmodeus rose to circle high overhead, screaming ferally.

"Shai-tan!" The bellowed command brought the griffin up, powerful wings sending a breeze that chilled my sweat. "Shai-tan!" The rider's left eye was gouged out. All that remained was a stringy mess lying limply on his cheek. Blood from a deep cut on the left side of his jaw welled down his throat, darkening his black shirt around the shoulder and upper chest. His right eye was crimson with blood but I saw no cut. His hands groped until they found a firm hold on the large saddlehorn. He screamed a harsh word. The griffin took one step, leaped the fence, ran four or five steps along the street, and flapped itself aloft with heavy wingbeats. I watched until it was a dwindling black speck in the clear sky.

I remember staggering to Ariel and holding her, crying on her shoulder for I don't know how long, until Malachi tapped me on the shoulder. "Pete."

I turned to face him, wiping my eyes. "You're okay?"

"I'll be fine." Both his eyes were blackening and he had a cut along his forearm, but the bleeding had stopped.

"What are we going to do now?"

"We bury Russ. We pull ourselves together. Then you and Ariel get out of here."

"You're not coming?"

He shook his head. "I'm going after him."

"Who is he? A necromancer?"

"No. I don't think we could have stood up to a necromancer." He glanced at Ariel, back to me. "He's a sort of right-hand man for someone in New York City. He scouts the east coast, doing whatever his master needs him to do. I've . . . heard of him before."

I thought he was going to elaborate, but instead he said, "There are shovels in the garage. Let's make it quick."

I studied his face. It was stony.

Ariel watched silently as Malachi and I dug a shallow grave in the back yard. We laid Russ in it, wrapped in a white sheet. The body was soft in the wrong places. Malachi looked at it a minute. The bundle was wrinkled, bulky, deformed. There was nothing there to show it had ever been Russ. An absurd thought tugged at me: it looked like a gigantic marijuana cigarette.

Malachi dipped his shovel into the piled earth; it made a chuffing sound. Red Georgian clay, chunks of granite, and black earth spread an irregular pattern on the white sheet. He dug in again: *chuff*. I held my shovel tightly and did the same.

Asmodeus screeched overhead.

Malachi stopped and looked up. The falcon was circling. She spiralled down slowly and landed on the mound of earth beside the grave, pecking at it with her sharp beak. Cinnamon wings spread, darting eyes questioned.

Malachi drew his sword.

"What are you doing?"

Ariel nudged me reproachfully. "Leave him alone, Pete. He knows what he's doing."

"But—"

The sword hissed like a taut wire breaking. Malachi cleaned it, returned it to its sheath, and picked up his shovel. He started to push it into the pile of earth, but stopped when he saw my face. "If a man's buddy dies," he said, "he'll live through it. The pain will lessen in a few years, and in maybe ten years he won't even hurt anymore. But if the man dies before the buddy"—he cast another shovelful of reddish dirt into the grave—"the buddy dies, too. Slowly, painfully. I've seen it before. Believe me, Pete, it was the best thing to do."

Ariel had turned away. I left Malachi to fill the grave and walked beside her. "Are you all right?"

"All this has been because of me. The killing . . . the blood . . . all my fault."

"Ariel?"

"A man has just died for me—"

I reached up and touched her twitching neck. She jerked her head as if suddenly realizing I was there. Together we walked silently around the yard. The chuffing sounds soon ended, replaced by light gongings as the shovel blade tamped down the piled earth. Then a clang and a thud as the shovel was thrown to the ground. Malachi appeared around the side of the house. He climbed the steps onto the front porch. I followed him. Ariel remained in the yard.

Faust jumped up against Malachi, front paws scuffing his thighs. He absently scratched the dog's head. He bent down and picked up the backpack he'd removed earlier. I was silent as he shrugged it on, adjusting the straps and belt. "We're going to New York," he finally said.

"All right. I'll get my gear."

"No. Faust and I. Not you."

"Why not?"

"You and Ariel need to wander around, like you said. Don't give anybody a chance to come looking for you."

"Why can't we come with you?"

"You'd hamper me. I'd be too busy having to keep part of my attention on you, and that might get me killed."

"I can take care of myself."

He shook his head. "You don't understand, Pete. I'm going to *New York*."

"So?"

"That's my point. You don't even know what you'll be walking into. No, you and Ariel are safer if you head away from here—and not to New York. Head west."

"Why are you doing this?"

"I work best by myself."

"That's not what I mean."

He looked at me carefully before answering. "Because if I don't, she'll never be safe. Because it gives me a little more purpose than just surviving here in this city. Because I promised—I swore by this"—he patted *Kaishaku-nin* at his hip—"to protect her. Plus a few reasons of my own."

I said nothing. He looked down. "Faust?" The dog sprang to attention. "We're on our way." The dog barked once and ran down the steps and into the yard, circling frantically at the front gate. Malachi and I walked down the steps. Faust ran back to us, jumped against me, and again headed to the gate.

Ariel looked at Malachi as he stopped beside her. "You're leaving."

"Yes."

"We're not coming with you?"

"It will be safer—for me and for you—if you don't."

She nodded, a glint of midday sun catching the tip of her horn. "I understand. Please be careful. And . . . thank you."

He nodded. "Pete—take care. Don't make yourselves obvious. Maybe I'll see you again."

"Yeah. Sure."

He studied my face a few moments, then turned and strode out the front gate. Faust trotted gleefully at his heels. They turned right, heading north. Their brisk pace put them out of sight in a few minutes. Malachi never looked back.

"Now what?" asked Ariel.

"Now we gear up and follow him."

"I thought you'd say that."

"You don't think we should?"

"That's up to you."

"Bullshit."

"All right. We'll follow him."

I nodded. "I'll need a map. I wonder if he has a road atlas around here?" I walked into the house. My feet thumped with a lonely sound on the wooden floor. Looking back, I saw Ariel still gazing down the block where Malachi and Faust had vanished. The bodies of the two we'd killed this morning lay in grotesque positions near the fence. Flies hovered around them. Five yards from Ariel the ground was discolored where Russ had fallen, been crushed, died.

"Come on," I said. She followed me in silently.

ten

Does the road wind uphill all the way?
Yes, to the very end.
Will the day's journey take the whole long day?
From morn to night, my friend.

—Christina Rossetti,
"Up-Hill"

According to the road atlas New York was eight hundred sixty-three miles away. If we did well we'd average about thirty miles a day. That meant New York was almost a full month away. I thought about riding Ariel, but no. She wasn't meant for it and I could never ask it of her.

So, backpack shouldered, blowgun slung, sword tucked neatly into the left side of my belt, Ariel and I walked along Interstate 85. We were on an overpass; I walked along the outside edge and looked out upon the quiet city. We'd passed no one along the road and I'd seen no more than a dozen people or so in the distance. I don't believe anybody paid any attention to us.

Ariel was silent most of the day. My comments and questions were answered by short, tight replies.

It had grown completely dark by the time we were ten miles outside Atlanta. I made camp beside the road, a process consisting mostly of propping up my backpack, unrolling the sleeping bag, and setting weapons at ready. I untied the tan-colored canvas pack from Ariel and propped the cocked crossbow against a guard rail. I'd made her wear her pack just so I could have the crossbow; I wanted it readily available in case I needed to stop something from a distance. I decided not to light a fire, as I didn't want to attract attention, human or otherwise. Dinner was a light meal of crackers, dried meat, and warm grape Kool-Aid. Afterward I lay with my head propped on a bundled section of sleeping bag, shifting uncomfortably on gravel biting into my back. The moon was a bright disk, often muted; silver light outlined the gray scarves of clouds.

Ariel stood by the edge of the highway, immobile, looking in the direction of a dark billboard. She'd been that way a while now.

"Ariel?"

No answer.

"Ariel, I'm sorry. But I've got to go there. Not just to help Malachi because he's our friend, but because if I don't, we'll be hiding as long as you're alive. Being on the road's fine, but being on the run stinks. It's not living, it's . . . I don't know. Existing by reflex, maybe."

Still nothing from her, even though she turned her spectral head toward me. The clouds passed in front of the moon so fast that she shimmered: gray, pale silver, gray, pale silver for a full minute, brief gray, silver again.

"I just wanted you to understand. I have to go there—but you don't. You could wait someplace for me—"

"No, I couldn't. And I won't."

"All right, then. But this sulking isn't like you. Once you make a decision you usually go along with it, no regrets. I can understand why you're scared, but you seem . . . resigned."

She twitched her shimmering head and walked over to me. A small comet's tail flared from her right front leg as it scraped pavement. Damn, I thought, looking at the play of gray and silver on her graceful form, those clouds really are moving.

She lay down a few feet from me. I turned on my right side to face her. She lay head up, legs folded beneath her. Her horn pulsed with intermittent moonlight and a tiny spark winked in her eyes. I remembered a line from *Romeo and Juliet* about the inconstant moon.

"Pete," she began, "that man, the one we fought today."

"The griffin rider?"

"Yes. I think I ran into him once before."

"Once before? But you were hardly more than a baby when I found you."

"Yes. I'd been wandering, looking for others of my kind. Those few I saw were timid, oddly frightened of me. I didn't know how to talk to them and they ran from me. One day—I don't even know where I was—I woke up and something was holding me. I remember feathers and fur, and that smell I smelled today for the first time since then. Like hot metal, stifling—"

"Hot brass. The griffin."

"Yes. It's all so dim. I was so young, and I've tried so hard to forget it since. I remember a man's voice, but not what he said. I didn't know what any of it meant back then." She said nothing for a few minutes. "I remember he tried to take me somewhere. I struggled. A unicorn isn't meant to be taken, Pete, not ever. The same thing happens that happens to a buddy when its human partner dies. We die. In captivity, we die. It takes a long time. I remember the pain of being captured. But the rest of it is so joggled, so dim. . . . I remember it was colder than it is now—I think it was winter."

"It was October when I found you."

"I don't even remember how I was being held, or anything, but—I was being taken somewhere and I didn't want to be, so I twisted . . . and kicked out. . . . Whatever I hit went flying, and I heard my leg crack. I ran miles and miles before I even began to feel the pain."

Realization hit with a surge of adrenaline. "Your broken leg. . . ."

The wind had been building as we talked. Now it gusted a little stronger, ruffling her mane. "I think I got it from the rider and the griffin, Pete. I think they were trying to take me to New York. And the necromancer there . . . he's powerful."

The growing wind was cold. The left side of my army shirt collar kept beating against my jaw. "And he wants you."

"He wants my horn. Even with me dead it has value to him. Properties that would give him a good deal more power."

The wind began to howl a sad dog's song. Ariel stood, facing into the wind. "Something's wrong. It doesn't feel right."

I stood also. The wind sent stinging hair into my eyes until I turned left. My hair blew back. It tugged lightly but insistently at my forehead, tickled my ears. "What doesn't feel right? The wind?"

"The wind, the weather—the night."

"Well, sure, it came up suddenly, but—"

"I feel it."

The wind's howl strengthened to a wail, then grew stronger still. The billboard Ariel had been facing vibrated from the force. Mercilessly the wind rampaged, flattening the grass of the wide median. It hurled itself in building gusts, hit like bricks, and bent the trees across the highway, spreading their leaves aside to reveal skeletal branches beneath. One swaying tree threatened to knock down useless power lines. Clouds skimmed in brief silver across the full moon's face. The roadsigns beat a rapid tattoo, back-and-forth, back-and-forth. The wind screamed across the corners of the roadsigns and cried into their hollow posts, mournful and lost. Ariel glanced my way and I managed a smile. Still, I couldn't hide my trembling, though the raging wind wasn't that cold. It whistled off the tip of Ariel's softly glowing horn. I stood my ground, leaning into the invisible howling. Ariel backed off a few steps as the buffeting grew stronger. Her hooves were darkly silver. "It's got to stop, Pete." Her voice was thin in the howl of the wind.

"It's a hurricane. Or the beginning of one. A tropical storm—"

"No. This was spell-cast. There's an intent behind it. Can't you feel it?"

I closed my eyes. Yes, I could. The wind had raised an unearthly insect buzz, eerie, angry, and insistent, but there was something else—a menacing something, as if the wind were somehow spiteful and searching.

I opened my mouth to speak but Ariel walked to the road. She struck sparks and lowered her head, muttering. Reflecting sparks flashed orange along her coat, then vanished. Her horn seemed to collect the moonlight with a steady, bright silver glow and she reared up with an uncharacteristically horse-like neigh. As quickly as it had arisen the howling ceased. All was silent and still, but when I looked about I saw that the tree branches were still being whipped about and the grass still rippled. Somehow, though, it wasn't affecting us.

"Something's searching for us," she said in midst of the odd quiet. "Something powerful, stronger than me." Her voice sounded as if we were in a small room.

"What do you mean, stronger? You stopped the wind."

"No. I was only able to calm a sphere around us."

"Same thing."

"No." The wind began to die down. The trees and signs shook less, the clouds slowed and the stroboscobic moonlight steadied. In two minutes it had dwindled to a light gale. "It was too powerful for me to stop; I could only ward it away for a small distance. And when I warded it off I could feel the power that had created it." She turned from the road, talking as she came toward me. "I'm not sure what it meant. It felt like something was looking for me, or for something, but I don't know why. Was it a warning? A show of force? I don't know. But I know I felt the power."

"But if our friend in New York did this, if he's that powerful, then why are we still alive?"

"I don't know. Maybe his power is weaker over this much distance. Maybe he needs to know exactly where we are for anything to work. It's even possible that wind was meant for Malachi and the necromancer doesn't even know we're headed his way." She lay down, folding her legs beneath her. No spot she picked ever had gravel to annoy her, rocks to dig into her ribs, or ants to use her for a midnight snack. "Or," she added, "maybe he does know we're coming and he's letting us. It would save him a lot of trouble. Maybe the wind was a dare. The question now is: do we keep going?"

"I—you know I have to."

"Then we go."

"But you don't want to."

"No, I don't want to. But you need to. So we go."

I zipped myself into my sleeping bag, perplexed. My sleep wasn't good when it finally came.

eleven

The implacable mutual hostility between man and dragon, as exemplified in the myth of St. George, is strongest in the West. (In chapter 3 of the Book of Genesis, God ordains an eternal enmity between reptiles and humans.) . . . With one exception, the Genesis account of the temptation by a reptile in Eden is the only instance in the Bible of humans understanding the language of animals. When we feared the dragons, were we fearing a part of ourselves? One way or another, there were dragons in Eden.

—Carl Sagan,
The Dragons of Eden

The white-tailed buck I'd been trailing for the last hour, trying for a good shot, finally stepped out from behind the tree that had been blocking him. I gradually raised the crossbow until the butt rested firmly on my shoulder. Head lowering until cheek rested against metal stock, I squinted through the scope. I know: a scope is cheating—but it also helped keep me fed. I'd run out of food a little over two days after we left Atlanta; I hadn't exactly been thinking about what to pack in all the excitement. Today was our fourth day on the road and my stomach was grumbling. At least water was never a problem;

I just dunked my flask in a nearby canal, creek, river, whathave-you. They were all clear, the water pure.

The buck lowered its head. The body was a clear shot in my sights. *Stay there, you pretty bastard,* I thought. Ariel knew I had to hunt to eat when we weren't around cities, but she didn't particularly like it, so she stayed around the Interstate or wandered about the woods while I sought game. I never worried about her scaring away my supper; no animal would ever know she was there if she didn't want it to. If she had her way I'd be a vegetarian, but I liked meat.

I curled my right index finger around the curved steel trigger and thought about all the kids who'd ever seen *Bambi*. I drew a deep breath and held it. Fuck 'em, I swore silently, they're all grown by now—probably eating Bambi's cousins to survive, just like me. I began to slowly squeeze the trigger: be smooth, be. . . .

The buck jerked its head right and bounded away into the thick tree growth. Small crackles and swishes faded away in its wake. I lowered the crossbow and stood up from behind the trunk of the oak tree that had hidden me. Cramped calf and arm muscles stretched. A scene from an old plantation movie, sunlight shafted lazily through irregular gaps in the moss which hung from tree branches like springy stalactites.

Last night we'd camped ten miles inside the South Carolina state line. By the time we camped tonight I planned to be at least forty miles inside the state, near a city called Greenville. Georgia's gently rolling hills had given way to more dramatic changes in scenery; South Carolina was no other word but hilly. Hilly but nice. The afternoon breezes were cool, especially after the sometimes stifling humidity of midday. Nothing compared to Florida's humidity, though. Nights were sharper, too, and I bundled up in my sleeping bag with Ariel beside me—I wasn't sure who was warming whom. The crickets seemed to chirp louder here, too, but once I was used to them they faded into a not unpleasant drone which even helped bring on sleep. My nights on the road had been restless. I'd been having bad dreams. I couldn't remember them after I woke up, couldn't even put my finger on why I knew they were bad dreams—but they were.

Another reason I liked South Carolina: it was sparse. Not barren—in fact, the foliage seemed heaped about in generous portions, giving the air a nice, thick but not heavy smell. Towns and cities were farther apart. Noticeable ones, anyway. I didn't count the ten-street affairs you missed if you blinked. Those were always around, though usually off the beaten path. Most of what lined the Interstate were dusty, empty gas stations and barren greasy spoons.

I yawned. It would be dark in a few hours. If I wanted to eat before I made camp I'd better get a move on after that buck. Hungry as I was I still knew that it would bother me to kill it. There was more meat on the buck than I would be able to eat, as I could only skin it, clean it, dress it, and cook enough for me to eat right then and next day. After that the meat would spoil, and I didn't have the time or salt to dry and cure it. I was in a hurry to get to New York, though I was damned if I knew why.

With clenched teeth I set out again after my prospective dinner, and had gone perhaps half a mile when a soft voice behind me said, "No wonder you haven't got anything, with all the noise you're making." I turned to see Ariel standing not three feet behind me, tail swishing. "Anything edible within miles has had plenty of warning to burrow, climb, or camouflage itself and laugh while you stomp by."

"Okay, smartass, you do better." Which was a stupid thing to say, considering.

"I don't need to," she said mildly.

"How long have you been following me?"

"Since you got up from behind that tree."

She'd been following me that closely for half a mile? Christ! I relaxed my grip on the Barnett and lowered it to aim toward the ground. "You piss me off sometimes, you know that?"

"Why?"

"Because twigs should snap, at least! Leaves and stuff crunch underfoot, that's why! For God's sake, from three feet away I should be able to hear you *breathe!*"

"Why don't you just give up, and we can go back to the road and get some more miles in and then make camp. We'll be in Greenville tomorrow; there'll be plenty of stores with food in them."

"How do I know that? They could just as easily be looted, stripped bare. And hunting in the city is practically useless unless you want to eat rat. Or maybe a dog or a cat, if you're lucky. Besides, I'm not going another night without something to eat."

"Okay, fine. Just—" She quieted suddenly. I listened: light steps crunching on dead leaves. I squinted, tightened my jaw muscles to open up my ears. Just ahead, about twenty-five yards behind that group of pines. . . . I looked at Ariel. Ha! Dinner after all.

"I don't think—" she began in a voice I barely heard. I motioned her to silence and brought the Barnett up, peering past the crosshairs. Yeah, a slight movement of shadow, betrayed by the latticework of sunlight above and behind it. My buck was back. I followed the movement with the Barnett. It should emerge from between the two trees right ahead of me in just a second. I began to apply gradual, steady pressure on the trigger. My mouth watered at the remembered tanginess of venison.

The crossbow was batted down with an empty sound—*clomp!*—just as the bolt hissed loose. It thwocked into the ground a few feet away. I jerked away from Ariel, holding the Barnett protectively. "Why the fuck did you—?" Before I could finish she nodded her head toward the knot of pine trees. Tingling redness flew up my neck to warm my cheeks and forehead. A boy not older than fifteen stood at the space between the two trees where I'd been aiming a moment before.

"It's not that you're dumb, Pete," Ariel replied. "You just don't think ahead sometimes."

"Gee, thanks. You're not even going to let me feel guilty."

She looked from me to the boy, who'd stopped, smiled, waved, and begun walking toward us. "Have it your way," she said. "You're stupid."

The boy wore a khaki Boy Scout knapsack, white T-shirt, and faded blue jeans. The legs were too short and his blue tennis shoes stuck out comically, along with a good three inches of white tube socks. His belt drooped down on his left side where he wore a large broadsword in a metal sheath. He stopped before us, still smiling toothily. Long, sandy hair and penny-colored freckles set off very white skin. "Hi," he said, accent turning the "i" sound into an extremely short "a." "My name's George." He looked at Ariel. Most people react strongly at first sight of her—they become short of breath, or they gape, or shake their heads, blink—overcome by her ecstatic beauty, or something. Hell, I don't know. She hit me the same way when I first saw her, though. But this George kid—he didn't look impressed one bit. "Hey," he said. "Your horse looks pretty neat."

Not again— "She's not a horse," I said, trying not to sound exasperated. "She's a unicorn."

"Uni . . . ?"

"Unicorn."

He repeated it. His accent made the vowels roll almost as much as the local countryside rolled. He said it again, feeling the word, tasting it, voice seeming to fold around its edges. "Unicorn." He nodded his head, perched atop a long neck. "I know they call it a unicycle 'cause it's only got one wheel, so I guess they call it a unicorn 'cause it's only got one horn." He paused, frowned, and smiled again. "Why isn't it a uni*horn*, though? Makes more sense that way."

I looked at Ariel but she was playing the dumb horse act, head bent to the ground, pretending to chew on grass. An air-brushed Mr. Ed, with extras. "Her name's Ariel," I told him, shooting her a disdainful look. She scratched at the grass and went on munching.

"Ariel." His voice changed it, put the accent on the first syllable instead of the last. He said it again, the same way: "*Ar*iel. Can I pet her?"

I folded my arms. This might prove interesting. Either way, I'd learn something. "Sure, go ahead. If she'll let you."

Still sporting that idiot smile he walked to Ariel and ruffled her neck. "Hey, she feels pretty good. You must wash her a lot. We used to have horses at home but Pop had to turn 'em loose when we couldn't feed them no more." He walked thin fingers through her mane and patted her high on the neck. "Yeah, you like that, don't you girl?"

Ariel raised her head and spat out grass. "This stuff tastes like shit," she said.

The kid damn near levitated. He jumped back, gasping, and his eyes widened. Suddenly they narrowed and he looked at me. "Hey . . . did you—"

"No, he didn't," interrupted Ariel. "I said it."

"Well. . . ." He couldn't decide which of us to look at, and finally settled his eyes on Ariel. ". . . hot damn! I ain't never seen nothing like this! I mean, those stories I heard from people, I thought they were all just . . . stories, you know?"

"Well, I guess some of them aren't," I said.

"Yeah." His face became thoughtful. "Hey, yeah." He turned to me with an urgent look. "Those stories they tell about dragons north of here—are those real too?"

"Well, I've heard that there were dragons in the Carolinas," I said. "Though I couldn't say for certain. Ariel?"

"I've never been this far north. How would I know?"

"Well, I hope they're not real." His expression reflected it.

"Why not?" Ariel asked.

"'Cause my dad says I gotta kill one."

She gave him her best surely-you-jest look, head lowered and lids drooping. "Whatever for?"

George spread his hands. "My dad killed a bear once with a knife. He wants to make it a . . ." he hunted for the word ". . . a tradition."

"Excuse me?" I said. "He killed a bear, so he wants you to kill a dragon?"

He nodded. "Uh-huh."

"And you're going to *do* it?"

He shrugged. "He's my dad," he said, as if that said it all. I guess for him it did.

Oh, brother—"I suppose that's what the broadsword's for?"

"Yeah. Dad found it in a store somewhere. It ain't very sharp."

"Do you even know how to use it?"

"I, uh—no, I don't," he answered in a small voice.

I sighed. "Right. Well, best of luck to you, George, my boy. You're gonna need it. I'm afraid we're in a hurry to get someplace, so we'll just run along—"

"Where you headed?"

"North on eighty-five," I answered vaguely.

He brightened. "Hey, could I go with you?

I started to say no, but Ariel stopped me with a look. "Excuse us a moment, George," she said. She closed one eye, regarding me speculatively with the other. "Private conference, Pete."

"Ariel, I *don't* want someone tagging along with us."

"Neither do I. But we can't just let him go off and get himself killed."

"He's not my responsibility."

"Lower your voice." She glanced at George, who studied a tree trunk twenty yards from us. "It's not his fault his father's got shit for brains. Come on, Pete—he's just a dumb kid."

"Who's gonna get us killed trying to slay a fucking *dragon,* for God's sake!"

She brightened. "Then he can come?"

Goddamn her—she knew me too well. "He can come," I said resignedly. "But I'll be damned if I'll play baby-sitter to him."

She trotted to George and told him the allegedly good news. He nodded happily.

Ariel woke me at sunrise. My sleep had been disturbed, full of twisting dream images, misty and elusive. I don't know if it was part of my dreams or if it really happened, but sometime in the night I awakened with an erection. It was so hard it was painful. I twisted about because it pressed uncomfortably into my stomach. It upset me that I'd had an erection; I didn't know why.

"Sleep good?" asked Ariel as I got up and stretched.

"Mmm." I rubbed sleep granules from the corners of my eyes and rolled them on the tips of thumb and forefinger. "Has it penetrated your mythical skull yet that we're going to attempt—and I stress the word attempt—to kill a dragon?"

"I don't like killing anything, Pete. But dragons are bullies. They get what they deserve."

We were in Greenville by a little after nine. It was a small town and had that kind of dead look that made me wonder if it had been just as lively before the Change. Probably; there were few cars in the middle of the streets, more in the parking lots of small shopping centers and car lots. Bird shit had made small white explosions on the windshields and helped turn the bodies to rust. Their South Carolina plates were red, white, and blue, with a palm tree and a banjo in the center, making me think of Dixie, mint juleps, and Tara. A lot of pickup trucks had a rebel flag front plate and shotgun rack holding, more often than not, an axe handle. There were also popular bumper stickers, faded by rain and torn by time: NRA; ONLY FREE MEN OWN GUNS; YOU CAN HAVE MY GUN WHEN YOU PRY MY COLD, DEAD FINGERS FROM IT; IF GUNS ARE OUTLAWED, ONLY OUTLAWS WILL HAVE GUNS, and the like.

"You say the town's completely deserted?" I asked George

as we walked through the main street.

"Pretty much. Some people live just outside of town, but I ain't heard of anybody living in it in a long time. My family never had no problem coming in and getting stuff if we needed to."

I stopped in a drugstore—the door was unlocked—and grabbed cigarettes (there were two packs left), new shoelaces (nylon—the old leather ones had turned out to be a mistake; they got wet, dried out, and broke), and a pack of peppermints for Ariel. The store owner had kept a snub-nosed .38 behind the register. I opened the magazine. Six bullets. I spun it and snapped my wrist. It clacked home. I brought the barrel to my temple and pulled the trigger.

Click.

But there'd been one heart-speeding second: what if, just this once, a gun went off?

I threw it to the floor. It clattered to the foot of the magazine section. I turned and left the drugstore.

"What are you laughing about?" asked Ariel as I joined her in the street.

"Nothing." I tossed her the packet of peppermint. She let it fall to the asphalt: what was she supposed to do with it? I opened it, still laughing, and began untwisting the cellophane packets. What a weird world.

We were back on the open road by ten. I walked on Ariel's right, George on her left. As we walked I practiced my daily regimen of drawing Fred and trying to return it to the sheath in one smooth motion without looking. I'd already cut my thumb once.

"Hey, Pete," George said as I drew the sword once more. "If you're in such a hurry to get up north, why don't you ride a bike? Ariel could keep up with you, couldn't she?"

I locked my wrist. Yeah, that felt right. Resisting the temptation to look at my left hip I slowly bent my sword arm at the elbow. The back of the blade slid along the top of my left wrist. "Yeah, she could keep up," I said, pulling the blade back and trying again. "But I won't ride one." I pulled the blade up until I felt the tip slide to the top of the scabbard.

"Why not?"

Now if I used my left thumb as a guide . . . yeah! It went

into place and I brought right hand close to left. The guard met the scabbard with a small clank. "Because you can't hide when you're riding a bicycle." I drew Fred again. My stride made the blade bob and I missed yet another attempt to return it to the scabbard on the first try. "Besides, I tried to ride one once. It wouldn't work." I cheated and looked. The sword went into the sheath. "Shit, I'll never learn how to do this." I walked in front of Ariel, who'd been watching me with amusement, then over to George. "Step away from Ariel," I told him. "I want to see you draw that thing."

He looked down at his hip. "Oh, sure." He grabbed the double-handed grip with his right hand and pulled. And kept pulling. His arm was straight out and the sword was still in the sheath. It was longer than his reach.

"You're going to have to get a bigger belt and sling it lower," I told him.

"It'll drag the ground."

"What can I say? It's one or the other."

Ariel scraped a hoof on the road.

"Oh, neat," George exclaimed at the trailing sparks. "Did you see that?"

I glanced at her. "Yeah. Whoop-tee-doo."

She looked over at me, mock hurt in her midnight eyes. "Whatever happened to the *Don Quixote* you were reading me?" Her voice was pouting.

"It's in the pack somewhere."

She looked at me expectantly.

"Jesus Christ, now?"

"What's wrong with now? I want to find out what happens. Besides, I like Rocinante."

We passed a Ford station wagon turned sideways on the left side of the road. With headlights knocked out and front grille bent it looked like a sleeping drunk. "Rocinante's just a stupid, worn-out horse," I commented. "She's hardly even dealt with."

She scraped a hoof. I ignored George's awed exclamation. "So? Rocinante follows Don Quixote faithfully—no matter how futile the quest." She looked at me pointedly, to use a bad pun.

I snorted. "That's because Rocinante's too dumb to know any better. 'A horse is a horse, of course, of course,'" I sang. "R-r-right, Wi-ilbu-u-rrr?"

"Why, Pete, you sound a little hoarse."

I groaned. "You're making an ass of yourself, kid."

She let out a horse-like fricative. "How can a kid make an ass of itself? Besides, I'm an equine unicorn, not a caprine one."

"So now it's goats, is it?"

"Fuck ewe." She looked smug.

George looked around, surprised. "Hey, you mean she talks like that?"

I ignored him. "What happened to your horse puns? They run out on you?"

"Yeah—they weren't very stable in the first place."

I groaned again. "No more. Please."

She shook her head. "Pretty fleece."

"You aren't even being consistent. Fleece is from sheep."

"You're full of sheep. Anything can have fleas."

"Stop, you're killing me."

A gleam in the black diamond of her eyes: "Whatever you say, Pete—just quit stallion around and read me some *Don Quixote*."

I made another pained sound. "All right. You win. Anything to stop the offal puns."

"I suppose you could try punishment."

I threatened not to read if she kept it up. She shut up. I asked George to reach in the lower left pocket of my pack and pull out the thick, dog-eared, paperback copy of *Don Quixote*. He did, then looked around at the scenery, gaze settling on the power lines ahead which played host to dozens of birds. "Lotta birds around."

"Mmmm." I opened the book where it had been marked, knowing George was bored. I hadn't asked to play nursemaid; he was going to have to think up his own ways to occupy time. I unfolded the marked page.

"When do we stop for lunch?" asked George. Ariel shot him an irritated glance.

"We don't," I said. "We eat while we walk. Only time we stop is to eat late dinner and go to sleep."

"What are you in such an all-fired rush about?"

"I'm trying to get to New York to meet a friend. Now be quiet." I cleared my throat and began reading. "'Chapter XVII. *Wherein is continued the account of the innumerable troubles that the brave Don Quixote and his good squire Sancho Panza endured in the inn, which, to his sorrow, the knight took to be a castle.'"* I glanced up to Ariel. She nodded attentively and I continued.

I'd begun smoking again when I could find cigarettes, but Ariel hadn't said anything to me about it. I knew she hated to be around it, but I needed it to keep my nerves calmed. Maybe she knew that.

That night—our fifth on road—the three of us slept in a motel in Spartanburg. It was deserted but had been broken into at some time. From behind the desk I grabbed a key to a room on the second floor. The room was pale blue, with two narrow beds and a seascape painting on the wall to the right of the door.

George flopped onto the far bed. "Heck, I don't know which I want to do first—eat or sleep." Three minutes later he was snoring.

Dreams again. They brushed a tickling feather across my nighttime awareness. Muted images of hot, rapid breaths, and softness.

I awoke to find Ariel pacing restlessly around the room, though that had not wakened me. You couldn't hear her move. George slept quietly to my left. When I sat up she stopped pacing and turned to face me. A little light came in from the curtained windows, just enough to give her the faint phosphorescence of crashing waves on a dark beach. "What's the matter?" I asked.

"My leg. It's begun to throb."

"Which one?"

"Right front."

Oh. The one that had been broken. "All that walking we've been doing, maybe?"

A faint shift of luminescence as she shook her head. "I think it will get worse as we get closer to New York. The memory gets stronger as the distance lessens." She paused a few moments, then said, "You moved around a lot in your sleep. You kept... rubbing yourself. You know, on your... crotch. It bothered me."

"Bad dreams again." I felt embarrassed, as if I'd been caught doing something wrong. After another pause I said, "Ariel, if you'd like to quit this whole thing, we will. I don't want to do this if it means—"

"We've been through this before, Pete. We'll go."

"But—"

"We'll go. Now go back to sleep."

twelve

Offering dragons quarter is no good,
they regrow all their parts and come on again,
they have to be killed.

—John Berryman,
"Henry's Programme for God"

Spartanburg turned out to be a lot like Greenville, but bigger. I saw a few people moving in the distance as we walked through what seemed the main drag, and once, on the sidewalk, we passed four men and a woman who stared at us openly, not saying a word. Ariel lectured George as we walked through the north end of town. "Never stand in front of one and swing your sword," she was saying. I kept looking left and right at buildings on both sides of the street—the presence of people made me nervous.

"Why not?" asked George. His low-swung broadsword clinked in time with his walk; the metal sheath hit the pavement each time he stepped forward with his left foot.

"Because it'll eat you. A dragon's main defenses are all oriented toward frontal attack. The front claws can swipe forward quickly, but they have difficulty striking to the side. Same with the head. It's on a long neck and it'll snap forward and strike like a snake, though not quite as fast. It also breathes fire. But the head has difficulty turning far to the side, close in toward its own body."

George took all this in soberly.

"Never try to stab or cut at the head. It's bony and the hide's tough; your sword probably won't go through. That, and it's easy to miss their brains, which are not exactly a vital organ where dragons are concerned anyway."

"Well, what am I supposed to do, then?"

She looked at the broken glass front of Sam & Sons Laundry and Dry Cleaning, then looked back at the road ahead. "Get it low in the side. You have to try to puncture the gasbag. That's what allows it to fly and breathe fire. If it gets airborne you're in trouble."

"Wait a minute," I said. "Gasbag?"

She nodded. "Most of the body is hollow, filled with hydrogen gas produced by chemical reaction within the body, the same way your body produces gas. Hydrogen gives it lift; without it dragons couldn't fly. Their wings aren't large enough. The gas is ignited in the throat and comes out as fiery breath."

I wasn't biting. "Hold on a second. Why the need for complex biochemistry? I thought dragons were magical."

"They are."

"Then don't they fly by magic, or breathe fire by magic?"

She shook her head. The point of her horn flashed as it caught the morning sun. "Magic is a resource, Pete. Waste it and it's gone. Why do you think I use it so rarely? Sure, dragons live by magical means—so do I. But nature isn't wasteful, whether it's labeled 'natural' or 'supernatural.' The magical power required to lift something as big as a dragon during the course of its lifetime would be tremendous. A dragon uses up magic just by existing, same as me. So rather than waste magic by using it up lifting a heavy mass, nature found an easier way."

"I still don't get it. I always thought of magic as unnatural."

"Don't be stupid. If it's unnatural it can't happen within nature. Magic is just a different set of physics laws than the one you're used to." She blinked and struck sparks. "But it still has to be consistent with itself, Pete; otherwise it won't work. There's no such thing as complete chaos."

I nodded, reminded of our first conversation with Malachi. The memory caused a sudden cold tingle at the small of my back.

"Anyway," Ariel said, dipping her horn at George, "you'll probably get off one poke, two if you're lucky. After that your sword will be pretty much useless. Dragon blood is pretty corrosive."

George accepted everything she said as gospel, but since she was in a mood for explanations I demanded to know why that was, also.

"Hydrochloric acid," she said patiently. "It causes the chemical reaction that produces the hydrogen and doubles as a defense mechanism."

"Oh." Until then I'd assumed she was bullshitting George on his dragon-slaying technique and that we were speaking academically; now I realized she was serious as a heart attack. Sometimes it surprised me to hear her speaking knowledgeably about something like biochemistry; she apparently remembered everything she'd read.

"Never look a dragon in the eyes," she continued.

It was George's turn to question. "Why not?"

"Just don't."

A couple hundred yards ahead was a roadsign: SPARTANBURG CITY LIMIT. Though the city proper continued a few miles past that, it made me feel better.

I looked up from the road atlas. "We're going to have to pick up our pace. We either walk faster, longer, or both." I had traced our route with a finger, only moderately pleased. Five days out from Atlanta, a little better than a hundred fifty miles. We could do better. I should have brought a skateboard. With my luck, though, it would be as workable as a bicycle.

"Faster," said Ariel.

"Longer," said George.

"It's unanimous, then—faster and longer."

Neither of them seemed too happy with that.

Our projected route would put us in Charlotte in two days. I didn't like that. Small towns were one thing; cities were a whole 'nother mess. I wanted to avoid them but I-85 went straight through Charlotte. Skirting around the city would just take up more time. Damn. But at least Charlotte would have places where I could pick up hiking boots—mine were nearly worn out. I also needed a change of clothes. I'd been wearing my ugly green Army shirt and black cords for six days. I tried not to think about what my underwear and socks smelled like by now; I even had to sleep in them. I'd also have to pick up cigarettes. I'd run out that day; I'd be having nicotine fits tomorrow. Peppermint for Ariel, too, to keep her from bitching about my smoking.

Hell, I might even pick up a skateboard. Purely out of curiosity, of course.

Ariel asked me to rub her right foreleg after we made camp. Nothing felt wrong, but she gasped when my kneading hands circled the ankle joint. "I'm sorry!" I said.

"It isn't you, Pete." She lay on her left side and I was beside her on my knees. George had run behind a group of trees to go to the bathroom. I had told him to be careful; it was dark and something might grab him while he was in an impossible position.

I bent forward, resting my weight on my left arm, and stroked her mane. It looked like moonlit fog in the early morning just before the sun rises. "Is there something I can do?"

She bent her head up and nuzzled my arm. "I'll be okay, Pete. Really. It's remembered pain, that's all. It's in my mind."

I followed the curve round her shoulder, along the length of her once-injured leg with my fingertips. My throat felt full. I wanted to clear it.

Suddenly I was holding her tightly, arms around her neck. My eyes stung; tears slid down my cheeks and onto her hair, beading like dew on a spider web, and somewhere in the back of my mind I thought, God, I look stupid. But I didn't care. I just felt scared, very scared.

"I wish . . ." I said, sniffling. My nose had plugged up. "It isn't fair!"

"What isn't fair, Pete?" Her voice was gentle; none of the underlying pain that had been there before was present.

I couldn't answer. I just cried harder.

"Tell me."

"I just . . . I wish so much that you were a woman!"

She was quiet a long time. I think George came back but respectfully kept himself scarce. After a while she spoke, and her voice sounded far away, as it had the time she'd brought me back from death and I hadn't wanted to come.

"So do I, Pete." She sighed. "Sometimes . . . so do I."

I stopped crying soon. Ariel felt like the soft stuffed animal every child should have guarding his sleep, and eventually, lulled by that warm security, I did sleep.

* * *

The dreams again. They grew worse each night. I only remembered fragments, but they became more and more detailed.

Hot breath mingling with mine. Sweat tickling my back, cooled by a light night breeze. A faint groan—mine? Sensations assailing me: infant-soft skin, warmth and wetness, and a persistent sliding . . . My name, said in a voice all breath—

My eyes snapped open. The lopsided waning moon shone down on Ariel, from whom I'd rolled a few feet during the night. The lumpy shape of George in his sleeping bag snored lightly six feet away, on the other side of Ariel. I realized I was cold. It hits you like that when you wake up: *Oh, yeah—I'm cold.* I got up quietly. My penis pressed against the fabric of my cords. I looked down at it. Those dreams. . . . I crossed the dark silver ribbon of black-bordered highway, went behind a tree, and unzipped my pants. I tried to urinate but the muscles wouldn't relax. Frustrated, I went back across the road. Fred was lying beside the cocked crossbow atop our piled packs and next to the Aero-mag. I picked it up and unzipped my sleeping bag. George snored on. Ariel's right foreleg jerked. Her head twitched. I crawled into the sleeping bag and zipped it up, left arm out and holding on to Fred. I closed my eyes. *Shit—I have to go to the bathroom.* Exasperated, I tried to unzip the bag, but the tab caught in the cloth and I had to crawl out. I took Fred along and went behind a tree.

As I zipped my pants back up a cry startled me. I turned around, drawing Fred as I spun. The sword arced out and a shock went through my hand as the blade cut through something. I danced grotesquely when something landed at my feet, and stopped when I realized my trained reflexes had caused me to murder a branch. The cry came again. It sounded like a hungry baby's wail. Some kind of bird. Or a squonk, maybe. I sheathed Fred and returned to my sleeping bag, hearing the eerie cry once more.

Tucked away again and beginning to feel drowsy, I realized that I hadn't had to look to sheathe Fred. Maybe I'd get the hang of this stuff after all.

NORTH CAROLINA STATE LINE, the sign read. We'd slept a hundred yards south of it.

The day was gloomy and overcast. Ariel, George, and I trudged along in silence. We're embarrassed, I thought, because of what happened last night.

It began raining about eight-thirty, starting off as a light drizzle and ending as a toad-strangler for most of the day. I couldn't read *Don Quixote* to Ariel and George. I also worried that Fred would rust.

Weary, soaked, hungry, and roadsore, we entered Charlotte by nightfall.

Sometimes I wish we'd never gone into Charlotte. I play *what if?* and wonder what would have happened had we avoided the city altogether.

We slept in a Holiday Inn at the outskirts of the city. It was out of the rain and we didn't have to go about setting up even the meager camp that none of us felt like making. We had neighbors in a room down the hall from ours, on the second floor. Three men and two women. They thought Ariel was "really neat." I didn't comment when they told me they'd shoved three beds together in their room. I made polite, noncommittal noises when they left me with an invitation to come over any old time.

I stripped in the room, towelled myself dry, and stumbled into the bed in an exhausted stupor. George was already out on the other bed. Within two minutes I'd joined him in dreamland. I didn't have bad dreams this time. I think I was too tired.

Next thing I knew Ariel was nudging me. Daylight pushed at the curtains. I whipped the covers back and sat up.

"Oh, Pete!" Ariel sounded hurt. My nakedness wasn't what upset her. It didn't bother me, either, but when I looked down I felt sick. My feet were a brownish mess of dirt and dried blood. Blisters on the knuckles of my big and second toes had burst and scabbed over. It looked as if I'd been shot in both heels. All that walking in worn-out boots.

"Wash them off in the bathtub," she ordered. "There might still be some water pressure. Make sure you put a stopper in the tub."

I wondered why my feet didn't hurt as I walked into the bathroom, rubbing sleep from my eyes. Just enough water coughed from the faucet to make a small puddle. I lathered my feet with a miniature bar of hotel soap. The lather turned pink. The water became murky. I swished my feet around to get as much of the soap off as I could, then stepped out and began to towel them dry—and that's when they hurt. I hissed as I drew the towel across the tops of my feet. It felt like an emory board sawing at an open wound.

"You all right, Pete?" asked Ariel from the doorway.

"My feet would probably still feel okay if you hadn't pointed them out to me." I looked up. Her black eyes were concerned. "Yeah, I'm okay. I'll heal, at least. It just hurts like hell."

"Do you think you should walk today?"

"I don't have a choice."

"How about we take it easy and get some things you've been complaining about not having? New hiking boots, for instance."

I wanted to argue and decided not to. It really wasn't a bad idea. Besides, my feet did hurt a lot. "All right. Get George up. We'll see if we can loot some stores."

"George is already up. I'll go knock down the hall and see if they know where we can get clothes and stuff."

I followed her to the front door and opened it for her. "And cigarettes," I called after her.

"And peppermint," she added.

I left the door open part way and got dressed, trying to imagine our neighbors' reaction to having a unicorn bang on their door wanting to know where there was a good shopping center. ("Harry, there's a unicorn at the door—wants to borrow a cup of sugar.")

George lay awake in bed. "Morning," he said.

"Good morning. Feel like going shopping?"

"Well, yeah, I'd like to get some stuff. How're your feet?"

"Lovely, if you like Sam Peckinpah movies." The comment drew a blank look. I'd forgotten he wasn't old enough to remember things like that very well. "They don't look so good," I amended.

"When are we gonna find a dragon?"

"We'll be coming up on the Smokies soon. Ariel thinks there are dragons there. Why the sudden hurry?"

He sat up and I saw that he was already dressed. "'Cause I want to get this stuff over with and go home."

"You miss your family?"

He nodded. Poor kid—he didn't realize his father was nuts. Ariel and I were fairly committed to helping him slay a dragon; he'd never make it on his own. Sure, he wasn't my best friend in the universe, but he was a good kid—I didn't want to see him get mangled. Of course, come to think of it, we might get mangled, too. Oh, yeah.

I looked down at my feet. "Fuck you," I told them. How dare they betray me like this; I wanted to catch up to Malachi. If my feet set us back we'd end up days behind him—if we weren't already.

Ariel nudged the door open with her horn. "They said there's a big shopping mall about three miles down the road. They went by there a few days ago. They don't know if it's occupied but according to them it's in pretty good shape."

"Three miles?"

She looked at my feet and nodded.

"I don't care if it's occupied. I want cigarettes. Let's go." I strapped her pack on, put in the Barnett, and looked at George. His broadsword hung ridiculously at his side and he'd shouldered his Boy Scout pack.

I turned the socks bloody side out and laced the boots so they were tight about the ankles and loose over my instep. It still hurt. I shouldered my pack and we left.

Charlotte was about a fourth the size of Atlanta, a little more sparse, less "cosmopolitan," I guess you'd call it. It was hilly but not mountainous. We headed north, walking between the frozen traffic lines on the street. Something I saw tickled me: someone had taken an old, white VW Bug, sawed off the roof even with the doors, dumped in a lot of dirt and rich topsoil, and turned it into a planter. The old Sixties slogan "Flower Power" had been painted on the side.

George had begun to look more and more worried; I knew it would get worse as we neared the Smokies.

The shopping mall was on the right side of the road. We turned beneath a dead stoplight and walked into the entranceway. Scores of cars were in a lot. The glass doors were unlocked. I held one open for Ariel. "Ladies first." She walked in with a superior air, nose high. My kick at her ass missed.

"It sure looks empty enough," whispered George.

"Then why are you whispering?" I asked in a normal tone.

He shrugged. We walked from the side wing of shops to the main arcade, our footsteps echoing—mine and George's, anyway; Ariel's never made noise unless she wanted them to.

"Are we gonna split up or stick together?" George asked.

I looked at Ariel. "It looks safe," she said.

I rubbed my chin. I needed a shave. "Split up and get what you need. It'll take less time. I want to get out of here as soon as we can. And be careful." I glanced at the fountain in the center of the mall. Scum had accumulated in the still water along the blue-tiled edges. On the bottom were pennies, dull brown in the murky water, tossed in years ago at wishful random. "We'll meet back at this fountain in an hour."

They agreed, and I headed toward one end of the mall, George the other, and Ariel down a side wing. Looking for a candy shop, I bet myself.

It was very cool in the mall. The sound of my footsteps mingled arhythmically with the echo of George's retreating ones. I tried to ignore it. I'd rather have silence than just a few sounds in all the quiet.

I drew Fred at the startling shape of several figures standing in a storefront window, then realized they were just mannequins in a dress shop. This place was making me jittery.

The door to Montgomery Ward's was open. I headed toward MEN'S WEAR and picked out two pairs of blue jeans from a rack. I leaned backpack and weapons against a register and took off my black cords, feeling both silly and naked—naked as in vulnerable. I took off hiking boots and socks and left them in the middle of the floor. I wouldn't be needing those again. One look at my underwear made me think twice about trying on the jeans immediately; I went to a display, opened a plastic packet of Fruit of the Loom, and put on a pair. The other two I rolled up and tossed into my pack. No doubt I'd be needing them later.

The first pair of jeans didn't fit. The second did. I left them on, picked out a new belt, put it on, and returned Fred to a belt-loop. I felt much better. Discarded clothes on floor behind me, I walked barefoot and shirtless through the store, dragging the backpack behind me with top flap opened. I tossed in an Atra razor for later.

Out in the mall I kept jumping at shadows, seeing motion where there was none. Once I saw Ariel up ahead and I waved. She nodded back. Unicorn in a shopping mall. Which way to the gift shop, please?

A stop at Thom McAn yielded new hiking boots and three pairs of white tube socks. At a drugstore I grabbed a carton of Winstons and a half-dozen small packs of peppermint to balance it.

There was a table of iron-on transfer shirts in the center of the store. They'd been on sale about six years now. I picked out a blue shirt in my size and held it in front of me. I'M WITH STUPID, it announced in red letters. Below that was an arrow pointing to the right. I put it on. The arrow now pointed to my left; I'd have to be sure to stay on Ariel's right side.

I imagined Muzak playing over the store's P.A., and a nasal voice over it: "Attention, shoppers. . . ."

There was a commotion in the mall: shouts, breaking glass. I ran to the store entrance and peeked out the door. George was barrelling toward me, arms loaded with booty. Every few steps something fell from his double-armed grip. He must have been messing around in one of the clothing stores; he was wearing tight blue dress slacks and a red silk shirt. It was unbuttoned, and as he ran it unfurled behind him like some disco flag. His broadsword screwed up his stride by slapping against his left leg.

Three men were running after him.

Something smacked against the glass door I held propped open with my body. I ducked—it would have been too late, but there was no controlling the reflex—and glanced up. The glass had spiderwebbed. One of the three men was trying to fit another arrow into his bow while running, which couldn't have been very easy. George saw me and veered my way.

"That way!" I yelled, waving toward the wing that led to the mall entrance. "That way!" He cut a corner, leaped over a bench (more things fell from his arms), nearly ran into a fountain but dodged just in time, and picked up speed.

Ariel appeared from the open doorway of a card shop a hundred feet to the left of the wing George had run down. Two men went after George. The third headed toward me. He loosed another arrow, which went ten feet wide of me. I decided you can't be accurate with bow and arrow while running full out. He wouldn't be able to fit another arrow before he reached me, even though he was still a good seventy-five feet away. I drew the Aero-mag calmly from its backpack sling, fitted a dart, and brought it to my mouth. Deep breath, wait . . . one, two, three, *puff!* The coat-hanger-wire dart hit him in the left forearm. He dropped his bow and screamed. It echoed down the length of the mall. The point of the dart protruded from his arm. I ran forward and punched him in the jaw. He went straight backwards, unconscious. I stopped just long enough to pull another dart from the pouch at my belt and tap it into the Aero-mag with a thumb. "Help George!" I yelled to Ariel. "He took off down there. Two men are after him."

She nodded and sprang forward as if she'd hit warp drive. I went around the bench George had jumped over and trotted toward the main entrance, one hand on Fred and the other on the aluminum shaft of the Aero-mag. The backpack bounced up and down in time. I crouched behind a smooth concrete fixture in the middle of the mall. Dusty odor inside: it held long-dead plants. A cautious peek over the top revealed the two men at either side of the B. Dalton's entrance. They held their bows ready but weren't firing. They must have seen George enter but weren't willing to go in after him; Dalton's was too crowded with full bookshelves to give any working room. They glanced at each other and I ducked to prevent the farther man from seeing me. They were probably waiting for George to freak and make a move. There was no sign of Ariel.

I brought the Aero-mag up and blew. The dart hit the nearer man and bounced off. They were too far away. The nearer whirled around and the farther swung his bow. I ducked and heard an arrow hit the concrete planter. Now, while he's fitting another one: thumb the belt pouch, slap in a dart, swing the blowgun out and pop up quickly—

I almost ate an arrow. The other one had fired when he saw me move; the arrow brushed my cheek and buried itself in the backpack. My entire body twitched and I dropped as fast as I'd come up. Fletchings tickled my left cheek. "Why, you son of a bitch," I said aloud. I exposed my head over the top of the planter and ducked again. An arrow hissed above me. *Now.* I ran from the planter to a water fountain twenty feet to my right, paused, then ran a zigzag pattern to the dusty display automobile by the fountain in the mall's center. I looked through the windows to see the nearer man heading toward me while his partner remained behind at B. Dalton's. I blew him another dart—it missed but made him cautious—and thumbed in another. Only two darts left now. He skittered, hugging close to walls and anything between him and me. I lay down behind a tire and looked beneath the car. Blue tennis shoes trotted toward me in irregular rhythm. It would be hard to get off a shot. His feet kept moving, my backpack kept me at an awkward angle, and that damned arrow was bothering my cheek. I tried pulling it out but the hunting-blade tip kept it firmly embedded. so I broke it off. I brought the blowgun to my lips and tightened them like a trumpet player. He stopped to change direction and I blew as Doc Severinsen never had. The dart hit his left shin and he did a near-complete flip. I ran to him and kicked his bow away.

Ariel jumped from inside B. Dalton's with George on her back, crossbow aimed. His red silk shirt billowed. Ariel leapt. Her back hooves hit a book display and sent paperbacks flying. The final man had been looking at me when Ariel streaked out. He spun and let fly a fast shot at Ariel. She twitched her neck and snapped the arrow with her horn. George pulled the trigger on the Barnett. The bolt hit the floor twenty feet behind the man, who sprawled backward with a hole through his neck. Ariel hesitated, looking toward me. I yelled for her to go on. She said something to George and he hurriedly returned the crossbow to her pack, leaned forward, and wrapped his arms around her neck. She plunged forward and struck the glass of the mall entrance horn first. It shattered and she broke into the sunshine amidst a diamond-shower of glass.

I looked back at the man I'd shot in the leg. There was no need to do anything else to him; he hugged the leg close to his chest and writhed on the floor. His eyes and teeth were clenched and his mouth was drawn back so that the cords on the sides of his neck stood out. Small grunts worked from his throat. I left him and walked out through the jagged hole Ariel had left behind, blinking in the sunshine.

Ariel made George get off her back. She would only carry him as long as necessary.

George was crying. He walked a little ahead of us in the middle of the highway. Ariel and I spoke in low voices. Her tone was accusing. "Was it worth it, for the things we came away with?"

I felt guilty and looked from her to the road flowing beneath my new boots. My feet still hurt.

"Peppermint candy," she said, "and cigarettes. You only wanted to loot that mall because you figured you'd have a better chance of finding cigarettes there. The clothes and things—you could have found those anywhere."

I didn't think she was right, but I said nothing.

"George found some good things. But about your cigarettes—" She closed her eyes and tossed her head, horn inscribing a brief circle in the late morning air. "There."

"'There' what?"

"I just got rid of them. No more smoking."

"Goddammit—"

"It's bad for you, Pete."

"Bullshit. You keep me healthy and you know it."

"That doesn't mean I should work overtime at it. It's neither my responsibility nor my duty. I'm not your doctor. And I don't want to be around it, either."

"I'm going to have to quit all over again!" Shit—bitten nails, piano-wire nerves, constant craving.

"Too bad. I'm not taking the blame for your addictions, either."

"Oh, for. . . ." I stopped. What was the use?

We walked through the city. George stayed ahead of us, head inclined toward the road. I think he'd stopped crying.

"Ariel, what are we going to do about him?"

"Leave him alone. He'll be okay."

"If you say so." I scratched my cheek. Sweat had begun to pour from me in the morning's growing heat and lessening humidity, and it stung where the arrow had brushed past. My shirt—about which Ariel had said nothing—was soaked in the back, damp as a washrag on my shoulders where the pack straps pressed. I shrugged out of them and turned the pack so the H-frame was braced against my stomach, leaning back and walking with knees bent to offset the weight. Holding it with one hand, I untied the flap and flipped it open. The arrow had dented my small auto first-aid kit and stopped against a hunting knife. I pulled the diamond-shaped head and broken shaft out and threw it onto the road. There was a nylon patch kit in the top left pocket of my pack; I'd fix the hole later.

The cigarette carton wasn't in the pack.

I reached in and tossed out the peppermint candy packets one at a time. "Fair's fair," I said.

Ariel snorted but said nothing, though she glanced at the candy on the road behind us.

George was walking with us again. He seemed all right but wouldn't talk, other than to give perfunctory answers. My feet throbbed and I was unhappy with our progress. Malachi was probably two days ahead of us by now. Maybe three. Shit.

We were out of Charlotte by noon. At the north end of town we came upon a young woman reading a hardcover book on a bus bench in the bright sunlight. She squinted up at us as we drew near.

I'd dug out *Don Quixote* and was reading it to Ariel. The woman gave a quiet little gasp and folded her book, marking her place with a finger. I followed suit. She looked at Ariel, looked briefly at me, and back to Ariel. She rose from the bench and stood before us, book dangling at her side. The clear plastic over the cover showed it to be a library book. She opened her mouth to speak and then shook her head as if fully expecting us not to be there when she looked again. Her shoulder-length brown hair fanned out as her head turned from left to right. She watched, mouth open, as we passed. I turned and nodded politely to her, but I don't think she even saw me. She was staring, of course, at Ariel. Gawkers, everywhere, gawkers. We walked on.

A few minutes later Ariel said, without looking back, "She's following us."

"Who? That girl on the bench?"

She nodded. I glanced back. She was a quarter mile behind us, walking with the book held absently in her hand. She still stared at Ariel. "Wonder what she wants?"

"Taken with my awe-inspiring magnificence, no doubt." She dragged a hoof on the asphalt. Sparks scattered.

"Hmph." I glanced back again. "Maybe if we ignore her she'll go away."

We tried it. I read from *Don Quixote* for an hour before looking back again. She was still there. "That's it," I announced, putting the book away. "I'm not being shadowed all the way to New York. Let's wait and find out what she wants."

"Sure. But I can tell you what it is." Her expression was smug. "It's me."

"Why, of course. What else could it be?" I coughed into my hand. We waited as the young woman caught up to us. She looked faintly embarrassed but said nothing, just stood before us.

"Is there something we can do for you?" I asked.

She flushed. "I'd like—I'd like to come with you." She smiled. Bright silver points glittered in her brown eyes.

I raised an eyebrow. "To come with us?"

She nodded.

"Why?"

"Because I've waited a long time for something like this to come my way." She looked longingly at Ariel. "You're a unicorn."

"Heavens," Ariel said dryly. "How astute."

"And you talk."

She snorted."Good trick, huh? You'd never guess it took two people to operate this thing." She turned sideways. "Look—no seams."

"I've never seen anything like you. I mean, I've seen magical animals before, but never a unicorn, never anything so . . . so. . . ."

"Beautiful? Noble, pure, that sort of thing?"

The young woman nodded.

"Okay," I broke in. "So you're both members of the Unicorn Admiration Society. I don't want to seem rude, and I'm glad you've finally seen a unicorn, but we're in a hurry."

"Fine. I don't need anything but what I have with me."

"I don't think you understand. We're traveling together. The three of us."

"Oh, no. I'm not letting an opportunity like this get away. I won't get another chance like this again. I know."

"We're going to New York," I said.

"Fine."

"It's dangerous. You'd slow us down."

"I can take care of myself."

George followed the conversation like an observer at a ping-pong match. I was getting angry. Who the hell was she to come out of the clear blue sky and demand to go with us? "Look," I said. "I'm not even going to argue about it. You can't come with us."

Ariel stepped forward slowly. The sun was just past overhead and her hooves spearpointed the light with polished chrome newness. "Child," she said—the young woman looked surprised at the word; she was at least my age—"you can follow us, but you'll never have me."

Her expression showed she didn't know what Ariel was talking about.

"Try to touch me," said Ariel. "And you'll understand."

She reached toward Ariel's muzzle, a child reaching for the shiny, golden ornament on a high branch of a Christmas tree. Her hand stopped five inches from the side of Ariel's face.

She frowned and pushed her elbow, but the hand only trembled and went no further.

"You can't have your dreams," said Ariel. "You'd only be wishful and frustrated if you came along."

"I don't understand," George said. "I can touch her no problem."

"Yeah, I know," I replied. "So can I."

"But why . . . ?" Her round-faced features drew in in puzzlement.

"You have to be pure to touch a unicorn," Ariel whispered. She looked intently at the frowning young woman. "I see what you need," she said, "and because of all you desire, I am for the first time in my life sorry this is so." Something seemed to pass between them; Ariel seemed to understand this total stranger as if she'd been inside her head. I didn't follow it too well. But the woman made a cutting motion in the air with her library book and said, "Okay, rules are rules and I can't touch you. But I've waited ever since I can remember for magic—real magic, not this spell stuff or bone throwing by candlelight—and I can't let it walk by without me, not after it's passed right next to me in the middle of the afternoon. I just can't." She jerked her head to me. "Look, I'm sorry if I'm coming on too strong. But you try reading fantasy books all your life—have a Bradbury dream walk by your bus bench on a hot day, with everything you've ever wanted tied up in a neat bundle—and see if you wouldn't do almost anything to have it."

"Ariel is my friend," I said. Something about her tone bothered me; it had that religious fanatic tinge. "Nobody 'has' her, dreams or not."

Ariel enunciated each word clearly: "I won't be worshiped. Not by anybody, ever."

George's face looked as if he were squinting at a bright light. "How come I can touch her and you can touch her, but she can't? I still don't get it."

"Aah—" I raised a hand, and dropped it quickly. "Because you've never been fucked, and I've never been fucked, and she has."

She flushed deep red. "I'm not ashamed of it. And my name is Shaughnessy, if you'd like to know."

"I wouldn't like to know. Look, this is crazy. We have to go." George still stared at me, open-mouthed.

"I'll follow you," she warned. "You can't keep me from doing that."

I thought about it. Short of violent means, I guess I couldn't. I sighed. Why did I always get the nuts? If we kept collecting people, Malachi would have a caravan strung out behind him from New York to Atlanta. I frowned at her. "Let's go," I said to Ariel and George. George looked uncertain but came along. Ariel cast me a baleful glance. I stared back until she looked away.

I turned my back to Shaughnessy's look and started walking. After a hundred yards I glanced back. She was just behind us, library book in hand. I turned back before she saw me looking and opened the *Don Quixote* to where I'd left off. I began reading.

"I don't want to hear it right now, Pete," said Ariel. There was something in her tone I couldn't quite read, a flavor between sullenness and melancholy. "Maybe later."

I handed the book to George and he put it in its pocket. After ten minutes I remembered to ask George what he'd got away with from the mall.

He turned away from where he'd been looking back toward Shaughnessy. "Huh?"

I snuck a glance: she was treading along about five hundred feet behind us, book open, eating an apple. I wondered if she'd had it with her, or what? "I said, what did you end up bringing back from the mall?"

"Oh." He grinned, sending large quantities of freckles closer to his forehead. "I got away with some pretty neat stuff. Here—" He opened Ariel's pack, excusing himself to her. An arm went in up to the elbow and came out with a package. "New boot laces," he said. "But you got new boots."

"That's okay. I can always use them when the others wear out. They will before too long, I'm sure." I was conscious of what's-her-name behind us.

George tossed them back into the pack and pulled out a Gyro Frisbee—a plastic flying ring. "I thought it'd give us something to do when we got bored," he explained to my heaven-cast gaze.

In went the Frisbee. Out came a wind-up Timex. "I want to put it on but I don't know what time to set it for," he said.

"It's two o'clock," said Ariel.

He brightened and pulled the button with his teeth, then set the dial at two and wound the watch. It made a noise like a lone cricket.

"Didn't you get yourself clothes other than the ones you have on?" I asked while he rummaged again.

"Nope." He had to reach up on tiptoe and pull down on the pocket to get into Ariel's pack. She complained that the straps cut into her side. I made her stop and bend down so George could reach in for more things. She grumbled to herself (something about it being A Matter of Principle) but complied. George pulled things out and we resumed walking, Ariel dragging a trail of sparks behind front left and back right hooves. I wondered if Shaughnessy saw that. Was Shaughnessy a first name or a last?

George tossed me a brown paper bag. Things inside clinked when I caught it. The paper crackled comfortably. "I looked at your blowgun darts and saw how you made them," he said. "Maybe you can use that stuff."

I looked into the bag. Foot-long pieces of steel, about a dozen of them. A pair of wirecutters (I already had a pair in the pack, but George didn't know that). A half-dozen strands of heavy plastic-beaded necklaces, the kind that are supposed to look like pearls and don't. "Hey, great stuff. Thanks, George!"

He nodded, pleased I was pleased. "I wasn't sure how big the beads should be, so I got different sizes. I got the wire from an umbrella."

"Good thinking." That had never occurred to me; until then I had used either coathangers or piano wire.

The final item was George's crowning glory: fishing arrows. They were the kind with four thin metal lengths that swept back from the sharp head. Once embedded they couldn't be pulled loose without leaving a hole the size of a baseball. Nasty things, but efficient. The only bow I had was the Barnett, and the arrows would have been totally useless to me had George not been lucky enough—or wise enough; I didn't ask—to find arrows with screw-on heads. I could remove the heads, throw away the long arrow shafts, and put them on my crossbow bolt shafts, which were also threaded.

I thanked George again, put the bag of blowgun dart materials in the lower compartment of my pack, and began unscrewing crossbow-bolt heads. Soon I was finished and Ariel asked me to read from *Don Quixote*.

Shaughnessy followed us all day.

* * *

I read to Ariel until sunset. We traveled a little over an hour into the night, then made camp. George pulled another rabbit from a hat: foil packets of freeze-dried camping foods he'd grabbed from some sporting-goods department. I got a fire started, heated water, and George and I ate chili-macaroni, washing it down with the last bit of Wyler's instant lemonade I'd managed to hoard.

Ariel and George got into another conversation about dragons. Saying I was going to the bathroom in the bushes, I slipped away with the last of the chili mac. I shielded it from view with my body.

Three hundred yards down the road a small campfire burned. She was nowhere in sight, but her library book rested atop a large rock. I picked it up and held it away from the campfire, reading the title in the dim orange-yellow glow. *The Little Prince*.

I set the book back and put the plate on top of it.

"What took you so long?" asked Ariel when I returned.

"Serious bowel movement." I looked at George, who sat cross-legged a respectful distance from the fire. "How're your feet holding up, George?"

He wriggled his toes. "Okay, I guess. They hurt, but they ain't nowhere near as bad as yours."

"Give 'em time; I've been on the road longer. Actually, though, I think mine are getting better. The new hiking boots will definitely help."

Thumb pinning spoon to aluminum plate, George searched around. "Hey, where's the rest of the chili?"

"Oh, I threw it out already. I'm sorry. I thought you were finished." Ariel threw me a look.

"Don't worry about it." He set the plate down. "I was just gonna fill up so I wouldn't be hungry tomorrow." He unzipped his sleeping bag. "We getting up earlier tomorrow?"

I nodded. "Five-thirty. You can set your watch by it."

He glanced at his arm and smiled before crawling into his sleeping bag. "See you tomorrow."

"Good night."

"'Night, Ariel."

"Good night, George." She got up and walked around the invisible perimeter of the fire's heat. I stopped in the midst of unzipping my own sleeping bag and looked up at her.

"Threw it away, huh?" she said.

I shrugged. "I thought she might be hungry. Is there something wrong with that?"

"Yes, as a matter of fact, there is."

"What?"

"Feeding a dog is no way to make it go away."

"Oh, come on. Even if you don't like her, she's not a dog. She's a person."

"She's following us like a dog. She wants to be blindly faithful to me like a dog. If you help her out she'll follow us all the way to New York."

"I can't let her go hungry."

"If she's lasted this long she isn't going to starve now. But she will turn back if she gets discouraged enough. Besides, she's not your responsibility."

The corners of my mouth tugged. "We seem to have traded places—that doesn't sound like you at all."

"I feel sorry for her," she said, "but I won't have somebody worshiping me, making me something I'm not."

"How do you know it isn't just that she appreciates what you are?"

"Bullshit. You saw how she acted. She was practically dazed. I don't need that."

"Maybe she does."

"I don't understand you. Just this afternoon you were raising hell because you didn't want her to come along, and now you're defending her."

I felt tongue-tied as I tried to sort things out. After deliberating a minute I said, slowly, "It's not her. It's you. You acted very strange today after she saw you. I think you might be letting what you are turn you into an egomaniac."

"What do you mean by that?"

"You've been acting like Miss America getting roses. 'But most of all I'd like to thank myself, because I couldn't do it without me.'"

"I don't even know what a Miss America is."

"That doesn't matter. The point is that, okay, fine, you're beautiful. But you've begun to take it for granted, and you're acting like everybody else should casually acknowledge it, too."

"What else can I do?"

I pointed a finger at her nose. "See what I mean?" I mocked

her tone: "'What else can I do?' That's what I mean by egomania. You're taking what you are right in stride."

"And I repeat," she said firmly, "what else can I do? Would you like me to bask in my own glorious radiance and remind myself every day what a wonderful creature I am? Of course I take it in stride; I've lived with it all my life."

"But people like what's-her-name, like Shaughnessy, haven't. Ariel, I've been with you close to two years now. In that time I've seen you grow from the equivalent of a five-year-old human to what you are now. I see what you look like at sunset, at sunrise, and by moonlight—and *I'm* not used to it. And furthermore, I don't ever want to be. I can't imagine the novelty ever wearing off. No, I don't want her to follow us to New York—she'll probably get killed if she does—but try to realize that she's probably never seen anything like you, and understand why she thinks she needs to go with us. I don't care that you're against her coming with us. Like I said, so am I. But don't be insensitive to why she's doing it."

"I've understood since the second she saw me. Why do you think I said the things to her that I did?"

"Well, if you understand, then will you please tell me why you're acting like you don't give a shit? Jesus, you've told me she's not my responsibility; you said to let her go hungry to discourage her from following us; you compared her to a dog—"

"And it gets back to what I said before." She spaced her words out. "I do not want to be worshiped." She shook her mane and tossed her head, horn arcing up at the night sky. "Besides, she's not a virgin."

"Ah, the truth emerges."

"That's only part of it. There's more to it than that."

"There must be. You gladly tolerated Malachi and Russ, and they weren't pure by any means." When I said it something dawned on me with the shock of certainty, and I drew in a deep breath before speaking. "She's a threat! That's what it is, isn't it? That's the way you see her—she's a threat to you."

"I never said any such thing."

"I don't give a damn what you've said. It's what you think. I notice you don't deny it."

She said nothing.

"You've looked down your avenues of possibility and haven't liked a few of the potential routes, haven't you?"

"You're faulting me for what I am, Pete. A creature of purity, of innocence—you've said as much yourself. Yet you've also said that I'm just as human as anybody else, and now you're blaming me because I am."

"Oh, you're human, all right, Ariel. Sometimes you're so damned human it amazes me. But jealousy doesn't suit you."

"It's not jealousy, despite what you may think. There's not enough there for it to be. But as you said"—she scratched at the grass—"I can see possibilities. Potential futures."

"The way any human being would who wasn't confident in their relationship—projecting situations, following what-ifs?"

"Maybe. But I'm a woman—that's something else you've said." She stopped scratching the grass and looked into my eyes. "And women fight to keep the things they love."

That night I dreamed again.

I lay my head back against the sleeping bag and closed my eyes, listening to the eerie silence. The wind, barely sighing among the trees, was all I heard. I felt myself sinking into sleep, and then the dream, worse this time. . . .

I unbutton her shirt with trembling hands.

She is a succubus, a demon lover of the night.

I close my eyes, feeling quickened heartbeat. Etched against the backs of my eyelids in liquid coldness, seen through fogged glass: her face, looking down on her face and seeing her mouth against me. A ring of softest fire cascades down the length of my penis. I moan and rake fingers across her shoulders.

I opened my eyes. The liquid cold pictures were gone; I was looking at Orion's belt in the night sky. Ariel stirred by me, and again I wondered what sort of dreams she had. A cloud went past the moon and her glow muted. I closed my eyes and returned to

the night, the night! And her molten warmth surrounding, succoring, demanding, controlling. Slowly, drawn out in delicate suspense, and then the quickening: of pulse, of breath.

And the day returns too soon.

I awoke once more. My breath was ragged. Again I was compelled to close my eyes and feel

the pinpricks of ivory canines, the warmth . . . Light kitten-scrapings of fingers cross my thighs, my belly, my chest. Cat's tongue rasps across nipples, neck, earlobes.

Somewhere in the darkness a wild dog howled. Feral eyes

gleamed blood-bright in the depths between the trees.

All the moonlight that has ever been is gathered in my head and exploded all at once. As I come, shock wave after shock wave spreading from mind to groin and back again, I know that she feels my orgasm with all its intensity.

Afterward I hold her for a long time, feeling both vampire and victim, the need and the willingly offered throat.

"Yes," whispers the night. "The day returns too soon."

Dreamless darkness ruled the rest of the night.

When Ariel nudged me awake next morning I found a plate beside my sleeping bag. On it was untouched chili mac. On the top of that were the remains of a rabbit. It had been neatly skinned and cleaned.

I put on fresh socks and slipped into my hiking boots. Dew had coated the landscape with a light flowershop spray.

Ariel looked at me looking at the plate. "Resourceful, isn't she?"

I said nothing. I looked at George, who was pulling on tennis shoes, having already put on tight blue jeans and by-now-dirty red silk shirt.

I carried the plate to the road. "All right!" A few startled birds took off at the sound of my voice. "All right, goddammit! You can come along." I heaved the plate onto the road. Ariel regarded me quietly, tail swishing. "She can come along," I repeated.

Ariel nodded but remained silent.

thirteen

Come not between the dragon and his wrath.

—Shakespeare,
King Lear

Her name was Shaughnessy Taylor. She was twenty-four years old and, like me, she'd been in school the day of the Change. She'd been in her first year of college, though, majoring in marine biology. She'd lived with a man the first two years after the Change. He'd become bored with her and one morning she woke up in the dorm room that served as their home to find him gone, no note.

She'd read *Don Quixote* before. "But go ahead," she said when Ariel asked me to continue the story. "I loved it." I read aloud and thought about other things than Don Quixote and Sancho Panza. In the first place, I wondered what to think of Shaughnessy. Strangely, she intimidated me. Though only four years older, she made me feel immature, inexperienced. She hadn't done anything to cause those feelings; it was mostly generated by self-doubt. The fact that she couldn't touch Ariel both elated and depressed me. I felt sorry she couldn't and special because she couldn't; I felt embarrassed because I could and because she knew it.

She'd read fantasy books ever since she learned how to

read. "In high school," she told me, "I started collecting fantasy animals. Especially dragons and unicorns." She played *Dungeons & Dragons*. Avidly. She'd seen *Star Wars* nine times.

Most of this I learned after darkness fell. I'd stopped reading when the light began to dim, but we still had a couple hours more walking to do. I was pushing to make up for lost time, despite what it was doing to my feet. Ariel never complained about walking and George had turned out to be pretty tough when you got right down to it. Shaughnessy just started talking about herself to all of us when I put the book away. I'd expected her to complain about the walking but she never breathed a word—not even to ask why we were in such an all-fired hurry to reach New York. I got the impression she didn't care; she was content just to be with us. Or rather, with Ariel.

We made camp a little after eight. Shaughnessy didn't have a sleeping bag. Mine was a down-filled bag with a nylon cover that zipped around three sides to open into a wide pad. The night was warm and, barring rain, I would probably sleep on top of the bag rather than in it. I could have opened it out and shared half with Shaughnessy, but I wasn't going to.

I boiled water and made instant coffee, black and sugarless. Shaughnessy had a cup also. George declined, saying he couldn't abide the stuff. I dug out my two collapsible metal cups and gave one to Shaughnessy. I usually tried to take it easy on coffee consumption; being a diuretic, it increased the frequency of urination and caused dehydration. I tried to hold it down to no more than a cup a day, but usually drank it just before bedtime—the worst time to. My urine had begun to turn bright orange days ago, but not from dehydration. Our thirty miles a day walking, at current elevation, was enough to cause my body to begin breaking down its own muscle protein. I'd had to calm George down because the same thing was happening to him. He'd thought something was wrong and blood was in his urine.

Supper was a feast of freeze-dried steaks (bless George!) and vegetables. For dessert I made the last of the Apple-Easy. After eating I lay back, shifting around to find a comfortable place. My head was propped against a large rock, and smaller ones dug in through the fabric of my sleeping bag at awkward angles. I stared into the crackling, flickering fire and did my best to think about nothing at all.

I'd piled rocks in a semicircle to help serve as a windbreak for the fire, and I'd found a couple of thick, green branches and put them over the ashes of the already burned ones. They'd keep the fire banked and smoldering through the night.

After a while, when it seemed as if everyone else had fallen asleep—George had offered Shaughnessy his sleeping bag; she declined politely and elected to sleep on the ground a few yards from the fire, though I'm sure George's intentions were pure—I picked Fred up from beside me and polished the blade with a rag and a little 3-in-One oil. Reflections of the fire ran in molten gold down the length of the blade as I turned it in my hands. The cricket equivalent of Woodstock was being held, with a frog supplying intermittent bass. The fire's sound was made for hot chocolate and quilts.

I'd taken off my boots when we'd set up camp and had carefully towelled my feet dry. They were healing, gradually. Still, salt from perspiration made the blisters sting during the day, and I had to keep them dry to prevent the sores from festering. Infection was the last thing I needed.

I was afraid to go to sleep. The dreams had begun to stay with me after I awoke and I feared to sleep again for dreaming. That sounded suspiciously like a line from *Hamlet* but was true nonetheless. I used to like to sleep; it was a time for recuperation, a time of pleasant but unsuspected images running rampant inside my head. Lately, though, those images had become cohesive, persistent ones, growing more detailed each time. Nothing bad ever happened to me in them—actually, I guess the opposite was true, depending on your point of view—but they bothered me. To occupy my mind and time I dragged my backpack around to my side of the rock, untied it, and began unpacking it to take stock. The inventory was scantier than I'd have liked, but I'd make it. I fished two tubes of Epoxy from the pile of unpacked things and repaired the hole where the arrow had pierced. While it dried I inspected the pack. A little worse for the wear, but holding up, though it wouldn't be too long before I'd have to find a new one. It was olive-drab nylon, patched in a few places with silver-gray duct tape. New backpacks were hard to find, so rather than let it give up the ghost on several occasions, I had repaired it, re-waterproofed it, taped it, and sewn it. It was the same one I'd left home with in South Florida, five-plus years ago. My parents had given it to me as a Christmas present when I was thirteen. I'd read *On the Beach* and *Alas, Babylon* and become convinced the world was about to blow itself up in a nuclear holocaust at any second, and that I needed to be ready in case it happened. I think my parents gave it to me to shut me up.

I wasn't being very realistic about nuclear war: we lived about fifteen miles from Homestead Air Force Base, a key coastal defense station, and though the blast probably wouldn't kill us, the firestorms or the fallout almost certainly would.

My parents never understood my morbid fascination with the concept of the end of the world. Because we lived away from the city, I sometimes walked down the street to the canal (the one at which I later saw the manticore), and it was easy, with no cars coming and no city noises, to pretend something had wiped everybody out. Everybody but me. I think I wanted it that way. I thought up endless scenarios: the typical and clichéd ones of nuclear annihilation, others involving humankind wiped out by mutant viruses, bacteriological warfare, invading aliens, or disappearance in some great exodus I'd somehow missed out on.

But I'd never figured on anything like the Change. And when it happened it turned out to be nothing like what I'd wanted all along. It wasn't some grand and glorious heroic struggle, One Man's Fight for Survival. It was work, and it hurt—emotionally and physically. I never found out what happened to some people I cared for very much. The end of the world turned out to be something I preferred to fantasize about rather than experience. In that wandering time before I met Ariel there was one thought that often ran through my head: I'd always wanted to be alone like this, but I'd never realized it was so *lonely*.

I sighed and threw a pebble into the fire. It was outlined ephemerally in black against the orange and landed with the sound of a heavy raindrop on wood chips. Better repack that shit, I thought, and set to it. I think I was up till two in the morning putting that damned pack back together. When it was done I tied it securely against possible rain and inevitable morning dew and returned it to its place on the other side of the rock. I checked the fire to be sure it was well banked and controlled. It had died down to a smoldering devil's pit which gave off an occasional flicker. It would be all right until morning, but to be sure I added wood shavings from a young branch and then set the stripped branch on top. I thought about going to bed and realized I wasn't tired. I grabbed the bag George had given me and sat by the fire. I took off my shirt, spread it out on the ground, and dumped the bag's contents onto it. I picked up a strand of fake pearls and began pulling them off. Half of them were either too large or too small; I threw them away. The others I set aside on the shirt. Beads sorted, I grabbed wirecutters and umbrella wire and began snipping off four- and five-inch lengths, cutting at an angle until I had three dozen lengths of steel wire and about as many hard plastic beads. I picked up a wire and held an end into the flame until it was cherry red. I touched it to a bead, using the hole where the string had been as a guide to be sure the wire was centered. It melted its way to the center of the bead; I set it aside and started another. When I was finished I had three dozen blowgun darts, which I put into a pouch that had originally been a carrying case for a pocket instamatic camera. I'd fitted a half-inch block of styrofoam into the bottom and pushed the tips of the darts in. The case was held shut by velcro, and the darts stood upright, embedded in the styrofoam.

A jet of flame in the distance caught my eye as I was pushing darts into the case. It was level with the horizon and just a touch above it, but it looked closer than that. It was a small streak of orange across the night sky, like a meteor, but with none of the sparkler-like shedding of a meteor. I fought the urge to blink and it flared again, a bright, even orange-red. No meteor; it was a tongue of flame. With the second flare came a distant sound, something like the sound you hear on a beach at night, the sound of a big wave beginning to build. A deep roar. I shut my eyes, seeing afterimages. *Son of a bitch,* I thought. *A dragon.* I looked at the sleeping figure on the other side of Ariel. Poor George—it wouldn't be long now.

I kept a lookout for another fifteen minutes but saw nothing else. Presently I went to bed.

Next day Shaughnessy and I debated whether or not we missed technology—she taking the affirmative, I the negative—while Ariel and George played ring-toss with his Gyro Frisbee. Shaughnessy believed that we had lost our humanity along with civilization; my position was that, except for a change in hardware, things were still pretty much the same. Ariel kept interjecting smart-assed comments while sporting the hoop around the base of her horn where George had scored a successful toss. Oh, man, would I give her hell about that—

she looked like something on a merry-go-round in Disneyland. The thought saddened me—Ariel and I had once been through Disney World in Orlando. It had grown dusty, dangerous, and useless—except to foragers.

Shaughnessy and I argued—pardon me, debated—the entire afternoon, and never our twain did meet.

Two days later: our eleventh night on the road. We had skirted around Greensboro; I wanted to avoid cities; something bad happened every time we went into one. Cities were where people were, and I didn't want to be where people were. They either posed threats, demanded to come along, or presented the possibility that news would reach New York that we—Ariel in particular—were on the way. Gossip traveled faster than we could.

Shaughnessy's feet had begun to hurt. I taped her instep just behind the toes where it was irritated and likely to blister. I lanced a blister on her right heel, taped that, and gave her a pair of my socks. I told her to tie her shoes so they were loose at the toes and tight farther up; this would keep blood circulating freely in her foot but would prevent the shoe from rubbing as she walked. My own feet were still healing fairly well.

At a store just outside Greensboro George exchanged red silk shirt and blue slacks for plain white T-shirt and jeans. Shaughnessy got another pair of tennis shoes. We were still on I-85, headed almost due east. We'd continue in that direction until we reached Durham, where the road turned northeast and remained more or less parallel to the coast. Not a lot had happened the past two days. Shaughnessy and I argued about damn near any subject either of us brought up, with Ariel chiming in occasionally. George grew increasingly restless but, as usual, said little. He would pace after we set up camp, and now and then his hand reached for the security of his sword's handle. I continued practicing with Fred each evening.

We had to settle for a lousy campsite that night; apparently somebody had been careless with a campfire, or maybe dropped a cigarette, and the woods had burned for miles. Not knowing how much further we'd have to travel to find unburned ground, I decided to make camp where we were. Getting a fire going was difficult but I managed it after several false starts, and we used the remainder of our water to cook our freeze-dried dinner. I hoped to find more on the way to Durham tomorrow, possibly in Durham if we hadn't found any by then.

We adjusted to the bitter stench of burned wood, but it was always there in the background, and Shaughnessy complained it gave her a headache. There was also something else, some underlying aroma I couldn't identify: a heavy, musky odor.

We all ate heartily and went to bed tired. Ariel annoyed me by sleeping on the charred ground; I knew it would neither bother her while she slept nor leave any traces of itself on her hide when she got up.

Simple consideration got the best of me and I unfolded my sleeping bag completely and let Shaughnessy sleep on one side. She thanked me and we went to bed back to back. It took me an hour to get to sleep; I was afraid to dream again with Shaughnessy behind me. I could feel her body heat across the six inches that separated us. After a while my uncomfortableness slipped into dim confusion and I was asleep. I think I dreamed again, but only vague stirrings this time, nebulous as ink in water. A vaguely familiar sound woke me in the middle of the night. I kept my eyes closed. There was sweat on my body, hot where I touched the down-filled bag, cool along my left arm and ribcage. I heard the sound again, and the reason it seemed familiar floated to the surface: my grandparents had had a furnace, a big one which grumbled loudly about having to warm their ancient, drafty, and creaky house. I was half asleep and the thought swam in my mind like a tadpole. I opened my eyes. An orange glow stretched shadows of the rocks and trees away from me. I rolled over, noticing that Shaughnessy had pressed against me for warmth and looked into the sky. "Holy shit!"

Shaughnessy jerked away, saying "What?" in a sleepy voice.

"George! Ariel! Get up, goddamn, get up!"

George jumped up quickly as another tongue of flame jetted into the sky. Ariel bolted up also. "Oh, shit," she breathed. George made inarticulate sounds and seemed to be trying very hard to swallow. Shaughnessy had popped up after Ariel and George. She asked me what the hell was going on. In answer I pointed behind her and up. She turned around and said, "Oh, my goodness."

It floated above us, flapping its wings lazily. Occasionally it buoyed on the wind; I saw what Ariel had meant about the gasbag. It vaguely resembled a leather Zeppelin being fucked by a sea serpent, but this is by no means intended to make the thing sound comical. Quite the contrary, it looked as if it could easily eat all of us in two, maybe three, swallows. As we watched, the dragon rolled its huge head in a lazy circle on its long neck, opened its mouth, and belched out a healthy flame-thrower's dose. It was too high for the flame to reach us, but I felt the heat. Its breath stank like the afterburn from a bad Mexican dinner.

I forgot Ariel's admonition to George and looked into its eyes. . . .

There was an animated Disney film, *The Jungle Book,* based on the Kipling story. It had a python with a funny name, though I can't remember what it was. It had those eyes. . . . You looked into them and the pupils dilated into multicolored bands. The dragon's eyes caught the firelight, drank it up until it spread into a pale yellow glow. The pupils were twin motes punched into the centers of the eyes. Ariel's voice came from a long way off. "It's the fire. I should have known."

"Known what?" Shaughnessy sounded as if she were under water.

"The campfire. Dragons use their fire breathing as a mating call." She paused. "The ground all around here—this is a mating ground."

My head turned to follow the dragon's every motion, eyes glued to its own strange and fascinating eyes. Toward the bottom of my peripheral vision I saw the tail curl, roll, and straighten like a deadly banner, scaled, ridged, arrowhead-tipped. I didn't move my eyes to look; I couldn't. Those beautiful and frightening eyes . . .

"It thinks the campfire is another dragon," Ariel continued, "and it's come to mate. They can't mate in the air; they have to land and—Pete!" Her sharp voice jerked my head toward her automatically, breaking the spell. "Don't look into its eyes!" George carefully averted his gaze from the huge beast and bent down to his sleeping bag. He picked up his broadsword and drew the blade. Sixty feet above our heads, the dragon had begun to circle. The breeze from its wings ruffled Ariel's mane. It rumbled as its bulk glided over us.

"Maybe we should put out the fire," Shaughnessy suggested.

"Good idea," said Ariel.

Having no water to quench the campfire, I grabbed a burned-out log and pressed it over sections of the campfire until the twigs, wood chips, and logs were only smoking. Slowly dying embers glowed dull orange.

I grabbed the crossbow from Ariel's pack. "Just in case," I said.

"You'll probably just make it mad," she said.

The dragon sent out another jet of flame, and then another, this one smaller, tentative. Ariel watched it; the eyes didn't seem to bother her. "It can't keep that up and stay in the air," she said. "It's using up hydrogen like crazy. I think it's wondering what happened to the dragon it thought was here. With any luck it'll forget about it and go away."

"If it came here to get laid," said Shaughnessy, "it won't forget about it that easily."

"I wouldn't know."

Shaughnessy gave her a sidelong look, one eyebrow raised. "How do unicorns mate, I wonder?"

Ariel looked away from the circling dragon. "None of your goddamned business."

"I think it's leaving," I said. Ariel and Shaughnessy were glaring at each other.

The dragon stopped flapping in a circle and angled itself upward. With slow wingbeats it pulled itself skyward. By the time I looked away it was a dark blotch against the night sky. "Well," I said, "so much for dragon-slaying adventures. How disappointing." I lowered the crossbow.

George sheathed his sword. "I'm never gonna be able to go back home."

Shaughnessy looked at him in amusement, looked to the blue-black sky where the dragon had vanished, then back to George. "Sorry you're let down, George, but personally I'm sorta pleased with the outcome, you know?"

Whatever reply he would have made was drowned out by a roar I felt in my bones. A new star blazed in the sky, falling to earth like a fastball pitched by Zeus. The ground lit up in Hallowe'en colors. I snapped the crossbow up, finger fumbling for the trigger. I had little time and I needed to put a bolt straight down its throat and hope it didn't burn to ash before it got there. If I missed, it meant a certain groundfight, because the thing wouldn't have enough gas left to get aloft. And I didn't want to have to battle those claws—each one was as long as I am tall. I squinted up at the orange light. The heat on my face increased. Aim toward the center of the flame... *squeeze*. The bolt flew, its hiss fading into the dragon's roar.

The earthquake bellow ceased, and so did the stream of flame. The dragon kept coming. We all ran in four different directions. It landed atop the smoldering remains of the campfire with a *whump* that jarred my teeth. My knees buckled and I tripped.

Its head reared stupidly and it tried to raise itself. Not ten feet in front of the automobile-sized mouth was George, sword in hand. He stepped forward and then stopped cold. His sword-point lowered slowly. He was looking into the dragon's eyes.

It tried to burn him. The head reared back on the serpentine neck, struck forward, and hissed. All that came out was the weak sound of escaping hydrogen. Embedded just in front of the tree-trunk-sized right foreleg was the rear half of the crossbow bolt. The beast brought the leg back to try to raise itself and the bolt snapped off. Smoke rose from the embers of the campfire beneath the furious thing. My eyes widened. "George!" I screamed. "George, run, get out of there!" He looked my way. My shout must have given him back his bearings: he looked back to the dragon's neck, avoiding the eyes, and brought the sword up in a two-handed grip. He stepped forward. "No, no, George! Don't—"

It went off like a reptilian *Hindenberg*. I saw the light of the explosion and managed to twist my head away just as the blast picked me up gently and slammed me down ten feet away. Pieces of dragon went in all directions, slamming into burned trees, plopping onto the grass, pattering the charred ground after being hurled skyward. My right shoulder burned as I picked myself up. I ignored it. A searing on the lower right of my stomach made me look down: the I'M WITH STUPID shirt was eaten half away. I removed it hastily and rubbed off hydrochloric acid—dragon blood—with the back of the shirt. Fortunately only enough had splattered me to turn my skin pink and itchy. I got up in time to see the remains of the fireball as it burned itself out. A thick, slaughterhouse smell hung in the air.

Ariel and Shaughnessy emerged from behind a knot of burned trees. They were arguing and didn't notice me.

"Don't you ever try to touch me again—do you understand me?"

"I'm trying to tell you," replied Shaughnessy defensively,

"I didn't mean to. I saw the explosion and grabbed you. It was a reflex."

"You don't know what it feels like."

"I can guess. It hurt me, too."

"Poor baby. Let me tell you something, child." Her eyes were haughty. "You don't deserve to touch me."

Shaughnessy planted her feet and raised her voice half an octave. "You know, ever since I joined you, you've acted like I wasn't worthy of your presence because you're pure as angel's piss—"

"Nobody asked you to come along. You invited yourself."

"Okay, fine. But in the midst of elevating yourself to such pure and lofty heights, you've proven to me you're just as human and fallable as the rest of us, because I think you're jealous."

"What could I possibly be—"

"Where's George?" I interrupted.

They turned to face me. "I . . . don't know," said Shaughnessy.

"Yes, I can see you're both busy with more important things, right? He could be hurt."

"I'll go look for him." Other than a small patch on the right side of her head where she'd been burned, she seemed all right. She turned and stepped over two pounds of cooked dragon meat.

I looked at Ariel with raised eyebrows. "Well?"

"You think she's right."

"I don't know. I don't know if she's right. But since she joined us you have been acting different."

"Different how? Jealous?"

"No. More like . . . threatened. I think you're still preoccupied with your avenues of possibility. It's not like you to stand there arguing with someone while somebody else might need help."

"Mmm." She looked thoughtful, as if she had an opinion of her own she was weighing against mine. "So why are we standing here?"

We looked for George. Scarcely a minute had gone by when Shaughnessy called out. She'd found him behind a boulder, thrown thirty feet from where he'd been in front of the dragon. His right wrist was sprained and he had a broken middle finger on the same hand, cuts, bruises, and a few burns where blood had spattered him. I dug out the first-aid kit and splinted his finger and swabbed his wounds.

"How about you?" I asked Shaughnessy when I finished with George.

"I'm fine, thanks."

"Uh-huh." I made her bend her head forward while I swabbed her scalp. "It'll grow back," I told her, and returned the medkit to the pack. "How about you?" I asked Ariel.

"What are you going to do, give me a band-aid?" She laughed. "I don't have a scratch."

"Figures. So what do we do now?"

She tossed her horn. "I guess we make camp again. I doubt we'll have any more—"

A jet of flame overhead.

"The explosion," said Shaughnessy. "It'll probably attract them from miles around."

"Lovely," I said. "Fucking lovely."

"I don't think they'll bother us if we don't light another fire," said Ariel.

"I can't tell you how happy that makes me."

"At least George got his dragon." She walked over to where George sat with his back against a rock and nudged him with a hoof. "Right, George?"

"I didn't have anything to do with it." He looked morose.

I re-tied the pack and examined the sleeping bag. A choice cut of dragon *flambé* had plopped onto one corner and the blood had eaten away most of the material beneath. I picked the sleeping bag up by the other end and pulled. The meat rolled off, feathers dropped out from the hole, and ashes and burned wood chips flaked from the bottom of the bag. I put it over one shoulder, pulled the roll of duct tape from a backpack pocket, and sat beside George. I started patching the eaten-away section. George stared glumly at his sword. An orange tongue of flame licked the sky and danced in reflection along the blade. I looked up, frowning. "What's the matter?" I asked, looking back to George. "Mad because you didn't get to play hero?"

"Well . . . I was supposed to kill a dragon and I didn't have anything to do with it. It just blew up all by itself."

I didn't tell him that it had blown up because I'd shot it in the gasbag and the leaking hydrogen had ignited on the remains of the campfire. It would have made him feel worse.

"Your father doesn't have to know that," I said, knowing as the words left my mouth that it was the wrong thing to tell him. He made no reply.

I tried again. "Look, nobody becomes a hero by setting out to do it. Circumstances make heroes. Some people just end up in the right place at the right time and they do something they think is perfectly natural for them to do, and suddenly they're heroes."

"I *could* have killed it," he said.

I nodded. "That's what counts, George. You did all you could do—I saw you in front of that thing with your sword out. Heroism isn't necessarily *doing* something. Sometimes it's the willingness to do it, when the occasion is right." Which, I added to myself, isn't often, thank God.

"Isn't it good to be a hero?"

"It's not good to go out of your way to be. It can get you killed—you came pretty close tonight, you know. Look, you've been paying attention to the *Don Quixote,* haven't you?" He nodded. "That's what usually ends up happening when you set out to be heroic—you get dumped on your ass. I've met people who've done heroic things—but never a real, live honest-to-goodness hero. Those only exist in comic books and hungry imaginations." I looked at the patch job on the sleeping bag. It would hold, at least until I could find another one.

I patted George on the shoulder and told him not to worry and to get some sleep, then I stood up. Before I turned away he said, "Pete?"

"Uh."

"Um, I was supposed to come back with. . . . I mean, my dad told me to bring back a piece of the dragon I killed, to prove I done it."

I nodded and yawned. It stretched my voice out. "We'll look for a piece of tail for you tomorrow, when it's light." I smiled at my own joke, but he didn't get it. He thanked me soberly and said good night.

I walked to the other side of the boulder, looking for a meatless piece of ground big enough for my sleeping bag. Ariel stood before me, tail swishing. "You certainly get preachy when you get half a chance," she said.

I unfurled the bag. "What do you want I should do? He was feeling pretty bad, so I gave him a pep talk." I smoothed out the sleeping bag.

She nodded. "I feel sorry for him. He tries so hard."

"He'll be okay." I drew Fred to check for damage, but there was none, thank goodness.

"I know." She looked at me a long moment. "Sleep well." There was a sarcastic note in her voice. She glanced at Shaughnessy, who was thirty feet away, looking up at the shapes of dragons in the air, their bodies like distant ships seen from below the water.

Ariel walked a short distance away and lay down with her back to me. I looked at the sleeping bag at my feet and looked back to Shaughnessy. I walked past Ariel to her. "We'd better get some sleep," I said.

My voice startled her and she spun, gasping. She put a hand lightly on my arm, placed the other against her chest, fingers spread. "I'm sorry. You scared me."

I glanced at her hand on my right bicep and leaned away just enough for her to lower it. "Sorry," I muttered. "Come on. We've got a lot of walking to do tomorrow."

"I don't know if my feet'll stand up to it." She smiled at the joke. I didn't smile back. We walked to the sleeping bag and she lay down on her side.

"Good night," I said.

She looked surprised. "Good night, Pete."

I went to Ariel and kicked a fist-sized piece of dragon out of the way. She raised her head to look over her back when I knelt beside her. I touched her neck lightly. "Lay back down. I need a pillow."

She lowered her head back to the ground silently and I lay my head on top of her neck. I lay on my back, staring at the starry sky. In some places the stars were blotted out: dragons. I turned onto my side because they made me uncomfortable.

I was exhausted. My sleep was dreamless, I think because of Ariel.

I shook George awake.

"Huh? What's going on?" He looked around wildly. "Another dragon?" He reached for his sword.

"Nope. Wake-up time."

He stood and, forgetting his broken finger, tried to crack his knuckles as he yawned and stretched. "Shit." His accent stretched it into two syllables. "'Scuse me," he said to Shaughnessy's amused face.

By daylight the ground was an awful mess. Pieces of dragon meat and internal organs were strewn haphazardly over an area the size of a football field. The stench of ruined meat mingled with the smell of burned wood, producing an odor I could do without smelling again. All of us—except for Ariel, of course—were filthy, ragged, and stinking like a slaughterhouse.

"What time is it?" I asked. "Looks like the sun's been up awhile."

George looked at his wrist. "I forgot to wind my watch."

"Five till ten," said Ariel. "I decided we needed the extra sleep."

I nodded. Desperate as I was to catch up to Malachi, we'd have been dragging by midday if we'd got up at sunrise. "All right. We'd better get packed and get a move on."

"I can't come with you," announced George.

We looked at him. He fidgeted. "I mean, I've got to get back home. They're expecting me back, and I've gotta let my dad know about . . . this." He waved his broken-fingered hand at the mess.

I nodded. "We'll help you look for a piece to take back with you, George."

"I ain't sure there's enough left to take back. I mean, most of it just looks like steak."

"We'll find something," promised Ariel.

The four of us searched in separate directions, scouring the blackened ground for something worth taking back, something George could show his father to prove he'd slain a dragon. A bone, a claw . . . No, too big, A scale from the tail, maybe, or the arrowhead tip. A section of leathery wing.

Naturally it was Ariel who found George's trophy. She called us over to the clump of burned-out trees she and Shaughnessy had run behind the night before. Embedded in a tree trunk was a tooth, its curved yellow-whiteness standing out against the black background. It was a foot long. I worked it loose and gave it to George. It was smooth, cool, and dry. The point was rounded. He stared at it.

"It's perfect, George," I said. "Nothing else around has a tooth like that. Your father will have to believe you."

He looked up at me with the tooth clutched in his hands.

We packed. George shouldered his Boy Scout pack with the tooth tucked safely away. I soberly shook his left hand; his right wrist was still swollen and the middle finger still splinted. Battle scars, I thought with amusement. You should see the other guy.

He shook hands with Shaughnessy and she pulled him in and gave him a hug. "You be careful," she told him.

"I will."

"Mind your wrist," I ordered. "You've got a week's traveling ahead of you even if you make good time. Here." I handed him the foil packet of beef jerky. "It'll keep you from having to hunt too much."

"Thanks, Pete." He turned to Ariel. He opened his mouth to say something—thanks, maybe—but she just blinked and nodded. He stepped forward and put his arms around her neck. Tears glistened in his eyes when he pulled away. I glanced at Shaughnessy but her expression was unreadable. Was she envious, I wondered?

We said goodbye again and walked away in opposite directions. I looked back once, and he saw me and waved.

His broadsword still dragged the ground when he walked.

fourteen

Now hollow fires burn to black,
And lights are guttering low:
Square your shoulders, lift your pack,
And leave your friends and go.

—A. E. Housman,
"A Shropshire Lad"

Walking, walking, and walking. My life since the Change seemed to consist of little more than putting one foot in front of the other and plodding onward. I could grow to hate it—but after more than five years it was the way I lived. I look at what I've written here and realize it sounds as if things all happened in rapid-fire sequence, but the truth is that most of it was boring. The dull parts have been left out because they're not worth mentioning, and there were plenty of them. What comes out in the telling are the highlights.

A river ran just outside Durham and we filled our flasks and continued. I let Shaughnessy carry the *bota,* the wine flask. We skirted Durham and I-85 turned north again just outside the town. We camped a few miles north of the town. I could tell Ariel's leg still hurt, but she never complained. Two nights later we made camp across the Virginia state line.

I finished reading *Don Quixote* to Ariel and Shaughnessy before we reached Richmond. Neither of them liked the way the novel ended.

"It feels like Cervantes just got tired of writing it. The ending's too abrupt," complained Shaughnessy. "I know I'm supposed to feel terrible that he dies, but all I feel is short-changed. I mean, he died in bed!"

I'd put the novel away and pulled out the road atlas, and was tracing our projected route with a finger. I-85 had just become I-95 and we would be in Richmond by late evening.

"Live a fast life, die a quiet death," said Ariel.

I looked up from the map of Virginia. "Mine ought to be pretty peaceful, then."

Guess that means mine'll be horribly gruesome," Shaughnessy mused. "Up to now my life hasn't been anything to rave over."

"Stay with us," I said, "and I'm sure it'll get more interesting."

She shook her hair away from her face. "Fine."

In Richmond we camped on a concrete bank of what the map said was the James River near the downtown area, not far from the Interstate. Ariel kept watch all night; she said she didn't need the sleep. I'd been sleeping the way I had our last night with George: head on Ariel's neck, Shaughnessy alone on my sleeping bag. Tonight, though, Shaughnessy and I slept on our respective sides of the unfolded bag, me facing away from her. The concrete was hard under my right side.

I dreamed again.

I unbutton her shirt with trembling hands. . . .

It went all the way through, exactly as it had before, the same movie rethreaded and played again.

At the end of it I woke up trembling and breathing hard. Ariel stood a few feet away, looking at me thoughtfully. Shaughnessy slept with her back to me. I got up quietly, feeling warm wetness in my underwear. I avoided Ariel's look and unzipped the bottom compartment of my pack, drawing out a baggie of folded toilet paper. "Have to go to the bathroom," I said.

"Sure, Pete." She continued gazing at me thoughtfully. "Be careful."

"Right." I tried to appear casual as I went to the other side of the overpass above the dark river. I pulled down my pants and underwear. Whitish goop was smeared on my pubic hair and the head of my penis. I wiped it off with a soft wad of tissue. I lifted it to my nose and sniffed. Heavy, starchy. I tossed it into the river, fastened my pants, and leaned against the concrete part of the sloping overpass bank, trying to think. I suppose it was what they call a "nocturnal emission," a wet dream. Nothing like that had ever happened to me before and I was scared.

Ariel said nothing when I returned. I went straight to her and put my arms around her neck, feeling her softness on the insides of my arms, her coolness against my cheek. "What is it, Pete?" she asked gently.

I could only shake my head.

"All right. I'm here."

I pulled away from her, hands still pressing the sides of her graceful head. "I'm scared."

"Of what?" That same gentle tone, lacking in reproach, filled with concern.

"I don't know. I really don't. Different . . . pieces of things, fragments. Too much of it is vague. Maybe that's part of it—uncertainty."

"New York."

I nodded. "I don't know what to do when we get there. If we get there."

"We'll help Malachi."

"We don't even know where to meet him. He doesn't know we're following him. Ariel, I don't even know if he's still alive! He might not have made it this far."

"You know better."

"We're probably so far behind him."

"He'll be on the lookout for us. I think he expected we'd follow him; he just didn't want us to hamper him on the way. If we don't find him, he'll find us."

"And then?"

"I can't say, Pete. We'll probably try to go up against Shaitan and her master. Knowing Malachi, that will be the first order of business."

"And after that?"

"If we win?" She blinked. "We'll have removed a domino from in front of one far more capable. The griffin rider serves someone, too."

"The necromancer."

She nodded.

I swallowed and dropped my hands from her face. "Ariel . . . I've been having . . . dreams."

"I know."

"You do?"

"Yes. Whether you know it or not, Pete, I guard your sleep. Even when I'm asleep I keep a part of me focused on you. When you're troubled I can keep your sleep dreamless so you'll at least be rested when you wake up. But lately—" She sighed. "I wake up in the middle of the night because you're moaning, or making small noises like an animal. Often"—she seemed embarrassed—"you have an erection. Next day we'll break camp and you'll be quiet for a long time, most of the morning at least. I'll know that whatever you dreamt is on your mind, and the peace you're being robbed of by night is troubled by day, too." She lowered her head and, with it, her voice, until she whispered. "And whatever those dreams are, I can't stop them," she whispered. "They're too strong, or too subtle, for me."

And so I told her about the dreams. About how they'd become more graphic, more intense, awakening feelings within me I didn't want disturbed. I described them in detail, and I told her they made me afraid.

"When did they start?" she asked.

I glanced at Shaughnessy's sleeping form. "Before she joined us, if that's what you mean."

"I was just wondering. It would be easier to explain if it was her. But I guess not."

"No. They began. . . ." I thought a minute. "I guess about the time we set out from Atlanta. At first it was just a vague something that disturbed my sleep, something I couldn't pin down when I awoke, except to know that I'd slept poorly. Like something below the surface of a dirty pool—you know something's there; you can see it. But it's hazy. Like that."

"I've been having dreams of my own," she whispered. "They began the way yours did, vague feelings that grew into a detailed scene." She shut her eyes.

"Ariel? What is it? What's the dream?"

She kept her eyes closed but relaxed them a little. "I'm in the woods. I'm running. I don't know what from or what to. Everything feels very immediate, very real. The wind is whipping my mane back and I can feel the ground as my hooves pound. I'm not quiet as I run, the way I usually am, but loud. I break out from the trees and into a small clearing, and there you are." She opened her eyes, looking at some invisible point past my right shoulder. "You're lying down, and when I head toward you, you get up. I try to say something but the words won't come. In the dream I always know what it is I'm trying to say, but when I wake up I don't know what it is anymore. You head toward me with your arms spread wide, but you run into something. It's invisible, but I know it's like one of those things you showed me once. People used to keep fancy old clocks inside them."

"A bell jar?"

She nodded. "It's as if you're in one of those, a giant one. And I can't get to you and you can't break out. I think, maybe I can smash it with my horn, and I step forward. Something in your face, in your eyes, makes me stop. I turn around and run away. I can't see because of the tears in my eyes, and branches crash into my face. That's where I always wake up, with branches hitting me in the face."

We were quiet a long time.

"What do you think they mean?" I finally asked.

"Who can say what a dream means? I only wish I knew where they came from."

"Our subconsciouses? Dreams are your mind's way of—"

"—Sorting out what happens during the day. I know; I've read the same books you have. But I rarely dream, Pete. And I've always been able to keep away the dreams that disturb you, up till now. I wonder if they're being sent."

"By what, or who?"

"Who sent that wind, our first night on the road?"

"Oh, come on. I'll grant you an evil wizard in New York, but to send us dreams—"

"It's just a thought. I don't think it seems likely, either."

"So what do we do, start taking sleeping pills?"

"No. They wouldn't work on me, and you need to be on your guard. I don't need you groggy if you have to jump up and fight in the middle of the night."

"They're getting steadily worse, and we've still got a long way to go."

"They get worse the farther north we go, yes. Which makes me wonder about their cause. But our anxiety grows the farther north we go, also, and that seems as plausible to me as the necromancer causing them. More plausible."

"Which reminds me—how's your leg feel?"

"Like it's broken all over again. I still remember how that felt."

"That has a lot to do with your being afraid of New York, doesn't it?"

"It has a lot to do with why I don't want to go there, yes. But it won't stop me from going. I guess I feel like I've got to make the world safe for unicorns, too."

I smiled. "Lower your head." She complied, and I gently kissed the base of her horn. One would expect the feel of cold bone; what my lips touched was warm and alive. I felt it through my skin like some barely contained, tremendous spark, some powerful healing energy beneath the fire-opal surface. "After this is all over," I said in a low voice, choppy because my throat kept trying to close, "let's just wander, the way we did before Atlanta. Just you and me on the road, no Causes."

"Where will we go?"

"We won't 'go' anywhere. No destinations. We can aim toward California, if you want. Go West, young man and unicorn."

"After this is over," she promised. "But not until. If we abandon this now, we'll never be safe again. Anywhere we went we'd have to hide."

For some reason her words made me remember what it was like to die, how it felt to have her there, trying to bring me back. "You brought me back to life, once," I said.

"Yes. But I don't think I could do it again, Pete. I think . . . it's one of those things you just can't do again. You've broken some kind of natural order the first time around, and death always has its due. Always. If you died again and I tried to bring you back . . . I think it would kill me. Some large part of me was left behind when I did it before, and I don't think I've got it to leave behind again. And if you died and I couldn't bring you back—I think that would kill me, too."

I looked at the silhouette of the overpass, black against the indigo of the night sky. "The thought of dying used to scare me because I didn't know what it was. Now it terrifies me because I do. It's dark out there."

"I know. I was there. I saw it, I felt it."

I touched her mane, ran fingers gingerly down its length. "Where are we headed, I wonder? I don't mean New York, I mean . . . you know. Destiny. That sort of thing."

She laughed softly, and the tinkling had returned. "Now who's trying to look down future roads? Too many side streets, Pete, too many places to branch off. Forks lead to forks lead to forks. It doesn't do to wonder. Just do."

"I can't help it."

"You could never be a unicorn. You think too much."

"Yeah. But you could be a woman."

She said she'd keep watch the rest of the night and I went back to bed. Shaughnessy tossed in her sleep as I lay down on my side of the sleeping bag.

And you, Shaughnessy, I asked silently. *Do you have your dreams as well?*

Shaughnessy nudged me awake. "People," she told me, stopping me in mid-stretch and yawn. "Over there." She nodded toward the overpass. Four men stood at the guard rail on the near side, all armed and wearing backpacks. As I watched, they stepped over the guard rail and started down the bank, keeping their knees bent to avoid slipping on the slope of dew-soaked grass.

"How long have they been there?"

"Barely a minute. Ariel hid; she doesn't think they saw her. I woke you up."

I nodded. "I'd better wake up George—" I stopped, remembering. "Never mind. Shit. All right, let's get ready for a scene, but keep it calm. You're my girlfriend. Stay close to me and look helpless and harmless. We're headed to Florida from, uh—"

"Canada," she suggested.

"Okay." I reached for the Aero-mag, keeping Shaughnessy in front of me to block their view. I broke it down—it separates midway down the length—and gave her the mouthpiece half. "Can you use one of these?"

"You aim this end and blow into this one, right?"

"Right. Blow hard. And be sure you inhale *before* you put your mouth to it." I handed her two more darts. "Stick these point-down into the back of your pants. Put your shirt over them. Yeah, like that. If it comes down to it, aim toward the chest; it's easier to hit." I watched them coming our way. Three of them carried swords. One wore a rapier, one a cutlass, and one—I frowned—a samurai sword. The last man had a double-bladed axe slung through his belt with the business end resting at his hip. They stopped in front of us and one of them, a short man with thin blond hair and a slightly darker beard, nodded to me. "Morning."

"Hi," I answered.

"You wouldn't happen to have a map we could sneak a peek at, would you? We're headed north a little ways and we want to make sure we've got our bearings straight."

"Sure, I've got a road atlas you can look at." I looked at Shaughnessy. "You want to get it from my pack, babe?"

She smiled, a wonderfully vacant look in her eyes. "Sure thing." She held herself very straight as she walked, trying not to reveal the broken-down blowgun tucked under her pants and shirt. It didn't show unless you knew it was there in the first place.

"Headed far?" I asked, trying not to watch Shaughnessy too carefully.

"We were thinking of maybe seeing what Washington's like. Heard anything about it?"

"Not a thing. We're headed Florida way, ourselves."

He nodded.

The one with the samurai sword jerked his chin toward Fred. "That yours?"

Time to dumb it up—"Yeah. I've only had it a little while. Never had to use it or anything. I used to have a cutlass like yours"—I indicated the blond man's hip—"but it broke when I was cutting firewood. Cheapshit thing." I felt I ought to be chewing on a length of straw.

Shaughnessy brought the road atlas and stood close to me, beaming. I put my arm around her waist and handed the atlas to the cutlass wearer. The two darts at the small of Shaughnessy's back pressed against my forearm; the blowgun rested against the bend in my elbow. I'm sure we looked the perfect Christian couple. *Take the picture now, Henrietta.*

"Yeah, if they're tempered wrong, the blade gets brittle," he said, thumbing through the atlas. He shrugged. "Happens."

"Mind if I see your blade?" asked the samurai swordsman.

My grip tightened against Shaughnessy. "No, go ahead." She cast me a quick, cautioning glance. I smiled down at her.

He went to Fred and picked it up. He held the scabbard at his hip beside his own and drew the blade. *Flash:* it caught the sun as it sped out. *Fast.*

He looked at me. I smiled. He nodded and then put his hand

on the blade. I gritted my teeth, still smiling stupidly. "Is it a good sword?" I asked.

He studied me briefly before replying. "Yes, it is. Very good. Where did you pick it up?" I had the strong impression he thought I wasn't worthy of it. The way he weighed it in his grip, obviously trying to look casual with it—he wanted it. I wondered if he would try to take it. "It was weird," I answered, thinking fast. "A couple days north of here we came across this mess. It looked like about five men; I really couldn't tell. They were all dead. Looked like they'd cut each other to pieces." I watched his face while trying not to look as if I were watching his face. "There was even a dead dog in the middle of them."

He glanced at his friend holding the road atlas. "No shit?" he asked.

"Really. There was this one guy, dead as hell, still holding onto this sword. I'd just lost mine a few days before, and so I just counted my blessings and took that one. I figured he didn't need it anymore, you know?"

The man with the rapier—short, squat, and looking like anything but a skilled fencer—spoke for the first time. "Do you remember what he looked like?"

"Sure I remember. It wasn't pretty, was it, hon?" Shaughnessy shook her head. I could see she hadn't the slightest idea what I was doing. "He was cut up pretty bad in a lot of places. Looked like he may have bled to death more than anything else. I couldn't make out his face; it was like . . . well, like I said, pretty bad."

"Hnh." He scratched the scraggly black growth on his jawline, then returned my sword to its sheath—without looking—and put it back beside the pack. Shaughnessy pretended not to notice my long exhalation.

"We'd best be on our way. We have a sort of deadline to meet." He looked at the leader with the cutlass. "Right, Chuck?"

Chuck closed the road atlas and returned it to me. "Yeah. I guess we found out all we need to know. Thanks."

"Sure," I said.

"Where'd you say you folks were headed?"

"Florida," said Shaughnessy and I.

"Long trip."

"We aren't in any hurry." I looked at Shaughnessy affectionately. "We just want to find a place without too many people, maybe an abandoned farm, and settle down, you know?"

"Yeah. Well, be seeing you."

"Sure thing. You all be careful on the road."

They turned away. The one with the samurai sword turned back to me as the rest walked away. "Your sword—would you be willing to trade it?"

I pretended to think about it. "I don't know," I answered slowly. "It's the only weapon I have. I think I ought to hang on to it."

"Would you trade it for another weapon?"

Shit— "No, I don't think so," I said firmly, momentarily out of character for the idiot I was portraying. "I really like it, for some reason."

He nodded curtly. "If you're going to keep it, then treat it with respect. Clean it." He looked at me contemptuously. "Don't let anybody touch the blade. It's a good blade, a good weapon."

"Oh." I left my mouth open for a second. "Okay."

He turned away. They climbed up the embankment and onto the overpass, then headed north. When they were gone I dropped my arm from around her waist. She dropped hers a second later. "Whew," she breathed, rubbing her forearm against the hip of her jeans to wipe off my sweat. "I get the feeling that was a close one, and I don't even know what the hell was going on."

"They thought I might be somebody else," I said. "Somebody they're looking for."

"Who?"

"You've heard me mention Malachi Lee?"

"A few times, yes."

"Him. They saw the sword and thought I was him. Christ, I'm glad I played dumbshit. I just hope they believe that story I fed them. If they do, then they'll believe Malachi is dead. Mentioning the dog seemed to clinch it for them; Malachi has his chow with him."

"I'm confused. Who is Malachi? Are you following him, is that why we're heading north? And who'd send somebody out after him?"

I rolled my eyes. "Malachi Lee is somebody we met in Atlanta. He's going to New York City to try to kill a man who rides a griffin who killed a friend of ours. The griffin rider serves a kind of sorcerer in New York called a necromancer, who offered a reward for Ariel's horn. Ariel and I are following Malachi to New York. Our reasons keep changing, but I guess we're doing it to help Malachi and to somehow get the price off Ariel's head. Does that make sense to you so far, because it doesn't to me."

"No."

I sighed. "Okay, let's try again. In order." I gave her a capsule description of most of what I have told so far, stopping with the Great Shopping Mall Raid of Tuesday Last. Or whenever the hell it was.

"I see," she said. "So they saw the sword and thought you might be Malachi Lee."

"That's what I said before."

"Yes, but it didn't make sense that time. So why didn't they kill us?"

"Some things didn't fit. No dog. I was headed the wrong direction, if they were to believe me. There was a woman with me." I shook my head. "They must know some things about Malachi, though. The way that fucker touched my blade—Malachi wouldn't have stood for it. Hell, he wouldn't have let him see it in the first place. I wish I hadn't." I frowned. "Damn."

"I take it you don't touch a samurai sword."

"No." I didn't bother explaining why not.

"But how would they know that about him?"

"I don't know." My frown deepened. "In Atlanta I had the feeling that Malachi and the griffin rider had met somewhere before. Maybe that would explain it."

Shaughnessy pulled the Aero-mag and darts from beneath her clothes. "Here. These are sticking me in the ass." I took them and put them into the belt case.

"Boo." Ariel had come back, silent as ever.

"Anything?" I asked.

"A little. I listened from behind a billboard."

"They didn't see you, did they?" asked Shaughnessy.

Ariel shot her a blank look. "Madame, if I don't want to be seen, I'm not." She looked back to me. "They think you were lying."

"Shit. About Malachi?"

"Parts of it. They think you were really part of a group that attacked him and got wiped out. They figured you looked stupid enough to get hungry enough to attack someone for his food. Your friends got cut to pieces, you ran away with your girlfriend until it was over, then came back and took his sword, his food, and some other things."

"Why do they think that?"

She tossed her head. "Your story wasn't convincing. They wondered why you'd be lying and that's what they came up with."

"But they think he's dead?"

"Yes."

I rubbed my hands. "Well, that's good, at least. I hope we did him a favor. Maybe now they'll haul ass back to New York and tell whoever sent them—Shai-tan's master, maybe, or the necromancer—that Malachi's dead. It ought to take some pressure off him."

"Something I don't understand, though, Pete." She slid a front hoof along the concrete. When I was little I used to take those disposable lighters and turn them so that the striker was bottom most, then I'd race them across the floor. The sparks they sent looked something like what Ariel did with her hooves. "Why didn't they seem to be looking for us, too? You'd think they would have been."

"I wondered about that myself. Either the necromancer doesn't know we're coming, or he's sent another bunch after us."

"Possibly. But why not tell these people, too, in case they came across us? Wouldn't that make sense?"

I shrugged. "Maybe he had his reasons for not telling them."

"That's what bothers me—what are those reasons?"

I saw what she was getting at. I'm slow, but I get there. "Oh. I see. What we wondered before: maybe there's no one after us at all—because we're saving them the effort of coming for us by coming to them instead."

She nodded.

"So what else can we do but keep on going? We can't turn back because of that. They win either way."

"We keep going," she said, "but we keep a good lookout. No walking by blind corners and stuff."

I bobbed my head, lips pressed together tightly. "Shit. That's my word for today, I think." I turned to Shaughnessy. "Well, I told you things would get more interesting."

"I'm not complaining yet."

"You'll probably never have time to. Don't go looking for adventure; you might find it."

"What if," Shaughnessy went on, unfazed, "Malachi is only a day or so north of us and that group does hurry back to New York? You just sent them his way; they might find him."

"I suppose there's the chance they will. What do you want; I was making it up on short notice. But Malachi's good at keeping himself scarce. I'm sure he'll see them coming. It's a lot easier for him to not attract attention than it is for us."

"Which is one reason," commented Ariel, "he didn't want us coming with him."

"Sue me. We'll meet him in New York come hell or high water."

"I'm sure we'll have plenty of both, and more, before we get there," she said wryly.

We packed quickly and got the hell out of Richmond, anxious to make up for lost time. I was worried we might run into our four merry men, so I diverted from I-95 to U.S. 301 until we were out of town. It was a shorter route through the city anyhow.

I spent an hour cleaning the fingerprints off Fred. If only things had been different. . . . But they hadn't been.

fifteen

The art of war is simple enough. Find out where your enemy is. Get at him as soon as you can. Strike at him as hard as you can and as often as you can, and keep moving on.

—Ulysses S. Grant

Three days later we were walking through concrete wasteland again. The green landscape had given way to the beginnings of megalopolis. The roads and cities were empty, dusty tombs of abandoned civilization. We were just south of Alexandria. I kept glancing in all directions. Sometimes we had to go off the road for long stretches because it would have taken hours longer to thread through the permanent traffic jam. Four-thirty had been early rush hour. My gaze kept drifting nervously to the Interstate and the empty, silent cars. I couldn't shake the feeling they weren't empty at all, that at any moment all the doors of hundreds of cars would jerk open at once and we'd be set upon by armed men from New York who had been waiting for just this chance. . . .

"Pete, will you for God's sake relax?" said Ariel. "You're making me more nervous than you are."

"I can't help it." I shrugged my left shoulder, adjusting the pack strap. "I'm so glad guns won't work—I'd freak completely trying to keep my eyes open for snipers."

Shaughnessy made a face at the piece of beef jerky she was

trying, without a great deal of success, to nibble on. "I wish I could say you were being paranoid. I'd feel safer." She clamped down with her teeth and wrenched the piece around, trying to tear off a bite. "This stuff's impossible. I'd die of starvation before I could get it down my throat."

"Suffer. Try hunting rabbits around here." I rolled my head slowly in a clockwise circle, trying to relieve some of the stiffness in my neck muscles. You'd think I'd be used to carrying a loaded pack by now. "Deer are a possibility, though."

"Don't get my hopes up."

"I want a piece of peppermint candy," Ariel whined.

"Sure," I said. "Get me a pack of cigarettes, too. And a banana split to go, hold the pineapple."

Shaughnessy bit her lower lip. "Oh, when was the last time I ate ice cream?"

"Or even ice?" I added.

She made a face. "I had ice enough last winter, thank you."

"Yeah—but in your lemonade?"

"What's a banana split?" Ariel wanted to know.

I told her in nostalgically pornographic detail.

"Sounds terribly indulgent," she said.

"It was. You'd have loved them."

We picked up momentum, and for the next half-hour listed things we missed. As I could have predicted, Shaughnessy missed a lot more than I did.

After a while Shaughnessy asked me to call a bathroom break. I conceded and she took off at a careful gallop, if you can imagine such a thing, behind a useless Mack truck three lanes over.

"You sure are quiet when she and I talk," I said when she was gone.

"That's because it's you and her talking."

"Bullshit. That never stopped you from sticking in your two cents' worth with me and anybody else."

She dipped her horn. A glossy white band of sunlight danced along her back. "It's interesting to watch her trying to get to know you."

"Interesting."

"Yes. She learns about you by arguing with you. I'm not sure I'd like being a woman, Pete, no matter what you think. They're too subtle."

I asked her if she didn't think perhaps she was generalizing from a single example, but Shaughnessy returned—looking enormously relieved—and we resumed walking.

Sometimes I felt I was a cartoon log-roller and the entire world was the log beneath my feet. I had to turn it under me, but the scale hadn't changed: it was still five-foot, ten-inch Pete and twenty-four-thousand-miles-around Earth. I watched this part of it slide beneath me at around three miles an hour and wished for roller skates, at least. Heck, Bugs Bunny used to do it. A little over a mile ahead was where I-95 turned due east. If we kept going straight it would become I-395, which ran smack into the middle of Washington, D.C., and I wasn't about to go into that. Instead we were going to veer west at the junction of I-95, I-395, and I-495, the latter of which would take us in roundabout fashion around Washington and straight back to I-95, which I intended to tread all the way into the Big Rotten Apple itself.

We passed a sign that read JUNCTION 395–495 1 MILE. "Look up ahead," said Ariel. "In the air."

We did. Slowly circling black glider shapes that flapped occasionally. "Buzzards?" I asked.

"I think so. Scavengers."

"Something's dead."

"Or dying." She blinked. "We might want to steer clear." Funny how she'd picked up expressions. She probably didn't know what "steering" was.

"We'll take it slow and see what's going on," I decided.

A few minutes later it was obvious from the shapes on the road that nothing there was about to bother us. The buzzards circled high overhead, and occasionally one swooped down to an abrupt halt on the asphalt and pecked leisurely at one of the corpses. The smell was pretty bad, but that wasn't what made me feel sick. In my mind's eye I'd seen close to this exact scene in Richmond as I'd lied to that group about how I'd found Fred.

Though there wasn't much left to make out, I recognized them. Three bodies sprawled on the road, and a small grave had been dug in the grass a few feet beside it. Flies buzzed a summertime drone. A severed hand still clutched a cutlass. A double-bladed axe had been cut cleanly in two through the handle. Dried blood darkened the asphalt in a huge patch. A white Chevy Impala in the left lane had been discolored by a streak of red on the left front fender. It had dripped as though from a sloppy paint job.

These were the remains of three of the four men who'd been after Malachi. Judging from the dismemberment, disembowelment, and decapitation, it was my guess they'd found him.

Shaughnessy turned around and clutched her stomach. I glanced at her and walked closer to the carnage. They looked as if they'd been cut down in mid-stride, but all had their weapons drawn.

Ariel called me from the side of the road. I went to her and looked. The rapier had been thrust point first into the head of a small grave. The metal was dark brown along the edge of the bottom half, broadening to a completely bloodstained six inches toward the tip. The grave looked hurriedly dug. It was poorly squared and incompletely tamped down. Probably shallow. I was surprised predators hadn't gotten to it yet. A torn-off back binding from a paperback book was tied by a piece of string to the handle of the rapier. It dangled from the bell-shaped guard, moving slightly in the warm breeze. Something was written in blue ink on the white side. A name.

Faust

I looked at Ariel. There was nothing to say, really. Finally I drew in a deep breath and said, "I, uh, I'm going to see if Shaughnessy's all right."

She nodded, not taking her eyes from the grave. "I don't know which makes me feel worse—Faust's death, or Malachi's loss." Her voice was a slender thread, barely audible. "Pete, I can think of a lot of people I'd rather see dead than this dog."

I touched the softness beneath her eye and went to Shaughnessy. She had stopped vomiting but was still on her hands and knees before the mess, eyes closed, absurdly reverent. I patted her back, ignoring her admonitions to leave her alone, removed the *bota* from its precarious sling—she had hung it diagonally across her torso and it dangled over the mess—and forced her to sip from it. She choked and spit, then took a few more long swallows. "Thanks," she gasped.

I screwed the top on the *bota*. "You all right?"

She nodded and stood shakily, stepping back a few paces. I removed the cap from the *bota* once more. "Here, cup your hands and splash some water on your face. It'll make you feel a little better."

She complied and then wiped her cheeks dry against her T-shirt sleeves. "I just—I've seen people who'd been killed before, you know? But never . . . not like this."

"It's okay. It's happened to me, too."

"Your . . . friend did this? By himself?"

"Yes. At least, I'm fairly sure he was by himself."

Ariel stood behind me. "Something's missing. Did you notice?"

"Yeah. Our man with the samurai sword."

She nodded. "One of the bodies—the one with the cutlass. His arm was cut off, but that's not what killed him. His throat was ripped out."

"Faust?"

"I think so, yes."

"Well, at least he took one with him." I put a hand on Shaughnessy's arm and handed her the *bota*. "We'd better get moving before somebody else shows up to investigate. Those buzzards can be seen from a long way off."

She nodded silently. I looked at Ariel worriedly and led Shaughnessy by the arm. After a few steps she shrugged me off. "I can walk by myself."

"Just trying to help."

Before we left I searched through their packs for anything we might need, feeling like the scavenger I was. I didn't need their weapons or clothes. I took some freeze-dried and canned food and a pair of binoculars, and we left the rest behind. Ariel kept glancing back at Faust's grave.

Half a mile from the Interstate junction Ariel called a halt. She craned her neck forward, looking down the car-littered road, her head cocked to the right as though she were straining to catch stray sounds. "Up ahead," she said. "At the junction—" She broke off. "Get behind a car, fast." I didn't question, just did as she said. Shaughnessy and I knelt behind a gray Cadillac. Ariel stood behind a white Chevy van, driver's door standing open in empty invitation. The two cars were side by side; I could see the van's keys hanging in the ignition.

"It's a griffin," said Ariel. "Shai-tan, I'm sure; it's wearing a saddle." She craned her head around the side of the van to look again. "There's a man standing beside it. He has those things—binoculars." She looked away. "They're waiting for us, Pete. They must be. Or for Malachi, if he found our dead friends back there. He could put it together the same way we did."

I tried to think. Shaughnessy looked at me expectantly. Shit. The mention of the griffin had sent adrenaline surging, a white burst within my chest. "All right." The fingers of my left hand tapped a nervous staccato on the scabbard of my sword while I said "all right" another two or three times. I pulled the road atlas from its flap, opened it, studied it. "All right," I said again. "We head east. No more highways, no more main roads. We cut across to Delaware and follow the coast the rest of the way up." I looked at Ariel. "Do you think they'll be watching the coast?"

"I can't see how they could. Too much area, not enough manpower. Besides, they have the griffin rider. He'd be much more effective from the air."

My teeth played with my lower lip. "So we still have to lie low."

She nodded. I turned to Shaughnessy. "You don't have to come along the rest of the way. It'll probably start to get pretty bad from here on out."

Her gaze didn't waver. "No. I'm with you two."

I nodded and looked back to the map. "Let's do this, then. Let's head back the way we came for a mile or so, then leave the road and head east until we reach the Chesapeake. Maybe we can find a small sailboat and cross—it'd save us some time. There's only one bridge on the map, so they might be watching it. We'll have to assume they are. From there we head northeast into Delaware, cross Delaware Bay, and parallel I-95 the rest of the way to New York. How about it?"

Shaughnessy shrugged. "Whatever you say."

I shook my head in exasperation.

"What's the Chesapeake?" Ariel wanted to know.

"An ungodly huge bay," I answered.

"Hmm."

"Something?"

"Just an idea. You think you can find a sailboat?"

"I think we'll find dozens. Finding a seaworthy sailboat is another matter."

She looked thoughtful. "Let me see your map." I got it out and unfolded it. She studied it carefully. Behind her I saw

Shaughnessy put her hand to her mouth to stifle a laugh. I narrowed my eyes at her and the laugh came out.

"I'm sorry," she said. "She looks like a surrealist painting." She put her hands out in front of her like a director framing a scene. "I want to put a frame around this and call it *Unicorn Behind Chevy Van: Rush Hour in Wonderland.*"

I frowned. Ariel looked up from the map. "I think I might be able to take us out of the bay and into New York Harbor, if you can find a good boat and get it to deep water."

I gaped. "You're kidding."

"No. But I'm also not certain I can do it. It's worth a try though, isn't it?"

"I'm sure it is. How are you going to do it?"

"We'll see when we get there."

I could see she didn't want to commit herself. "Whatever you say." I took off my pack and stretched; my legs had begun to stiffen. I touched my toes and did stretches to loosen my knotted calves. Before putting the pack back on I untied the main flap and removed the binoculars I'd taken in Alexandria. I peered around the right side of the Cadillac and brought the black-bordered lenses to my eyes. They pressed against the bridge of my nose; I moved them further apart. I was looking at a sideways figure eight, blurred, as the separate images overlapped. I adjusted the focus; the blur became the rear end of a car. I moved the view down the road to the junction, and there they were. The griffin stood alert, head flicking as it looked about, a Greek guardian sculpture come to life. The memory of hot brass flared my nostrils. My eyes met eyes of bright, predatory gold. They blinked once, lazily. I saw the feathers on the beast's neck ruffle in the breeze, slid my view down its length to where feathers became leonine fur. The saddle arrangement was on its back, riderless. The rider was at the road's edge a few yards from the griffin. Adjusting the focus a touch, I noted with satisfaction that there was dark discoloration around his left eye. Score one for our side, I thought. One day we'll finish the job begun in Atlanta, you bastard.

As I watched he raised something to his good right eye. Not binoculars, as Ariel had said. A telescope. Still, Ariel's vision must have been incredible, considering it took eight-by-forty-millimeter binoculars to let me make that out.

He was directly facing me, and I ducked back behind the car as the telescope came to his eye. If I could see him, he could see me. I told Ariel and Shaughnessy not to move. We were still for five minutes, until I decided to risk another look. His back was to me. The broadsword hung from his left side. He turned slowly to his right, scanning with the telescope. Shai-tan opened her beak and flapped her huge wings. I lowered the binoculars and the dim sound of the screech reached my ears across the silent distance. "All right, let's go. Stay low until I say, Shaughnessy. Always keep a car between us and them to block the view. Ariel—"

"They won't see me."

I handed the binoculars to Shaughnessy and she put them back and re-tied the flap. I left the waistbelt untied and walked half-crouched, causing most of the pack's weight to rest high on my shoulder blades. Ever try to maneuver while wearing a backpack, blowgun, and samurai sword?

I made Shaughnessy go ahead of me so I could keep an eye on her without constantly having to look back. She kept low and hugged close to the cars along the road's edge. She deserved more credit than I gave her, I guess.

The outside lane gave the advantage of a narrow angle of view from the vantage point of the rider. If we tried to walk in one of the inside lanes he might see us as we darted from one car to another. There was no way he'd spot Ariel. We barely saw her ourselves. She kept pace with us, but did it by streaking to the rear of a car in the next lane in a white blur, pausing until we caught up, and speeding to the next car, appearing there as if she hadn't covered any space between the two.

It took us an hour and a half to travel a mile. Behind a rusted-out yellow taxicab with the hood open, I called a ten-minute rest and removed my pack. My back and hamstrings were rubber bands stretched almost to snapping point. I wiped sweat from my face with the tail of my ragged T-shirt, salt stinging my eyes. Shaughnessy became an X on the asphalt. Ariel just stood behind a car and looked at us, impassive.

"Goddammit," I panted, "can't you at least *look* tired?"

She said nothing, tail swishing restlessly. I saw that, though she understood that we were only human and therefore tired quickly, she was anxious to move on, so after ten blissful but unfairly short minutes, which had mostly served to let me know how tired I really was, Shaughnessy and I stood, groaning, and we set out away from I-95. We paralleled the highway for five miles before returning to it. We saw no one; empty streets, empty buildings, empty houses. The area around Washington seemed deader than it ought to be. Usually this fact wouldn't bother me a bit, and even now I found some security in it, but that only served to make me more wary. Any black speck in the distance automatically became a waiting griffin; as we approached it would resolve into a building. I tried to calm myself, knowing that Ariel would warn us if Shai-tan and her master were up ahead. I kept a hand on Fred.

I'd handed the crossbow to Shaughnessy. "It's already loaded and ready to fire," I told her. "Just aim it like a rifle—look through the scope if you have time—and pull the trigger. Aim a little higher than your mark if your target's a good distance off."

"Stop talking to me like I'm an idiot."

"Excuse me?"

"You talk to me as though I can't understand what you're trying to tell me. You overexplain. I'm perfectly capable of comprehending a crossbow, thank you."

"I just want to be sure you know how to use it in an emergency. Don't be so defensive."

"Me defensive!" She brushed a strand of hair from her eye. "You've got this attitude that I'm a burden to you. If you feel you've got to look out for me, that's your problem, not mine. I can look out for myself." I started to protest; she held up a hand to stop me and continued. "You seem to feel that if we got into a fight you'd have to both fight and look out for me." Her voice hardened. "It is *not* your manly duty to protect me. I expect to be helping out, too."

"That's an easy thing to say. But would you be in the middle of it all if it were really happening? Would you put a bolt in a man's back while I'm busy fighting him?"

She frowned.

"See? I'm not talking chivalry, I'm talking survival. I don't expect you to like it; I don't like it either. I just want you to understand it. There aren't any rules, no 'honorable combat' bullshit. I'm not a fighter, so if I'm in the middle of a fight it's because I had no choice."

"How naïve do you think I am? Do you think I could have survived six years without at least being aware of that? Do you honestly think no one's tried to rape me?" She was almost crying; I ducked my head, feeling embarrassed. "God *damn* you, Pete, do you really feel so holier-than-thou that you need to justify your every act by preaching to everyone else?"

"You're trying to make it sound as if I think I'm the only one who's had to kill to survive," I said. "Certainly I know that's not true. But if you want to know the truth, yes, I think you're that naïve. You say you've got that 'protective paranoia' attitude, but you don't even carry a weapon. You were reading on a bus bench when we met you, for Christ's sake!"

Her eyes slitted. "I carry a knife."

"Oh, boy. A knife."

Her eyes were bright, glistening with tears. "Yes, a knife. And I hate it. I hate having to carry it, I hate the idea that I'm supposed to be good with it, I hate the fact that I'm vulnerable without it. You walk around with your 'you gotta kill to survive' bullshit, and I resent it. I can't tell you how many people—always men—I've heard rationalize it that way. I've survived as well as you, and I haven't had to kill, or fight. I've run away. I've hidden. I've lied, I've done anything I could not to have to be in that situation, because I know you don't really have to kill. I resent hearing you say how much you like the Change, because I despise it. I always have to be on guard. I can't get close to anyone. Sure, you can romanticize the Change. Try it from my end."

I should have shut up, but I didn't. "You think this is different than it used to be? You're the one who said that people were people no matter what the circumstances. There were rapists before the Change. There were people who'd shoot you six times in the head because you honked behind them when the light turned green. There are people who'd kill me the second they saw me because there might be food in my pack, and sometimes you have to hurt people to keep from being hurt yourself."

"I haven't had to."

"That's you, then. It doesn't seem to work that way for me."

"If that isn't rationalization, nothing is. You could avoid killing as easy as I do, but you don't. I avoid it because I loathe the idea, and you just seem to accept it as the way things are."

"What, do you think you can change it? Do you think it's uncivilized?" I swept my arms around. "Look around you—no civilization. Do you think the Change should be this neat

Disney movie with animals like Ariel? Come on, Shaughnessy—it's not Disney. It's Dante. And if you don't realize that, if you act as though it's Disney, they'll win. Every time."

"I do realize that. *Why do you think I carry a weapon?* That doesn't mean I think it has to be this way. It's not some unwritten law that says things are like this and can't change."

"But it *is* like this. You can be as idealistic as you want—but if you don't act realistically in a world of reality, unicorns or not, magic or not, you won't be able to act at all."

We let it hang there, but the argument still ran through my head. No matter how many times I went through it, not understanding why I felt obliged to defend my position, I couldn't shake the feeling that she was right and I was wrong.

We were at the Woodrow Wilson Bridge. It made me nervous: no place to go except toward an opponent or back the way you came—by which time, if they were even moderately smart, there'd be a greeting party there, too. Unless you wanted to dive over the side. I looked at the massive concrete of the car-filled bridge and wondered. In the cars? Possible.

"How 'bout it, Ariel?"

"Feels okay. Which is why it feels wrong."

I nodded. "It says a lot when you can't trust a safe feeling anymore. Keep your eyes peeled." She stepped alongside me, followed by Shaughnessy, who held the crossbow with the butt clamped under her right arm, hand on the trigger guard, other hand on the stock. She'd been silent for the past few hours. I made her follow a different path through the cars than the one I took, then began threading my own way through, trying not to think about her. I concentrated on the cars, looking intently into their interiors as I came up on them.

I kept glancing at both banks of the Potomac to see if perhaps we were being watched. I just couldn't shake the feeling. Motion out of the corner of my eye caused me to bring Fred up to guard position. I relaxed: Shaughnessy, looking nervous but resolute.

We crossed the bridge without incident. Ariel was already waiting on the other side. All was as still as an early scene from *The Omega Man*. I sheathed Fred, reached out, and gently dislodged Shaughnessy's hand from around the crossbow's trigger guard.

* * *

We made camp well out of sight of the Interstate. Ariel assured me she would keep the night vigil, and Shaughnessy and I collapsed on our sides of the sleeping bag.

We reached the Chesapeake about two-thirty the next afternoon. We smelled it long before we saw it; something in the very atmosphere, in the feel of the landscape, changed as we neared it. Weathered houses indelicately pulled their skirts up against the eventuality of flooding. The bay was deep blue and serene.

"Nice, huh?" I asked Shaughnessy, hoping to get some sort of enthusiasm out of her. I was rewarded by a broad smile.

"Yes! I'd be happy just to stop here and sit around for a decade or so."

"I like looking at this," said Ariel. "It looks . . . serene. Timeless, or something. As if your civilization could start up again tomorrow and I'd disappear, and this would still be here. And things could Change again, and again, and that"—she nodded at the indigo horizon—"would still be there, regardless."

I realized then that she'd never seen the ocean before. All that wandering we'd done in Florida, and we'd never been to a beach. I wanted to see her on the beach in moonlight, waves unfurling behind her with foam on them like the fluff of her mane, her silver hooves firmly in the wet sand and she a ghostly silhouette against the eternal crescendo of wave after wave.

We did nothing but look at it for a long time. It was Shaughnessy who finally broke the spell. "Well, what now?"

I looked at Ariel. "Find a marina, I guess. You can forget about any boat in the water, but a boat in dry dock might not be in bad shape."

She nodded. Shaughnessy and I got up, slapping sand from our pants, and the three of us walked along the beach.

Its name was *Lady Woof* and it hung twelve feet above the water. It was at least forty feet long and held from a crane by steel cables.

"Good-looking boat," remarked Shaughnessy. "How do we get it from there to there?" She pointed from the crane to the water.

"Let's just count our blessings," I said. "At least we've found a seaworthy boat—I hope. After so long she might ship water like a clothes basket, for all we know. The sails may have dry rotted."

"Most sails are nylon, not canvas," said Shaughnessy. "Nylon won't dry rot in six years." She grinned. "Besides, there's no rigging on that boat, in case you didn't notice. They had to remove the masts when they raised her."

The *Lady Woof* turned out to be in good shape. I clambered up the framework of the crane and lowered myself down the cable and onto the deck. Boat fixtures are built to be waterproof, so half a dozen years' worth of storms had barely affected her. There was a lot of birdshit crusted on deck. Surprisingly, the wheel and rudder moved freely. The cabin was luxurious. Dust had settled about the rich wooden cabinets and countertops. The plush green sofabed was faded. I found a few hurricane lamps tucked away, and a bottle of lemon-scented lamp oil. Whoever had owned her had, at the risk of a bad pun, gone overboard on the interior. Varying tones of wood were everywhere, and the musty air smelled of cedar. Yellow curtains trimmed the left and right windows—I mean, the port and starboard hatches—drawn in at their centers.

I returned to the deck and leaned out over the starboard side. Ariel and Shaughnessy looked up at me from the dock. "Looks seaworthy," I said. "But how we'll get her to sea I don't—"

"We'll do it," Ariel insisted.

"How come you're Miss Mystery all of a sudden?" I asked. "You have an antigravity device tucked away somewhere?"

Shaughnessy interrupted and suggested I check out the interior of the crane—perhaps there was some kind of release lever. I climbed down.

The crane's mechanisms wouldn't work. Big surprise there. Well—"If it doesn't fit, use a bigger hammer." I found a ballpeen hammer and lugged it back from the deserted boatyard. I had to stand in an awkward position with one leg braced against the side of the crane in order to swing it against the gear holding the winch in place. I was relying on the combination of six years of salt air plus no lubrication or maintenance. Sure, the weight of *Lady Woof* was locking those gear teeth in place—but nothing supported the gear if I smashed it from the side. I pulled back the hammer and swung. The solid steel impact made me blink involuntarily. I swung again, and again, the gear gonging in bell-tower rhythm. On about the tenth swing there came a faint, sustained squeaking which rapidly grew to a nerve-rending metallic shriek. I swung once more and the small portion of the gear that still bit into the winch gave way before I hit it. The winch began turning quickly. I was tugged toward it as it caught the hammer and ate it; I let go quickly. Steel cable began spilling from the winch. I ducked, rolled, and got the hell out of there.

Next thing I knew, my back was soaked with cool water. There was the long, wet hiss of a huge splash. I turned around.

Bobbing and rocking slowly, the *Lady Woof* settled herself into the water of Chesapeake Bay.

sixteen

We are coming, lovely Isle
And in thy Harbour for a while
We lower our sails; awhile we rest
From the unceasing, endless quest.

—cited in Stanley M. Babson,
"Where Sands Are Pink"

Shaughnessy applauded. Ariel cheered. I grinned, bowed, and clambered aboard the boat. Not that I'd be able to tell if there was any hull damage from the fall, but it wouldn't hurt to look. Everything seemed all right, though.

Aboard were two large coils of rope. Ariel made me take a third from another boat and Shaughnessy helped me carry it to the *Lady*. I didn't ask what they were for, though I had my suspicions.

The breeze cooled as night fell, and we brought our gear aboard. Shaughnessy tied us securely to the dock for the night. I went to the cabin and fell upon the sofabed. Shaughnessy and Ariel could do what the hell they wanted—I was going to sleep.

I awoke to gurgling noises and Ariel's insistent prodding. "Come on, get up," she urged. "The tide's going out." I was disoriented: the sea sounds and faint rocking motion were unfamiliar. My hand went automatically for Fred. I clasped air and remembered that I had left it by the backpack on deck the night before.

"Pete," said Ariel again. She had to crane her head in the cabin to keep from hitting the ceiling with her horn. Only her head and neck were in the little room; her body wouldn't fit through the door. "Wind and tide are in our favor," she continued. "We've got to put to sea."

"I don' wanna go to school," I muttered to her blurry image, and stepped past her and onto the deck. Early morning yellows lanced my eyes.

"Good morning," said Shaughnessy cheerfully. She sat against the bulkhead, wearing a yellow tank top and cut-off jeans. "I found these in the cabin," she explained to my raised eyebrow. "There were a few other things, but they didn't fit."

Shaughnessy and I lowered the *Lady*'s dinghy into the water—which sounds pretty suggestive, I admit—and I settled myself slowly into the little rowboat, keeping my weight in the center, picked up the oars, and held them over my head threateningly. "Where's me faithful cutlass Fred?" I bellowed. "Tie the scurvy dog to the yardarm! Hoist the Jolly Roger! Arrrh!"

"Oh, Captain," called Ariel, "don't you think we'd better cast off first?"

"You have in fact anticipated my next command—Cast off!"

Shaughnessy pushed us off and the *Lady* moved slowly from the dock. Shaughnessy scrambled aboard.

We maneuvered the *Lady* by kedging. Once we had her away from the dock and able to head out to open sea, we took one coil of rope and tied it to a bow cleat, passing the end through the ring in the stern of the dinghy. I lowered myself back into the little rowboat, positioned myself, and began rowing. After twenty seconds the *Lady* began to move toward me, and I began rowing away until the connecting rope went taut. Shaughnessy waved encouragingly. I gritted my teeth and began to put some muscle into it. Towing a forty-foot boat with oars and a dinghy isn't impossible.

Being possible doesn't make it easy. I felt every ounce of her twenty thousand pounds on the blades of the oars as I strained to keep us at our snail's pace. Humphrey Bogart and the *African Queen*. I was beginning to appreciate why the boat was named *Lady Woof*.

Ariel stood on the bow to provide moral support. Ah, she was a sight! Standing nobly behind the rail, horn catching the light, wind rippling her mane, land so very gradually receding behind her.

Around ten-thirty I shipped oars and forced my hands to unclench. They felt as if they were burning off. I stuck them in the cool water and screamed. Burning salt water dripped from my hands and ran down my forearms. The *Lady* was beside me, her momentum having carried her a little farther. I grabbed her rail and stifled a cry: the metal was searing cold-hot, as if I'd grabbed dry ice. I straddled the rail, swung my other leg over, and fell on my ass. I lay back until I was looking at the sky, lacking the strength to get up, right forearm shielding my eyes from the sun. An unmistakably-shaped blot appeared above me and I smiled tiredly at Ariel. "Well, so far so good. What now, Skipper?"

The three lengths of thick, strong hemp sank lazily into the water and began to lag behind *Lady Woof*. Ariel had had me tie the three coils of rope into huge nooses, tie their other ends to the two T-shaped metal cleats in front, one rope on the left and two on the right, and toss them overboard. We'd been drifting out to sea for an hour but were hardly making progress. We were still well within sight of land, so I was at least sure of our direction. The sun was almost straight overhead. I watched the three ropes slanting beneath the *Lady*. "Well," I said, leaning back to prop myself up on one elbow, the other hand holding onto a bright metal cleat, "now we just wait for three good Samaritan killer whales to wander into the nooses and pull us merrily on our way, right?" I squinted at Ariel. She'd spent most of the last hour deep in thought, focusing her concentration. This was the only time I'd interrupted her; watching the three ropes trail languidly along made my curiosity itch. "Actually," she said, "I'm hoping for humpbacks. But killer whales would do."

I sat up.

Ariel rose unsteadily, trying to compensate for the boat's hardly noticeable pitching. She had a keen sense of balance but seemed quite out of her element at sea. She stepped cautiously to her left, and looked out over the rail. "I need to get closer to the water."

"Whatever for?"

"I need to touch it."

"Oh. Of course." I stood. "Whatever you say, Cap'n Skipper

Ma'am. How do you propose to do that? Jump overboard? Can you swim? Could you get back on board? Or would you rather I leaned the whole boat a little—my arm muscles ought to be capable of that by now."

She glanced back at me. "Don't try to make me feel guilty. It won't work."

"What are we doing?" asked Shaughnessy. She'd snatched the Coppertone from my backpack and was greasing herself liberally.

I shrugged. "'Ours is not to reason why. . . .'"

"Quiet," snapped Ariel. She craned her powerful neck forward to look at the water and dipped her horn. *Flash:* it caught sunlight. Shaughnessy squinted just before I did. Ariel was thoughtful a minute. I tried to picture her pursing her lips. "Get a bucket and some rope," she ordered.

"Aye-aye, sarr." I fetched a bucket from the cabin and a length of line from my backpack. She ordered me to tie the line to the bucket, lower it into the water, and bring it up full. I complied and held the bucket of seawater before her. "Set it down," she said. Her eyes narrowed in concentration, and she lowered her head until the first six inches of her horn were immersed in the bucket.

Landward was a flock of seagulls, their greedy cries reaching us like the sound of a hundred rusty gates swinging in the distance.

A muscle rippled in Ariel's neck. It spread to her shoulder like a small wake in a silken pond. She closed her eyes tighter and let out a long, silvery breath. She raised her head. "There," she said. A few drops of salt water dripped from her horn; a few more traced an incomplete spiral down its length.

I looked into the bucket. It still looked like seawater to me. "'There' what?"

"That ought to do it. Just toss it overboard."

I eyed her doubtfully, but picked up the bucket and emptied it over the side.

The gulls stopped crying. For a few seconds everything—the sea, the wind, the birds—was silent and still. Then it passed and the gulls resumed their searching, hungry calls.

Ariel walked gingerly back to the center of the deck and lowered herself to it, front legs and bottommost rear leg tucked delicately. A reddish-gold glimmer of sunlight traced the graceful length of her right hind leg, becoming reflected magma at the hoof. "Well," she said in answer to our unspoken but obvious next question, "now we wait."

"For humpback whales." Shaughnessy was skeptical.

Ariel regarded her blankly. "We'll see when they get here."

I sat on deck with my back against the curving bulkhead. "Pass the Coppertone," I said. Shaughnessy tossed me the brown plastic bottle. *Tan, Don't Burn!* Right. I squeezed a healthy glop onto my left hand, rubbed both hands together, and spread the stuff over my face. It felt cool at least. Ten minutes later Shaughnessy shielded her eyes from the sun and looked out on the water. "Something's coming," she announced. "No, correct that—a bunch of somethings."

Ariel got up carefully. I shaded my eyes and squinted in the direction Shaughnessy was looking. Bright flashes, a half-dozen, now a dozen, now nine, leaping in silver arcs from the water. "Dolphins!" I grinned at Ariel. "Dolphins!"

"Hmph. The call was for whales, but this might do."

They jumped from the water in well-timed groups, performing intricate maneuvers that made the best Olympic-level divers look like cerebral palsy victims. Shaughnessy grinned, too, looking all of eight years old. Then they were by the *Lady* and we could hear the razzing noise of their playful chatter. They moved like shadows through the water, gliding gray torpedo shapes which left almost no wake. One nudged a trailing rope playfully with its snout. Ariel watched it a few seconds, then—I found out later—called to it. The call was ultrasonic, above the normal human hearing range. Though she stood in the center of the boat, she was large, and it must have seen her. "Seen" is the wrong word; I later discovered a dolphin has terrible eyesight. More correctly, it perceived her with its echolocational ability—a sense no human being can quite imagine, as it is alien to our physiology. It must have signaled its comrades, for when Ariel "spoke" to it, it stopped playing with the rope, shook its head from side to side, and dove below the surface with a flip of its tail. The rest did likewise. The water was calm again, as if they'd never been there. The gulls cried in the distance.

"What'd you do, insult it?" I asked.

"Him. No. Wait."

All at once they sprang from the water, a precise circle of two dozen dolphins diving for air. Simultaneously, they executed a complete back flip with a half twist. I could hardly distinguish the splashes from each other; they were so well-timed it sounded like one big splash, and again the water was still.

"What just happened?" I asked.

"I said hello," said Ariel. "They said hi back."

"Oh."

Presently they surfaced again, blowing air in bull snorts from the top of their heads, frolicking, nudging one another like elementary school kids at recess. The leader separated himself from the group. It—he, rather—rolled left, looking up at us with his dark and intelligent right eye. His mouth was molded in a natural, friendly smile. He raised his right flipper, almost as if in greeting, and slapped down hard. A jet of water hit Shaughnessy in the face. She brought a hand to her eyes, sputtering. The dolphin let out a Donald Duck-ish exclamation and dove beneath the surface.

"They love to play," said Ariel.

"Noticed that, did you?" asked Shaughnessy, drying her face with the tail of her shirt. She saw me regarding her with a too-innocent smile, looked down, and tugged her shirt back down to her waist.

I laughed and turned to Ariel, who wasn't laughing. "You know they can't pull this boat all the way to New York," I said, changing the subject.

"I know. But they're great messengers."

"How do you know? You never saw the ocean before yesterday."

"We're birds of a feather, so to speak. We understand each other. There's a lot more to it than that, but it goes beyond words. We're . . . friends. Allies."

"How is it you can talk to them?"

"Language is language. Now be quiet; I need to talk with the bull some more."

I stood out of the way and watched while Ariel palavered with the dolphin. It was a silent, five-minute exchange. Ariel turned away at the end of it and the bull submerged to join his herd.

"So what's the story?" I asked.

"They're checking the area. Be patient."

Fifteen minutes later I saw it and nearly shit my pants. Beneath the water a shadow moved toward the *Lady Woof*. It looked like a frigging *submarine*. It broke surface a hundred yards from us, slapping its tail on the water, and dove again.

"A humpback whale!" Shaughnessy shouted in delight.

"Ariel, that thing's bigger than this boat!"

"Yes. Beautiful, isn't it? There ought to be one or two more on the way. We should make good time."

My jaw ached; I shut my mouth.

The leviathan circled and came at us from beneath and behind. I tensed, waiting for the impact, but none came. It was an effort to fight the urge to shut my eyes. I compromised and held a tight squint. It was hard to accept the reality of a living thing bigger than our forty-foot boat. Oh, sure, the dragon had been bigger—but we'd been on our element, on dry land, at the time. The sea was alien territory to me.

One of the trailing ropes began to swing forward. I watched as the blue-gray shadow sped silently ahead of us, almost creating the illusion that the sun was setting alarmingly fast and our shadow was lengthening before us. Then the rope grew taut and my knees buckled as we surged forward.

"Thar she blows!" yelled Shaughnessy, and it was true. A white geyser shot up from the whale.

My heart pounded wildly. I was frightened and exhilarated at the same time. "Your friends seem to have connections in high places," I said.

Ariel said nothing. Instead she inclined her horn to the sea. I looked. Out beyond the humpback pulling us along, two more leviathan shapes broke surface with Brobdingnagian majesty.

Night at sea. There were few clouds and the stars were a riot of varying magnitudes. Ahead the phosphorescent shapes of three humpback whales pulled us onward. We must have been doing five or six miles an hour. I'm not sure what that is in knots. They seemed to be able to maintain that speed almost indefinitely, though occasionally one would back out of its noose and swim freely. The dolphin herd remained with us, their silvery shapes speeding about the *Lady*.

Ariel had spoken to the leader for a long time after we were under way. She came back to me after an hour and a half of conversation. She seemed disturbed, but when I asked her what was wrong she only stared through me dazedly and said, "They're very . . . different . . . from you," and that was all.

* * *

Ariel had gone to sleep. The summoning spell had exhausted her and she retired early from the conversation. I stayed up and Shaughnessy talked to me about dolphins—they'd been the subject of a morphological report she'd written in college. After a while she realized I was no longer listening.

"Am I boring you?"

"Huh? Oh, no; I'm listening. I just . . . have a lot on my mind." I stared at my hands.

We were silent a long time.

"You've been with Ariel a long time, haven't you?" she finally asked. She looked at me steadily. There's something about moonlight and what it does to a woman's face, her eyes.

"Almost two years."

"You two act like partners. Listening to you talk is like watching a ping-pong match. It has that . . . that interplay you see in people who are lifelong friends, who've been roommates for a long time."

"Partners." I tasted the word. "Yeah, we're partners. Familiars is the proper term. A friendship. . . ." I shook my head, looking at the pale form of Ariel lying on the foredeck ahead, at her mild, comfortable glow, so much like the dolphins swimming around us. "It goes deeper than that, Shaughnessy."

She looked at the deck. A dolphin broke surface beside the boat, its back a silver crescent as it curled into the water with a small splash. The motion startled Shaughnessy and she jumped.

This is where she jumps toward me and I reach out to hold her protectively, I thought. *And I look into her eyes, awkwardly for a moment, and we start to separate, but instead we pull closer together. . . .* It would have happened like that in the movies. But it wasn't a movie, and she just smiled a brief smile, an apology for jumping, with a small duck of her head. Was I disappointed? I didn't know.

"I like it here," I said, much too loudly. I took an exaggerated, deep breath. "The sea air—it's fresh, it's invigorating, it's . . . Old Spice." I laughed.

"Please, I'd almost managed to forget about TV commercials."

I smiled and it faded away quickly. So did the conversation, again.

A cry came from the sea ahead of us. A mournful, echoing thing, the ghost of a dead baby calling for its mother. My heart leapt. "What's that?" I tried to keep my voice calm.

"One of the whales. They do that. Sometimes sailors in old wooden sailing ships could hear them at night. The shape of the hull acted like a kind of microphone to make the cries echo inside."

I shivered. "It's eerie."

"Yes. I think it's beautiful, too—the way some kinds of books are wistful and leave you sad and wondering, but they're beautiful, too." She leaned toward me.

The kiss was short. Just long enough for me to feel her warmth next to me, to want it to go on longer. The muscles in my shoulders and arms tightened, and I felt strangely stiff and wooden, liking it but reluctant.

We broke apart. Her eyes opened after mine; the lids lifted slowly, darkened by the moonlight. Somehow it separated her lashes from each other, made them distinct. She started to lean toward me again. I turned away. "We—we'd better get some sleep," I said, glad the darkness hid the flush I felt creeping up my neck to my ears.

"Yeah." Her voice was flat. "Big day tomorrow." She glanced at Ariel, who stirred restlessly. "Good night," she said. She stepped carefully past Ariel and into the cabin, where she had claimed the sofabed. I moved to the stern, watching the thin wake trail behind us, seeing the stars, listening to the mournful sobs of the whale. My ears were ringing. The night had a strange, surreal quality to it, as if suddenly it was something I could grab with both hands. I felt I could rip the fabric of reality in half, crumple it up, throw it away, and look at the blackness behind it. I looked straight out and tried to find where the horizon met the sky. I gave up when my eyes found nothing to focus on.

I fell asleep to the cries of the whale song.

On the morning of our third day at sea Ariel let me sleep late. I got up and stretched, interlacing my fingers and turning my hands palm outward, yawning. "What time is it?" I asked. Force of habit; I never really cared what time it was.

"Eleven-thirty."

I twisted my upper body and vertebrae popped. "We should have grabbed George's watch from him before he left."

"I wonder if he's all right."

"I'm sure he is. He ought to be home by now; it's been

almost two weeks. Where's Shaughnessy?"

"Swimming."

I looked ahead. Silver streaked the water; apparently the dolphins were going to escort us all the way to New York. "There's no way she can swim this fast. She'll be left behind!"

"She'll be fine. Look—here she comes."

And, indeed, there she was—being pulled by a dolphin. I'd half-expected her to be nude, but she still wore the yellow tanktop and cut-offs she'd found on board before we put to sea. She opened her mouth to call out just as the dolphin dove, giving her a mouthful of salt water. She came up coughing and spitting, rubbing her eyes. The dolphin nudged her concernedly, making sure her head stayed above water. "I'm all *right!*" she complained, but the dolphin hung around to make sure. She stroked it along the side, then grabbed the dorsal fin. "Come on in," she called out. "The water's fine!"

I waved back and she tugged on the dolphin. It made a sound like a high-pitched lamb's bleat and raced away, Shaughnessy skimming along behind it. "Looks like fun," I said.

"Yes, it does. I wish I could do it."

I patted her flank. "Poor thing. Must be rough being a unicorn."

"Yeah, well, it's a dirty job, but someone has to do it."

I laughed. "You won't get mad if I go for a swim?"

"Mad?" Her nostrils flared. "Are you kidding? I'd be grateful."

"Okay, I can take a hint."

"Go ahead, have fun, leave me here. See if I care."

"Can't have it both ways." I rummaged through my pack, found my dirty blue gym shorts rolled up at the bottom, and changed.

I frolicked in the water with the dolphins and Shaughnessy until the sight of an object poking up from the distant sliver of coast made me ask to be brought back to the boat. Shaughnessy followed. Ariel came up to me as I clambered aboard. "Something wrong, Pete?"

"Look landward—see where the land ends, there?" She nodded. "What's that white thing sticking up a little bit?"

She peered forward. "I don't know what you call it. A tall cylinder, tapering toward the top. The topmost section is darker than the rest."

"A lighthouse," I said, and told her what that was. I went

dripping back to the cabin and got out the road atlas. My finger traced up the coast until I found the only lighthouse marker corresponding to the lighthouse on the outcropping of land in the distance. The small red print beside my finger read: *Sandy Hook Light/National Historical Landmark.*

About an inch above that were bold, black letters which spelled out: **NEW YORK.**

"Fun time's over, huh?" asked Shaughnessy.

I nodded. "Ariel, are the dolphins staying with us all the way to New York?"

"No. I just talked with the bull. They'll be leaving shortly."

"And the whales?"

"They know where to go."

"Terrific." My voice was heavy.

A few minutes later we said goodbye to the dolphins and the herd turned as one and sped away. We watched, silent and sad, as they sped quickly out of sight.

The whales pulled us on. Land crept closer.

All too soon we weren't on the open sea any longer. Land squeezed in on both sides of us and there was a bridge overhead. Though both shores weren't really all that close, I felt constricted.

And then we were in New York Harbor and I was looking at the Manhattan skyline and the Statue of Liberty, all clearly visible. Because pollution had vanished with the Change's advent, the water was clear, no Coke cans, no traces of oily residue; but the water itself was dark.

Shaughnessy and I had changed into dry clothes. The three of us stood on the center of the deck. The three whales plowed along diligently. Further up rose the Empire State Building and the twin towers of the World Trade Center. I couldn't help but laugh when I saw the latter, though my heart wasn't in it. Ariel and Shaughnessy glanced at me curiously. "Tolkien would have loved it," I explained. They said nothing.

Onward. . . .

Governor's Island to our left, the Statue of Liberty to our right. I looked up at the gray-green figure and thought of Charlton Heston scraping at the sand on the beach in the last scene in *Planet of the Apes,* screaming, "You did it! You bastards, you finally did it, you blew it all up!"

No, I thought. Not with a bang, but a whimper.

Onward. . . .

A few minutes later the three ropes on our prow slackened as the whales backed out of their nooses. Our momentum carried us beside a boat docked on the concrete shore. The Liberty Island Ferry. *Miss Liberty* was stencilled in white on the prow and stern. The water gurgled as we stopped.

The three whales remained thirty yards away. Ariel dipped her horn in silent thank you and goodbye. Shaughnessy and I waved as they slipped silently away.

I moored us to the *Miss Liberty* and helped Shaughnessy on board. Ariel leapt the distance. I'd have accused her of showing off, but it was the easiest way for her to disembark, and I felt too sullen to say anything.

Though the ferry was in water, it was stationary and solidly anchored, and walking on its deck was a whole new experience. When you bounce on a trampoline for even a few minutes you get used to the feeling; your brain adjusts to the ground giving way beneath you. And when you jump onto the ground it jars your teeth because your brain expects it to give and it won't. It was like that.

We walked to the other side of the ferry and down the ramp. We looked at one another before any of us moved from the end of it. Finally I nodded and took a deep breath. I stepped off. Ariel and Shaughnessy followed me onto the concrete dock.

We were in New York.

seventeen

How doth the city sit solitary, that was full of people!

—Lamentations 1:1

"Well," I said with mock cheerfulness, "I don't see Malachi Lee. Maybe we got here ahead of him." I stood beside the metal rail along the dock, turning slowly to take in the lonely greenness and brownness that was Battery Park, half-expecting to see bums in trenchcoats on the weatherbeaten benches, their grizzled faces nuzzling wrinkled brown paper sacks concealing bottles of bad wine. A squirrel or two should have been evident, a couple walking hand in hand, but there was nothing. Except for the pigeons. Pigeons and pigeons, everywhere. New York had a lot of roosting places high up, and there were few things left to check their population growth. The wide black asphalt of the Heritage Trail ended a hundred yards to our right. I surveyed the dock, the silent ferry, the *Lady Woof* moored just behind it, the seasick-green Statue of Liberty facing seaward with torch held high in greeting, Governor's Island to its right.

"What now?" asked Shaughnessy. "We take the world by storm, or something?"

I gave her a stony look: words didn't belong, not here, not now. All things were coiled to maximum tension here; all roads had led to New York—and it seemed just as dead as old Rome. Black skyscrapers reared behind the trees of the park, looking like a badly matched matte painting in a cheap science fiction flick, a painted backdrop that didn't quite fit the foreground scene.

"I suggest we find somebody," said Ariel, "and see if we can find out what's what in this place."

"From what I've heard about this place," said Shaughnessy, "we may not want to find anybody."

"We'll have to look around anyhow," I said. "Keep a low profile, though." I couldn't take my eyes from the skyscrapers. "But this place feels so empty we'll stand out like blood on snow."

"It feels desolate, not empty," said Ariel. "There are people in this place, somewhere. I can feel it."

I studied her carefully but she didn't return my gaze, instead turning her head slowly from left to right, surveying the park. "Shaughnessy, will you get our gear from the boat? I want to look at that monument over there." I'd slung Fred at my left side but was without backpack or blowgun. I'd put Ariel's pack on her, empty except for the Barnett on the right side, the one closest to me. It was cocked and fitted with a fishing-head tipped bolt.

Ariel and I walked across the black asphalt, gray pigeons scattering about our feet, cooing as they half-flew. Everything looks so gray, I thought, like a half-hour after sunrise in Georgia. Except for the park. That's green—green and brown, live leaves and dead ones. And even in the midst of that ran gray concrete paths. I couldn't shake my moodiness. It was the depression you feel in the heavy humidity after a big rainstorm. I wiped sweat from my palms and clutched Fred's twined grip. *It's a city,* I told myself. *You've been in dozens before. This one's just bigger, that's all—it's still empty.* I glanced at Shaughnessy as she walked back up the ramp of the ferry toward *Lady Woof*. Her brown hair fanned out as she vaulted over the rail.

The monument to American military seamen killed in the service was just ahead of us. It was a small granite court—more gray, I couldn't help thinking—with four tall granite slabs on either side. Names were carved on both sides of all eight silent monoliths, thousands and thousands of names.

"These were all killed in wars?" Ariel asked.

"In the military, yes."

She shook her head slowly, silently. A warm breeze scattered crisp brown leaves across the court, startling me. The sound was like chitinous beetles scurrying, like rat claws scraping on concrete.

At the far end of the court, between the last two slabs, was a statue—the Battery Park Eagle. It was the classic American Eagle, head arched forward and wings raked back, frozen in the midst of a killing dive with claws clenched. It was about a third the size of Shai-tan and with time and weather had gone the same pale green as the Statue of Liberty. Something was carved into the black marble of its base, but I couldn't read it from where I stood. I asked Ariel what it said.

"'Erected by the United States of America in proud and grateful remembrance of her sons who gave their lives in her service and who sleep in the coastal waters of the Atlantic Ocean.

"'Into Thy hands, O Lord.'"

I started up the short flight of steps and froze as someone injected Freon into my veins with a chilled needle.

"Yes," said a familiar voice, "straight into our hands." From behind the eagle's base stepped Shai-tan's master. His right hand rested on the haft of his broadsword. "Hello again," he said, his one-eyed gaze taking in Ariel and myself. "You've saved us a lot of trouble."

Sweat on my palms. I tried to swallow.

At least twenty armed men filed onto the court from behind the last of the monoliths on the left and right, scattering pigeons and dead leaves in their wake. I looked up at the four black skyscrapers framing the scene in the background behind the park trees.

Ariel started forward without a word. Hands went to swords, axes, spears, chains, clubs.

"No," I said. "We can't. Ariel, look—we can't—we'll get killed."

She looked at me, a penetrating, disquieting gaze. "Pete," she said softly, "I can't be captured. I'll die in a month if I am."

"If we fight, we'll die now." I lowered my voice. "If we let them take us we can try to get away later."

"Fat chance."

"It's better than our alternatives." I turned around and cupped my hands to my mouth *"Shaughnessy!* Cast off! Push away!" I glanced back. The rider was motioning to a group of men, who broke away and ran toward the dock, ignoring Ariel and me. Shaughnessy appeared on the deck of the ferry. She hesitated, hands going to her mouth when she saw the dozen armed men heading her way. "Cast off!" I waved her away sharply. "Get out of here!"

She seemed indecisive, then turned and vaulted the rail and went out of sight. The twelve men were at the foot of the ramp, now swarming up it, then pouring onto the ferry deck.

Shaughnessy must have cut the rope and pushed off; the *Lady Woof* began to drift slowly away from *Miss Liberty*. The pursuing men stopped at the far side of the ferry deck. Two of them threw down their weapons and dove into the water. The rest were wearing a variety of heavy body protectors and couldn't follow without sinking to the bottom. They stood at the rail, watching their two comrades swim after Shaughnessy. The *Lady* was only twenty-five feet from the ferry and moving slowly. I wondered if the current would bring her back to the dock in a few minutes anyhow.

The faster of the two swimmers reached the stern of the *Lady*, grabbed with both hands, and pulled himself up. Shaughnessy popped up in front of him. In her hands was a rod. One end of it was against her mouth. The Aero-mag! The man's head snapped up and he arced backward into the water, thrashing.

The second swimmer had reached the starboard side and was pulling himself up. Shaughnessy must not have had another dart ready, or else she just reacted blindly; she reversed the blowgun and swung it like a baseball bat. I heard the faint smack as it hit him on the jaw. He recoiled but held on. She brought the blowgun back and jabbed him in the eye. He fell away with a splash.

"Let her go!" called the rider. His men turned to look at him from the deck of the ferry. "Let her go," he called again. "We don't need her." He lowered his one-eyed gaze to Ariel, lowered his voice as well. "We've got what we need."

I took a deep breath and walked forward two steps. The rider eyed me carefully, but a slight smile was on his lips. I reached slowly to my left hip, drew Fred, still sheathed, from its belt-loop sling, and laid it gently on the granite. "Let's go," I said, not looking at Ariel. I couldn't bring myself to.

He nodded and picked up the sword.
It was the hardest thing I ever said.

We were marched through the silent pathways of Battery Park and onto the desolate streets, where we headed north, walking in the middle of the road. Piles of olive-drab plastic garbage bags slouched on some street corners, twist-tied and lumpy. Occasionally a breeze wafted down the corridors of streets. There wasn't a store without a broken window. Some had been smashed from inside, and glass had sprayed onto the sidewalk.

I kept glancing to the World Trade Center as we walked. I'd always expected something . . . huge, massive, you know. These were merely tall. The twin towers—again I thought of Tolkien—with the pinstriping effect of alternating light and dark blue-gray lines, played tricks on my eyes the way a *moiré* pattern does, causing the perception of motion where none was.

And then we had passed Trinity Church, and the Trade Center was even with us, and we were heading north on Broadway.

I glanced at Ariel, who walked silently beside me, head up and noble, both of us surrounded by men with their weapons at ready or drawn. I looked down at the asphalt moving beneath my feet, trying to keep the images of heroic hindsight from coming, the "I shoulda dones." Maybe I should bolt for it now—go for the rider and kill him. That'd be enough.

I laughed aloud. Right—I no longer had Fred, and he had a broadsword and fifty men—and, most important, I would be forcing myself to perform an act which would result in my losing Ariel. Or, more likely, her losing me. And I just couldn't bring myself to do that. Time had become so valuable: the time I was spending with her now might be the last.

One of Ariel's rear hooves trailed along the street, scattering sparks. The men around us clenched their weapons tighter and muttered among themselves. The rider, who had been walking just ahead of us, turned back curiously. He questioned one of his men briefly and frowned. "Don't do that again," he said to Ariel. She stared blankly at him, blinked, and very deliberately extended her left front hoof and raked it across the asphalt. Red-gold sparks flew. There was a disturbed mumbling among the men.

The rider said one word: "Smith." A tall, burly man separated himself from the rest. He carried my crossbow in his right hand. He nodded to the rider and got behind me, not quite bringing it to bear, but holding it level at the hip. "If you do that again," said the rider with a forced smile, "we'll kill your friend, here." He jerked his head toward me.

She looked as if she were going to say something and apparently thought the better of it. I tried to walk without looking behind me, but it wasn't easy. Five kinds of warning bells were going off in my head and the small of my back, where I'd been hit before, was nearly screaming.

The rider turned around and we resumed walking. I tried to puzzle it out—why would Ariel striking sparks upset them like that?

The men walking with us were mostly silent and wary. Some glanced at Ariel with a strange mixture of wonder, curiosity, and fear.

We were in the outskirts of Chinatown, amid shops which had sold clothes and martial arts equipment—the latter no doubt looted. The rider slowed to walk with us, rubbing his left eye socket with an index finger. He saw me trying not to look and his other eye narrowed. He wiped the finger on his pants. "The bird who did this to me," he said. "That was its owner we killed?"

I mumbled something.

"What?"

"I said yes, you son of a bitch." I glanced around self-consciously. The men looked almost amused—yeah, brave little fuck, so what—we're gonna kill him anyhow. The rider half-smiled. There was something cold in his single eye, as if he were pleasuring himself by picturing me cut to dogmeat. Except for the eye he had that German *übermenschlich* look about him—he could have been a figure on a Hitler Youth poster, but the broadsword at his hip and the ruin of his eye gave him a vaguely piratical look which jarred with his Aryan features. I smiled inwardly as I regarded his eye. Give me half a chance, bastard. I'll do the rest of you, too.

He just nodded at my attempt at bravado, that same half-smile on his pale face. "Good, good. The falcon was his buddy; that means it died, too." The glint in his eye grew stronger.

"No," I said, glad at being able to contradict him, "we killed the falcon. Malachi Lee did. It didn't feel a thing."

"Malachi Lee." The smile thinned but the eye remained cold. I looked away from him.

They must have seen us coming in by sea—but how? I looked at the skyscrapers all around. The streets looked like deserted hallways with the ceilings somehow ripped away, leaving behind jagged walls. If not for our present situation I'd have been impressed by the grandeur of the city's architecture.

I asked where we were going, but the rider said nothing.

"Where do you think, Pete?" said Ariel. "He's taking us to his employer, his liege lord, the one he bows to. The necromancer." I could see Ariel was trying to irritate him. Nobody with power likes to be reminded that they have superiors, too.

Very distinctly, he hawked, turned his head, and spat at her. My hand went for Fred at my side and clasped air. The phlegm looked as if it were deflected by the wind and it curved left, splattering on the street ahead of her.

The men muttered to each other. I thought I was beginning to understand.

"*Nobody* spits on a unicorn," said Ariel proudly. One day her pride will be her downfall, I thought.

The rider glared and turned away. "We'll see what good being a unicorn will do you soon enough," he said to the empty street ahead of him. "You can protect yourself for now—but you can't protect him."

I knew the "him" was me and felt the pang of adrenaline shooting into my heart. It had just hit me that I was the only thing holding Ariel back. Her fear for my life had caused her to be captured and kept her from trying to escape. She'd have been able to get away easily if not for me.

I caught some of the men who surrounded us eyeing Ariel speculatively. They looked away quickly if Ariel looked at them. They were afraid of magic. It was what kept them in check, I felt sure. Most of them had the look of long-time loners about them—the wary eyes and mistrustful glances, the conservation of movement, the constant checking of terrain in all directions. Most loners don't trust magical ability, fearing it for the unknown that it is. These loners guarding us associated magical ability with people in authority, with their superiors—people with the power to *make* them do things. Now an enemy was in their midst—two enemies, actually, but I didn't count—

an alien thing. And it performed magic.

"How much farther?" I asked.

"A few miles," he said grudgingly. "You can see it from here." He pointed at a building ahead. My eyes followed the line of his finger to the Empire State Building.

Empire State Building.

Yeah, I could see it, all right. We'd turned onto Fifth Avenue. An absurd thought kept running through my head like an annoying jingle: Gee, I've always wanted to see New York! Gee, I've always wanted to see New York! Gee— I walked like an old man, shoulders slumped, head hanging, feeling beaten. I *was* beaten. I was tired. I'd given up.

Off to see the Wizard. The worm in the Big Apple. I walked like an automaton. *Welcome to the Machine, Mr. Garey.* Why, thank you, nurse, I'll take a double—left bicep this time, please. Free Will, my ass—Fate led me here, that malicious bitch.

Dozens of armed men walked the streets in front of the Empire State Building. They became alert when they saw us, gesturing to one another and pointing to Ariel. The double revolving doors of the Fifth Avenue entrance were guarded by two armed men dressed in a hodgepodge of collected homemade armor. One even had a hockey goalie's mask pushed back on top of his head. They looked vaguely like English knights.

How many men could you fit into a building one hundred two stories tall? Thousands, at least. Tens of thousands, probably. I couldn't be certain the entire building was occupied—it posed too many practical problems, such as how to get from the bottom to the top. Elevators wouldn't work anymore.

Magic? Ariel had once said that magic was a resource like any other and shouldn't be wasted. Employing magic for routine elevator-type operations seemed a bit extravagant. What else, then? Pulleys and ropes in the elevator shafts? No way—the amount of rope necessary would be too heavy for any group of workers to pull. It never occurred to me that the necromancer would set his quarters, his "sanctum sanctorum," as Dr. Strange used to say, at the bottom of the building. Anybody utilizing this skyscraper would instantly recognize the military and psychological advantages of being master of all he surveyed. No, I never doubted for a second that we were going to the top.

The answer was so obvious I missed it.

Seeing the broken windows of a McDonald's on the other side of Fifth Avenue made me realize I was hungry. The last time I'd eaten was a small dinner at sea on the *Lady*.

We passed a restaurant called *Leo Lindy's* at the base of the building and turned left onto Thirty-fourth Street. A sign above the revolving doors ahead read: TO OBSERVATION DECKS. Orbach's was right across the street, Macy's a little further down. Preening itself in the middle of the road was a griffin. Shai-tan.

I hesitated, glancing at Ariel. She remained silent. Our guards pressed closer around us, probably thinking that if there was any one time we were likely to make a break for it, this was it.

They were right—Ariel reared. Men backed away unthinkingly, all but one who pulled a hand axe and drew it back. Ariel twitched her head and the man fell with his skull caved in.

This is it, I thought, and I side-stepped the crossbow bolt I pictured heading my way at any second. Turning around quickly, I saw that "Smith" had turned the Barnett toward Ariel, whose back was to him. His hand was going for the trigger when I leapt, kicked it to the side, and gave him a right to the temple. He sagged to the street and the crossbow went sailing. I went for it—and found my way blocked by a bloody broadsword an inch in front of my face as I knelt on the street. I tried to look past it at the rider, but I couldn't. There was nothing else in the universe but that point, two inches from my eyes. I couldn't breathe, couldn't even think. My ears told me the shouting had died down, that Ariel obviously wasn't fighting anymore because she'd seen me, but it didn't register, nothing registered but the blade, *the blade*. The rider's voice was a world away, made throaty by his heavy breathing. "All right," he said. "I may not have your power—I'll give you that. But if you say another word, make a wrong move, do anything other than walk to that building, I'll kill him." The blade shook before my eyes. I flinched. "Get up!" I stood, not taking my eyes from the end of the sword, and it followed me up. "Move."

I moved. I stepped over a body. The remaining men had their weapons drawn. I felt them on all sides, at my back, ready.

We left three bodies behind. Blood covered Ariel's horn.

It was all too much for me and I cried.

The rider strode ahead of us, heavy broadsword bobbing in time with his swagger. He stopped at the huge, leonine bird, reached up, and stroked the feathers at the bottom of its throat. He stroked down, ruffling at the place on Shai-tan's breast where feathers became golden-brown fur. The beast arched its powerful neck and blinked its eyes, a sleepy killer. It saw Ariel and spread its huge wings, hissing from deep in its throat. The rider calmed the griffin, stepped forward, and untied the long reins from around the right stirrup, standing on tiptoe to reach them. He held both reins in his right hand and turned to face us. The reins grew taut as he stepped forward. The griffin stood reluctantly and stepped forward slowly, not being pulled, but not exactly following. Our guard looked nervous as the beast approached, but they merely exchanged glances and kept a watchful eye on us. The rider stopped in front of me and lowered the hand clenching the leather reins. I smelled hot brass. "What's your name?"

I looked him in the eye and said nothing.

He shrugged. "It doesn't matter." He gestured with the reins. "Get on."

I glanced at Ariel.

"She'll follow you up," he said.

"How do I know that?"

He smiled. "You don't. But you don't have much choice, either."

I looked at the griffin's molten gold eyes. Why didn't the cavalry ever come over the hill in real life?

The griffin settled itself down on the street, bringing the stirrups level with the top of my chest. "Get on," he said again.

I grabbed the stirrup and the bottom of the saddle, jumped, and pulled myself up. I swung my right leg around and settled onto the saddle. It creaked beneath me.

"Hold on to the saddlehorn," said the rider. "Use both hands. Don't pull on the reins or you'll get thrown—it's a long way down." He turned to Ariel. "We're going to hold him on top while Shai-tan comes back for you. I know you can probably keep yourself from being lifted if you want to, but if you do we'll throw him off. Understand?"

"I understand." She looked over to me. I tried to nod confidently but I knew she wasn't fooled. She nodded back slowly and looked to the rider. "If you do anything to him, I'll kill you. Griffin or not, men or not, you know you won't be able to stop me."

"We don't care about him."

I swallowed hard. By then I had made up my mind to go for him. I truly didn't care what happened to me as long as Ariel was all right.

She must have seen it in my eyes, for she shook her head slowly and said, gently but firmly, "Go on, Pete."

Shai-tan stood, craning her neck, head flicking about alertly. I rocked in the saddle and grasped the long horn in both hands. The rider released the reins. "Take him up," he told the griffin mildly.

The street wheeled as the griffin turned and took two running steps that jarred my teeth. Two great flaps of the sail-sized wings and we were aloft. We climbed steeply. I looked down and managed to glimpse Ariel looking up at me, the rider and our captors around her. Shai-tan began circling and I had to look away because the ground began to revolve slowly and I thought I'd be sick if I kept looking. The griffin made two complete circuits in an upward spiral around the skyscraper. To my left the building seemed to rotate clockwise. We were about three hundred feet up when Shai-tan headed north, away from the building. We were still climbing. Skyscrapers rose ahead of us. I recognized the Pan Am and Chrysler buildings. Soon they began to give way beneath us and I saw Central Park ahead. The view was marvelous, unhampered by smog. I held on to the saddlehorn for dear life, rocking in time to the griffin's surging wingbeats. Shai-tan called out, a predator's cry echoing into the canyons of the city. We banked right, turning a hundred eighty degrees. We were now about three-quarters of the way to the top, around nine hundred feet up. The World Trade Center was bluish gray in the distance. Beyond lay Battery Park. I searched the blue expanse of water farther on, but saw no sign of a boat. I hoped Shaughnessy was all right. If she'd been with us when were were captured she'd have gone with us, and if we'd tried to fight our way out of it she'd have fought alongside us. And died alongside us, too. I'd seen no reason for it; it wasn't her fight. I'd sent her back to the *Lady Woof* in case there was a trap, so at least she could get away.

My hair streamed back in the wind rushing at my face. The powerful back muscles of the griffin flexed beneath me as its wings grabbed air. To have a Familiar such as this! The feeling of power it would give to soar above the cities, to command the pent-up fury within this creature!

I remembered Russ Chaffney and felt ashamed.

Cars had become motionless beetles; people weren't even large enough to be called ants in comparison. Men waited on the perimeter of the eighty-sixth floor observatory, the only suitable place to land; the protective metal fencing that had once been set in the guard wall had been removed.

The cathedral-like Chrysler Building and the blue strip of the East River were now to my left. Except for the sound of the wind rushing past my ears, it was deadly quiet down there.

As we neared the eighty-sixth floor it became apparent that the only place with enough room for Shai-tan to land was one of the corners; the guard wall jutted irregularly and the walkway was too narrow, only about ten to twelve feet wide. The building slid underneath and Shai-tan cupped her wings, braking by air drag. The griffin landed smoothly on the near corner, one of her claws gripping either side of the angle of the guard wall, and folded her wings to her sides. A dozen armed men stood on the brick-colored deck before me. I gathered I was supposed to dismount where I was. It meant swinging out over open air and stepping onto the six-inch-wide wall, then stepping down from there. I glanced up at the thick needle of the TV tower rising above the observation deck and felt as if I were pitching over backward. I lowered my gaze to the wall on the left-hand side and eased out of the saddle, probing for the top of the guard wall with my right foot, slowly lowering myself until my feet touched the wall. I tried looking back over my shoulder so I could see just the wall and the observation deck without having to take in the cityscape below and ahead, but it was impossible—it was there in my peripheral vision.

Shai-tan shrieked just as my feet settled on the wall. I jerked and lost my footing. There was time only to push away from her and pitch myself backward onto the observation deck, where I was caught by the waiting men. "Thanks," I said, and then felt stupid.

Shai-tan spread her wings and jumped over our heads. A brief gust spread across the deck and she was aloft again. She rose twenty feet, flapped twice—just enough to clear her from the building—and then pulled her wings in and plummetted in a dive toward the street. I stood on tiptoe and leaned out over the wall as she dove, just managing to catch a glimpse as she cupped her wings and began to level off, and then she disappeared below one of the lower terrace levels. I was grabbed from behind and my arms were pinned behind my back. "All right, let's go," someone said. I tried to struggle but my hands were held fast. And there were at least a dozen of them, all armed. "I'm supposed to wait here!" I said over my shoulder. "They're bringing Ariel up—my friend—a unicorn—and I'm supposed to wait until she gets here."

"Get him out of here," said the voice.

"No, wait—"

They pulled me. Again I tried to protest and was punched in the kidney for my efforts. I gasped and my insides locked up when I tried to inhale. They dragged me up a short flight of steps and into a metal and glass area that used to sell souvenirs of New York City. A double elevator bank slid past, blurry, and then I was jarred as they dragged me down several flights of stairs. Keys rattled and a door opened. I was brought to my feet and turned around to face somebody. His face was blurry. I blinked to clear my vision, and when I opened my eyes again I just had time to see the flesh-colored blur before his fist hit my face. Colored explosions spread from jaw to eyes, and everything went black.

I was roughly shaken awake. Reflex took over before I was fully conscious, and I grabbed the arm tugging my shoulder and pulled. Whoever it was pitched forward, striking his head on the wall, and then they were all over me, five men crowding around me pinning me down with their knees on my arms and legs. I began struggling, then relaxed. "All right," I said. "All right. I'm not gonna resist."

I was pulled to my feet and pushed into a corridor lit by lanterns set on the floor at irregular intervals. The effect was eerie: the five men surrounding me were lit from below in pale orange, shadows making empty black sockets of their eyes.

"Where are you taking me?"

No answer. They indicated the direction I was to walk by shoving me. I stumbled, caught myself, and began walking. Our footsteps echoed in the long, empty corridors.

We stopped at a door guarded by two men in homemade

armor. One of them nodded to my escort, flicked his eyes to me briefly, and opened the door outward. My escort led me in.

The room was dimly lit by five candles near the walls on the left and right. The door clicked shut behind us. The flames wavered. I smelled burning wax. The pale yellow light barely revealed an office desk with a large black chair behind it at the far end of the room. It sat before a large window which looked out on the night sky.

"That's fine." The voice came from the chair. The guards, who shifted nervously as they stood more or less at attention, turned and left the room. The candles flickered again as the door opened and shut with a final sound.

The room had been a large office. The carpet beneath my feet was plush. I tried to make out the figure behind the desk, but he was lost in the blackness of the chair. I stood my ground and said nothing.

"So you're Pete," he said. Telling me, not asking.

I took it as a question. "Who wants to know?" I asked, trying not to sound afraid. My voice cracked on the second word like a boy hitting puberty.

There was the impression of motion as hands were clasped together on the desk. "Please. I'm not impressed." His voice was low and mild. It had a persuasive, soothing quality to it, sounding faintly like a priest on a late night TV sign-off. He stood. Yellow candlelight from both sides highlighted his pale button-up shirt and dark pants. He was thin. He wasn't tall. His hair was light brown and caught gold on the ends from the candle flame. He was clean shaven. I'd walked almost nine hundred miles to confront him, and here he was.

I don't know what I'd been expecting. A tall, pointed hat, maybe, festooned with stars and crescent moons. A long, flowing robe and beard. Saruman the White.

"What have you done with Ariel?" My voice shook.

"I talked to her. That's all." He smiled. It looked genuine, unlike the rider's false cat-with-a-mouse smile. "The first thing she asked me was what I'd done with you. Obviously you both mean a great deal to each other."

"We're Familiars."

He nodded. "If you were anything else, if she were anything else, I might try to bargain with you."

"What kind of bargain?"

"Your life for her horn."

"Eat shit."

He shrugged. "It never hurts to offer. I don't have a vendetta against you. I don't care about you, or your unicorn. All I want is her horn. If I could take it and leave her alive, I would."

"What do you want it for?"

He ignored me. "She's strong, though, and she has abilities I hadn't expected." He slowly walked around to the front of the desk and leaned back against it. "But her defenses will weaken now that I have her. She's beginning to die." He paused to let that sink in.

"I'd like to make a deal," he continued. "But not with her."

"With me."

"Yes. I can't deal with her, but I can with you." He scratched his head. "I can take her horn and leave her alive, but only if she's willing."

"Why don't you ask her, then?"

"Because she wouldn't agree, of course."

"And you think I will. You want me to talk her into it."

"Think about it. You could have her, she could have you. Both of you would be alive. As I said, all I want is her horn."

"Why should I agree to that? You can't take it while she's alive. And you're not powerful enough to kill her."

"True," he acknowledged. "But, as I said, she's a captive now, and she's dying. I could wait until she's too weak to defend herself, but I don't know how long it would take. I'd rather she let me take it and have it now."

I looked down at the floor. He seemed to delight in twisting the knife.

"So I'm prepared to bargain," he continued.

"Not with me you won't." My voice quavered. "She's told me she'd die without her horn."

"I can promise you she wouldn't. If it were taken from her, yes, but not if she gave it willingly."

"I don't believe you. She wouldn't be a unicorn without her horn. No deal."

"I guess I will have to bargain with her, then."

"She'll never do it."

"I think she will. I'll offer a trade I think she'll go for, the same one I offered you—your life for her horn." There was no trace of uncertainty in his voice. "As I said, when she and I talked it was evident that you are her prime concern. I could have had you killed at any time, you know. It would have been easy to lie to her and tell her we'd kill you if she didn't co-operate."

I said nothing.

"But I think she would have known if you were dead. Or if I lied. I think she'd be able to tell that."

"I don't care what you do to me," I said, meaning it.

"That may be true, but it doesn't change anything. I'm going to put you in front of her so there'll be no mistaking my intent. If she gives in I'll have her horn and you can go. If she remains stubborn she'll die anyhow, eventually—and I'll still have her horn."

"Fat chance you're going to let me go."

"I might. You'll never be able to harm me. And after I have her horn, nothing will be able to harm me. Nothing in the world."

I went for him. I'd decided the second I realized where they were taking me that I was going to kill him regardless of the cost. Ariel would be able to get away; I would no longer be holding her back. I took two running steps and leapt for his face. He didn't flinch, didn't so much as bat an eye. Instead, he waved his right hand nonchalantly and I ran face first into an invisible brick wall. My feet kept going and I pivoted in midair and landed on my back. He waved again and an unseen something sent me sprawling. I tried to pick myself up. My arms gave beneath me.

Behind me came a knock on the door. I was still trying to focus my eyes when it opened and a man walked in. My vision didn't need to be clear to recognize him, though: a dark discoloration over one eye made his face skull-like. He glanced at me on my hands and knees on the side of the room and looked away. "You wanted to see me?"

"Yes, I did." He had sat back down in the depths of the black executive chair. "I understand you discovered a loner in the city yesterday."

"Nothing special about that," he replied carefully. "There are loners all over this city." The pale candleglow mannequinned his Germanic features.

A creak in the chair, a suggestion of leaning forward: "Captured loners are supposed to be brought here for questioning. You know that."

"He was a forager, half-starved. He was hunting for food."

"I don't care. There's been an increase in loner activity in the city these last few weeks and I want to find out why." He paused. "We can't find out anything if captured loners have their throats cut before they're interrogated."

The rider said nothing.

The dark shape of the chair leaned back, squeaking. "You're getting a touch too smug to suit me. A little too greedy. You can do what you want with prisoners after I question them, not before."

"I'm not trying to overstep any bounds," the rider protested. "I don't want your power. I'm happy where I am, thanks. With Shai-tan."

"Whom I gave you."

The rider nodded. He looked at me as if I were a piece of bad meat he'd just chewed and spat out. "What about him?"

"I'm taking care of him now. You can stay and watch, if you want."

I still fought waves of dizziness. My throat constricted at the metallic tang in my mouth. I swallowed. I didn't want to stay hunched over in front of them the way I was; I loathed the thought of the satisfaction it gave them. I struggled to my knees. Flashbulbs went off in my head. My jaw was swollen and tender where I'd been punched.

I think I passed out. My next recollection was of seeing several men carrying in a large, round table of thick, heavy wood. I was on my back, looking up, and the room was a carnival ride gone haywire, revolving around an ever-changing axis.

The rider had my samurai sword in hand. He saw me looking at him and grinned, then pulled the blade six inches from the scabbard and spat on it. I got mad enough to stand up, ignoring the headache piercing behind my eyes. I staggered a step toward him, intent on doing my level and wholly inadequate best to kill him. Two things stopped me. The first was Ariel. She stood in front of the door, flanked by armed men. She looked bad. Her hide caught the pale candle flame reluctantly, reflected it as a flat, rusty orange; her mane hung limply and dried blood stained her horn, but in that dim light her eyes were dominant. Her space-black gaze was still prideful and vitality still burned there. Those eyes went soft with hurt when they saw me, and I was conscious of what I must have looked like.

"Oh, Pete." A weight Atlas had never felt was in her voice;

that, and the contained rage and pain of a chained Prometheus.

The second thing I noticed was the table. It was made of some dark wood—ebony, perhaps—and was directly between Ariel and me. It was round, about seven feet in diameter, and three and a half feet high. A pentagram had been drawn across it in blood. A candle burned at each point. Ropes were secured in the wood at four of the five points. At a word from the necromancer three guards lowered their weapons and took hold of me. I struggled and cursed, but was too weak to do anything more than writhe feebly against them. Not that I could have done much had I got loose. I was dragged to the table and tied to the pentagram. Once I was secured, the guards returned to stand beside Ariel. I felt the candles burning by each hand. I was bound spread-eagled, hands and feet tied at four of the five points of the star within the circle. I lifted my head and saw the rider looking on in satisfaction, face half shadowed.

The office chair creaked as the necromancer stood. He held a black book in one thin hand. Those were surgeon's hands, pianist's hands. He walked around the desk and stopped before me. I looked up at his calm face, wishing I could work up spit.

The book was bound in old leather. He opened it and looked at Ariel, then shifted back to the book and began reciting, tilting the book forward until it was lit by the glow from the pentagram candles. The words he spoke were vaguely Latin-sounding and all too familiar:

"I summon thee,
O Dweller in the Darkness,
O Spirit of the Pit.
I Command thee
To make thy
Most evil appearance."

It took a moment for the shock of recognition to wear off, and when it did I began struggling against the ropes cutting into my wrists and ankles, renewed strength flowing from my pounding heart, but the ropes were tied too tight.

"In the name of
Our mutual benefactor,
In the name of
Lucifer the Fallen,
I conjure thee."

"No!" It was Ariel, eyes smoldering. She sent one of her guards sprawling with a toss of her head. The necromancer looked to the rider, who came forward, drawing his broadsword. Ariel stepped purposefully toward him, almost casually batting aside the spear that was aimed for her side. The rider kept me between himself and Ariel. He brought the broadsword up and held it poised over my head, staring evenly at Ariel.

> *"By his blood-lettered sacraments,*
> *By hell and Earth,*
> *To come to me now,*
> *In your own guise*
> *To do your will."*

Coldness began spreading deep within me, as if I'd swallowed an ice cube whole. I felt isolated within the pentagram. A hurricane's-eye stillness settled around the table. I struggled harder but the bonds held. I jerked my right wrist; it had been burned by candle flame.

Candle flame?

I looked around quickly. Nobody was paying any attention to me, not even Ariel. She and the rider were absorbed in each other, a test of will. One guard was unconscious or dead, a second was picking himself up from the floor with the help of one of his mates, and the last watched the silent game of cat and mouse played by the rider and Ariel. The necromancer was immersed in the conjuration.

> *"I adjure thee*
> *In the name of*
> *The foulest of masters. . . ."*

I looked at the candle ahead of my bound right hand. A steady, even glow. My stomach was numb with cold. My lungs breathed Arctic air. The space a foot above my midsection pulsated, and a swirling gray mist slowly took form. I strained my hand past the candle flame. It seared my wrist. I turned my arm so that the rope was against the flame.

> *". . . By his loins,*
> *By his blood,*

By his damned soul,
To come forth."

Burn, damn you, burn! The skin began to blister along the inside of my wrist. I smelled burning hemp. Disturbing movements began coalescing within the stormy gray above me. Once the spell was complete the pentagram would be sealed and the demon would appear.

"I order thee
By all the unholy names:
Lucifer, Satan, Beelzebub—"

The mist began to solidify into something resembling ink in water. The rope was burned through! I pulled it but the twists of the knot held fast. I worked my hand quickly from side to side and finally it pulled free. My fingers trembled as I untied the knot from around my left hand. A glance up at the rider: he still eyed Ariel, waiting for her to make her move. She had to have noticed me untying myself, but would have been careful not to register it.

"Belial, Shai-tan, Mephistopheles—"

The air was freezing. I twisted beneath the inky mass and began untying my ankle bonds. My movement caught the eye of both the rider and the necromancer. The latter looked quickly back to the black book and intoned evenly:

"Thy hair, thy heart,
Thy lungs, thy blood,
To be here
To work your will
Upon me."

And with the last word the temperature plummeted. I breathed mist and trembled from more than the cold as I untied the last rope. The thing in the pentagram with me began to assume a smoky humanoid shape, massive and dark.

The stand-off between Ariel and the rider reached a head when I leaned forward to free my legs. I saw him about to swing the sword for my head and jumped away. I should have landed on the floor. Instead I ran into an invisible wall. The conjuration was finished; the pentagram was sealed.

I must have seemed to defy gravity as I leaned at an impossible angle with my back against the edge of the pentagram. The rider's sword stopped jarringly midway through its arc. A flash of sparks screaming from grating metals illuminated the room, and suddenly I was falling backward to the floor. The sword had breached the integrity of the pentagram, and I landed at the necromancer's feet. Before he could react I knocked the book from his hands and sent him flying over his desk.

An enraged bellow came from within the pentagram, then faded away.

Ariel had bolted for the rider the instant he began to swing. Through the haze of smoke I saw the rider jerk the sword from the wooden edge of the pentagram. He pulled back and swung, and sword met horn. I stumbled over something in front of the office desk. Fred! I drew the sword from its sheath and intercepted a guard heading toward Ariel with his blade held ready to thrust. I deflected it, reversed my blade, and slashed, cutting through half his neck. Ariel backed toward the door. She used her horn as a counterpart to the rider's sword: block, slash, thrust. She must have already started to grow weak; she was much slower than usual. I had to help her.

I turned around, grabbed the edge of the office desk, and lifted. It toppled over onto the necromancer. I had to keep him too distracted, enraged, and busy to be able to cast a spell, or we were lost. Ignoring the curses—profane rather than arcane—from beneath the desk, I turned and ran to Ariel. The three remaining guards were behind the rider, trying to fan out and outflank Ariel but having a hard time of it because of the large table in the middle of the floor.

Fuck honorable combat. I dove to the floor beneath Ariel, rolled onto my back, and slashed straight up. The rider stopped in mid-swing, gasping as my sword brushed his thigh. Blood flowed down his leg. I'd been aiming for his groin. I thrust up and back, toward the soft part beneath his chin, but he jumped clear. Blood spattered my face. I rolled out from beneath Ariel and stood. The rider stepped toward me, skidded in his own blood, and fell. I stepped forward to deliver the *coup de grace* and stopped hurriedly. Three guards were on us and the necromancer was struggling to stand upright.

Ariel twitched her head. A deflected spear scraped along

the wall. I risked a glance and saw the necromancer standing, arms raised above his head. Using her body as a shield against the guards, Ariel backed up quickly, crowding me against the door. It flew open as the doorguards burst in, and I fell backward, rolled, and came up slashing, catching the right-hand guard in the stomach. Fred cut through his mail and he dropped his cutlass.

Ariel kicked straight back while engaging the remaining guards ahead of her. She caught the left-hand doorguard in the ribs. Bone snapped and blood ran out of his mouth.

"Run, Pete!"

I had time to glimpse the rider, on his feet again, eye blazing, sword swinging, and Ariel's horn coming up to meet it, when the necromancer spoke a foreign word and the door slammed shut.

The elevator shafts and stairs were my only way down. I was on the eighty-fifth floor. No alarm had been spread and I made it to the elevator doors with no trouble. I pried the doors open with Fred, silently apologizing to Malachi Lee for demeaning the blade. I felt sure he'd understand.

The shaft was dark. Looking up, I could barely make out the bottom of the elevator, forever stuck on the eighty-sixth floor. A narrow peg ladder ran the length of the shaft; I grabbed it and swung inside. The door proved difficult to re-close but I managed somehow, holding onto the peg ladder with one arm. I'd slung Fred through the familiar and worn belt-loop.

I descended in total darkness. I found it was easier if I closed my eyes. The shaft only went down to the eightieth floor, so I climbed up to the eighty-first floor, pried open the doors just wide enough to pass through, and stepped into the corridor.

Nothing.

I walked to the stairs, trying not to appear hurried. Women's voices came down the corridor as I reached the stairs. I opened the door quickly and stepped into the stairwell. They passed by. I counted to thirty, then began walking down flights of stairs slowly to keep my footsteps from echoing in the stairwell. I expected at any moment to hear them thundering down on me from above. Surely they'd be scouring the elevator shafts and stairwells by now. Possibly, though, word hadn't got around yet and there hadn't been time to send parties into elevator shafts and stairwells.

I crept on cat feet—maybe frightened mouse feet is closer—when I passed the eightieth floor. Men's voices came from the corridor beyond the stairwell door. I hugged the wall and went slowly down the stairs, expecting the door to open at any second. Nothing happened. I'd made it all the way down to the sixty-fifth floor when I heard voices and footsteps above me. They were perhaps four floors up and descending fast. I couldn't afford a confrontation. I was fatigued, had been beat up twice within the last twelve hours, and didn't want the sound of a fight tipping off others in any case, so I pushed open the door that led to the sixty-fifth floor and closed it quietly behind me. The floor was deserted. I kept my right hand firmly on Fred as I walked past office doors. Ignoring the first set of elevator doors, I walked around a bit instead, eyes peeled for movement among the dark shapes. There was none. I found another elevator on the opposite side of the building. I shook my head wearily and used Fred to pry open the elevator doors, sheathed the blade, and stepped in.

Forty-seventh floor: it had taken me over an hour to descend less than twenty floors. My fingers were hopelessly cramped, palms blistered beyond redemption. My legs were holding up relatively well. All that walking.

I had just stopped for a breather when something struck me hard on the shoulder. It felt like a brick and probably was. I stifled a cry behind clenched teeth and saw searing white bands. I lost my grip and fell.

I landed on my back almost immediately. Moist things lay all around me. The stench was terrible. Voices came from a long way above me, echoing along the shaft. One spoke something loudly and all fell silent. Three seconds passed, then something smacked into the metal by my foot. Another brick. I stood quickly. It hurt. I stepped over the junk around me and pressed myself against the wall opposite the peg ladder. Another brick slammed next to the first. I felt it through my feet when it hit.

The voices reverberated again, and then they were gone.

I'd landed on the elevator. I bent and groped around in the muck until I found what I was looking for: the emergency exit. I smiled to myself. It made me wince.

I picked Fred up from the shit. The fall had broken my belt loop. The sword seemed in good shape but the scabbard was cracked. I lowered it into the square hole until it touched bottom, then let go. It fell over and landed with a hollow clank. I lowered myself into the elevator with one arm. The other didn't want to work.

Using Fred again, I opened the two sets of doors—the elevator was only a foot above being even with the forty-sixth floor—and stepped into the corridor. Again, no one was there. I was having a hard time understanding this. A contingent of possibly five thousand people, and I'd seen no more than—what? Fifty, sixty, something like that. A hundred, tops. I realized the building was big, but they should have been concentrating on the elevators and stairways to find me. I should have been running into them everywhere. Unless the army was nowhere near five thousand strong. One thousand? It began to sound more and more likely. Yeah, great, Garey, now the odds are only one thousand to one instead of five. Whoop-te-doo.

I made it out by cutting long lengths of phone wire, tying them together, and lowering myself out a window from the fourth floor as soon as it got dark. It wasn't easy, but it was just about my only workable option. My left arm still tried to convince me that it was on strike; I had to force it to reconsider. I dared not go any lower than the third floor; there were bound to be guards at all possible methods of egress from there down. I had been mildly surprised that the fourth floor was unguarded. Either they figured I'd have to descend further to get out of the building or my revised estimate of one thousand men divided between top and bottom floors was accurate. Either way, I wasn't about to stick around to find out which speculation was correct. I wanted *out* of there. So I could come back. And get Ariel. And head west, and we could go anywhere, nowhere. And the entire rest of the world could go even further to hell and I wouldn't care.

It seemed a long time before my feet finally touched the sidewalk. During my careful back-step descent I kept remembering old *Batman* reruns, half-expecting celebrities to pop out of windows and deliver one-liners. Then I was outside, on the ground, and couldn't help but breathe a sigh.

Voices were headed my way. I walked away from the phone wire climbing the wall like straight plastic ivy. I deliberately walked so that I came close to them. Two men, both armed. They nodded a greeting to me and I returned it, heart pounding, trusting the darkness to hide my beat-up face.

It isn't like in the movies: lone man in enemy territory is sighted by soldiers, recognized instantly, and pursued. These people were loners, as I was a loner. And, while they were part of what I suppose you could call an "army," there were no uniforms to distinguish me from them. I did nothing to invite suspicion, so I wasn't suspected. I kept walking past them, trying to keep my pace slow and deliberate, a curious, cold feeling between my shoulder blades.

So, after an inglorious arrival and an impotent confrontation, I walked straight out of enemy hands. But I vowed I would be back.

New York is a big city. There's too much of it to search realistically; almost anywhere I wanted to hide after leaving the Empire State Building would prove reasonably safe. Or as safe as anything ever is, which isn't very.

I hid in the manager's apartment of an old brick apartment house three blocks from the Empire State Building, just off Fifth Avenue. I collapsed on the musty bed, clutching Fred close to me.

Just before I became unconscious I heard the terrifying shriek of a huge nightbird in the distance. Its name appeared in formless letters, black on black, fading out as exhaustion forced me into sleep:

Shai-tan.

eighteen

. . . In which is continued the narrative of the misfortune that befell our brave knight.

—Cervantes,
Don Quixote

Wedges of sunlight, escaping from between the tall buildings, came through the window to rest upon my face, and the jolt of awakening whisked away the twisting memories of sleep. I sat up. The pain in my jaw had lessened only slightly. My hands looked like raw hamburger. The blisters had popped long ago. Blood crusted my palms. I rubbed white granules from the corners of my eyes.

I tried to get out of bed and my calves cramped. I hopped back onto the musty, red and black bedspread to take the weight off the muscles. The bed creaked in protest. Something clinked beside me: Fred. I picked up the sword and looked at it. The scabbard was cracked three inches from the tip. Wood showed through the black lacquer in places. I drew the blade and held the handle close to my eye, closing the other one and sighting down the curved length. No bends, no nicks, a few scratches. A small smear of blood at the tip. It blurred as tears formed in my eyes. I clenched my hands, one on the scabbard, the other on the sword handle, and slid the blade back in. The tears came then, slipping through the cracks in my restraint. The fingers of my left hand rubbed the scabs on the knuckles of the right. No, no, don't punch something. That won't do you any good.

I took three shaky breaths. It calmed me down, some. I set Fred down and rubbed my calves. They felt like closely packed Superballs. My leg muscles began knotting when I got up again, but at least they didn't cramp. I went into the bathroom to look in a mirror. I stared stupidly at it for a long while, then lowered my head, shook it, and walked painfully out of the bathroom, shutting the door behind me as if it would block the view from memory. I looked as if I had miraculously managed to drag myself away from a plane crash.

I gazed down at my hands. They balled into fists, almost as if recoiling from the sight of me. I wanted to smash something. I wanted to see something break. There was a metal lamp on the writing desk on the other side of the room. I picked it up and went back into the bathroom. A stranger faced me on the other side of the sink. His face was varying patches of black, blue, and sickly green. Blood had crusted down around both nostrils and both eyes were blue-black. His jaw was swollen and greenish on the left side. His long hair was filthy and matted, so dirty it was hard to tell what the true color was. His clothes were worn through and filthy. He held a lamp in both hands.

I closed my eyes in a slow blink and opened them to see the haggard stranger completing the motion. I tightened my grip on the lamp (he tightened), reared back (he reared back defensively), and swung. He swung as I did and our lamps met with a jolt. Traitor, traitor, *traitor!* The stranger broke into a hundred irregular fragments with the teeth-sliding-on-metal-file sound of shattering glass. I pushed the lamp away. It hit the wall where the mirror had been, bounced against the sink, and splashed into the open toilet bowl.

I grabbed Fred and left. As I passed the bathroom door pieces of mirror winked at me knowingly. Like unicorn hooves, I thought. My mouth tightened. I left the apartment.

From the tops of trashcans along the street I gathered metal boxes and cans, anything that had collected even a little rainwater. I poured their contents into a round metal cookie box and used it to wash the blood and dirt from my face and hands.

The remaining cloudy water I used to clean the dried blood from Fred. On the blade were fingerprints I hadn't noticed earlier. I wiped them off, face tight.

The streets were empty of life. The only sound was the wind whistling between the buildings.

I muttered to myself as I half-stumbled along the sidewalk like a bum speaking to invisible listeners, not caring, but wanting to cry. The mirror pieces whispered to me from up the block.

By nightfall I had meandered my way northwest of the Empire State Building, muttering to myself on the dark sidewalks, searching for food. The predatory scream of a huge bird froze me. I jumped back, flattening myself in shadow against a recessed doorway. A dark, massive shape lowered from the night sky, blotting out stars. I caught my breath. Wings beat with the sound of strong gusts flapping a huge flag. The shadow swooped down. It let forth another echoing scream. Molten eyes blurred past. I smelled hot brass. By the time I thought to look for a rider it had lifted again, heading off toward distant skyscraper peaks.

After a while I found I could breathe again, but my heartbeat stubbornly refused to slow. Ten minutes went by before I worked up the nerve to step onto the sidewalk again and scan the starry sky.

Nothing.

But it had left behind a prickly sensation that spread up my spine until it felt as though hairy tarantulas crept across the back of my neck. After several minutes of nervously looking at the distant, dark outlines of the cityscape, I began to walk. I found myself standing in front of an old Honda car and wondering what had happened to the time it had taken me to get there. I shook my head and opened the door, intending to crawl in and try to sleep. The odor that spewed forth chased me back. An all too familiar smell, thick and vaguely sweet: decay. A decomposed body was in the car.

I found a taxi, stopped forever in the midst of a right turn, and clambered into the back seat. I shut my eyes and sobbed silently until I fell asleep.

I woke up hungry. That was my first realization as I grew aware of my surroundings: God, I want something in my stomach. Anything. Grass. Cardboard. Yes, cardboard would be fine. My eyes were sore and heavy from crying the night before.

I emerged from the yellow and black taxi, carrying Fred blade side up in my left hand. My eyes watered in the sunlight and I turned my head and shrugged my shoulder, wiping my eyes on my sleeves.

Where to now?

I knew, of course. I looked at Fred, gripped the scabbard tighter, and headed southeast.

On the way I found a delivery truck parked on a back street. Shop-N-Go, it said on the side. The double doors at the back were padlocked. I broke into a garage and came out with a pair of bolt cutters.

The truck smelled stale inside. I paid no attention, wiping my mouth on my sleeve.

Lunch was Spam on crackers, cold Hormel chili, and a small can of chicken and noodles. I washed it down with canned orange juice and vomited it up in five minutes. I tried eating a little slower next time.

I felt better when I was finished. Taking one last sip of orange juice, I mournfully said goodbye to the truck and resumed my walk, feeling refreshed and determined.

The two-mile walk was a montage of absurd thoughts: We're committed now, Pete, old boy. Yeah, well. Shoulda been committed years ago. Ah, New York in the summer! The neon lights no longer shine bright, but God, is there magic in the air! My vision began to mist and I felt the burning of more tears brewing.

Walk. Time for that later. I felt the way a long-distance runner feels when he hits second wind. I was giddy, almost drunk. Exhilarated. Fuck it; I could take on the world. Having an objective, no matter how ill defined, was better than the helpless wandering, the wondering what to do next. I drew Fred, slashing a wide, neck-high arc, and let the motion continue to my right as I turned my wrist and brought the blade down in an overhead strike, "splitting the reed." I hacked at an invisible opponent's jugular, gutted the rider from crotch to throat, rolled the necromancer's head from his shoulders, and returned the blade to the scabbard without looking.

The raw scabs on my palms had opened up from the swordplay. I looked at the slowly pooling blood, thin and watery from pus.

A block away from the Empire State Building I saw five armed men. Their backs were to me as they peered around the corner of a brownstone building, looking at the skyscraper a few hundred yards away. I didn't bother to move quietly as I came up behind them. One noticed me and tapped a comrade on the shoulder. They turned to face me, hands going to swords. I kept my hands at my sides and cleared my throat. "Hello," I said. I nodded toward the Empire State Building. "You've got a friend of mine up there. I'm going to kill you." My heart raced at the sound of my own words, but I drew in a deep breath and resolved to go through with it. *If I do this right,* said the rational half, *I might get myself captured and end up where I started from.* Then again, I might get killed. If only for Ariel's sake, I didn't want that. I needed to fight incompetently, badly enough so that they would subdue me with only a little difficulty. The necromancer had said that all captured loners were to be brought to him. I must allow myself to be captured. I was flattering myself, I realized, by thinking that I was in any condition to dictate the events of a multiple opponent fight, but I felt resolved nonetheless. I walked forward and all five drew in response. None seemed to want to attack. I hawked and spat. What was their problem? I couldn't possibly have been an intimidating sight.

One man, black bearded, stepped forward, rapier firmly in hand. The others fanned out behind him, trying to form a semicircle around me with the building at my back, no place for me to run. Black Beard's eyes remained steadily on my sword. His was a straight, one-handed blade, lighter and faster than mine. Fred was sturdier and more powerful because of the two-handed grip. One strong engagement could snap the rapier. His eyes showed him weighing advantages and disadvantages.

Two of the others had successfully flanked me on my right side and the wall of the building was no more than four feet from my right shoulder as I faced Black Beard, left foot forward. Letting myself become enclosed had been stupid, but I'd had no choice. I hoped the necromancer's standing orders would make them cautious.

Rather than be rushed—or possibly stabbed—from my blind left side, as I knew I would be any second now, I turned so that my back was to the wall and stepped slowly toward Black Beard. The slight shift of his eyes away from me revealed what I'd been expecting: somebody coming from behind. I turned, and there he was, Scottish claymore at ready. I brought Fred up and sword met sword. He was open for a fraction of a second and I jabbed, intentionally slowing it. He backpedalled and deflected my blade. A blow to the back of my head sent me reeling. I'd expected that. I whirled around again, dazed. A voice in my head said, oh, good, they're not going to kill you, because they've had a few opportunities by now.

I saw the right hook heading for my chin. Reflex is almost impossible for a normal person to check; I blocked it without thinking. Then I dropped my arms and the next punch connected. My knees buckled. I was only stunned, but I fell to the curb. *I could have blocked it,* I thought with some satisfaction as I sank to the ground and lay there, motionless. *I could have.*

I kept my eyes closed, listening.

"I don't believe this."

"What the fuck is his problem?"

"I don't know. That was weird, Mac."

"Yeah."

Silence for a few seconds.

"Look, we can't just leave him here. If he talks, they'll know we're here, or at least suspect. They'll tighten up security, maybe send out more patrols."

"So what do we do?"

"Take him with us."

"You can't be serious."

A strong, gruff voice: "Mac, if we take him to Deecy and he gets away, we're finished."

"Not to Deecy. Just to the warehouse. You heard him—he's not one of them. He thinks we are."

Murmurs. The voice—Mac's, I assumed—continued. "Look, if he is with them we can do away with him any time. If he's not, he might be able to tell us something useful. And we can always use an extra man."

"We were only supposed to scout," said a dubious voice.

"And that means getting information," finished Mac. "Come on, give me a hand with him."

Strong arms lifted me. I tried to remain limp.

"This is bullshit, Mac. We were supposed to be back yesterday."

"You got a date? You saw what was going on yesterday. We would have been seen trying to get back. Something was up, I tell you. We can't chance leading them to Deecy."

"I still think this is risky."

"And coming to New York in the first place wasn't?"

After what must have been at least a dozen blocks of carrying me they stopped. I heard what sounded like a huge, rusty door opening, and was carried out of the light and into a cool space, where I was deposited on a cold concrete floor. I was startled by the sound of horses whinnying; I hoped no one saw me jump.

"You can get up now." Mac's voice reverberated in the large space. "We know you're awake."

I opened my eyes. We were in a large warehouse. Five horses were tied to support posts toward one wall. The garage-like aluminum door was open to let in the morning sunlight. One of the men turned and closed it, leaving the inside concrete-gray. Before me was Black Beard, rapier at his side. He must have been Mac. The rest of them clustered around him, watching me warily. I stood up, rubbing my chin. Goddam; another sore spot, another bruise.

"Who are you?" asked Mac.

"My sword."

He shook his head. "Who are you?"

"Give me my sword first," I insisted.

He smiled. "Give him his sword, Walt," he ordered. The lithe man with the Scottish claymore looked dubious. Mac looked around at him. "Go on," he prodded.

Walt produced Fred and tossed it to me. "Okay. My name's Pete Garey. Happy?"

Mac shook his head. "What are you doing in New York?"

"Wasting my time with you, right now. Look, I've got things I need to do. It's obvious you people aren't who I thought you were—"

"Who did you think we were?"

I said nothing.

"From the Empire State Building, maybe?" he prompted.

I lowered my guard a little. "All right, look. I've got a friend up there. They captured us and I got away. I want to get her out. Now please, just let me go."

He considered. "No, we can't. You might be saying this so you can get back to report. We can't allow that." He gripped the handle of his rapier meaningfully.

"I'm not lying. And I don't have time for a stand-off. She's dying and I've got to get her out of there."

"How do you know she's dying?"

His calmness infuriated me. "Because, you shit head, she's my Familiar; she's a unicorn; because I was with her and got away, and now I need to get back, because the longer I wait, the less her chances are—now get the fuck out of my way." I stepped forward. He didn't move. I drew Fred.

"What makes you think you'll do any better this time?" asked one of them.

"He let us take him," Mac said. "Didn't you? If you were captured, they might take you back up there. It figures." He frowned, folding his arms, and stepped out of my way. "No, let him go. Somebody wants to commit suicide, it's none of our business."

Walt glared at me. "Mac, we can't just let him go. Even if he's telling the truth he can tell them we were here, if they torture him."

Mac stared at me evenly. "He won't tell them. He doesn't know anything about us anyhow." He stepped back, turned away from me, and raised the warehouse door. "You can go if you want. But I think we can help you."

I didn't leave, of course. Not after an offer of help. They demanded I tell them who I was and how I came to be there, which was only fair. It took a while, though, and there was a long silence when I finished. Then they all began at once: You say you've met the griffin rider? You've *fought* with him? They took you to the necromancer? You've been up there, in the Empire State Building? You've seen the layout, the deployment of manpower, the locations of the big shots? How did you get down? How did you get *up?* Why'd you leave in the first place if your friend—this unicorn—was still there? I tried my best to answer them, but the questions came too fast; they seemed desperate to know a lot of tactical information about the building itself that I just didn't know.

Mac quieted them down. "Look," he said to me, "we don't mean to give you the third degree like this. But you know some things that are important to us. We're a scouting party sent over to look at the situation here—a recon team, if you like."

My eyebrows knitted. "I don't like. I don't know what the hell's going on."

"You've come in on the ground floor of a war, Pete, and you're a gold mine we could use. We think we can help you rescue your unicorn, if you'll go back with us to Deecy and tell what you know." He paused. "Are you with us?"

"I don't even know who 'us' is!"

He walked to the support posts and unhitched a dark bay horse. He led it to me and offered me the reins. For some reason—don't ask me to explain it because I don't know why—that decided me. "All right," I said evenly. "I'm with you."

He nodded. "Good. Walt, you're going to have to double up with Esteban. Pete will use your horse. He and I will ride ahead of you as fast as we can; we've got to get him to Deecy soonest."

Walt nodded. "Be careful getting out of here."

"Right." He began unhitching another horse. "Mount up, Pete."

"Now? We're leaving now?"

"You said you were in a hurry. We are, too. We were due back some time ago."

I stood there stupidly for ten seconds, then bit my lip, put a foot in the stirrup, and swung onto the saddle.

Mac gave last-minute instructions. "Take your time. We're the ones hurrying, not you. We'll try to go out the same way we came in; you try to do the same. Remember the vantage point they have and try to keep out of sight. There are four of you and three horses, so you won't be able to go fast if you run into trouble. Give us ten minutes and then get out of here."

"Yes, mother," said Walt. "We'll be sure to wear our rubbers, and if we fall down we won't get dirty."

"And if we break our legs," added Esteban, "we won't come running to you."

Mac flushed. "All right, all right. But I don't like splitting up."

"Neither do I," said one man whose name I never did learn. "But all of us booking outta here at the same time like something out of a John Wayne flick would be asking for trouble."

"Let's go, Pete."

The reins were tight in my hands. The saddle had a sling

at the side and I'd hung Fred there for easy draw. "Who's Deecy?"

"You mean where's Deecy."

I frowned, and then it hit me—I hadn't been listening right. I almost missed his next words: "Washington, D.C. That's where our army is."

nineteen

If Murphy's Law is taken into account, and plans are made accordingly, then things will run smoothly—and that will screw everything up.

—Tisdel's Constant

Too many things all at once. My mind reeled as I warily and joyfully accepted events and facts, hoping, wanting, desperate.

Events first. We rode our horses slowly along the sidewalks of New York City, speeding up little by little as we got farther away from the Empire State Building. Mac rode ahead of me. We didn't talk; the need for silence outweighed my need for information, or his. We headed south, then east. After half an hour we stopped and dismounted. Olive-drab and khaki-colored trash bags were piled high on a corner across the street. Most were split open, their contents splayed across the sidewalk, sometimes spilling over the curb and into the gutter. Dogs had been into them.

I looked uncertainly at Mac. He approached me, leading his horse by the reins. *"Qué pasa?"* I asked quietly.

"Nada." That elusive smile widened his black beard. "We're just stopping a few minutes to get our bearings. I want to sketch out for you just what we're trying to do. Our first priority is getting out of Manhattan unseen. That's not quite as easy as

it sounds; that skyscraper gives them one hell of a view. So far we've been sticking close to the sides of buildings and not rushing it, and that's good, but it's two hundred and thirty miles to Washington and we're going to have to take it easy—if we push the horses too hard they'll founder, and then where'll we be?"

I looked at my horse. He twitched his ear at a fly. I patted his flank. I had thought it might remind me of the feel of Ariel, but no. The horse's shape and feel seemed a rough mockery of the unicorn, as if an eight-year-old had molded the image of a man with Play-Doh and considered it a perfect likeness. Still, even having the comparison to work with troubled me. Stay troubled, I told myself. Stay mad. You'll need that later.

I realized Mac was looking at me carefully. "What?" I asked, thinking he'd asked something and was waiting for a reply.

"I didn't say anything." He mounted up and gestured for me to do likewise. I swung onto the saddle and saw that he was still watching me. "I've seen that look before," he finally said. He shook his head. "I don't ever want to be that hooked on something."

I looked away from him. "How are we getting out of Manhattan?" I asked lamely.

"Holland Tunnel."

"You're kidding."

He shrugged. "Could be worse."

"Could be raining," I finished. His face fell and I laughed. "I saw *Young Frankenstein* at least four times."

"That's Fronkensteen."

"Yeah, well—let's get this over with, shall we?"

His smile returned. "Yes, let's. 'Onward, ever onward, into the jaws of death,' and all that."

I mirrored his grin. "Rode the two," I completed. "Never liked Coleridge anyway."

"That's Byron."

"That's what I meant."

Leading the horses we threaded our way through traffic in the Holland Tunnel without incident, unless you count my echoing yelp when a rat skittered across my foot. We emerged squinting into the light at the tunnel's end. Mac blinked for a while, then said, "Well, let's trip the light fantastic."

"What?"

"Let's skedaddle, vamoose, split. Let's go." He swung onto his horse.

I remained where I was.

"Come on, Pete, we've got to get a move on."

"You got any food?" I blurted.

He leaned forward in his saddle, looking at me as if he'd never seen me before. "Any idiot could see you were pretty beat up, but I didn't notice you were so thin. When was the last time you ate?"

"This morning. I can't remember when the last time was before that. It blurs."

He frowned. "There's food and water in your saddlebag. Go easy on both or you'll puke your guts out."

I nodded, not telling him I had found that out for myself just this morning. I began untying the saddlebags with greedy fingers. He said nothing as I drew forth a tin of Spam spread (!), a small jar of Armour dried and salted meat, and a cellophane packet of hardbread slices. *Bread!* Oh, baby, it's been so long. . . .

"Canteen's slung right next to you," said Mac. "Eat and drink while we ride."

I wanted to argue, but he was right. I opened the tin of Spam, scooped out the contents with a finger, and spread it onto a slice of hardbread. Mac stopped me from discarding the empty tin on the road and made me fling it as far away as I could. I put another piece of bread on top, ate it, then made another sandwich of the dried meat and swung into the saddle, holding fast to my food and trying not to slobber all over myself.

We kicked our horses and trotted off. Hanging on and eating at the same time was tricky, and my stomach didn't like it much, but the food stayed down.

We followed the Jersey Turnpike toward D.C. The eerie stillness of the Newark Airport crept up on our right, drew abreast, and slid silently away. Quiet jets rested idly on runways, poked curious long noses into repair hangars. Along the end of one runway, and continuing for blocks past the neighborhood proper, was a great deal of wreckage. Gnarled, twisted metal, plastic melted shapeless, burned bits and pieces fanned out, scattered over an area of a few square miles. The only section recognizable as once having been an aircraft was the rear of the fuselage and the truncated wedge of tail, lying smoke-blackened three-fourths of the way from the end of the runway. Beyond that, thirty yards of airport barrier fence was missing, torn by hurtling metal. Parts of the wreck gleamed in the sun, winking to us as we hurried past.

It must have just left the ground, I thought. Point of no return, four-thirty in the afternoon, plane lifting off right on schedule—and the Change occurred. How did the pilot feel, I wondered, when he saw the horizon drop satisfyingly below him, then rush upward again, too fast, filling his windshield with the irrefutable knowledge that he was about to die.

Mac's face was grim as he trotted up the circular ramp and headed in a more southerly direction where the Jersey Turnpike and I-95 became one and the same. We thudded along the left side of the six-lane highway, a constant line of cars gliding past. It's been a long time since I've moved this fast, I thought.

I wearily hitched my horse to a guard rail for our first night's camp, regarding it with a mixture of appreciation and wariness—call it cautious respect. "Horses always made me nervous," I said. My ass and the insides of my thighs would never be the same.

"Good beasts. Need 'em, nowadays." The grayness of his eyes was striking, and I found myself surprised I hadn't noticed it before. I blinked. It seemed to me then that his face was old, much older than he probably was. Black beard aside, there was a grizzled, weathered look to him. His shaggy head belonged on a big man, yet he himself was of medium build.

"Tell me about Washington," I said as we tried to get a fire going. "What's there? Is there really an army? And why? Who's fighting for what?"

His dark eyebrows crept closer together. "All right, all right. They're going to pump you dry when we get there; it's only fair you know what you're walking into." He took a deep breath and let it out, considering. "Well. It was, shall we say, a bit of an overstatement to call us an army, exactly—"

"You were bragging."

"Exaggerating. Don't quibble." He ran fingers through his beard. "We began—they began, actually; I wasn't there at the start—as a sort of artist's colony, a group of people who wanted to pool together to use their creative talents and resources in the aftermath of the Change. They began with around a dozen people. The idea was to do whatever you wanted, they didn't care, as long as you contributed something to help the group survive."

"Sounds like a commune."

He pursed his lips. "Sort of. If you've got the stereotypical image of organic types 'finding themselves,' no, it wasn't. But if by 'commune' you mean a collection of individuals working for the group—a community—then yes. They eventually established themselves outside the city as a small farming community. It began to work. Word got around that there was this group who didn't have to worry about where the next meal was coming from, who had learned to get by without being parasites, and more and more people trickled in to join them." He paused. "You know, most people are like mushrooms now, living off the rotting remains of this big dead tree." He waved toward the buildings across the street. "Pretty soon they had seventy or eighty people, all trying to help one another out."

"You sound like a commercial."

He shrugged. "What can I say? They were idealists. The world had gone crazy and they wanted to pull good people together so they could make it. They had a good thing and it worked. But—ah, yes, the inevitable but—there was this other group, see? A large group of loners—I know that sounds contradictory, but that's what they were—began forming in New York. They started out, in principle, the way our group did—pool together, to scavenge food, not to raise it. Pretty shortsighted of them."

"The city's running out of food."

"Yes. That's something we learned by scouting. Their main priority seems to be gathering food. Between them using it up but never replacing it and the other loners in the city bleeding off the rest, they couldn't have lasted long. But then they got the necromancer to get the trains running on time, so to speak."

"Who is he?" I asked. "What was he before the Change? Why has he organized an army?"

Mac turned his palms up. "I don't know. I'd lay odds he's somebody who was nobody before the Change, and now he's got his chance to get even. A little knowledge, you know? As to his 'army,' I'd say it was closer to the Mafia than the military. One of the things the necromancer did to 'improve' the organization was to do what any don would have done—he looked for strong-arms. He offered them bribes, spells, Familiars—"

"The griffin rider."

"Uh-huh. One day, not long after I'd joined up with our group, something happened. I was out in the field with friends and we were trying to figure out a way to build an efficient rainstill. Somebody pointed out something in the sky, a dark spot that looked like it had huge wings. It was headed our way."

"Let me guess."

"He landed right in front of us. He said he was from New York and he wanted food." He snorted. "Hell, we told him he was welcome to share some. We'd even feed his griffin, if we had anything it could eat." Mac put his hands in the front pockets of his jeans and balled them up. "He stayed on his griffin and shook his head. 'You don't understand,' he told us. 'I want all the food you have, and I want it by tomorrow.' We tried telling him we needed what food we had, that we had just about enough to feed all of us plus a little extra that he was welcome to." Mac looked at the ground, talking more to himself, it seemed, than to me. "He just laughed at us. Told us we had to give him all the food we had, once a month, and that it had better be enough. And then he said something to the griffin and it stepped forward and slashed with one of its claws." He shook his head. "It cut a man into three pieces. He fell apart—there was blood everywhere—and we just stood there. It slashed again and I barely jumped out of the way. It got the woman beside me." He broke off and raised his head suddenly. His gray eyes were bright. "He told us to have the food ready by tomorrow, and then he flew off. We held a conference and decided to pack up and move first thing next morning. Some people didn't want anything to do with the whole mess and left the group entirely, heading off in small groups, pairs, going loner, whatever. Most of us stayed, though, and we moved to D.C."

"Why Washington? You couldn't farm—you'd have to scavenge."

"We aren't interested in being agricultural at the moment." He pulled his hands from his pockets and held them at his sides. "We've only been there a few months. We don't plan on being there much longer. We're going to have it out with Our Gang in New York."

"That's why you were sent to scout?"

He nodded. "A bit Tolkien-ish, isn't it? Washington going to war with New York. A lot of us wanted to just move on, either south or west. We could be farmers anywhere. But we decided against it—principles, and all that. Who knows how big their outfit would be in another year, two years, if they were left alone? Maybe we'd be farming in Grand Shebongle, Kansas, or someplace, and one day we'd end up with this griffin guy again, demanding food, selling protection, who knows? So we've been banging strategies about for a few months, getting our shit together, and we were a scouting team for last-minute developments. We're about as ready as we'll ever be in D.C."

"Yes, but are you ready?"

He shrugged. "Only one way to find out. I was worried while we were scouting that they were onto us, somehow. Over the past few weeks they've increased their activities. We thought they might be readying an assault on *us*—one of the reasons our team was sent. We'd been in New York a week when we came across you, Pete. Until then we didn't know what to make of it. They were sending out armed scouting parties and the rider was on the wing, but the organization around the Empire State Building was as lax as ever. They definitely weren't preparing for a full-scale assault."

"That was something I noticed," I said. "Hardly any door guards, not a lot of discipline. I'd hesitate to call them an army, exactly; I never should have made it out of there."

His smile was wry. "That's one of the points in our favor. Because of the necromancer, the rider and the griffin, the fact that they occupy the Empire State Building—big deal—they're convinced they're the most powerful group around. Whether or not it's true, it's made them careless. I don't think it's that they think they can withstand an assault; I don't think they've considered the possibility that they might be assaulted. They seem convinced they're the only organized group around."

"Then why the increased activity?"

The wry smile remained. "Haven't you guessed? It's you. They were after you—you and your unicorn."

"Oh." I felt stupid. (Later, Ariel, I promise you. I need these people's help.) "How are you going to deal with the necromancer?"

The smile disappeared. "We're sort of going to have to ad lib in that department," he said lamely. "There's too much we don't know about him—which is why you're being carted to D.C. You've seen him, talked with him, been in his castle, so to speak. No one in Washington has ever seen him. At least," he added thoughtfully, "no one who ever returned to tell us about it. Some of our scouts didn't come back. So I think you'll be able to help us out quite a bit."

I shrugged, one corner of my mouth drawing in. "I'll tell you what I saw. I don't know how helpful it'll be."

"You're a gold mine, Pete, believe me. We didn't even know where in the Empire State Building he was until you told us." He bent over, touched his toes with knees straight, straightened up, bent backward a little, and righted himself. "We'd better get some sleep. We start early tomorrow."

"One question," I said.

His eyebrows lifted.

"How many of you are there in D.C.?"

"Counting men, women, and children, about four hundred. The kids won't do any fighting, of course, and some of us will have to stay behind with them. Subtract ten or twenty sick, injured, or elderly, and we'll have a little over three hundred people in the assault."

Three more days we thudded along the highway, riding, resting, riding again. My saddle sores felt as bad as my feet had not two weeks ago. I gritted my teeth a lot. We parallelled I-95 on U.S. 40 and avoided Baltimore by swinging around on State Road 151. From there it was almost due south on the Baltimore-Washington Parkway, straight into D.C.

It was night by the time we entered the city. Mac led on unflaggingly, leaning forward in his saddle as if it would make his tired horse move faster. Our mounts' hooves echoed tumultuously in the dark, silent city, and soon pieces of a dead and fading national culture were gliding past, dim white shapes that marked the grave of a nation. To our right, the Capitol building slowly wheeled by as we clopped along the circular street strewn with dark, dead cars.

We turned left onto Independence Avenue.

What do any of the monuments mean now? I thought.

A straight mile along Independence, made slow by the permanent traffic jam, a few turns, and we stopped before what was one of the few famous buildings in Washington that wasn't white. Few people were in sight around the brick building. Pale yellow candleglow shone through five or six somber windows. People were startled when they heard us trotting up;

some ran inside and emerged immediately with weapons in hand. We reined up before them, our horses sweat-slick and breathing hard.

"Hold on, hold on, don't get trigger happy," said Mac. His voice was dimmed by the pounding in my ears. "It's Vic Magruder of the scouting party, and a friend."

One of them lowered the mace he'd held ready and stepped forward, peering at us. "Mac!" he whooped, and dropped the mace entirely. "Christ, we figured you guys weren't coming back."

Mac grinned and dismounted. After a moment's hesitation I followed suit—slowly, favoring the blisters. The big man continued walking toward Mac until they were shaking hands, and the handshake quickly slid into a friendly hug. While they exchanged bear hugs and insults the rest of the dozen or so people around us looked on with a blend of wonder, admiration, and disbelief. Some gazed at me speculatively. More people appeared from the huge entranceway; word was getting around.

Mac and his friend turned to face me, arms around each other like reunited brothers, both smiling idiotically. "Tom," said Mac, "this is Pete. We found him in New York. I think you'll want to hear what he has to tell us. Pete, meet Tom Pert, self-appointed head of operations here."

He disengaged himself from Mac and extended his hand. I stepped forward.

"Pete!"

I turned at the yell and glimpsed long brown hair streaming behind a woman as she charged down the steps of the Smithsonian Institution, and suddenly I had a double armful of Shaughnessy, crying and laughing at the same time.

twenty

Sebastian: *Now I will believe*
That there are unicorns.

—Shakespeare,
The Tempest

Things got sorted out eventually.

Shaughnessy had got there the morning before. She caught me up, following the confusion of our unexpected arrival. Her story spilled out in a run-on stream. "The *Lady Woof* drifted out a little," she told me. "I was afraid they'd come after me again, but when they were sure they had you and Ariel—" She broke off. "Where is she, Pete? What's happened to her?" She searched my beat-up face, my eyes, looking for something.

"They still have her." I tried to keep my voice steady. "If I can't get her out of there soon, she'll die."

"Ah. . . ." She bit her lower lip. "They might be able to help you here, Pete. They're—"

"Going to war with New York. Yeah, I know. Mac told me already. He's part of a scouting team they sent in. I—I got away and came across them. I guess I ought to count my blessings; I don't know what I'd have done if I hadn't found them."

She nodded. "They told me there was a chance you might,

if you escaped, but I don't think any of them believed it. I kept my fingers crossed."

"So get on with what happened."

"Well, I waited an hour on the *Lady* and then swam ashore. She'd only drifted a couple hundred yards." She frowned. "I tried to bring your backpack with me but it was too heavy. Everything got soaked. I'm afraid I had to let it go."

"That's okay. There wasn't anything in it I can't replace. Thanks for trying."

She brightened. "I did manage to save your blowgun, though. I'll give it to you later; it's in my room. Anyway, I hid in a looted jewelry store all night, all next day I tried to find you. I walked around almost all day, but there was no sign of anyone."

"You were lucky."

"So I've been told. Toward the end of the day, though, I ran into Drew Zenoz. He'd just been sent as a scout from here and had found out their increased activity was because of you and Ariel. And because of Malachi. I told him who I was, and about you and Ariel. I wouldn't have thought he'd believe me, but he knew all about it. He'd been told to be on the lookout for you, and to get you to come back here with him if he saw you."

"He knew about us?" I was confused. I had images of this legend of a Boy and His Unicorn working its way north by word of mouth. Bullshit.

Shaughnessy nodded. "I came back with him and told what I knew about you and Ariel to Tom Pert, but he'd already heard."

"But how did—"

She anticipated the question. "About a week ago—" Her eyes went wide. I turned, automatically reaching for Fred. I barely saw a metallic blur, and before I could think I drew Fred and blocked the slash aimed at my head. The sword lowered and its wielder laughed.

I exploded. "You shit head!" I raised my sword. "You think that was funny, then try—*Malachi!*"

And, for then at least, it seemed everything would be all right.

I fidgeted in a lecture room within the Smithsonian. Mac had already made his report to Tom Pert and it was being reiterated before the hastily assembled group. Most of the army/

commune/whatever was in the room, listening quietly. Mac had been right; there were about four hundred of them. I hadn't seen such a large assembly since before the Change. A baby's wail was punctuated by its mother's shushings. Most everybody looked as if they had been rudely awakened—as, no doubt, they had.

I looked down at my fingers. The wood of the straight-backed chair I sat in pressed against my aching back. Mac's report went on; I heard but didn't listen. I glanced at Malachi Lee, who sat to my right. He wore a dark blue jumpsuit and carried *Kaishaku-nin*. He was the only person I saw who was armed, excepting Mac and myself, who had had neither time nor opportunity to remove our weapons. Not that I'd have wanted to.

Old home week had been short lived. There were things that needed doing; these people were readying what was by present standards a large-scale assault and they needed any and all information as soon as it arrived. Even if it meant being roughly shaken awake at two in the morning. Tom Pert had wanted to talk to me, so Shaughnessy had broken off with a promise to provide a more detailed account at her first opportunity. I twisted my neck and saw her sitting four rows back on the left side. She'd found a T-shirt somewhere with an iron-on transfer of a unicorn on it. When she saw me she smiled, waved, and pointed to it. The gesture turned into a heartening thumbs-up. I smiled tiredly and nodded.

"The rest of the party will probably be here tomorrow afternoon at the latest," Mac was saying. "I don't know what the target date for leaving for New York is—"

"Four days from now," supplied Tom Pert.

Mac nodded and continued: "—but I figured it was worth the risk of splitting up with the rest in order to get Pete here as soon as I could. Hell, for all I knew I was going to run into you guys on the road, headed my way." A few chuckles. "Most of you know the rest." He stopped. He looked tired. "Questions?"

Tom Pert stood. "It can wait, Mac. We'll shove bamboo shoots under your nails tomorrow. And thanks."

"You'll get my bill."

Tom smiled and began talking to the assembly. I barely heard. My mind was on "record," taking it all down for later.

I became aware of an expectant silence in the lecture room.

I looked up sharply. Tom Pert smiled gently at me. "You're on, Pete," he whispered.

I nodded, not understanding. Numbly stood. Stepped forward. Turned around. Panorama of waiting strangers. Mute glance: Malachi Lee, straight backed, one hand on his sword, face blank. Mac leaning forward, elbows on knees, eyes expectant. I opened my mouth to speak. Something blocked it. I cleared my throat, swallowed, and tried again "I—" There was Shaughnessy, hands gripping the back of the chair in front of her. "I met Ariel . . . a long time ago." Puzzled looks on the faces of strangers. "She . . . her luh, leg was broken."

"Pete." Tom Pert, *sotto voce*. "You can just tell us what you saw in New York. Malachi's told us the rest."

I shut my eyes. "Her leg was broken! I went to a house and found some wood to make a spuh, splint!" Curious stares. Shaughnessy biting her lower lip, tears blearing her eyes. "I taught her how to speak English. We used to just walk on the roads together, and, and—" The last word heaved out in a great convulsion of my lungs. My eyes burned as everything misted over. Strong hands gripped me as I sobbed, led me down the aisle. My nose dripped on somebody and I wanted to stop, to apologize for getting snot all over them, but I couldn't stop, I could only blubber. I pushed my tongue at the back of my mouth to clear my nose but it was too clogged. My bottom lip quivered. Oh, this is great, this is wonderful, right in front of everybody, Shaughnessy, Malachi Lee. . . . I stumbled and the hands gripped harder, steadying, guiding. "It's all right," said a voice. "He's exhausted, is all. He's been through a lot."

"The fuck you know," I tried to say, but more snot dripped on my forearm. They led me out of the room, through hallways, and finally left me alone in a quiet room. The glow of a single candle refracted through a film of salt tears. Left to myself, I sobbed into the pillow for another minute, and then it cut off. It figured: nobody was around now.

I didn't hear the door open but felt the small breath of air it made when it moved, disturbing the candle.

"Pete?" And Shaughnessy was kneeling beside me, trying to hold me, to stroke my hair, wet at the temples where tears had streaked as I lay on my back. I twisted away from her, cheek muscles tightening, mouth drawing in.

"Pete, it's okay. It's—"

"It is not okay!" I sat up and looked at her through leaden

eyes. "That's easy for you to say because I'm here with you, but that doesn't mean a fucking thing to me. You *followed* me up here. I don't give a damn about you. What I want is in New York, and I'd die to get her back. Don't take it on yourself to replace her, because you don't hold a candle, bitch." I drew a deep, shuddering breath. "Now why don't you just leave me the fuck alone?"

She looked at the steady burning of the white candle in its pewter holder. I wanted her to react, to become enraged, or cry, or anything. But there was only a sad, wistful look on her face, in the brown eyes catching the candle glow in twin points of light, cat-like. "All right," she said softly. "If that's what you want."

"That's what I want."

She blinked. Stood. Turned. Reached. Pulled open the door. All measured, precise.

"Bitch," I added before the door closed softly, punctuated by an understated click as the spring-loaded catch slipped into place.

I turned back to my pillow and cried again.

A knock on the door awakened me next morning. I automatically reached for Fred and was mildy surprised when my fingers clasped the twined handle—somebody had thoughtfully placed my sword by the head of the folding cot. A Malachi Lee touch. The thought elicited a small smile.

A second, softer knock.

"Come in." My tone made it a question.

I'd expected Shaughnessy. Instead, the door opened and a large, red-faced woman came in, pushing a silver tea service. "Room service," she said brightly. Her bright floral summer dress was two shades short of gaudy, but would nevertheless mark her as a tourist almost anywhere she went. Or would have, I should say, before the Change. She stopped the tea service beside the folding cot, where I had propped myself up on one arm. "I'm sorry if I woke you," she said, "but we let you sleep as late as we could."

"What time is it?"

"Just after one." Her face worked itself into a distasteful look. "You can put that thing away. I'm not here to assassinate you."

I felt sheepish. "Oh, look, I—" I returned Fred to its original position against the wall. "Force of habit," I offered in explanation.

"Mmph." She turned and poured steaming water from the sterling silver pitcher into a cup. "Coffee or tea?"

"Excuse me?"

"I said, do you want coffee or tea?"

"Umm—" I wiped my mouth with one hand. "Coffee. Please. Black." She obliged by stirring in a spoonful of instant. I accepted the cup gratefully, blowing on the dark brown liquid at the edge and slurping in loud sips. Its warmth spread through my insides. I paused just long enough to notice her waiting patiently and politely for me to finish. Feeling rude, I raised my cup. "Have some?" I asked, and thought, damn, that sounds awkward! Social nuances were a thing of the past for me; I'd forgotten most of them. But she shook her head. "No, I had more than my share last night. We were all up pretty late talking about you. Mac thinks you can help us."

"What do you think?"

"Like the silver? Thomas Jefferson used it."

I set the cup back onto the stand, three-quarters finished. "You don't trust me," I said, "because Mac found me in New York."

"We've learned not to get our hopes up, that's all." She held one arm at her side, clasped the bicep with her other hand, and walked around the room. I remained quiet, noticing the room for the first time. It had a business desk which had been shoved against the wall by the head of the cot. Sunlight from the window behind it illuminated orange carpeting and mostly empty space. Beside the cot was a small stand, Early American, on which rested the remains of the candle that had melted down to a small puddle of wax during the night. It was an administrative office they'd cleared out. I wondered if they all slept in emptied offices, and decided they didn't. There probably weren't enough to accommodate four hundred-plus people. But the Smithsonian had lots of space, and plenty of rooms full of now useless memorabilia which could stand being removed—or at least pushed into corners.

The woman turned to face me. "We've spent a lot of time and planning to move against New York. Some of our people have been killed trying to get information to help us, and now you pop up at the last minute, poof! A whiz kid with all the answers—"

"I don't have all the answers."

"But you can still see why a lot of us think it's too good to be true."

I said nothing.

"Do you feel good enough to walk?"

"Sure—" I stopped. "Do I look that bad?"

I saw her looking for a mild way to put it. "Never mind. I don't think I want to know. Yeah, I can walk fine. I hurt, but I probably look worse than I feel."

She smiled. "I sure hope so . . . because you look *terrible*."

I stood suddenly. It hurt a lot. "Okay, where to, coach?"

"Rubber hoses and bright lights, I'm afraid." She saw my blank look. "Our council of war, so to speak. They want to turn you inside out."

"Figured they would, after I blew it last night."

Her look softened. "I guess that was understandable." She opened the door and gestured to the hallway outside.

"Well. 'Lay on, Macduff.'" I followed her through hallways and huge rooms packed with fragments of American history. The few people we met nodded politely—and curiously—toward me, but shot her wide grins and, without exception, a cheerful, "Hi, Mom!"

"What's with the 'Mom' bit?" I asked after the third person had greeted her this way.

"Oh, I'm sorry," she said, still hurrying her bulk through the maze of hallways. "My name's Maureen Redbone, but everyone here just calls me Mom. Come on, they're waiting."

"Right, Mom." It sounded funny. I hadn't called anybody that since. . . . I suppressed the memory. That's gone now, I thought. A different life. I tagged along behind Momma Redbone.

A huge pendulum swung before me. It was a top-shaped weight attached to a long cord which disappeared up into the high ceiling. It swung leisurely like God's Own Planchette between bright orange highway safety cones arrayed in a twenty-foot circle. Some of the cones had been knocked onto their sides.

"They tell me the earth's rotation keeps it swinging back and forth," Mom told me as we passed it. "It's supposedly been swinging like this for years and years. I always liked to think the nightwatchmen at this place used to stop it at closing time and then give it a push to get it going again before they left."

I laughed, shaking my head slowly. I didn't get it—this thing was proof that *some* of the laws of physics still applied. In fact, so was the fact that objects fell down when I let them go. How could the Change have been so selective?

Beyond the pendulum, looking as absurdly out of place as the spaceship in the living room toward the end of *2001: A Space Odyssey,* was a locomotive. It looked too huge, larger than life in its dark contours. I wondered if it really was oversized or if being indoors just made it appear so. In front of it stood Malachi, Tom Pert, and Mac. Malachi had his sword with him—of course. I felt somewhat reassured; I'd brought Fred.

Mom cleared her throat. "Here you go," she said, voice reverberating in the huge room. "'Neither rain, nor snow, nor sleet, nor gloom of night...'"

All three men smiled. "Thanks, Mom," said Tom.

"No trouble a'tall." I had to suppress a smile—this woman ought to bake gingerbread cookies for a living and give them out to little kids. She squeezed my shoulder. "Just go easy on him. He's not as tip top as he'd like us to believe."

I wanted to say aw, shucks. Mom did that to you.

"We'll be gentle," said Mac.

Mom "hmmph"ed and left us. "Neat lady," I said when she had passed the pendulum and was out of hearing range.

"Yes," said Tom. "Her husband was killed by the griffin at our farming community. Mac says he told you about it."

I nodded. There was an uncomfortable pause. "I, uh, I'm sorry about last night."

He waved his big hand. "Don't be. We've all been under a lot of pressure these past few weeks."

"Let's get this over with, Pete," said Malachi. "We've got to rake you over the coals."

My smile was mirthless. "Rake away."

Tom let out a long breath and began. "Between Malachi, Mac, and the young lady—Shaughnessy—we know enough about you to save you a lot of story telling. What we need from you is what happened between the time you set foot in New York and the time you found Mac."

I told them, in as much detail as I could, what had happened, trying not to embellish but to remember exactly what I'd seen.

They listened without interruption. When I finished Tom offered me a drink of water from a dark brown canteen set behind him on the sideboard of the locomotive. I accepted gratefully. "Anything else?" I asked, wiping water from my mouth with the back of my hand.

"Tons," said Tom.

And *then* the interrogation started: Where was the necromancer, exactly? At the top? What floor? Where on the eighty-fifth floor? Could you draw us a map? Could you show us the route you took from the eighty-sixth floor observatory deck to the necromancer's room? Could I draw them a map of the observation deck—the eighty-sixth floor, which I'd landed on atop Shai-tan. What about the strength of their group? Why a thousand? Why not more, or less? Supplies—what sort of arms did you see? How is their food supply holding up in the city—you mentioned their difficulties with loners working away at what they needed to scavenge. How about division of their manpower?

They digested my responses for a few minutes, and then Tom folded his bowling-pin-sized arms and said, "Go over your escape again, Pete. Maybe there's something there. As you said, you shouldn't have got away."

I went over it again, trying not to seem testy. "I don't know if that's any more help," I added after I'd finished. "I still think I got away because they're not well organized and didn't have the manpower to effectively cover something the size of the Empire State Building, as I said before. That, and I was descending, which made it a little easier—for me. I'd say it would be difficult to damn near impossible for us to fight our way *up* elevator shafts and stairwells. They almost killed me by just tossing bricks down the shafts. Having three hundred people's not going to help; it'd be like shooting fish in a bucket."

We were interrupted by the hollow echo of running feet. The poundings seemed to underscore the Smithsonian as the dead museum it was. He was about my age, I noted as he stopped before us, breathless. "Sorry to interrupt," he panted, "but the rest of Mac's scouting party is back—what's left of it."

"What? What happened?"

"They were ambushed. Walt came in with Esteban tied to the horse in front of him. He's been wounded pretty bad. Walt's okay but he can barely talk, he's so exhausted."

"What about the others?" demanded Mac.

The kid—funny I thought of him as a kid, despite the fact that he was about my age—tightened his mouth and turned palms up helplessly. "Walt says it happened about thirty miles north of here. Everyone else was killed."

"Were they followed?" Tom wanted to know.

"Walt's pretty sure they weren't."

He stopped, thinking. "Send out six people, and make sure they all have bows. Have them retrace Walt's route for twenty miles. Tell them to shoot anything that looks like a scouting party heading for New York. Have them report back to me immediately when they return. And make sure Esteban's getting whatever help we can give him."

"Doc Mundy's working on him now."

"How bad is it?"

"He took an arrow in the chest—Doc says he'll do what he can."

"All right."

I pictured a doctor working frantically and swearing because medicine was nearly a frontier practice again—only hand-powered instruments, a shortage of drugs, no anesthesia save alcohol or ether.

Tom looked thoughtful while the messenger bit his lip and eyed me openly. I stared back, blank-faced.

"Tell Walt I'll see him soon," said Tom.

"Right." He nodded importantly, turned, and trotted away, leaving behind the echoes of his running and one last speculative glance at me. Tom watched him go, then turned back to us. "Christ, I hope they weren't followed. All right, then, gentlemen, we've got to step things up. Unless we can think of a practical way to reach the top, I'm afraid we're going to have to stick to the only plan we've got: fight it out floor by floor, all the way up."

Malachi and Mac said nothing, but I knew what they were thinking: it's literally uphill all the way—and at more than three to one odds. We'll be slaughtered.

"Well, obviously we can't use their methods," said Mac. "Pete, you're sure the griffin was their only way up and down?"

I shrugged. "I didn't see anything else. You could go down easily enough by walking down the stairs, but I didn't see another way up besides Shai-tan. I can't think of anything else that might work, except a hot-air balloon, which would be just plain—wait a minute! You could hang glide!"

They were already shaking their heads. Their expressions were a mix of despair and urgency. "We talked about it," said Tom. "It won't work."

"Why not?"

"Because the only point in Manhattan higher than the Empire State Building is the World Trade Center."

"Right! You could—"

"Let me finish. The World Trade Center is three and a half miles south of the Empire State Building. If you jumped off the top *you'd be descending all the way*. Oh, you'd probably make it to the Empire State Building—but at best you'd only be halfway up."

"But that still cuts your climbing time in half," I protested. "Plus it gets rid of about eight hundred enemy soldiers below you."

Tom shook his head. "Still no good, Pete, believe me. I've done it a few times. Hang gliders are maneuverable, but they can't dodge arrows—and three hundred people in the air aren't going to take anybody by surprise, no matter how unorganized they might be. And there's nothing to land on halfway up. The sides of the buildings are too smooth. The windows are too small to afford entrance. A small force might work because it might retain the element of surprise—but only if it could come in from above. That means landing where you did—the eighty-sixth floor."

"But—" I shut up, frustrated. He was right.

"Then it's uphill all the way," said Mac.

"Back to square one," said Tom. "No worse off than before." He stood from where he'd been leaning against the locomotive. "Okay, we've all got things to do. I need to see Walt and Esteban. We'll meet here at noon tomorrow and see if any of us has anything new to kick around. Pete, be thinking about your experiences in New York. Maybe you'll think of something else that may help us. As it is you've given us a lot of information we needed."

We broke up and I left with Malachi Lee.

"I guess we have some catching up to do," I said. We sat on the front steps of the Smithsonian. Fred lay across my thighs. I'd found some duct tape in a maintenance closet and was wrapping the wide, strong, gray stuff around the end of Fred's black scabbard where it had cracked.

White plastic spoon in hand, Malachi scooped beef stroganoff from the paper plate on his palm, pushed it automatically into his mouth. We'd found the food piled in the East Storage Wing. Malachi said they were freeze-dried emergency rations retrieved from underground bomb shelters beneath the government buildings. Tom Pert had led the foraging parties that had stockpiled the preserved foods.

I chewed a bland spoonful from my own plate, waiting for him to reply. When he didn't, I washed it down with warm Tang from a styrofoam cup and tried again. "Of course, you already know most of what happened to me."

He finally looked at me as if just realizing I was there. "What happened to your sword?"

I felt guilty. "I fell down an elevator shaft in the Empire State Building. The scabbard cracked. This is the first chance I've had to repair it." I pulled more tape from the roll. As a saving grace, and because I felt foolish, I added, "The blade's in good shape, though."

"Let's see it." I tried to think his eyes weren't accusing. His gift of that sword had been a trust. I pulled the blade out smoothly and held it vertically, edge toward me. He took it from me and lay the backside of the blade across his blue-clad left shoulder. He bent his face closer, closed one eye, and sighted down the edge. "Mmm."

Now what the hell did that mean?

He straightened, nodding. Favorably, it seemed. I hoped. "Still straight. A few nicks, but a blade's the better for those." He smiled ruefully. "If you're alive then they were well-earned."

I started to reach for it. He shook his head. "You've tried to clean it but there's still the trace of blood—it smears the tempering pattern. Go ahead and finish fixing your scabbard," he said, not taking his eyes from the slightly dull mirror-metal. "I'll clean your sword." He frowned. "Needs sharpening, too."

His backpack leaned beside him on the dark old steps. He reached into it and began removing things: a black silk rag; two small, milky plastic, thin-nozzled bottles, one with liquid the color of motor oil, the other clear. Both were half-full. He moved my sword gently onto one knee and turned it to one side, blade toward him. The dark twined handle lay in the corner formed where right leg met hip. He squeezed fluid onto the silk rag and began rubbing it onto the blade slowly and methodically. I finished taping the scabbard.

"The night Faust and I left Atlanta," said Malachi abruptly, "there was a wind. I never saw anything like it. It seemed confined to a very small area. Faust kept growling and howling. I kept an eye on him. He kept turning, sniffing the air. He looked as if he wanted to attack something but didn't know where it was. I felt something searching, but I couldn't tell what it was or who it searched for. And then it was gone, as fast as it had come. It headed south; I could see it bending the trees as it went.

"Faust and I kept walking until two in the morning. I slept beneath a tree." He paused. His rubbing ceased. "Faust would always bark when the sun came up. I still don't know why. Some dogs bark at thunder or lightning; he barked at the sunrise." The rubbing resumed. "He was my alarm clock the entire trip. I'd make camp at one a.m. and get up at sunrise. We hunted along the way. Faust ate rabbits." The black silk was now three-quarters of the way to the tip of the blade. "I thought you'd follow me."

I watched him cleaning the blade, fascinated by the deft movements of his hands, the patience exhibited as he worked one small area and moved on to the next. I blinked, realizing he'd been talking and I'd tuned him out.

"—didn't want to, because a horse would have been too noisy, too conspicuous. Hard to find, hard to feed, hard to get rid of in a hurry. And it would have been hard for Faust to keep up that kind of pace." The rubbing paused once more. "Saw dragon fire in Tennessee and went across some scorched ground. Saw a roc once, in the late afternoon, but it was flying away."

Roc: picture that prehistoric flying reptile, the pterodactyl. Now picture it twenty times bigger and add a taste for fresh meat—whole cows, for instance. You've got it.

"The only incident we had was in Alexandria." I remembered the aftermath of the swordfight which Shaughnessy, Ariel, and I had come across in Alexandria and knew what was coming next. "I got caught sleeping. I usually looked back every few minutes to make sure nothing was headed up the road toward us. I hadn't looked in at least ten minutes. Too much faith in Faust's nose. But they were upwind, and by the time I looked back and saw them they were too close for me to make myself scarce without raising eyebrows. It was all open road, anyhow, and no place to hide—no exit coming up I could pretend to take, just the highway and more streets off of that. I had to let them come up on me. When they were close enough Faust started growling. I hushed him up. I turned around about the time I knew I had to, and there they were. There were four of them, all armed, of course. Their weapons were out and there wasn't going to be any bullshitting; they didn't want to stop and palaver. There was a man with a double-bladed axe, one with a cutlass, another with a rapier, and one with a katana. I drew. Faust crouched down low." He began rubbing the blade with the clear fluid from the other bottle. The smeared look he'd given the entire blade began to glisten where he rubbed. "They never said a word. The one with the rapier brought his arm back for a side strike. It was meant to distract me; he was too far away to touch me. The one with the axe swung, hoping I'd shift my eyes, maybe my blade. I crossblocked. I cut through his handle, reversed direction, and took him off at the shoulders.

"Faust got to the one with the cutlass as he lunged for me. Faust went for his throat; I saw what was coming and didn't have time to stop it. He just kept his blade straight and Faust speared himself. I got to him just as Faust was sinking his teeth into his throat. I came down and cut his arm off, but it was too late. I turned and met the thrust of the one with the rapier—the fall of his axe-carrying friend's body had cut him off from me and he'd stumbled over him. I barely caught the thrust—it nicked my arm—and sliced him across the belly. His guts fell out and he landed on them.

"I turned. The last one was standing there. He hadn't moved the entire fight, except to return his sword to the sheath. He looked from the man I'd belly-cut to me. He nodded. I turned around and cut low and the man on the ground stopped moving. I looked back. The remaining man hadn't moved, other than to put his right hand on the handle of his sword. 'I figured,' he said to me, 'that if you got through them you'd be worth it.' He told me I was as good as he'd heard I was, but from the way he said it I could tell he thought he was better. I nodded at him and asked if he had a clean rag. He gave me one—this one"—he held up the black silk rag—"and I wiped *Kaishakunin* clean and sheathed it. We stepped away from the bodies and onto the road where there were only a few cars. We bowed—

neither of us took our eyes away from the other. When we straightened up he told me his name was Jim D'Arcy and that his sword's name was *Migi-no-te*. It means 'right hand.' I told him it was a good name and gave him my name and *Kaishaku*'s. After that there wasn't much left to do, so we hit our stances and started playing mind games. We stared at each other for two or three minutes, waiting for a waver, a blink, a passing bird. Or for the other to draw." He straightened a wrinkle on the silk rag. "A draw is a committal move. I was going to wait until he began his and counter-draw, trying to beat out his blade on speed alone. You know what my draw's like."

I nodded.

"His was at least as good. His arm twitched and his sword was out, and so was mine. They met half-way. For a second there, while our blades were locked, I saw the surprise in his eyes—and I knew he could see it in mine. I tried to come in over his blade and thrust. He backstepped, batted my blade aside, and almost took my head off in the same motion. No surprise there, though—as soon as our draws had met I'd known he was at least as good as me. I ducked the head slash just in time and brought *Kaishaku* up, sliding in as I did. Anyone else I'd have cut from hip to opposite shoulder; he just stopped the slash midway and blocked down, then tried to do the same to me. I jumped back and we squared off again, blades pointed at each other's throats. We had already been fighting twice as long as it had just taken me to kill three men—about ten seconds. Once it's actually started and metal begins to swing, ten seconds is a *long* time for a swordfight." He was quiet a minute, finishing up one side of Fred. The blade was bright now, like a new dime. He turned it over. Another spot of the clear fluid on the rag, and he resumed speaking as he began to rub. "We circled each other like alleycats, attacking, trying different combinations, counters. It was always the same. No ground yielded on either side. Once, when we were circling, we saw each other—I mean *saw* each other, our fighting concentration broken—and I knew he was thinking the same thing I was: should we quit? We were both good, had pretty much proven ourselves equal—it would seem a waste if either one of us died. A kind of honor among thieves, a mutual respect, I guess you'd call it. We stopped circling and he and I came out of our stances at the same time. 'I get the feeling one of us will live to regret this,' he said. And he sheathed his blade. I didn't say anything, but I sheathed mine, too. He turned around and walked away. He didn't look back." He finished cleaning my blade and tossed the rag back into his backpack. "How's that?" he asked.

It took a moment before I realized he meant Fred, which he held before him to catch the fading sunlight. "Um. . . ." I looked at the blade. It was better, a hundred percent better, gleaming like captured moonlight against the daytime sky. "It's better, it's much. . . . Thank you. Thank you very much."

"It still needs sharpening." He pulled a small grinding block from his pack.

"We found the bodies," I said. "And Faust's grave."

He hunched forward and began sharpening Fred, holding it by the handle across both knees. "Hold this for me," he said. I took the handle. He leaned to his right, retrieved the black silk rag, and wrapped it around the blade, holding it with one hand to steady it while sharpening with the other. I tightened my grip so the sword wouldn't move as he worked on it.

I thought of Russ Chaffney, and of Asmodeus. It reminded me of something Malachi had said: if a person's buddy dies, he'll live through it. The pain will subside in a few years, and in maybe ten years he won't even hurt anymore. Faust hadn't been Malachi's buddy; he hadn't been held to him by a loyalty spell—but the relationship between the dog and the man had probably been stronger because of that. He'd lost a friend, and I wondered if his outward hardness was because he was trying not to let the hurt show.

He stopped grinding the blade with the stone. "Turn the blade over," he ordered. I complied.

"Right after the fight in Alexandria I headed north. I decided to go as directly as possible to New York, cutting across anything that might be in the way. I didn't need to run across more scalp-hunting parties. It turned out to be a good decision; I'd no sooner left the road than Shai-tan and the rider flew overhead. There was a pyramid of sewer pipes not far from me and I hid in one. They landed on an overpass ahead of me and stayed there for about half an hour. The rider looked around with a telescope, then they flew away. I waited another half-hour to be on the safe side. Or as near to it as I ever get. I don't know if he was looking for you and Ariel or me."

"Both, probably. We came close to having a run-in with him in the same place a few days later."

He nodded. "I crawled out of the sewer pipe and headed north. When I came into Washington I was spotted by a road watch—one of about two dozen they have watching the main roads through here. I talked with him a bit. He was friendly but guarded, which made me suspicious—sentries are posted so *somebody* gets warned. I tried to convince him I was one of the good guys and that I wasn't stupid. I kept at him, trying not to invite any more suspicion. The name Tom Pert came up somehow." He shook his head. "Tom and I were in the Society for Creative Anachronism together."

"The . . . ? Those nuts you told me about, the ones who played King Arthur before the Change?"

"Yes. But don't call them nuts. If you ask, you'll find a lot of the people still around were S.C.A. members at some time or another—not a large percentage, certainly, but enough to be noticeable. They had learned medieval combat before it was forced back into being; they were—combatively, at least—ready for the Change before it occurred. Some of them couldn't have been happier when it happened; it was tailor-made for them."

"Like you."

He shrugged. "Tom and I were knighted at the same tournament."

"Tournament?"

He nodded. "We used to make our own armor and go at it with rattan swords. I was one of the few Japanese personas around; most people were European knights. Tom was one of those. Combat was mostly honor system—if somebody hit you a shot that would have put you out of the running had it been real, you were expected to fall down and die. Or lose the use of the limb you'd been hit on."

Apparently my mind didn't work chivalrously. "What if you didn't want to honor his shot?"

"It happened. Tom once fought someone who wouldn't honor his shots. It irritated Tom; he was running circles around the idiot and nothing was being acknowledged. Tom's Society character—we called them personas—was a pre-Arthurian warrior named Beowulf Brassmountain. You can see why." I could indeed—Tom Pert was *big*. "The guy he was fighting was bigger than him. Tom kept banging away at him, killing him half a dozen times, and he just kept swinging back. Tom called a temporary halt, found an official, and protested. The official asked Tom's opponent why he wasn't honoring shots. Tom's opponent said they weren't hard enough to be counted as killing blows. The official just grinned and told Tom to keep hitting harder, until his opponent had no doubt whatsoever that he was being dealt killing blows. So Tom strides back onto the field, engages his opponent, blocks a slow swing, and gives him a Babe Ruth special on the ribs. Everybody watching heard him gasping for breath, but he stayed up and tried to swing again. So Tom reared back and sent one to the side of his head. The impact went through his helmet and knocked him cold."

I laughed, but not without some bitterness. It must have been fun when all that was for pleasure and not for keeps.

He paused, eyes looking into the distance. It was as close as I ever saw him to nostalgia.

"Anyway," he said, and he was his old self again, "I was taken to him here. I told him everything, he told me everything, and he said that if I'd help him, they might be able to help me. They sent out a few more scouts to New York and Tom told them to be on the lookout for you and Ariel, to mention my name and get you back to Washington if they found you. Mac's team had already been sent when I arrived, so they didn't know about me when you met up with them." He looked up from his sharpening. "We'll do something about Ariel, I promise you—but you better realize something. These people will do what they can for you, but they have other allegiances as well. People they cared for have been killed by those in New York. I have my own reasons for going up against the necromancer and the rider. But I'll do what I can to help you get Ariel back."

I lay awake in my cot, staring at the dim ceiling. The lone candle burned pitifully a few feet from my head and darkness threatened to engulf the room. I'd lit it from one of the paper-covered Japanese lanterns in the hallway outside my door. After a while it was extinguished by its own build-up of liquid wax and the room was swallowed as if by a great whale.

Whales—there was an unbelievably huge reconstruction of a blue whale on one mammoth wall of the Smithsonian, fully ninety feet long, Nature's biggest and most prideful possession. I had talked a while under it with Tom Pert just before coming to my room. He told me the latest on the ambush of the returning scouting party: apparently they'd been attacked by a roving band of scavengers. Esteban was dead; Doc Mundy had been unable to stop the bleeding from the arrow wound.

I turned on the stiff cot. So much, so fast. I resolved to go to sleep, as it would bring the day of the march to New York a little closer.

I unbutton her shirt with trembling hands. . . .

I dreamed it again, more graphic than ever this time. When it ended, another came—a brief image, almost a photograph:

I am in a huge bell jar, and Ariel is on the other side.

Malachi woke me up at eight a.m. by charging into my room with his sword out and screaming like a homicidal maniac. I had Fred out and ready before he could reach me, and before I was fully awake and knew what the hell was going on. He smiled grudgingly, lowered his sword, backed away, and bowed, indicating the door. I returned Fred to its sheath and stared at him. "Ah, shit," I finally said. "I wouldn't have got back to sleep anyhow." I used the chamber pot, covered it, and followed him outside. We began limbering up on the dew-soaked grass.

Somebody had made him two wooden swords, or perhaps he'd made them himself. Not a lot to it, really—a yard-long stick with a circular wooden guard ten inches from one end to prevent smashed fingers. He tossed me one.

He put me through my paces for three solid hours, pressing attacks that took everything I had to block, not giving me time to counter, then easing up and allowing me to work on strategy and technique. About a dozen early risers had gathered around to watch by the time we finished. They maintained a respectful distance. I didn't notice them until we disengaged and Malachi lowered his wooden sword. My concentration relaxed as the sword lowered. I was startled by the staccato of applause. They were making fun. . . . No, they weren't; their applause was sincere. Malachi nodded curtly to me and walked away without a word. I was exhausted, but it felt good. New York had left its mark; I was not in the best shape I'd ever been in.

Hunting up lunch later on, I met Shaughnessy.

"You've been keeping yourself scarce, Pete," she said.

I was conscious of my sweat-soaked body. I probably stank. "I've been busy. There's a war in a few days, you know."

"Yes, I'd noticed."

The cat and mouse distance between us irritated me; I didn't feel like playing games. "I, uh, I've got to be going, Shaughnessy. Got to eat and then see some people."

"Will you come see me later? I'm staying in Archives. I've still got your blowgun, remember?" Her face was blank, not matching her tone.

"Will do."

We went our separate ways down the hall.

I ate lunch on the steps where Malachi and I had talked last evening. A plastic spoon and a paper plate of beans and franks. I could have found something else, I suppose, but I'd grown to miss the little buggers. Someone sat down beside me.

"Mac! How's it going?"

"Hey, Pete. Where were you? You missed the meeting."

"The—oh, shit."

"You didn't miss much. Nobody had any new ideas."

"We're still stuck with fighting all the way up, then, I guess." I snorted. "Mac, that's suicide."

He shook his head. "I don't think so. Neither do Tom and Malachi. If they're as loosely organized as you said, we at least have a fighting chance. It's just going to be a long, drawn-out battle."

"'Just?'"

He spread his hands. "Okay, so it won't be easy. What other choice do we have?" He hesitated. "I don't want to say this, Pete, but it's sort of obvious why you're so anxious that we raid the top."

My fork paused en route to my mouth. Would I use these people like that?

Yes. To get Ariel back, yes. Oh, that's shitty, Pete.

Yeah. I chewed on beans and franks.

"When you finish eating," said Mac, changing the subject, "you want to give me a hand with some stuff?"

I swallowed. "Sure. What do you need?" Why did I get the feeling that everyone was trying to keep me distracted, to keep me occupied instead of dwelling on Ariel? Dammit—I didn't need anyone's sympathy.

"Some help putting together equipment."

I stood. "I'm finished." I walked down the steps and threw the rest of my lunch into a green metal garbage can.

He nodded and rose. "Follow me." We went indoors. He

began leading me through the maze of corridors.

"What made you people choose the Smithsonian?" I asked as we walked. "I'd think it would be pretty inconvenient."

"It has disadvantages, sure. But this place is a gold mine. It's full of relics from times when the Change wouldn't have made that big a difference—pioneering days, colonial times. It's loaded with ideas. Just take a random walk through this place and you'd find things right and left that'd help you survive." We stopped in a large chamber. Mannequins were arrayed along the walls, dressed in clothes of bygone days. A black sign with white letters said that they were gowns worn by previous First Ladies. In front of one wall was a long stretch of tables. Almost two dozen people sat at them. As we neared, I saw they were using short lengths of wire, snippers, and pliers to make chain mail garments. They looked up as we approached. One of them, a short woman with long brown hair and bright blue eyes, stood. "Hi, Mac. Coming to work with us lowly peons?"

He chuckled. "Yeah. Every now and then I like to remember what the low life was like."

"Hmmph." She looked at me, eyes . . . cautious? Something; I couldn't recognize it. Appraising, maybe. "You're the one they brought in from New York," she said. "I saw you at the assembly the other night. Paul, isn't it?"

My heartbeat increased. "Pete." Aw, come on—what was there to feel flustered about?

She looked at Mac expectantly. "Oh," he said, "uh, Pete, this is Terri—Theresa McGee."

"Hi." She smiled at me. "Okay, let's put you two to work. Grab a chair and the stuff you need. You ever make this stuff, Pete?"

"I'll show him how," said Mac.

"I'll show him, Mac. You get busy."

"Sir, yes sir!" He grabbed a vacant chair, sat down, and started to work.

"Come on, Pete," said Theresa. "Sit next to me and I'll show you how it's done."

"I'll bet you will," Mac muttered under his breath.

I followed her to the table. We made chain mail vests for the next three hours. I finished one that had already been started. They were easy to make, but time consuming: cut off a short length of wire—an inch and a half or so—slip it through a previous ring on the vest, bend it into a circle with the pliers, repeat the whole thing. Turn the mail the way you want it to go and leave holes for arms.

After a while Theresa put down her pliers and looked at me. I didn't really notice until she'd been motionless for almost a minute. I looked at her expectantly. "You need a haircut," she said.

I blinked. "Excuse me?"

"A haircut," she repeated firmly. "You can't go into battle with your hair that long."

"Oh. Is it a breach of etiquette?"

"It'll get in your way. You want hair in your eyes when someone's trying to take your head off?"

I drew a deep breath. "You have an eloquent way of putting things."

"You need a bath, too."

My cheeks warmed. True, I'd managed to rinse off once since New York, but I hadn't had a real bath since . . . since . . . hell, I couldn't remember the last time. "I suppose," I answered defensively, "that I don't want to smell bad if someone's trying to take my head off, either."

She smiled. "Don't get mad. I was just telling you. I know what you've been through; you've probably been too busy to notice."

I started to ask her how she knew and stopped. Everybody in Washington probably knew by now.

"I'd be glad to give you a haircut, if you'd like."

I looked down at the lengths of wire I'd snipped off and began bending them to form more links. "I. . . . Yeah. Yeah, that'd be nice, thanks." I looked up and smiled. "I can take my own baths, though."

She returned my smile and shrugged. "Can't win 'em all."

Mac appeared very interested in bending wire into links.

My hands were clammy. I tried to busy them in making mail and fumbled with the pliers. Wire fell to the floor. "Shit," I muttered, and picked them up. Theresa seemed not to have noticed, having returned to her own chain mail vest, almost completed. Across the table and four chairs down, Mac appeared to want to say something, then apparently thought the better of it. We kept working until I had completed one vest and started another. Mac put his tools down and announced that we had to leave.

"I knew it was a token effort," chided Theresa.

"Sorry, hon. We've got other things to do to turn them ol' war machines. Coming, Pete?"

"I—" I glanced at Theresa. "Sure, Mac. Nice meeting you, Theresa."

"Terri."

"McGee," I decided.

"Nice to meet you, too, Pete. I meant what I said about that haircut."

"Okay. I'll . . . be by when Mac's finished with me. How long will we be, Mac?"

"A few hours. Three at the most."

"That's fine," she said. She gave me directions to her room.

"Where to, Mac?"

He was silent for a minute, leading us back outside the Smithsonian. "Horses," he finally said. "We're going scavenging."

"For?"

"Weapons. Bows, arrows, knives, anything we can find to make life easier for us in New York." He stopped walking. "Look, Pete, this is none of my business, but—"

"McGee," I said.

"Well, yes." We were out on the front steps now, blinking in the sunlight.

"Look, Mac, you don't have to be diplomatic. If you don't want me to see her, I won't. I mean, if she's one of your prospects, don't worry about me. I'm . . . spoken for."

He made a sour face. "It's not— Ah, hell. She's not a prospect. I've known her since I've been here, but . . . she's—" He broke off. "Never mind," he finished. "It's none of my business."

He went down the steps ahead of me. I stared at his back, confused. "Hey," I breathed. Then louder: "Hey, wait up!" He turned around and I caught up.

Riding wasn't so bad this time, or perhaps my nerve-endings had gone on strike. For hours we searched every department store, pawn shop, and sporting goods shop on the outskirts of Washington proper. Our efforts yielded little; previous scavenger parties had been thorough. I made Mac detour on the way back to the Smithsonian and we headed west until we reached the east bank of the Potomac. I tied my horse to a guard rail, threw off my clothes, and cannonballed in with a huge splash. The water felt fine.

I scrubbed myself all over with a bar of soap acquired during our foraging, swimming under water to rinse off, and scrubbed myself again. "What are you looking impatient about?" I asked Mac as I soaped my hair. "Why don't you jump in, too? Or do you think you smell like Chanel No. 5?"

His tone was rawthuh snotty. "For your information, I had a bath three—no, four days ago."

"All right, I'll just be a few more minutes."

"Take your time. I'll appreciate it as much as you will."

"Up yours." I took a deep breath and went under, frog-kicking toward the center. I surfaced, wiping my eyes.

I was bathing in a lake when I saw the unicorn. . . .

I swam back to the bank.

"What's wrong, Pete?" asked Mac when I reached him and began wiping myself dry with the blade of my hand.

"What? Oh, nothing. The water just irritates my eyes, that's all." I remained nude until I dried off, then got another set of clothes from a store along the way.

JUDITH RAY, announced the sign on the door. A.P.B.S.C. I knocked tentatively, wondering what the letters stood for. I waited three seconds. Oh, well, she's not in. Guess I'll—

The door opened. "Well, hello there, stranger," said McGee. "Come to get your ears lowered?"

"Just a little off the top, thanks."

"Sure—you want me to stop when I reach scalp?" She opened the door wider. "Come in to my parlor."

I walked in and looked around. A rumpled bed, a huge poster of Beethoven, an Early American dresser, the inevitable chamber pot, candles, oil lamps, and a straight backed wooden chair in the middle of the floor.

"Have a seat."

Fred clacked against the back leg of the chair when I sat down, and she gave a small smile. "You can put your sword in the corner, if you like. Here, I'll do it." She reached for my sword and I pulled it away protectively. She laughed. "You men and your swords. Heavens to Freud."

I colored and handed Fred to her. She took it as a lowering of my guard—which I guess it was—and brightened as she accepted it and leaned it carefully in the corner. She got on her knees and reached under her bed, pulling out a box. The denim stretched nicely where she bent. "And what would monsieur prefer?" she asked, straightening. "Zee cue ball, perhaps?"

"How about just evening it up and getting it out of my eyes?"

She pursed her lips. "Oui." She opened the box and removed the scissors and a black, large-toothed comb. I sat straight while she arranged a white towel around my neck and half into my shirt collar so the hair wouldn't fall down it. She played with my hair a minute, seeing which way it fell naturally, then leaned forward and sniffed gently beside my neck. "Somebody smells much nicer," she said. Her voice was low.

Mentioning my smell made me sharply aware of her own: a light, fragile odor, with a soft of overtone of musk. The clammy feeling was in my palms again. I clenched them together.

"You aren't nervous, are you?" she continued before I could reply. "I haven't lost a patient with these yet." She snipped the scissors.

"'Yet,'" I observed. *Damn*—my voice broke.

"I give haircuts all the time. Don't worry." She dunked a towel into a pail of water, twisted it to drain some of the water off, and stepped behind me. "Lean your head back. I can work with your hair better if it's wet." I leaned back until I looked at the ceiling, feeling skin pull from chin to larynx. She rubbed the damp towel through my hair, briskly at first, then more and more gently. I was sorry when she stopped. I became conscious of my own increased heartbeat. She started pulling the comb through my hair.

"Ow, shit!"

"Sorry. But it's very tangled and I have to comb it out."

"Sure. I'll bite a bullet or something. It's been a long time since my hair was combed, but I do brush my teeth on occasion, if it's any consolation."

She chuckled and went back to work with her comb, trying to be gentle, separating tangled strands of hair with her long nails, grabbing my hair with one hand and pulling hard on the comb with the other when gentleness wouldn't work. Eventually she could run the comb through my long hair unhampered. "Forward a little," she ordered, nudging the back of my head softly. I nodded forward. My thigh muscles bunched as my hands attempted to cover my erection. My breath caught, but she gave no notice. Hair fell in front of my eyes, landing on my lap. I brushed it away. She noticed me brushing and said, "Oh, I'm sorry. Let me get you another towel." She removed a thick white towel from a stack atop her dresser. I reached for it as she unfolded it, but she ignored me and spread it across my lap, smoothing it over my thighs. My breath was ragged. An obvious lump showed beneath the towel. She appeared not to notice and walked behind me again. The snipping of scissors resumed. Two-inch lengths of hair fell to the towel.

My legs echoed where she had touched them. Her touch lingered on my skin like a sweeping whisper of distant bells. A drop of water from my hair fell onto the back of my left arm, spreading goosebumps for ripples.

"Are you cold?" she asked.

I could only shake my head slowly. The snipping resumed. Her body heat warmed my neck as she lifted the hair and began to even it up. "There you are," she said, a few age-long minutes later.

"Finished so soon?" I stood and turned to face her, plucking the towel with one hand as it dropped. I held it in front of me. She only comes up to my chest, I thought.

She blinked. "If it were six years ago I'd blow-dry it, but the best you can do now is ride a horse fast. It was just a trim cut, no big deal. Want a lollipop?"

"You're kidding."

"Nope." She opened the first drawer of her dresser and pulled out a green lollipop, the round candy part covered in square cellophane.

"Got a red one?"

She smiled. "Ingrate." She fished around and finally brought up a red one. I accepted it, grinning like an idiot. When had I last had a lollipop? "McGee," I began, putting it into a back pocket for later, "thanks a lot. Really. I don't—" I stopped. She was looking at me funny—looking at my mouth?

"Would you like a shave?" she asked.

"Uh—" I was about to tell her I needed to go eat dinner

because it would be dark soon—was already beginning to grow dark—and I didn't want to go hunting up food in the dark, but she was already removing a bright steel straight razor and shaving soap from her wooden box. I sat down in the chair without another word, holding the towel the way Linus used to hold his blanket. "Not there," she said. "On the bed. I have all my close shaves there."

I rose uncertainly. She opened a window—her room was along the edge of one wing—and shook out the towel she'd put across my lap, then shut the window and spread the towel over her pillows and part of her cot. "I shave men better if they're lying down," she explained. "They're less likely to move unexpectedly."

"Oh." I lay down self-consciously. McGee set the pail of water beside me on the floor. She rubbed the lower half of my face with a damp cloth, then applied shaving soap with an antiquated, horse-hair shaving brush with an ivory handle. "Supposedly," she said conversationally, stroking my jaw softly with the brush, "this once belonged to Abe Lincoln, though I have my doubts."

"I'll pretend it did and maybe it'll make me feel important."

"You seem pretty important now. To us, anyway." My face lathered, she rinsed the brush off and put it and the soap away. She unfolded the straight razor.

"You ever read *A Clockwork Orange?*" I asked nervously.

"Shh. You can't talk once I start."

"Wouldn't dream of it."

She folded her legs beneath her, sitting Japanese style, and began gently shaving the softer skin beneath my chin with the bright steel. I remembered the griffin rider's sword twitching before my eyes and tried not to swallow. The blade was a gruff whisper across my skin. I felt the heat rising again.

"You know, you have a nice jawline." Her voice was a half whisper.

If it was a question, I couldn't answer. But no, I didn't know I had a nice jawline. Suddenly conscious of my breathing, I felt it was an awkward process, an action I had to constantly control. *Don't turn your head, Garey. She'll cut your throat.* Oh, wouldn't that be fantastic—come all the way from Atlanta, get away from New York, and have some pretty woman accidentally slit your throat while shaving you. It was just ironic enough to seem likely.

And yet—there was something strangely . . . erotic . . . about the gentle, skillful way she held the potentially deadly instrument. I dared not move my head. My erection strained harder against my underwear. The lollipop in my pocket pressed against my butt. I had to leave it that way.

McGee finished the left side of my face, dipped the razor in the water to clean it, turned my head to face her, and leaned forward slightly to start on the other side. Her breasts pressed against my shoulder and elbow. The delicate musk of her filled my nostrils. I felt, strangely, annoyed. I closed my eyes. Worse—it made me more aware of my erection, of her warmth against me, of her smell, the soft push of her against my arm. I wanted to sit upright and push her away, but I couldn't. And something underneath felt differently, didn't want to push her away at all.

I was only dimly aware of her folding the razor. Her long hair tickled my throat, moving as she moved.

It was so gradual: wiping my face dry with a soft cloth, continuing the motion with her hands long after my face was no longer wet. Her cheek replaced one hand, brushing back and forth until her lips slid like silk scarves across my own, then paused, making the motion halt to become a kiss. Something caught in my throat when her lips parted and my own followed after the barest hesitation. Her tongue found mine and danced wetly around it.

I slit open my eyes when the kiss broke; she breathed my name and her breath filled my mouth. Her hand rested lightly on my chest, feeling my heart pound, making her smile. Her other palm was cool against my cheek. My hips pressed into her. The hand on my chest slid slowly down, long nails rasping faintly on my shirt; then the hand stroked my erection through the corduroy. Her breath trembled with her hands, her skilled fingers.

Trembled—

I sat up. She had to grab the edge of the cot to keep her balance. "What—Pete, what's wrong?"

I stood. Looked . . . at the walls, through the walls, anywhere. "No," I breathed. "*No!*" I looked at her blue eyes, framed by her brown hair. They were very bright. "Ariel," I whispered. The name rode unevenly on my choppy breath. Confused, I looked down at myself. "I—" Eyes slammed shut.

A great roaring in my ears. Hands clenched. "No." A flat statement this time. My eyes opened. They stung. They didn't want to focus. I stepped forward. Stopped. Confused.

And then I ran from the room.

twenty–one

All of these goddamn theoretical analyses are taking the humanity out of warfare.

—Unidentified admiral,
responding to a Center for Naval Analyses lecture.

I wandered around in a dull fog as darkness fell. I was confused and trying not to cry.

Something crackled as I walked. I patted my back pocket and pulled out the red lollipop. I looked at it a full minute, then heaved it away from me as hard as I could. It clacked onto the street a few seconds later.

My testicles ached dully, a mild, underlying tug of pain like a bruised shin, a feeling I didn't understand. They felt heavy. I craved a cigarette. My knees trembled as I walked, looking down at the dark pavement sliding aimlessly beneath me.

Bitch, bitch, *bitch*.

Somebody passed me. I barely looked at him as I asked if he knew where I could find a cigarette. He led me indoors and got one from someone else. I grabbed it without thanking either of them, went into the hall, and lit it from a Japanese lantern on the floor. The man I'd followed stood in the open doorway, silent as I drew in a deep lungful of smoke and breathed it out in a wispy cloud tinged by the flame's light. I grew annoyed at him watching me and looked at him to say thanks, but get lost.

Malachi Lee.

Somehow that was worse than him being a stranger. I stared dumbly. He stared back. I dropped my gaze, turned, and left, almost running. I smoked the entire cigarette as I walked briskly, no destination in mind. The smoke made me cough. My lungs felt scratchy. I liked it.

I stopped and flicked the still burning cigarette from my fingers, staring at a dark building without even realizing it was a building. It was just a shape to me, a pattern my brain hadn't taken the effort to label.

What did she do, Garey? I asked myself. Really, what did she do that was so wrong?

Nothing. It's me. She couldn't have known. I was making a big deal out of nothing.

No—it wasn't nothing.

True. But it wasn't her fault, either.

Mine, then. Was I so naïve? It would seem so. I just didn't understand. It all happened so fast.

It felt good.

Face tightening, I stepped forward and brought my foot down hard on the glowing cigarette and ground it satisfyingly beneath my heel. "Fuck sex," I said aloud. That made me laugh, but mirthlessly. I turned back around to regard the building before me: The National Air and Space Museum. "I suppose that's where they keep all the national air and space," I muttered.

A dry laugh from behind startled me. I spun, hands groping for a non-present Fred. Shit—I'd left it in her room.

The oversized form of Tom Pert resolved from the darkness. "And the National Hot Air Museum is just down the road a piece," he added. "Better known by its branch names: the Capitol and the White House." He wore a heavy one-handed broadsword at his side. Malachi had told me that, like himself, Tom Pert had had his sword long before the Change.

He came closer. "Malachi said you had headed this way. Want some company?"

I wanted to say no, that he had no right to be here, but realized he was only trying to help. "Everybody's trying to help," I said, not realizing I'd spoken aloud until he answered.

"That's because you're helping us."

"I want my magic back," I said accusingly. "Can you understand that?"

"I can recognize it." Something in his voice made it seem like a compromise, an incompleteness on his part. "I can try to help you get it back. I want to try. So does Malachi. And Mac. And that young woman who's in love with you. Shaughnessy."

Well, there it was. Out there on the floor for the cat to sniff at for the first time. "I can't help what anyone feels," I said heavily. "I can't help how I feel, either. And I don't want to." I looked up at him. "Is that selfish?"

"Yes. But we're all entitled to some selfishness. But I won't lecture you, Pete. I think you want someone to tell you that what you're doing is okay, someone who'll advise you because you don't want to commit yourself. I won't do it, nor would anyone who saw your predicament. I don't understand it and I wouldn't pretend to. I'm a little jealous of you for your unicorn. Most of us are, a bit. But I wouldn't be in your shoes for the world."

I nodded. Yeah, I guess I could understand that.

He touched my shoulder. "Come inside."

The door was open. I followed him in.

Da Vinci would have died content had he been able to see this place. All the ways human beings had ever flown were represented here in full scale. Near one wall the dark, ghostly shapes of two biplanes engaged in a permanent dogfight. Ahead sat the stubby cone of a Gemini capsule. We almost had that, I thought as we walked past it. Those points of light were at fingertips' edge, then snatched away. Our footsteps clattered eerily as we walked.

"I like to come here," said Tom. "I don't exactly know why; it depresses the hell out of me."

Because there's poetry here, I thought; melancholy remnants of the crowning achievements of a civilization rested here, wasting away. *Nevermore to grace the night*—where had I heard that before?

I stroked the dark wing of a mock-up of Pappy Boyington's F4U Corsair, the terror of World War Two. Tom and I stared wistfully at a model of the Apollo-Soyuz docking. The Starship *Enterprise* hung mournfully, a reminder of broken dreams. A half-scale mock-up of the Shuttle *Enterprise* stood beside it in mute testimony.

It made you sad, this place, and threatened to provoke anger by taunting you, yet it drew you in, eager to satisfy your morbid curiosity. It was so dark in there we barely saw where to walk, but we took our time and felt out the shapes of the useless aerial silhouettes like blind men tugging at an elephant.

I was crying again and couldn't help it. Tom respected me by saying nothing, doing nothing, until it passed, and the last of my sobs had stopped echoing in the dark and my eyes had dried, and then we walked on.

We stopped before an impossible thing. It looked as if it was built for a world with no gravity, as if it would collapse under its own weight. The pale moonlight, which illuminated the inside just enough to keep us from bumping into things, sparkled on the incredibly thin dragonfly wings.

"The *Gossamer Condor,"* I said. "I remember reading about this. It was the first man-powered aircraft."

Tom nodded. "It was seventy-five years after the Wright brothers flew before they did it," he said. "The designer got the Kremer prize for it."

I studied the fragile thing. Its ninety-foot-wide main wing glistened as if wet. It had taken high technology to produce this craft which had realized one of humankind's oldest dreams. The wings were thin mylar plastic; the rest of it was incredibly light metal, woods, and plastic. The whole thing weighed about seventy pounds; I could have pulled it along with one arm. "Wouldn't it be nice if we had about a dozen of these things?" I asked. "We could come in on the Empire State Building from above."

"I don't think so," said Tom. "The ability to produce this thing simply doesn't exist anymore. And even if it did, it took a *very* small, *very* strong person to operate it. He was a jockey who weighed about one-thirty, I believe. Offhand, I can't think of anyone in Washington that small and that strong. That, plus I don't know if it'd go high enough to reach the top of the Empire State Building." He stroked his beard with thumb and forefinger. "The wings would snap in strong winds. Even if you could get it up on a still day, the convection currents rising up the sides of the building would be more than enough to break—" He stopped, thoughtful. A smile crept across his face. "Well," he said distinctly. "I will be dipped in shit." His eyes glittered like the wings of the dragonfly aircraft. "I didn't even think of it. It didn't even *occur* to me." He turned to me like a man in a dream, one who liked it there and didn't want to come back. "Convection currents," he said, as if that explained everything. I waited for more, but nothing else came.

He needs a pipe, I thought absurdly. He should be a huge, easy-going psychiatrist, or an English professor, smoking a pipe and staring out the window without seeing the world outside.

Displayed in front of the *Gossamer Condor* were Da Vinci's designs for man-powered flight, arrayed in light, carefully crafted wooden replicas: the dream and the dream realized.

"Come on," said Tom. "If they were holding an exhibit on man-powered flight, then there has to be a hang glider around here somewhere."

I looked past him at a dark silhouette by a corner wall. I pointed at it. "Will that do?"

He turned, with a religious fanatic's look on his face. Behind a glass stand with a picture of Francis M. Rogallo and accompanying text was an assembled hang glider with an eighteen-foot wingspan. A mannequin hung in the center. The hang glider was suspended in front of a painted backdrop, but it had grown too dark for me to make out what the painting was.

"Go find Malachi and Mac," he ordered suddenly, as though he were shifting gears. "Bring them back here."

"What are you going to do?"

"I," he said, smiling, "am going to try to get that thing down. Now get."

At the main building of the Smithsonian I asked around until I found Malachi and Mac and explained to them that Tom wanted them at the Air and Space Museum. On the way to the museum Mac could stand it no longer and demanded to know what was going on.

"Your guess is as good as mine," I told him. "What's a convection current?"

He shrugged. "You got me. Malachi?"

Malachi pursed his lips thoughtfully but didn't answer.

We found Tom at the man-powered flight exhibit. He had managed to put on the mannequin's harness and strap himself into the hang glider, and he stood before us like a stylized Hawkman from *Flash Gordon*. He was giggling. It was unnerving. He just kept chuckling at some private joke as he unbuckled himself from the giant kite and gestured pridefully to it like a magician setting up his best trick.

Mac and I looked on wonderingly. Malachi watched interestedly, nodding to himself as though everything were happening according to his expectations.

Still wearing the harness, Tom stood in front of us, the dark wedge of the hang glider behind him. "Convection currents," he said.

"You'll need to go in the late afternoon," said Malachi calmly. "The heat will be best then."

Tom nodded. Mac and I exchanged looks. "What?" we asked.

"Tell them, tell them." Tom gestured impatiently.

"Convection currents," said Malachi. "Updrafts of warm air replacing cold air, rising from sun heated areas of land. Or, in the case of New York City, concrete."

"Oh." A light bulb clicked on in my head. Mac still looked confused. "Warm air rises," I told him. "It provides lift."

"Oh," he said, echoing me, as his own little bulb winked on.

Tom spoke in a rush. "Warm air constantly replaces cool. There's a continuous rush of air up the sides of tall buildings. It's especially strong in the late afternoon, when the concrete is hottest. Actually, early evening would be best. The air would be cooling while the concrete still radiated absorbed heat. But we don't want to fight at night, not given a choice."

His enthusiasm was catching. "We can send an air team," Mac said. "There was a place—a sporting goods shop—they had hang gliders, at least half a dozen of them."

"Elite Sports," supplied Tom. He thought a minute. "An updraft up the side of the World Trade Center," said Tom rapidly. "We could jump off and circle to get initial lift. The Empire State Building would provide more, so that, even if we lost enough height to put us below the eighty-sixth floor, we could circle and lift."

"Hold on," said Malachi imperturbably, the eye of the hurricane. "Don't count your chickens yet."

"But—" we all began in unison.

He went on, crowding out our voices. "We leave day after tomorrow," he said. "We'll have that long to round up a team and learn to fly these things. We have to figure out if the lift will be enough. We have to find someone here who's done it enough to know what he's talking about. An assault team has to be trained; we need a plan of action."

"There was a place not five miles from me when I lived in California," interrupted Tom, "that used to offer hang glider flights down a slope for fifteen bucks. Minimal instruction provided. As I said, I tried it a few times. There's not all that much to it, Malachi."

"Perhaps not, for simple flights," he admitted. "But you're talking jumping from one skyscraper, flying three and a half miles, and landing on another." There was a pause. "But"—he gave a grudging half-smile—"it's all we've got. We'll want to get an early start tomorrow, so I suggest we get the gliders tonight and then go to bed. Pete, I'll bring one back for you."

"I'm coming with you!"

"No. You're going to put a notice up on the bulletin board telling anybody with any experience at this to report to Tom." It was everybody's duty to keep abreast of announcements on the bulletin board in the huge Smithsonian lobby.

"Oh." Why was he always so infernally reasonable? "Okay."

Tom nodded. Grinning like a bandit, he began to applaud himself. Mac joined in and I was a close third. Malachi remained stony. "Tomorrow's going to be a long day," he said.

We each shot him the same sour look: *party pooper*. Yet we knew we needed his hard-headed pragmatism. I couldn't help but hope—for myself, for Ariel—yet I couldn't afford to hope. Not too much. Leave it to Malachi to keep our feet on the ground long enough for us to see what we were doing.

Just the same—and I only saw it because of where I stood—a smile crossed his face as he turned and stalked out of the dark museum.

The first thing to hit me when I walked into my room was the smell. It wasn't the chamber pot; I'd emptied it that afternoon and covered it when I put it back. It was me. Or rather, traces of me. McGee, I reflected wryly, had been diplomatic and most restrained when she'd suggested I take a bath. The room smelled as though somebody had shit in a football player's locker. Where's the body? my nose demanded.

Okay—the sheets go first. Might as well throw them away; I doubted washing them would do any good.

Fred lay on the stained white sheets. I picked it up. A note dangled from the handle. I removed it and unfolded it. Ruled notebook paper and a disgustingly neat handwriting:

Pete,

I feel I must write you this note, as I do not want animosity between us. I couldn't understand why you fled the room as you did, though it was obvious you were quite upset. I didn't understand, that is, until Mac came by later and told me about you and your unicorn.

Believe me, Pete, I didn't know. There are some women who would attempt to seduce you with malicious intent, knowing full well what it would cost you and your Familiar. I am not one of those.

Mac was angry with me. He called me a whore, though he's too much a gentleman to say so in those words. I make no apologies, just as none are expected from you. What I am sorry for is your consternation. If only I'd known!

And—truly!—I would like to meet your Familiar someday. She must be marvelous.

McGee

P.S. I brought your sword back. Don't worry—I know better than to touch the blade.

I sat on the stained and smelly sheets and read it at least five times by the flickering light of my lone candle before folding it and wedging it beneath the pewter candle holder. Then I stripped the sheets from my cot, tossed them into a corner to be dealt with in the morning, and turned the mattress over. I slept on the bare bed, hugging Fred as though it were a Teddy bear.

Mac burst into my room just after dawn and almost lost his head. "Goddam!" he yelled, leaning back severely. "You and Malachi are just alike with those things."

"Habit," I mumbled sleepily, though mentally I felt alert. "You should cultivate one sometime."

He made a rude noise. "Try sneaking up on me sometime and see what happens."

I sheathed Fred. "'Do unto others . . .'"

"Come on, get up. We go the Icarus route today."

"Chirp."

The morning chill was invigorating. Tom and Malachi were

already waiting at the foot of the stairs. On the sidewalk were six brightly colored nylon bags, thin and about twenty feet long. Six hang gliders, which meant we'd have seven people—assuming the one Tom had retrieved from the Air and Space Museum was operable.

"Ah, Pete," said Tom. "Would you care to act as our step and fetchit this morning?"

"Sure. What am I fetching?"

"The rest of our team."

"I take it our bulletin yielded some results?"

He nodded. "First there's Walt."

"Is he well enough?"

He shrugged. "He's been up and around since the day after he came back; it was just exhaustion that got to him. I want him; he's an excellent swordsman. He's never hang glided, but he used to fly an ultralight, which is good enough for me." He paused. "Next is Drew Zenoz. He's the one who solo scouted New York and brought Shaughnessy back. He's young—a little older than you, Pete, but reliable. I think he's in it mostly to make an impression. Still, he's serious, and I'm not in a position to turn down volunteers. Plus he's been to New York recently, which helps. Familiarity might prove an asset."

I nodded, warmed by the implication that my own age meant nothing to them. "Who's third?"

"Hank Rysetter. He looked me up late last night after you posted the notice on the bulletin board. He's got a Hang II rating, so he gets to play teacher. He's a good fighter, and one of the best bowmen I've ever seen. I've watched him put out candles from over fifty yards."

He told me where to find each of the three. I left as they were compiling small tool kits for each team member. The hang gliders, folded and waiting in their long, colorful nylon bags, lay side by side at the foot of the steps.

I knocked softly at Drew Zenoz's door. He answered sleepily, unarmed and in his underwear. They sent this guy to scout New York? I was surprised he'd made it back; he didn't seem nearly paranoid enough.

He woke up considerably after I explained what was going on. I told him to meet Tom, Malachi, and Mac on the front steps and left him as he struggled into a pair of pants.

* * *

Hank Rysetter answered the door nude, alert, and with a Bowie knife held nonchalantly in his free hand near his thigh. He was my size but more muscular, and had curly black hair and bushy eyebrows. There was something of the ideal Byzantine in his features.

He relaxed when I introduced myself; apparently he knew who I was. I rapidly explained why I'd rudely awakened him and he nodded and invited me in while he dressed, opening the door wide and turning his back on me. He picked clothes from a heap on the floor at the foot of his cot. The original office furniture hadn't been removed, but had instead been pushed against one wall. His target bow stood by the head of the cot. It would have cost a pretty penny before the Change.

I told him where to find the others and left to find Walt.

His door was open. I rapped on it anyhow; one learns not to walk into people's rooms unannounced. He was already up and dressed, and he seemed pretty fit.

"Well, hello," he said when I entered. "How're you getting along?"

"Fine, thanks. I heard about what happened."

He frowned. "Yeah, it was pretty bad. Is this a social call? I'm not trying to give you the bum's rush, but I wanted to get an early start today. There's a lot to do before we set out tomorrow morning. I'm helping a bunch of people finish building shields."

"I think you can skip shield making today."

We sat on the front steps of the Smithsonian while Hank lectured to us. He showed us how to assemble the kites, how to carry them, and how to put on the harnesses and buckle ourselves in. After going over the basics for flying the kites he said, "All right, I could talk till next week about how to fly one of these things, even though there isn't that much to it, but nothing's going to teach you how to fly better than flying. So everybody pick out a kite, and let's *fly*."

I stood up. The sun was directly overhead. People bustled everywhere, hurrying to get things done before tomorrow. They looked worried and impatient.

Tom gestured at the long bags. "Pick a kite, any kite."

According to Hank the ideal length hang glider for my weight—about 155—was eighteen feet, measuring along the central keel. These all had twenty-foot keels, easily capable of supporting the weight of the heaviest of us, which was Tom, who weighed in at one ninety-five. I would do well with the twenty-foot keel; the low wind loading on the larger sail area would mean better soaring performance—I could stay up longer. I picked out the nearest kite and separated it from the rest.

"All right," said Hank, "the next step, obviously, is to find a good hill and learn it the real way now."

"I think, too," said Malachi, "that we ought to find a building we can jump from. Apparently that's an entirely different thing, and I want to at least have an idea of how to do it before New York. I don't want to jump blind from the World Trade Center."

"Sounds reasonable," agreed Tom. "Any suggestions as to which building? There's nothing here to compare with the World Trade Center."

"There's an office building a few miles from here," said Mac. "The roof's flat and one side faces a bit of a slope, though the slope itself wouldn't be any good to us. But at least there aren't any power lines around."

"We don't have to worry about power lines anymore," said Drew.

"Oh, yeah? You try untangling yourself with a twenty-foot kite on your back."

"How about a slope?" asked Tom.

"On Louisiana Avenue," Hank suggested, "there's a hill that ought to be good enough for a short flight."

"Then what are we waiting for?" We picked up our hang glider bags and set out.

The hill was perfect. A dozen cars were stopped on it, though, so we put them in neutral, released their emergency brakes, and pushed them one at a time. They picked up speed and rolled downhill until they smashed into the cars stopped at a blind red light. We began at the bottom and worked our way up, sending cars crashing behind us. I'm a little embarrassed to admit that it took a while because we stopped to watch each car glide smoothly down the hill until it smashed into the others below. Eventually there was a twenty car pile-up at the foot of the hill, but it wouldn't present a problem—if we made it that far on our trial flights, we ought to be able to fly over it. We dug out our minimal tool kits and began assembling the gliders. I put the frame together, fitting the wing spars and keel into the nose plate and tightening it securely. Rigging wire, which helped relieve the pressure on the wing edges during flight, went to each angle of the A-shaped frame, held there by turnbuckles. They were held taut and away from the sail itself by being attached to the triangular "trapeze" control bar at the bottom and the king post at the top. I made sure the flying wires were secure and not about to slacken from being hooked around turnbuckles. The rigging was thousand-pound test stainless steel, and helped the paraglide sail maintain its shape. The sail was made of Dacron, the same material used by many sailboats. It had the advantage of being light, strong, and non-porous. It stretched across the A-frame of lightweight aluminum tubing. Jesus bolt through the channel bracket, trapeze bar fitted and rigging wire anchored, and swing-seat strap and link fitted and adjusted to what I hoped was centered for my weight and bulk, and I had a fully assembled Rogallo-winged hang glider. Putting it together took about fifteen minutes. I gave a walk around inspection to make sure everything was tightened and fitted correctly. Malachi was right; I didn't want to fuck up and miss the only chance I was going to have to get Ariel back. Having assembled our gliders, we examined each other's. Better safe than sorry.

The trailing edges of the sails flapped in the breeze. We faced them nose-down into the wind so they wouldn't be flipped over or cartwheeled away. Next we fitted ourselves into the swing-seat harnesses which, along with crash helmets, Malachi, Tom, and Mac had also brought from Elite Sports. The harness was an ingeniously simple device. It looked like a sort of combination jockstrap/suspenders and felt about the same: standing straight made it pull in on the insides of my thighs and press down on my shoulders. I asked Mac to loosen the leg straps a little for me and he obliged. My harness was yellow and black; the helmet I strapped on was bright red, and the gliders themselves were bright, vibrant colors. We were going to sneak up on the Empire State Building in day-glow camouflage.

We were ready. I grinned nervously at Mac. He grinned back, just as nervous, I think.

"Well, Hank, m'boy," said Tom, clapping him on the shoulder, "since you're the one with the most experience at this, I think you ought to be the first, so we can follow your shining example."

Hank smiled thinly. "Yeah, okay, okay. First things first. Help me carry the glider to the middle of the road. Only carry it by the rigging wires."

I grabbed the rigging on the left side, Mac grabbed the right, and Hank held the two wires leading from nose to bottom corners of the trapeze bar. The kite was surprisingly light, but difficult to maneuver because of its bulk. It wasn't a creature of the ground, but of the air. "There's a decent breeze today," Hank said, after we set the glider down in the center of the asphalt. "When we finish our flights we ought to be able to 'fly' the kites back up the hill. You do it by holding on to the nose wires and keeping the nose up and into the wind. Let it fill with air and then walk forward slowly." He buckled his chin strap. "Let's do it. Somebody want to hold the nose up for me while I climb in?" Tom came forward and held the nose level while Hank carefully picked his way through the rigging, knelt down before the trapeze bar, reached behind himself awkwardly, and grabbed the heavy-duty clip buckle attached to the back of the harness. He attached it to the link hanging from the keel just behind the trapeze bar. "I can't stress this enough," he said. "The first thing to do is to always make a hang check. Be *sure* to clip yourself on; it's easier to forget than you might think. If you jump off the World Trade Center without hooking yourself to your kite, it'll keep going and you won't." He lowered himself into a prone position, placing his hands at either side of the trapeze bar. He hung four inches off the pavement. We gathered closer to see. "Let the glider take your weight," he said. "See how you're hanging or, better yet, get someone else to stand in front of you and see. How's it look, Tom?"

"You're hanging in the center, not leaning to either side, with your chest even with the bar."

"Good. Now, this is the tricky part." His grip tightened on the trapeze bar. "This thing is really sensitive to your commands. You're what steers the kite; you're its center of gravity because of the way you hang here. So if I want to turn left, I shift my weight to the left." He straightened his right arm, pushing his body toward the left side of the kite. "Make sure you move your hips and legs over, and not just your chest, or your body will compensate by doing this." He deliberately did it wrong, so that his chest moved to the left but his hips remained centered and his legs moved to the right. "See? You haven't done anything; my weight's still centered." He returned to neutral position. "This is your flying position: relaxed, not forcing your body anywhere unless you want to alter your flight. Your hands should stay at either end of the bar. You're going to be excited but don't grab it in a death grip. It takes a few seconds for the kite to respond when you want to turn, but when it does, it turns fast. Don't turn too much or you'll stall.

"The mistake most beginners make is overcorrecting—moving the bar too far forward or back. It's hard to get used to the fact that it hardly takes any effort to make this thing stall or go faster. If you stall, pull in on the bar. The answer to almost everything is to pull in on the bar. You're better off being high and going fast—the more speed you have, the more control you have. Like riding a bicycle."

"I can usually get up afterward if I wreck a bicycle," Mac muttered.

Hank ignored him. "No matter what happens, don't panic. We'll be high up, and that's actually better—you have lots of time to correct. If worse comes to worst and you stall and don't know what to do, just relax and let it stall. The kite parachutes down. But *don't* try to turn on a stall—I saw one woman crush her wrist because she got about thirty feet up and stiff-armed the bar.

"Position the nose so that it's just a little above level. Don't look down—look straight out." He picked up the kite. "Heads up, Tom. Okay, I'm going to run full-out, even after my feet start to leave the ground, and as soon as I'm in the air I'm going to push the bar out just a little bit to get height, then go to neutral position to glide on down. To land I'm going to push the bar all the way out and stall, and—I hope—I should flare up and parachute down." He grinned. "Ready, set . . . *go!*" He took three running steps and was airborne. His next few steps were imaginary ones taken in the air. His kite—red, green, and blue striped—angled out from the hill for a few seconds, gained height until he was about twelve feet up, relative to the slope of the hill, and angled down again. He raced along, level with the slope of the hill, and sailed smoothly over the mass of collided cars, and then his descent seemed so rapid and steep that it looked as if his crash was inevitable. His chest was two feet from the asphalt when he pushed the bar forward. The kite, which had been riding along on its own cushion of air, flared up. Hank swung his feet down and touched the asphalt, light as you please.

I realized we were all cheering. All but Malachi, of course, who nevertheless looked awfully pleased.

Hank stumbled a bit, but recovered quickly and set the nose down immediately. He unbuckled himself. *"Whoooooooeee!* Make sure you put the nose down, or you'll get blown over." He walked around to the front of the kite, lifted the nose, walked his hands down the lead rigging wires, and let the wind lift the sail. He began "flying" the kite back up the hill. "Who's next?" he asked when he reached us, setting his kite to the side with the nose down into the light breeze. "Tom?"

"Oh, what the hell." Tom carried his glider to the middle of the road, picked his way through the rigging, and buckled himself in. He lowered himself into prone position. "How's it look?"

Hank eyed him carefully from in front of the glider. "Perfect. I'll run down the hill and call up to you. If I tell you to do something, just do it, okay?"

"Right, coach."

Hank trotted down the hill and sat on the hood of a white Maverick. "Ready when you are," he called up.

Tom grimaced. He positioned his arms on the bar, set the angle of the nose, and ran. Four sprinting steps, and up he went.

"Pull out!" Hank called from below. Tom complied and the glider gained height. "Now in!" The blue and white sail dipped, gliding down the hill. "Left! Left! Okay, neutral! Perfect! You're flying it; just ride it out." Tom sailed over the cars and continued past the intersection, barely skimming the road. Hank called after him. "Push the bar out! You're—oh, hell." Tom pushed the bar out, but was much too late. He belly-skimmed on the asphalt for ten feet before the nose plunked down in front of him and he stopped. He unbuckled and came out. "Well, my goodness," was all he said. Hank ran to him and they carried the glider back up the hill. Tom's shirt was a little worse for the wear and his stomach could have used a squirt of Bactine, but otherwise he was fine. "Malachi?" he said.

Malachi nodded and set up his glider, which was bright yellow with a red V in the center. He methodically checked himself out, picked up the kite, set himself, and ran. Suddenly his feet were off the ground and he was speeding down the hill. His straight line trajectory wavered for a second, but he corrected and landed light as a feather, a dozen feet past the spot where Tom had touched down. He unbuckled and nosed the kite down. "He makes me sick," muttered Tom. He trotted down the hill to help him with the kite.

"Pete next," he said as they set Malachi's kite to the side.

I swallowed, suddenly feeling it was much easier to watch than to do. Hank returned to his spot on the hood of the Maverick. "Just listen and do what I say," he called up, "and everything will be fine."

I stepped to the center of the road and climbed through the rigging. My foot caught on one of the wires and I pulled it free before I tripped. I twisted around, grabbed the buckle, and clipped myself on.

"Hang check," Tom reminded me.

I nodded and lowered myself into prone position. The harness tugged on my shoulders. I kept my head up.

"Looks good to me," he said.

I knelt and lifted the bar as I'd seen the others do. It was heavier than I'd expected. I felt awkward with the added weight above me; my center of gravity had shifted from the pit of my stomach to the top of my chest. I felt strangely buoyed. I let the sail fill with air until it was rigid, two arcs spreading seagull-like from the central keel to the wing spars. I took a deep breath. It's really easy, I told myself. Just remember what Hank told you. Nothing to it. You have to develop familiarity with the kite, and a sense of how to react, but the basics are easy as hell. A twelve-year-old could do it. Twelve-year-olds *had* done it. I nodded to myself. I experimentally moved the bar, feeling the balance shift in the kite above me, stopping when it felt right. The wind was nice and smooth—now or never. I ran.

Holding the bar in and down made it awkward, but after no more than three steps the weight began to lighten from my feet. I felt I had no traction. Keep running, I told myself. Run until they aren't touching the road any longer. I kept the bar in firmly and tried to keep the nose up. *Angle of attack,* Hank had called it. How appropriate.

My harness grew taut as my weight settled into it. My feet dangled: an odd, helpless feeling. I remembered to push the bar away a few inches to gain height. The angle of attack became higher as the kite's center of gravity—me—moved toward the rear.

"Keep your head up," called Hank. "Don't look at the ground!"

I looked away from the pavement blurring beneath me and relaxed until I was in neutral position. I was gliding down the slope, I was doing it!

I'd been in the air no more than five seconds when I was speeding over the wrecked cars. Hank flattened himself on the hood as I sailed over him. The road rushed up. I had to fight a momentary panic that screamed for me to abandon ship. I pushed the bar away and slowed as the ground-cushion effect took hold, and then the kite became a parachute and I settled vertically. I had flared too high, though, and felt myself back-sliding, slipping backward. I pulled the bar in and landed easy as a snowflake.

I unbuckled quickly. My ears pounded. I felt giddy, as if I'd hyperventilated. When I'd been flying, I had been preoccupied with doing it right; all that information had been running across my head and it hadn't really hit me that I'd been flying, I had *flown!* Now that I was down and out of the glider, the sensations sleeted across me. I grinned like an idiot and applauded myself. Hank jogged up to me, returning my grin, sharing my exhilaration. He helped me tote my kite back up the hill. I grinned at Malachi Lee. He rolled his eyes, shaking his head as he tilted his face to the sky.

"You're up, Mac," said Tom.

I looked with different-seeing eyes as Mac positioned his kite—an arc of rainbow with a ball of gold at one end. Now I knew what it felt like, and watching was a vicarious thrill.

Mac waited for the wind to stop gusting. I looked at Hank, who had resumed his position at the foot of the hill. Why, he wasn't even a hundred yards away! As Mac rushed forward I realized my flight had lasted no more than ten seconds. The sensations had been enough to fill several good hours.

Mac ended up dry running it. His last few steps lost their oomph, and instead of lifting off, the tops of his shoes dragged the ground for ten feet. He pulled back on the bar to gain lift, but he had neither speed nor proper angle of attack. His kite nosed up and we watched him dangle like a hung-up marionette for two long seconds, and then the tail of the kite hit the ground, with Mac not far behind. He got up quickly before the wind could flip him onto his back like a Raid-sprayed roach. Cursing, he walked the kite carefully back to us and tried again. This time he lifted smoothly, glided down swiftly and evenly, and settled down onto his knees. He unbuckled and stumbled from the glider. "Oh, well," he said cheerfully. "Any landing you can walk away from." He declined Hank's offer of help and walked the kite back to the tip. His eyes were bright. "I think," he said seriously, "I've found a suitable replacement for sex."

I found myself blushing.

"Walt," said Tom mildly.

Walt's flight was something out of the instruction book. Nice.

"Okay, Drew. Curtain up."

Drew got off to a good start, coasted down the slope—and freaked when he saw the cars heading toward him. He shoved the bar away to gain height, but he overdid it and stalled.

"Hold still!" shouted Hank."Pull in on the bar!"

Drew's legs continued to flail as if he were trying to tread water. He came down on his ass on the roof of a black Cadillac. He hit hard. We ran down to see if he was hurt. The wind had been jarred out of him, but he was okay. Hank helped him out of the rigging and onto his feet, making an obvious effort to be patient. "You can't panic," he said, trying to keep his tone reasoned. "You're going to jump from a fucking fifteen-hundred foot tall building, and if you land on the roof of a Cadillac from there you're going to be a permanent part of it. Relax, pay attention, and remember what you've been told."

We went five times apiece, trying for a little more height each time, a little more speed, before calling it a day and deciding to let the jumps off the office building wait until tomorrow. We spent the rest of the evening working out an attack strategy.

No one got killed, or even broke anything, so I guess we did okay.

The air was charged in the assembly room. A nervous hub-bub waxed and waned. Tom had announced the assembly on the bulletin board when we returned from our strategy session, the purpose being to go over the plans for the attack and make sure everybody knew who was doing what.

Tom faced the assembly and cleared his throat. The murmuring died down. "Well, here's the story," he said, electing not to mince words. "We've assembled a hang gliding team."

He was drowned out by the excited babbling which followed the announcement. He waited until it died down. "The team consists of myself, Malachi Lee, Vic Magruder, Hank Rysetter, Walt Bonham, Drew Zenoz, and our latest addition: Pete Garey."

The murmuring rose again. I saw people counting on their fingers as he called our names out, and I heard a few commenting to each other: "Seven people? *Seven?* Oh, come on. . . ." And one voice from the rear: *"Go-o-o-o mice!"*

"The rest of you leave for New York early tomorrow morning."

Again his voice was lost. It was like a nominee's speech at a big political convention; every statement was emotionally charged and brought a response. Tom went on when it died down. "Don't rush the march. It's eight days if you make good time without wearing yourselves out. Don't push it any faster than that. Remember, you've got a battle to fight when you get there."

I looked around and saw Shaughnessy sitting with a woman I didn't recognize. She didn't see me. I kept looking around and saw McGee, who smiled and waved when she saw me. I waved back, surprised at how pleased I was to see her.

"You should reach New York in the early morning," Tom continued. "Make sure you get a good sleep the night before; take longer to camp. Because when you get to New York I want you to attack without delay."

He waited until the noise died down enough for him to be heard, then turned to a map of Manhattan mounted on an easel. He pointed to the intersection of two streets. "This is Fifth Avenue," he said, indicating one, "and this is Thirty-fourth Street. The main entrances open out there. That's probably where you'll do your heaviest fighting; it'll be a bottleneck until you can get through. From then on I'm afraid it's a fighting push up the stairs. According to our information from Pete they have a possible eight hundred to a thousand men on the bottom three or four floors."

It was several minutes before it grew quiet enough for him

to speak again. Beside me, Mac said, "He ought to have a gavel." I nodded. Tom had upped my estimate of their number a bit, but who could blame him? Better safe than sorry. At least he wasn't bullshitting them about what they were walking into.

"Do all of you know Avery Stondheim? Stand up, Avery." A small, bird-like man stood, turning so the seated people could get a good look at him. "Avery will lead the attack from the Fifth Avenue side. Roger Dawson—stand up, Rog—will lead the Thirty-fourth Street. We'll split our forces equally. Once you're on either the Thirty-fourth Street or the Fifth Avenue side, your respective leaders will tell you what to do." He paused. "The hang gliding team will leave the day after tomorrow. We'll be traveling on horseback, so we'll probably pass you on the way."

"Why do you get to ride?" someone called out.

Tom ticked off on his fingers. "Because we're carrying twenty-foot-long hang gliders. Because we need the extra day here to practice jumping off buildings. Because we need the extra time to climb the World Trade Center, set up, and jump off."

Silence this time. Amazed stares.

"At three o'clock that afternoon," he continued into the hushed audience, "we'll jump for the Empire State Building. It should take us less than ten minutes to get there. With a little luck they won't notice us, because they aren't expecting an attack from above. Right now, surprise is our only real advantage, both in the air and on the ground. Mr. Garey has estimated that there are two hundred men in those top floors—"

"Two hundred?" said an incredulous voice. "Against seven? That's suicide."

Tom looked toward the voice. "The hang gliding team, I should say, isn't intended as an effective attack force. I guess it would be more accurate to call it a hit squad. Our primary goal is the necromancer."

The babble in the auditorium sounded as though an astounding fact had just stunned the courtroom on *Perry Mason*. "Our chances aren't good," continued Tom, raising his voice, "and we don't know nearly as much as we should. But it's the best chance we're likely to have. He has powers—" The talking had died and the last three words were spoken too loudly. "He has powers," Tom repeated in a lower voice, "and at the very least we can serve as a distraction while the rest of you fight your way up. If we can keep him busy enough, he might not get a chance to try to stop you." He stopped to let that sink in.

He had neglected to mention something we had discussed earlier: that the fighting on the lower levels would also serve as a distraction in the hang gliding team's favor—the battle might cause reinforcements to be sent down from the upper floors, decreasing the chance of our being spotted as we came in, and increasing our chance of being able to fight our way through.

"But," he went on, "we also might not make it. There's a good possibility we'll be picked off before we even reach the Empire State Building. In which case it's up to you, and you'll have to fight it all the way up."

"That's a hundred stories!" somebody protested.

"Eighty-six, in the main building," Tom responded levelly. "And, as far as we know, the enemy are only located on the bottom three or four and top two or three floors. The middle ground should be the easiest part. Once you get past the bottom four floors, you ought to be home free."

I noticed he said "once" instead of "if."

The next thing I knew the assembly was breaking up amidst loud arguments, speculation, expressed fears, and optimism, and Tom was asking that members of the hang gliding team and the two leaders of the ground forces—how quickly we form our military jargon, I thought—stay behind to go over the whole thing again. Everyone cleared out but the nine of us. I stared at the map of New York as Tom gave instructions on the ground attack to Avery Stondheim and Roger Dawson.

You're it now, you bastard, I thought, looking at the grid of streets. *You're all there is.*

"As for us," Tom was saying, "we have to go light. No armor, no shields. No heavy weapons. Carry a bow and arrow if you're any good with one; we'll find a way to strap them down so we can get them off quickly but won't fall off before that. Take your sword, of course—I think you can wear it without having to tie it to the glider."

"Tape it to the trapeze bar with duct tape," said Malachi,

"and turn an end up so you can pull it away quickly when you need your sword."

Tom nodded. "Hank, you're our archery expert—could you fire a bow while flying one of those things?"

"I don't think so. The kites respond pretty quickly, and if you let go I doubt you'll stay in neutral position. One good gust of wind and you're gone. You could probably recover, sure, but I don't think you'd be able to do that and land on the eighty-sixth floor. Maybe you could do it if you had the bow out and already fitted, but I wouldn't want to try to do that and fly the glider at the same time."

I stared through the far wall. Tom stepped into my field of vision, lifted the map of New York, and set it behind another drawing. "This is a rough map of the eighty-sixth floor, based on a drawing Pete did for us. We're going to have to—Pete, where are you going?"

I looked back at him, only half aware I'd started for the door. "Huh? Oh, I . . . I've got to . . . my blowgun. Shaughnessy has my blowgun." I turned and left. My feet pounded numbly down the hallway, echoing in the huge empty spaces, and I was only dimly aware of reaching my room and sitting down on the edge of the bed.

I sat there for an hour, hands clenched, with the worse case of the shakes I've ever had.

I knocked on the door.

"Who—oh, hello, Pete."

"Hi, McGee. I came—" she opened the door to let me in and closed it behind me "—I'm not sure why I came," I finished lamely.

She studied me.

"I, uh, read your note. I guess that's why I'm here. I mean, what I want to say is, well—thank you. Thank you very much."

"You don't have to thank me, Pete." Her voice was soft.

"I know, but I want to. I—shit, I don't know. McGee, I'm confused."

"You don't have to explain anything to me," she said gently. "I understand."

My jaw worked. "Well I'm glad *you* do. Maybe you can explain it to me."

She looked at me for a long time. "I don't think I'd want to be in your shoes for anything," she finally said.

"What makes you say that?"

"Because I know what I want. *My* choices are usually pretty clear; I rarely have any major conflicts." She went to the door and opened it. "And I'm sorry, but I think you'd better leave."

"But. . . ." I stepped toward her.

"No, Pete. I wouldn't do that to you, and I wouldn't let you do it to yourself." And she held the door open for me.

I stood on the other side of it for a few minutes after it closed, still confused.

Archives Section:

"Uh—" I didn't know her name. "Do you know where I could find Shaughnessy? I've got to get my blowgun from her."

She looked dubious but told me. "She's been rooming with me," she added. I wondered why she did.

The "room" turned out to be a sectioned off space, a hastily made cubicle of sheets, wood partitions, and curtains, arranged to provide some semblance of privacy. How do you knock on a sheet? I cleared my throat. "Um, anybody home?"

Shaughnessy pulled a sheet aside. "Pete." The distance still seemed to be there. "Hold on a minute. I'm not dressed." She closed the sheet before I could respond. A minute later she emerged, wearing shorts and a blue T-shirt.

"I came for my blowgun," I said without preamble.

"Oh." She looked as if I'd just punched her in the stomach. "I'll . . . get it." She disappeared behind the sheet again and was back in fifteen seconds with the Aero-mag. I looked it over, squinting down the tube to see if anything had got lodged inside, and to make sure it was still straight. It was in fine shape. A little scratched up, maybe, but we'd been through a lot together. I had made darts from piano wire I'd found on the scavenger hunt with Mac, and I pulled one from my back pocket, fitted it, and looked around for something to shoot at. An antique headboard and bedframe leaned against a wall. The mattress had probably been procured by someone with the room for it. I raised the Aero-mag to my lips and puffed as if sounding a low note on a tuba. *Thock!* It reverberated through the Archives Section. Ignoring Shaughnessy, I walked to the headboard, grabbed the end of the dart, braced one foot against the wood, and pulled, twisting. The bead came loose and I fell onto my back.

I got up quickly, dusting myself off. Shaughnessy looked as though she were trying hard not to laugh. Her face was red.

"What's so damned funny?" I demanded, feeling cloddish.

"You take yourself so seriously," she said when she caught her breath.

"I'm doing serious things, Shaughnessy."

"Oh, Pete." She looked exasperated and changed the subject. "That's really something, being able to hang glide. Maybe you'll be able to get to Ariel." She watched me carefully, gauging my reaction.

"That's why I'm going," I said evenly.

"Is there another glider?"

She looked insulted when I laughed. "No, there isn't. At least, we didn't find another one. Besides, you could get killed."

"For your information, Mister Garey, I am marching with the rest of this army tomorrow."

"You can't."

"I can and I will. And who the hell are you to tell me otherwise?"

"Shaughnessy, look—you don't have to do this for me. This is my fight."

"Your fight! *Your* fight! You arrogant son of a bitch, what makes you think I'm fighting for you and Ariel in the first place?"

"But I thought—"

"'But' nothing. Do you think all three hundred of these people are fighting to get Ariel back for you? They'd be fighting if you'd never existed, and I happen to believe in what they're fighting for. But I suppose you haven't stopped to consider their reasons for any of this." She snorted. "You don't even care about Ariel—you're trying to save your own feelings, your own selfish interests."

"That's not—"

She wouldn't let me get a word in. "You don't care about her, you don't care about these people and their cause; you don't even care about me, and I've tried everything I can to—" She stopped, eyes widening. "Oh . . . shit!" She disappeared a final time behind her sheet.

For the second time in fifteen minutes I stood behind a closed entranceway, feeling stupid and confused.

I tried to use the chamber pot in my room and couldn't relax enough. I tried to sleep. I couldn't relax enough, but I had to go to the bathroom. I lay awake and stared up at the blackness, thinking how nice everything would be if only I could use the fucking bathroom.

I was scared. I was surprised at how hard it was to admit that to myself.

I got up and dressed.

"Shaughnessy?" I whispered beside the silent sheet. "Shaughnessy?"

"Who is it?"

"It's me. Pete."

Another voice, sleepy: "Wha? Time to go already?"

"Shh. No, Deb. Go back to sleep."

She appeared quietly, drawing the sheet aside and stepping into the huge room. She wore the T-shirt and white shorts she'd had on before. "What do you want, Pete?"

A single Japanese lantern burned behind me, casting my shadow upon the sheet, upon half her face. I moved a little to see her more clearly. She looked as if she had been crying.

"Shaughnessy, I—I want to apologize. For the other night, when you came into my room and I yelled at you. I was upset. I'm sorry. I shouldn't have done it. You didn't deserve that."

"It's okay, Pete. I understand."

"No, it's not okay," I said, echoing the words I'd used to begin shouting at her that night. "I need you to understand. I haven't been thinking straight." I tapped my temple with a forefinger. "I feel like I can't see things as they are."

"You need Ariel back," she said simply.

I nodded in the darkness and she shut her eyes. "I understand, Pete. Yes, I do." And without saying any more she turned back inside her little cubicle. I heard her beginning to cry.

I stood there a long time, listening. When it stopped I realized there was a wet streak under each of my own eyes. I wiped them away with my sleeve. And then I left.

* * *

We sat on the front steps and watched them go, Mac, Walt, Hank, Drew, Tom, Malachi, and myself. Occasionally someone would look back and we gave them a heartfelt thumbs-up.

"Well," said Tom after the last of them had turned out of sight, "what are we waiting for? We've got a building to jump off of."

twenty–two

I wandered lonely as a cloud
That floats on high o'er vales and hills
When all at once I saw a crowd. . . .

—William Wordsworth,
"I Wandered Lonely as a Cloud"

Ice water chilled my lungs as I drew a shuddering breath and jumped off the top of the World Trade Center.

The building dropped below me. The street was a nine second, screaming fall away. The skyscrapers pointed away from me, their angle of tilt increasing with their distance, as though I looked at the city through a fish-eye lens.

The wind caught the kite above my head as I stepped off into the dizzying height. It threatened to lift the sail's nose, to carry me backward over the roof where the vortex winds whirled unseen, which would slam me back onto my starting point. I pulled the bar, moving my body forward six inches and picking up speed by increasing the angle of attack.

The journey to New York had been uneventful, made mostly in silence, only the uneven drumbeat of the horses' hooves pounding in time to the steady clinking of our swords in their slings. When we passed those who had left on foot before us they cheered, and for those few minutes I felt good.

We reached Manhattan before nightfall the next day, abandoning the horses at the Holland Tunnel. After freeing them, we walked the rest of the way to the World Trade Center. The front doors were open. We walked into the huge, blue-toned main floor and began climbing.

I went straight toward the Empire State Building for twenty seconds, then began a gentle turn to the right. If I turned more than about thirty degrees I would be losing more height than I'd be able to make up. I made sure it was more gradual than that, inching to the right side of the kite. After a second it responded: the right wing spar dipped slightly, and there was the city, spread out in high relief, wheeling ever so slowly almost two thousand feet below. Ice cubes formed in my stomach as I looked down at it. I tried to relax in my prone position, resisting the irrational impulse to kick my feet as though swimming. The wind blew into my face. I felt as if my shoes were going to fall of.

Stall speed increases on a turn—that is, it's easier for the kite to lose lift while banking. I compensated by pulling forward on the trapeze bar to gain speed. The kite lost altitude, but I'd gain that back when I passed over the western edge of the tower I'd jumped from; the air rushing up the sides would provide lift. If I did it right, I'd gain more than I had lost. I continued the gentle curve until I saw the rear of a yellow kite with a red V in the center. A G.I. Joe figure in a warm-up suit dangled beneath: Malachi Lee. He was climbing at a good angle as he passed over the World Trade Center, playing it smart by keeping the nose up slightly and letting the wind do the work. Far ahead of him, just beginning his second right-hand curve toward the eastern side of the opposite tower, was an even smaller figure beneath a white paper airplane with a diagonal blue slash: Tom Pert.

The top of the building was now above me by a few stories; I'd lost the height in the turn. Each of us was launching as the one before him began his first half-turn of the circle, and as I steadily approached the building another delta shape glided from the edge. A rainbow-arced kite with a ball of gold at one end of the colorful crescent: Mac.

We'd managed to climb up the first forty-four flights before Tom decided it was too dark to go on and we set up "camp." Exhausted, we set our long, thin burdens on the floor and slept in a hallway. We hadn't seen another human being since passing the ground forces the day before.

An upsurge of wind lifted the sail. I raised the nose just a tad, climbing. In only a few seconds I was back at rooftop level, fifteen hundred feet from the street. Another of the kites swooped, bat-like, from the top. Red, green, and blue stripes: Hank. Behind me, Mac should be midway through his first turn. I was too busy to watch; the air gusted unpredictably and the glider required my constant control. I couldn't afford to let my grip relax on the control bar.

I climbed until I was about two hundred feet over the top of the tower before the upsurge died down. Malachi and Tom had been right: the updrafts more than compensated for the altitude we lost during turns. By the time we came over the eastern edge of the other tower, straightened out, and caught the convection current from that side, we should have gained at least three or four hundred feet from rooftop level. Possibly more, if we could keep our turns gentle.

My speed had put me a little ahead of the game: Tom was just reaching the opposite edge of our lift-off tower's twin. He should have been just leaving the influence of the updraft, but the difference shouldn't prove crucial, as long as I didn't overtake him. Or run into him.

I leveled off and flew straight. Ahead of me, Malachi Lee completed his second one hundred eighty degree turn and straightened.

I'd got up early next morning, having slept little, and what sleep I'd had was troubled. Everyone else seemed edgy also. Except for Malachi Lee, who looked like a relaxed cat. Drew seemed the most nervous. He was defensive and easily agitated. We left him alone.

We picked up our zippered nylon bags and took the stairwell again. The climbing was dreary and mindless, which was bad—not because of the drudgery but because it left your mind free to roam. Fear played volleyball in my imagination. Ironically, I was relieved when we finally reached the top.

The final door was locked. We took it off its hinges. It opened onto a small area that, like the Empire State Building, had been a concession counter selling souvenirs. We walked on through double glass doors and blinked in the sunlight glaring from the roof. We set the kites side by side. Each of us walked to the edge and looked down silently, alone with his thoughts.

On a clear day, you can see. . . .

The Empire State Building. No more pollution to mar the scenery; the Change had provided a grand view. Funny—it seemed even smaller from here, though it dwarfed the buildings around it.

We still had five hours to go before we jumped. Rather than sit around and become even more jittery—Drew had developed a pronounced twitch in his right eye—we unzipped the long bags and began assembling the rigs.

I banked into the second turn. Drew ought to be launching about now. I risked a glance toward the farther of the twin towers. His kite—green on the wingtips and along the keel—rested on the roof beside Walt's, nose down, two technicolor moths.

Goddammit—he's chickened out.

I shouldn't have been so disdainful, but I was. I could understand the reluctance to take that first and irretrievably committed step, but not the lack of fortitude in being unable to overcome it.

Hell, Garey—he doesn't have as much at stake as you do.

Now the green and white kite was moving, being lifted up and carried to the sheer drop of the edge.

Drew jumped, only a little behind schedule. I completed my turn and straightened out just as his feet left the roof.

It was small talk only as we lay out our respective A-frames, making them rigid by affixing nose plates and crosstubes, tightening nuts, running rigging wire, securing the sail, attaching trapeze bar. We took our time and did it right, then went over it again, tightening a wing nut here, tautening a wire across a turnbuckle there, and then we inspected each other's kites as we had before. I excused myself once and went to the other side so they couldn't see me vomit.

Soon it was time to jump.

I approached the eastern of the two towers a good seventy-five feet above rooftop level, higher than either Tom or Malachi had been. The wind was favoring this side and the convection currents pushed a bit stronger, helped by the additional flow of air from below. I kept the nose high and climbed. Ahead to the right, on the opposite tower, the last of the kites jumped away. Blue and red stripes radiated in a sunburst from the nose: Walt.

By the time the strong updraft began to lessen I was four hundred feet above the rooftop of the World Trade Center, almost two thousand feet from the ground. I kept the nose up a little while longer to gain as much height as I could. It would decrease my speed, but I would end up ahead—the higher you are, the farther you go. I was thankful for the haircut McGee had given me as I looked forward, the wind rushing across my face, pushing the hair sticking out from the crash helmet toward my eyes. I was higher than Tom or Malachi. I decided to keep it that way; I might need all the height I could get. It was easier to lose than gain, and I could always lower myself later, when we were closer and I could better estimate how I'd have to come in.

I glanced at Fred for reassurance, and to see that it was still secure against the left side of the triangular bar, held tight by four bands of masking tape. I hoped I would be able to remove it easily when it came time to land on the eighty-sixth floor observation deck and ditch the kite.

As I buckled myself onto the kite just before jumping, I noticed on the wing a small decal that I'd managed to miss before:

WARNING

Hang gliding is a dangerous activity and can result in serious injury or death even when engaged in under ideal circumstances. This equipment is manufactured in accordance with the safety, material, construction, and flight standards established by the Hang Glider Manufacturer's Association, Inc. This equipment should be used only under proper conditions after proper instruction and practice supervised by an experienced hang gliding instructor. The manufacturer has no control over the use and maintenance of this equipment and all persons using this equipment assume all risks for damage or injury. The manufacturer and the HGMA, Inc., disclaim any liability or

responsibility for damages or injury resulting from the use of this equipment.

I felt I should make a joke, but it didn't seem very funny, really.

The rigging wires hummed beehive tunes as they cut through the air. The trailing edge of the Dacron sail flapped rapidly, like a drum roll at a circus. Manhattan was a three-dimensional grid beneath me. I felt as if I were some huge kite flown on an invisible string held by a child on the streets a third of a mile below. A backward glance revealed the four remaining hang gliders, pop-art candleflies at various heights, spaced more or less at five-hundred-foot intervals. My own kite was sky blue, but with a bright yellow V along the leading edge.

The East River was to my right, the Hudson on my left. It was quiet down there. Quiet and gray. Washington Square slid silently beneath my feet: the halfway mark.

I patted the Aero-mag at my thigh to be sure it was still in place, then felt the pouch to be sure it was securely closed. The blowgun and the sword: my weapons. They would have to do.

The mammoth dart of the Empire State Building neared steadily. A few men were visible on the eighty-sixth floor. A good sign. There would have been more had they noticed us.

From below I thought I heard noise. Somewhere down there, two "armies" fought. Shaughnessy. McGee.

Tom, leading us, looked to be just a little low. Immediately ahead of me, Malachi looked to be just where he needed to be. Of course. Behind me, in order of proximity, were Mac, Walt, Drew, and Hank. Drew looked a little low, but it was hard to tell because I was higher than any of them and relative altitude was hard for me to gauge from above.

Those four were going to have it roughest. Tom and Malachi would probably land before any alarm was efficiently sounded. I figured I might squeeze by before any sort of organized resistance could be massed. But Mac, Hank, Drew, and Walt would almost certainly have to avoid archers. A hang glider is maneuverable, but hardly evasive. Especially when you're in a hurry.

I was the only one of us without a bow. The rest carried light hunting bows with thigh or bow quivers, which made the arrows much easier to get to. Tom carried an extremely short bow. It required strong arms to pull it to full draw, but Tom could yank it to his ear without batting an eye. Hank Rysetter carried his tournament target bow taped on his trapeze bar. Pulleys at the ends made it a compound bow; peep sight, levels, a distance/elevation gauge, and a bow quiver made it look like a damned machine, as if it ought to be able to load and fire itself. I thought all the gizmos were cheats, but whatever works, I guess.

Tom was close now. My arm muscles tightened and my hands clenched harder on the bar. I shivered.

The white wing with the diagonal blue slash was now even with the eighty-first floor. Tom raised his nose and began listing in a narrow angle curve. He began to lift. I was close enough—no more than a thousand feet—to see that he'd been spotted: two people stared out a window above his climbing kite. They disappeared.

I concentrated on the scene ahead just long enough to realize that Tom and Malachi were going to land at about the same time, if neither one was shot from the air, and then I had to think about how the hell I was going to descend. Maybe I could spiral down in a tight curve. . . . I pulled the bar toward me. The nose dipped and I picked up speed. I was still fifty feet higher than I needed to be when the building's updrafts caught me and lifted me still higher—shit! I'd overshot—the building was nowhere near as wide as the World Trade Center. I could have stalled and parachuted straight in, but I'd have been a flashing neon sign: HIT ME! HIT ME!

No choice: straighten out, circle to lose height, and try again.

I was being lifted still higher. The wind here was strong. I flew straight for five hundred feet and began to turn. As I came back around I saw Malachi's kite spiralling down the side of the building. It was empty. Tom was quickly dumping his, and the battle was joined.

I was too busy concentrating on what I was doing to get more than fleeting impressions: Malachi pulled his bow and a man dropped; Tom pulling his bow, and the same; Mac's rainbow kite skimming over the edge and him kicking someone in the head even as he somehow unbuckled himself and shucked his kite, dropping onto the deck; Malachi now swinging his hunting bow at someone's head, dropping it, and his sword magically appearing in his hands.

I was still too high, and the goddamn upsurge lifted me again. I pushed the bar away in a deliberate stall, holding it stiffly with one hand while the other ripped the broken-down Aero-mag away from my left thigh. I had fitted a dart before I jumped, and it was held in by a rubber stopper.

Somebody down there saw me and began to raise his bow. I yanked out the stopper and puffed hard. The vortex winds spilling over the sides of the huge building grabbed me and shook me like a kitten in its mother's mouth. I pitched forward just as something ripped through the fabric of my sail. I had to grab something, and quick, or else I was going to be slammed into God's own hypodermic syringe: the tower. I scraped down its length, hands flailing. Something rammed into my right arm and slowed my fall. I shot my left arm over to it and grabbed for my life.

I was clinging to one of the slanting, T-shaped, black metal guards around the perimeter of the top floor, the one hundred second floor observation deck. The gusting wind tugged at the sail on my back and threatened to pull me off. I locked my legs around the guard and let go with my hands, hanging upside down. I reached up and strained the kite toward me to slacken the strap I was buckled to, and managed to get my harness clip off. I put the Aero-mag in my mouth and held onto the kite's control bar just long enough to remove Fred. With the sword loose and held tight in my right hand, I let go of the kite. It descended in a slow spiral toward the ground, over twelve hundred feet below. I made the mistake of following it with my eyes.

Picture hanging upside down, at almost the tip of one of the largest buildings in the world, and raising your head—looking *up* to the far away ground to watch a giant kite spiralling away. Every survival instinct I had screamed for me not to move, not to twitch a muscle, not even to breathe. I hung motionless for what seemed like minutes, listening to shouts from below.

I forced myself to move. I tightened my grip with my ankles and leaned forward. My stomach muscles clenched. I grabbed with my left hand. The right was busy trying to hold onto Fred. All this with a blowgun in my mouth. Saliva dripped from the corner of my lip and flowed across one cheek. I hoisted myself upright slowly, worming my legs. The black metal guard I'd latched onto was square, and the corners dug into the insides of my thighs.

Upright and straddling the slanted T of the bar, I saw the developments on the eighty-sixth floor, two hundred feet below. Walt had sped up, obviously having to lose height, and was coming in just as Hank dropped in midair from his glider and landed atop a man who was trying to draw a bead on Tom Pert's back. At least a dozen bodies were already down. There was no sign of Drew.

Hank's kite sailed on until it dropped on top of two men. I quickly tucked Fred under my arm and brought my hand down to the dart pouch—and discovered that it had come open and was almost empty. A few left, though, so don't waste time. I slapped one into the Aero-mag with my palm, raised it to my mouth and puffed, just as the two men moved Hank's kite aside. One of them slammed to the concrete as if he'd been hit by a baseball bat. If the shot had been true I'd got him just above the left ear. I rammed another dart home and fired as the second one looked from his fallen comrade to me, and he pitched backward onto the other still form, grabbing at his chest.

The bar I sat on was just beneath a circular observation window about a yard wide. Praying it was breakable, I returned the Aero-mag to my mouth and drew Fred. I brought the handle up and began pounding it against the glass. It spiderwebbed at first, and then started falling inward in jagged fragments. I cleared the shards away from the edges. It was going to take both hands to climb in. I saw no one in the small room, so I dumped the blowgun and sword inside. I grabbed with both hands, feeling glass cut into the left one, and hoisted myself up, in, and through. Glass crunched beneath my feet.

The room was thirty feet in diameter, circular, and painted an ugly shade of blue, into which graffiti had been etched everywhere. The floor was metal. The room was featureless except for the viewing ports around the perimeter, the graffiti, and the very top of an elevator shaft. Beside it was an iron stairwell.

I held out the lip of the dart pouch and looked in. Six left. Better make 'em count.

I removed the hang gliding harness and tucked Fred in at my left side. I'd grabbed a wide leather belt from a Western clothing store and it was buckled tightly around my waist. A belt loop would no longer serve.

Footsteps clanged on the metal staircase. I looked around. Between the elevator shaft and the wall was a narrow space where I could stand. I hurried to it, keeping my footsteps quiet. I fumbled within the pouch until I came up with a dart pinched between thumb and forefinger, and I carefully inserted it into the Aero-mag. I kept my back to the wall and waited to see which side they'd come from. Both, probably. The shattered observation window would give me away, so they'd be prepared. I tried to hold my breath, waiting. Eyes straight ahead; don't favor any one side or you're dead. I concentrated on my peripheral vision—and saw the harness on the floor where I'd shed it. Shit. I hurried to pick it up.

Movement from the corner of my eye: my head jerked right, and there he was, spear in hand, in the midst of drawing back for a thrust. Blowgun up and *puhh!*

He spun, hands covering the space between his nose and upper lip where a four-inch piano-wire dart was wedged, and crumpled to his knees with a cry of pain. I didn't waste time fitting another dart, but dropped the blowgun and pulled Fred from my belt. Holding it in my left hand, I leaned back and began inching the sword forward as though I were walking forward and carelessly keeping the blade in front of me, not realizing it could be seen before I was. When most of the length of the blade was exposed, it was batted aside by an axe. Its wielder stepped out from around the corner and swung at where my chest ought to have been. The axe thumped into the side of the elevator and I stepped out and swung the hang gliding harness with all my strength. The heavy buckle hit him on the head. He brought his arms up to ward it off, rendering his axe ineffective. I brought the blade back and pushed. The point went into his chest. Something popped as the steel slid in, and there was a second quick jolt as the point came out the other side. He opened his mouth and blood bubbled out. I felt his weight in my forearms as his knees buckled, and when I was sure he was dead I pulled the blade out and finished off his writhing comrade.

I dropped the harness, retrieved the blowgun, and tucked it at my right hip. I ran down the stairs with Fred in both hands and cursed myself for not pulling the dart from the first man. Five left now. At least the one hadn't been wasted. How wonderful. Oh, the economy we learn in battle.

Someone was heading up the stairs, making so much noise that he couldn't have heard me coming down. I was ready for him as, spear cradled in one arm, he rounded the corner onto the level space where the staircase turned. His head was down so he could watch his footing. I gripped the rail with one hand and said, "Hey!"

He looked up and I caught him full in the face with the sole of my boot. I thrust hard, trying to straighten my knee as I made contact. His head snapped back with a bone-cracking sound and his body tumbled the way it had come, stopping hard against the wall. I ran past it and kept going until I reached the door with "86" stenciled on it in white. Fred in left hand, I held my breath and pulled on the knob with my right. A silver blur almost cut me in two. It *wheet*ed past as I jumped back. I slammed the door. "Malachi, it's me!"

"Pete." His voice was muffled. "Wait."

Leaning against the door, I heard the clash of steel from the other side, then two grunts: Malachi's, a controlled exhalation, and another, punched-in-the-kidney sound.

"Tom!" Malachi's voice. "This way."

The door jerked open. I flinched. Malachi stood with his back to me, fresh red staining his sword. Tom was next to him, one-handed broadsword at ready, also stained. Past them I saw Hank and Walt fighting their way into the metal and glass souvenir counter that was the indoor section of the eighty-sixth floor. Walt engaged like a classic fencer, incongruous with his heavy Scottish sword: block, parry, block, and leap nimbly in, pushing the blade into his opponent's sternum almost to the hilt. Walt pushed him off the blade with a foot, turned, and ran inside, shirt snagging on the shattered glass door.

Hank hadn't even drawn his blade yet; he was still picking them off with his target bow. He was all fast, fluid motion, deftly pulling an arrow from the thigh quiver, sliding up the length of the bowstring with two fingers to notch the arrow, and barely taking time to draw, aim, and release. His latest aggressor had been running for him full out; he jerked backward on invisible strings not three feet from him, landing on his butt and staring stupidly at the arrow that had sprouted from his solar plexus. He started to reach for it, then his eyes rolled up in his head and he pitched sideways. Hank remained impassive, pulling, fitting, drawing, sighting, and releasing again without even glancing at the man he'd just killed. Another fell with a hunting arrow lodged in his throat up to the feathers. Hank turned a complete circle, sweeping the bow, but no more opponents were to be seen. Only then did he walk calmly toward the stairwell door where we waited.

I kept glancing backward into the stairwell, waiting for reinforcements to arrive any second now—*their* reinforcements. "Malachi," I began, "where's Mac? Shouldn't he . . . ?" I stopped. Through the shattered remains of the glass door I saw Mac.

Malachi looked at me without expression.

Hank joined us. "Any sign of Drew?"

"He didn't make it," said Walt. "He panicked and stalled. I saw it just before I came in. Last I saw of him, he was cartwheeling down the side of the building."

Tom, Malachi, and Hank merely nodded. *Now we are five,* I thought.

"One floor down," said Malachi. I stared beyond him at the red-soaked figure neatly framed by the glass door, as if he were posing for a picture and would wipe off the fake red and get up, laughing, once it was taken.

"We'd better hurry," said Hank.

They turned and began descending slowly and quietly down the steps. I trailed after them, after taking one more look through the block of light which narrowed as I closed the door.

The shaft was dim, but there was still enough light to see by. I'd taken no more than a half dozen steps when the other four came running back up.

"What's going on?" I asked. "What happened?"

"Ran into two people coming up," said Tom. "They saw us and ran back down to the eighty-fifth floor. Hank got a shot off, but we don't think he hit either one of them. Doesn't matter—they know we're coming."

"That door'll be guarded like a harem," added Hank.

"There're two stairwells in the building," I said. "Starting on the eighty-fifth floor. One in each corner. We could go down a few floors, take our chances getting to the opposite stairwell, and come back out on eighty-five."

"No," said Malachi. "By then they'll have both doors guarded too well." Suddenly a six-inch-wide stripe illuminated his face. I whirled around—I was the closest to the door that had just opened. A silhouette was framed by the doorway. He took a half-step in and jumped back when he saw us. "Shit," he said.

I jumped out after him, Fred readied. He held a long black spear and fumbled to gain distance and bring the point up level with my chest. He waited until I was four feet from him, and the point darted forward. I almost impaled myself, just managing to twist out of the way in time. I was off balance and realized there was no way I'd regain my footing before he ran me through, so I went with the motion and rolled on the floor, holding Fred at arm's length above my head so I wouldn't complete his job for him. He jabbed again, but I was already out of range. He jumped forward and tried once more. I was in the midst of getting back on my feet and used my momentum for a rising block which deflected his spear over my head. I stepped in and slashed at his ribs, missing by a foot. His spear gave him too much range. I danced out of the way and we squared off.

He twitched the spear at me, trying to make me react and then check myself. It would freeze me just long enough to be shish kebobbed. Instead I stood my ground, ready to block and try to create another opening.

A black arrowhead and six inches of shaft sprang from his chest like an ineptly rigged knife-throwing act at a circus. He didn't seem conscious of it and twitched his spear at me one more time. Then his breath caught and the spear clattered from his hands. He closed both hands around the bright yellow shaft and tugged half-heartedly. He stared at me, eyes widening.

"Pete." Hank, from the stairwell door, target bow lowered. He'd fitted another arrow. "Pete, we need a hand taking the door off. We're going to try something." Reluctantly I took my gaze from the dying man. Hank's face was impassive as ever. He'd just saved my life and I should have felt grateful.

The man pitched forward onto his face, gurgling. I walked past him.

I saw nothing but the door Walt and I held before us. It was a heavy, metal-lined fire door; we'd removed it from its hinges and toted it downstairs to the eighty-fifth floor. I held onto my side with both hands. It pressed heavily against my right shoulder. Walt held the other side. We had it angled just enough to let us through. Though I couldn't see it, I knew

Tom's hand was on the bar of the door ahead of us. "Now!" he hissed, and pulled it open. Walt and I chop-stepped through, using the door as a shield. Arrows thumped against it, a lead-rain sound I felt in my hands. They'd been waiting, all right. Oh, had they.

I had no idea how many of them were in front of us, and was given little time to worry about it—there was one near me, swinging an axe as we cleared the doorway. I shrugged in and it glanced off the door. He pulled back to try again. I decided he didn't deserve a second chance and dropped my end of the door. It thudded onto the floor and fell forward, given an added boost by Walt. No time to draw Fred before the axe came down. I rushed him and took the impact of the handle on the shoulder. It wasn't too painful, as it caught me just above where his right hand held it, where the power in the swing was least. I grabbed his arm so he couldn't choke up on the axe and kill me, then pulled Fred straight out. The metal-capped handle caught him in the side. I hit him again, in the same spot, and ribs cracked. Once more and he bellowed and tried to club straight down with his axe handle. I kneed him in the crotch, stepped back quickly, and drew Fred, slicing his carotid artery in the same motion. I'd meant to take off his head.

I turned. An archer had managed to get enough distance to draw again and sight; his bow was levelling at Hank. He saw me running at him and tried to shift aim. He was too late. I jabbed with Fred and jerked right, severing his bowstring. I pulled both hands in and thrust.

I glanced at Hank as the archer fell. *Debt paid.*

A low, soft breath as Malachi made a final slash, and all was quiet. They had been ten. We were still five. Walt had a bad cut along one bicep. Hank pressed his palm over it while Tom used his sword to cut a strip from a dead man's shirt to make a bandage.

"Just a graze," Tom said. "You'll live."

Walt winced, teeth gritting as Tom secured the bandage.

Footsteps heading up the stairwell. A lot of them.

I looked at Malachi. Stand and fight?

They were getting close. No time to deliberate. Angry voices, pounding footsteps, and clanking metal echoed in the stairwell.

I turned when Malachi did, facing the open door. The floor was slick. The sprawled bodies would be easy to trip over.

The door we'd removed lay on the floor at an angle, a dead archer beneath.

Malachi glanced through the doorway. He jumped back. "Too many—run."

We ran. I ran down the corridor to the right. They ran down the corridor to the left. I stopped and looked back. Thirty feet away, our opposition had reached the stairwell door. Malachi, Tom, Hank, and Walt had turned a corner and were out of sight. I couldn't double back, and I had to get out of there *now*.

I ran.

They were going the wrong direction, dammit! The necromancer was this way, the way I was headed—but who'd had a chance to get his bearings?

I turned left at the first opportunity, hoping I wasn't being followed. Running down the corridor with Fred clenched in my left hand, I had a chance to wonder why we weren't running into more opposition than we had. Were they spread that thin?

No time to think—find Ariel.

I came around a corner and almost ran into three feet of swinging steel. I ducked at the last possible instant and the blade rang as it hit the edge of the wall two inches above my head. Reflexively I brought Fred up in a diagonal upward slash, but my assailant had regained his balance and sprung out of range.

Fast! The impression washed over me in a cold wave. I stepped back to gain time and brought swordpoint level with his throat.

He grinned past the unwavering point of his own katana and my knees gelatined as I recognized him: muscular, black-bearded—

The one who'd wanted my sword, beneath the overpass in Richmond. The one who'd equalled Malachi's skill after the fight that had killed Faust. He recognized me, too. He relaxed, but the blade never wavered. "Well, well, well. You. Ever name that blade I touched?"

I didn't want to talk to him; conversation during a fight is just another strategy, another way of getting mind fucked. But I couldn't hold my tongue. "It was named well before that. And you'll regret ever touching it." I was glad my voice stayed even.

His voice rose. "You'd better hope your technique's as quick as your mouth, *boy.*"

I had decided to clam up after my last words. He decided to rush me after his. I stepped back, barely stopping his overhead strike with a rising block. My body jolted with the force of it, wrists threatening to bend so far that I would no longer be able to control my blade. His speed was only a touch greater than mine, really, but he was also far more powerful.

I tried a quick inside cut to the arm but he'd anticipated it and deflected my blade with the slightest turn of his wrist, as though he were brushing away butterflies. He countered immediately, and the bright tip arrowed for my throat. I hit overdrive and everything slowed down. My arms were almost at full extension; I didn't have time to bring them back for an effective block. Options snapped into my head so incredibly fast I didn't know they had been there until later: I could try to block anyhow and sacrifice an arm to save my neck—literally; I could dodge, leaving me off balance and an easy kill; or I could duck, which might get me in the clear. It would also restrict my movement so that a slight change in his direction of thrust would finish me.

I chose the latter and ducked anyhow—

—and kicked him on the kneecap as his sword brushed over my head. Close.

He leapt back with amazing agility. The knee I'd kicked buckled as he stopped, and I jumped in with an all out straight lunge.

I tried too hard. Every nerve in my body screamed for me to kill him. My muscles tightened with the effort and with anticipation. As a result the thrust was slow and poorly timed, and he blocked it easily, off balance as he was.

I made an animal sound when our blades met, a snarling, mindless noise.

(Malachi Lee's voice hissed in my head: "*Control!*")

We stood three feet apart, blades and eyes locked, muscling each other with subtle motions, playing mind games. Who goes first? Which one of us thinks he's faster? Both of us knew that, from this position, the initiator would have to leave some area of his body open no matter what the sword position. We stood in "closed" stance: right foot near right foot, blades crossed and leveled at each other's throat.

The razor tip of his blade wasn't six inches from my Adam's apple. Mine was the same distance from his.

He tried to spit on my face. Stupid—his mouth worked, his throat muscles tensed, and as his head went forward to spit I turned my right wrist inward to parry his blade. It was like trying to move an iron pillar. He stopped in the act of spitting, expecting my counterstrike. I leaned forward slightly and twitched my blade toward his head. His sword flashed across to block the slash that never came; instead I leapt backward and slashed down.

I opened up the top of his right foot.

He looked surprised. His eyes were on me intently, and I knew he was waiting for me to look down to see what damage I'd done him. I kept my eyes on his, drew in a long breath, deepened my stance, and dropped Fred into low guard position.

He responded in kind: a deep breath to clear the mind, then setting his stance. He set most of his weight on his back leg, bending that knee, and drew his blade back in a guard I had never seen before, a sort of awkward batting stance with the blade held vertically. His left elbow pointed away from me, right arm reaching across his body to grasp the hilt firmly just beneath the guard. The fingers of his right hand straightened, then wrapped around the twined handle slowly, almost caressingly. The muscles bunched in his right arm. As he exhaled his eyes seemed to unfocus, as if he could see through me. Malachi Lee's eyes had done that.

I took advantage of the chance to flick my gaze down to his foot; if I had hit him well enough, I'd be able to wait him out while he bled to death. But it was only a nick: blood seeped from a cut on top of his boot, not nearly fast enough.

I took in a long breath to bide for time—both to play his mind game along with him and in the hope that the blood welling from his foot might make him slip on the floor—and found to my surprise that things actually did seem to become clearer in my mind. The pieces fell into place. My grip relaxed against the twine. The swordpoint steadied, leveled at his throat. My katana had become an extension of my arms. Without actually looking at him, because it was more than just looking, I noticed that his stance left his entire right side completely open—which was probably what he wanted me to think. Yeah. And his stance, though defensive, would also afford him a hell of a lot of momentum when he did swing. You had to be fast to use it—and apparently he thought he was.

All right, then. Fake left, draw his guard, and go for the open right side. I was about to try it when something stopped me.

Behind him was an open door, and through it I saw Ariel. Pure white, shimmering mane, silver hooves, head high . . . She couldn't see me from where she stood; she faced someone hidden beyond the doorframe.

My hands worked by themselves; what I did I felt as a puppet master feels through his marionette. I swung for his right side, not even trying to hit it, just waiting for his power block—and power block it was. Edge caught edge; unhesitatingly I turned my wrist, pushed his blade away, stepped in, brought Fred back, and slashed—block, parry, and slash.

He opened his mouth, not yet knowing he was dead. His knees gave, his body fell, and his head followed, both gushing blood. I hardly noticed.

Ariel.

She was speaking to someone. Her voice broke over me in silver waves. "No one," she breathed, "no one commands me!"

I stopped short, eyes filling as she drew in a proud breastful of air. Her voice gained strength. "I am a unicorn! I am of those named by Adam before all others were named. We didn't need your puny Ark; we don't need you to know what we are. I am the theme of all Nature; her Truth and her Light. *No one shall take what is mine!*" Her head lowered until the gleaming spire of her horn rested at human throat level. "You aren't fit to touch me." The last was spoken with a feral intensity I wouldn't have thought her capable of.

The necromancer. You won't take her horn. I tightened my grip on Fred and stepped forward.

"Pete, no!"

The shout brought me around, sword poised.

Malachi Lee. Red covered the length of his sword. His navy blue warm-up was torn and cut. A cut below his right eye had bled down to his chin and dried. Both his hands were bloody, but I don't think it was his own. I took it all in in a quick, grateful glance. "I've found her—come on!" I turned away, reassured that he would be behind me.

"Pete, don't go in there."

The very calmness of his voice, the sureness, stopped me.

I wanted with all my being to go to Ariel, to face whoever she spoke to, but a doubt formed about Malachi, a lump of suspicion that was just enough to keep me from turning my back on him—and his sword. I looked at him. Waiting. Very much aware of the feel of the rough handle of my sword, of the front-heavy weight of the blade. Of the body of the swordsman I'd just killed, lying in a red pool between him and me. "Why not?" I asked, matching his calmness. I heard the threat in my tone.

He heard it, too, and was careful not to move. "Pete, I wouldn't keep you from her. You know that. Just listen to me. Back away from the door and listen to me. It's a trap."

I tried to interrupt but he shook his head and went on without pause. "A trap," he repeated. "Think. *Think,* you goddamned idiot, and get away from that door."

I stayed where I was.

"Think about the last time you saw her. What did she look like? She's been a captive more than *two weeks now,* Pete—what would she look like?"

I remembered the last time I'd seen her. Limp mane, dulled coat, the red-brown and dried blood staining her spiral horn. Pained eyes, slow reactions. And after over two weeks of captivity, what then?

I stepped away from the door and joined Malachi Lee. We watched the proud white image of Ariel waver uncertainly and then melt into the floor.

A lithe man stepped into the doorway, gloating.

Malachi's hand went beneath the waistband of his warm-up jacket and snapped out in a blur. A whirring sound descended rapidly as something sped toward the necromancer. He caught it in his hand. A small, flat, metal star with six points. A *shuriken.*

He spoke an ugly word and the six steel blades wilted in his palm. He wiped away a few drops of blood where the tips had scratched him. He dropped it to the floor. Ting ting! He smiled coldly.

Malachi returned the smile. "We'll see how strong you are now," he said. "You have garlic poisoning in your bloodstream; I smeared garlic on the edges of the star. There's no cure, and it takes a long time."

The necromancer brought his hand before his face. He turned it. He blinked once. He stepped back into the doorway and looked to the side. "They're all yours," he said. And he retreated.

They'd been in the room with him, waiting for me to come after the illusion of Ariel he'd created. Now they poured from the doorway. Had we been right there, on just this side of the door, they would never have got out. We could have killed them easily as they tried to emerge. Now it was too late to try to get that close, and we had to thank our good fortune that they were at least bottlenecked in the doorway.

Malachi got the first two with throwing stars. One in the mouth, one in the sternum. I pulled the Aero-mag and used my remaining five darts. I made all but one count and then had nothing left but Fred, and I had to stand there while Malachi hurled his remaining stars: one, two, reach for the hip, three—that one missed, slamming into the edge of the door.

The adjacent door opened and we had to run for it.

We headed the way I had come, running side by side. We dashed ten paces and Malachi darted left around a marbled corner. I hadn't expected it and swung wide, having to push off the far wall to avoid colliding with it. Something *wheet*ed past my shoulder as I rounded the corner.

I followed Malachi as he turned right, then left. He cut a man down without breaking stride, reached the stairwell door, and held it open for me while I sped past him and started up, taking the stairs three at a time.

"Down!" he said, shutting the door behind him.

I turned and headed down, intending to descend two flights and come up the other staircase. I stopped when I saw people coming up, turned back around, and ran up the stairs to the eighty-fourth floor. I opened the door, ducked in case somebody was waiting there to hack whoever came through, ran out—

Nobody in sight.

Malachi was right behind me, and we sped away. We reached the opposite stairwell, went in, and climbed back up to the eighty-fifth floor. We went out the door the same way, Malachi first this time. Someone was waiting there; he turned when Malachi barreled through and I cut him down as I emerged.

Our run became a brisk trot. I was growing short of breath. Much more of this and I wouldn't be able to fight anything.

Turn, straight, turn, turn, straight—I couldn't have traced

our route if I'd had a map; it was totally random.

"What happened," I gasped as we hurried past doors I kept expecting to fly open as we went by, "to the others?"

"Split up when we met more opposition," he said between breaths. "I don't know who's where." He slowed. "Start trying doors. But be careful."

"You don't have to tell me twice." I tried a door. It was locked. He tried a door across the hall and it opened. He peeked in quickly, looked back, and beckoned to me. We locked the door behind us and turned around.

Oh, man. The low, round table of heavy wood, with the pentagram in the center, was still there. Behind it was the office desk. Behind that was the large, black swivel chair, and behind that a picture window with a dizzying view of the East River and beyond. "Malachi," I whispered. "This is it. This is the necromancer's . . . where he was, where *I* was, before."

He raised an eyebrow. "Is that so?" He walked around, surveying the room. He ended up staring at the desk interestedly. "Good."

"Good! Christ, we're—"

"Guard the door. Let me know if you hear anyone coming. And keep quiet."

He reached beneath his warm-up suit top and drew forth a length of wire resembling a packaged guitar string. He straightened it and inserted an index finger into a loop at each end, then got behind the office desk and turned the swivel chair sideways.

"What are you—"

"Quiet, I said."

I shut up and kept my ear to the door. He began sawing at something—metal, from the rasping sound. What I'd thought was some type of garrote must have been a loop saw, and a damned good one, too, if it could cut through metal. I wondered what else he had tucked away.

I cleared my throat. The rasping stopped. "What's garlic poisoning?" I asked.

"Garlic juice in the bloodstream," he said from behind the desk. The sawing resumed.

"But . . . that means. . . ."

"No, it doesn't. It was a lie. If I'd thought of it, I would have rubbed garlic on the *shuriken*, but it didn't occur to me until we were about two thousand feet over New York." His head popped up from behind the desk, lips smiling thinly. "But it ought to keep him occupied."

I leaned closer to the door. "Someone's coming."

The smile vanished. I listened as the voices and hurried footfalls of two men went past. I waited to be sure, then told him they had gone. "They're looking for us, though. They think about thirty of us came in from above."

The sawing resumed. "Good," he muttered. "Let them keep thinking that."

Half an hour later—during which I'd had to stop him once more—he stood and carefully set the chair back upright once more behind the desk.

"What did you do?" I asked.

"I made a nasty. Come look, but don't touch."

I joined him behind the desk and knelt to see what he was pointing at. I swallowed. Yeah—nasty.

"Let's go," he said.

"Malachi—" I hesitated. "What are we looking for—the necromancer, or Ariel?"

"We'll have our hands full enough without having to look for anything, especially. Come on."

We made sure the hallway was clear. I looked back once before closing the door. The upper half of the black chair was outlined against the picture window.

I followed Malachi.

We came upon the bodies of the ten men we'd fought at the stairwell entrance. "I don't get it," I said. "Where's everyone else?"

"They must have scattered. Searching for us, probably. Tom's strategy must have worked; I get the feeling most of their men left for the lower levels when the fighting started earlier."

"So what now?"

"I guess now we look for trouble. Start opening doors again. Sooner or later we're bound to run across something."

He opened a door. Empty office room.

I shook my head and opened a door on the other side of the hall. I was halfway through closing it when I realized there were men in there. Armed men. They got up when they saw me. I slammed the door.

It opened again quickly and a man started out. On the side of the doorway across from me, Malachi crosscut and the head rolled. Blood emptied into the corridor. Voices came from inside the room.

The door behind me opened and three of them came out. Fuck—adjoining rooms. I backed up to have more fighting space. I saw motion in the corner of my eye just before I engaged, and a wordless shout came from the end of the hall. Tom Pert's voice.

And then Malachi and I were busy as hell and I didn't have time to look. A spear thrust for my chest. I pivoted, blocked with Fred, and drove the spear to the floor. The end snapped off. Now a quarterstaff, the stick came back and struck me in the waist. A little lower and it would have struck bone. It knocked the wind from me as it was. I forced myself to breathe as I slid my blade down the length of the stick and cut off his fingers. I stopped his scream quickly as I swung again.

The rest was like some demented Laurel and Hardy parody. Turning to face the next man, my feet slid out from under me as I fell to the floor in the blood. Above me I watched a thrust aimed at my back, coming from a man I didn't even know had been there, slide into the ribcage of the man I'd been turning to face. I swung blindly at the one who'd accidently killed his comrade, opening him up across the stomach. He dropped his weapon and clutched at himself. The ends of his intestines poked through flaps of skin. A swordpoint appeared from his chest, lengthened, and shot back in. He dropped. I looked up foolishly at Tom Pert. The blood on the floor had seeped through the seat of my pants and I could feel it on my skin. It was warm. More had spattered my thigh as the man above me was pierced.

I got up. Hank and Walt had arrived with Tom. Hank was covered with blood—I realized I was, too—but didn't seem hurt himself. Walt was pale. The bandage around his bicep had turned crimson. It dripped from one of the tied ends.

The noise of our fight had brought more opposition. They crowded at us from all directions and all the swordplay and scrambling and vying and killing and blood blended into one continuous swing of metal. There were fifteen of them, I think, and like Hercules and the Hydra it seemed two replaced each one that dropped. There were still only five of us.

I remember little of it. I could only react. I had to stay alive, so I maimed and killed.

At one point I was fighting back to back with Walt. At another I managed to catch a glimpse of Malachi Lee. A ring of bodies surrounded him. Hank fought calmly and methodically, guarding himself at all angles. Tom snarled bear-like at his opponents as he fought. The sound of battle brought more of them, two and three at a time, from wherever they had been looking for us.

It became hard to move because of the bodies.

We were at the intersection of two hallways and they came from all sides. The man running toward me skidded as he tried to stop to engage me, and I ran him through almost without a thought. I was granted a brief respite from the carnage and looked toward Malachi Lee. He'd become separated from us by both the bodies and the tide of opponents. Tom, Hank, and Walt fought with me at one end, and Malachi fought alone at the other. Five men were trying to get at him, but all were hesitant. They'd seen him dispatch others as quickly as they approached. But I could see how tired he was and that some of the blood on his clothes was his own.

Behind them stood a man: tall, Germanic, one-eyed. The griffin rider. He looked annoyed.

Malachi batted aside a blade, sheared off the wielder's wrist, and arced smoothly through his throat, all in less than half a second. One of the remaining four, the nearest, attempted to seize his opportunity and move in. Malachi blocked and swept down, just missing the man's shin. He was slowing.

Tom, Hank, and Walt were still engaged with their opponents. No more were coming. We stood in the midst of a buzzard's feast; some of the bodies still twitched like Galvani's frogs.

I deserted my comrades-in-arms, heading for Malachi. I slipped on the slick floor and moved Fred out of the way quickly so I wouldn't land on the blade. I got up from the twisted limbs and spreading organs. The air was thick, sour-sweet.

The number of men in front of Malachi had grown to eight. One of them reeled backward suddenly, a spear embedded in his chest. To my right, Hank's arm completed a follow-through arc.

And the rest descended on Malachi. He rolled backward, swinging his sword wildly to ward them off, and ended up on his knees, bleeding from a half dozen new wounds. The men he fought paused uncertainly as he held his sword out to the griffin rider, turning it so that the handle pointed away from himself.

The griffin rider nodded, smiling, and stepped forward.

Malachi thrust. The point disappeared into his warm-up jacket. Narrowing his eyes at the rider, he worked the blade to the left across his stomach. He brought it around in a half circle, pulled it out, and thrust again, lower this time. He yanked the blade up and his insides spilled out onto his thighs. He shuddered. His head lowered, his jaw went slack, and he fell to one side among those he had killed.

I brought my blade up, seeing Malachi beyond the reddened edge.

He didn't have a *kaishaku-nin,* a second—the one who assists, who cuts off the head before the pain becomes too great. The rider had taken that from him.

I headed for him. Hands tugged at my shoulders, stopping me— We have to get out of here Pete there's nothing we can do come on walt give me a hand with him he's—

I twisted away from them and faced the men who'd killed Malachi. The rider looked gleeful. He taunted me with his broadsword. "Get through them," he said. "Get through them and you can have me. Otherwise you aren't worth it." He nudged Malachi's body with a boot. "He didn't make it." He laughed.

The men attacked.

Tom, Walt, and Hank formed a flattened diamond with me at the head. There wasn't room in the corridor for us to fight side by side.

The first man to reach me died before he completed his initial swing. The second had a sword and shield. I raised my blade high for a downstroke and he covered up. When the blow didn't come he looked over the edge of his shield and I killed him.

They kept coming, gradually forcing us back. A stumble over a corpse would have meant death for any of us and we were bitterly tired. In less than thirty seconds I found myself with my back to a door, three attackers trying to press in on me. Before they reached me, I found the knob and pushed open the door, jumped in, slammed it, and locked it behind me. They pounded a few times, then stopped.

I turned around. Adjoining rooms to either side. Which

meant more doors leading into the corridor. I hurried to the room on the left, leaving bloody footprints on the carpet. I opened the door.

Ariel.

No illusion this time. No mistake. Her horn was rust-brown with caked blood. There was no glow like a moonlit snowfield in her coat, no light in her eyes. She held her right front leg up the way a dog holds its leg when it is injured.

And for the first time in all the times I ever saw her, she looked, not like a unicorn, but like a horse with a horn.

Chains lay on the floor behind her where she'd been shackled, but she had apparently grown too weak for even those restraints to be necessary.

"Ariel." A whisper.

Her head was lowered almost to the floor. Slowly it rose. She looked at me. A touch of the old light returned to her midnight eyes. She spoke with the trembling voice of a little girl, afraid and alone. "Peeete."

I ran to her. My sword clinked to the carpet in front of her dulled mirror hooves, and suddenly my cheek was against her and my hands clasped across her limp mane. I left blood smears where I touched her. I hugged her and said her name over and over. My eyes burned.

I drew back and looked into her eyes. There was something uncomprehending there, a puzzlement. "It's all right," I said. "Everything's going to be all right."

She blinked. "Peete?"

"It's me, it's me," I soothed. Something swelled inside my chest. She was startled when I touched her muzzle. Her head turned away and she looked at some point beyond the wall. I moved toward her. Her eyes didn't follow me.

"Ariel?"

She looked back at the sound of my voice, but not quite at me. I reached for her. She didn't register the movement.

She was blind.

She'd grown weak enough for his powers to work, and he'd blinded her. He'd had her shackles removed, and he'd blinded her.

I screamed. It broke into a long sob and she tentatively stepped forward and lowered her head, brushing the side of her face against mine.

The door to the corridor burst open and men poured in. I

grabbed my sword from the floor and turned to face them, holding it high. They avoided me, fanning out to line two of the walls, weapons readied. Behind them came the necromancer. I heard fighting in the corridor beyond. The necromancer walked calmly into the room, unable to keep a certain arrogance from his stride, until he had walked around me and stood, eyeing me, with his back to Ariel. "My friend and his Familiar have flown down to help with the battle below. As for you and yours . . ." He glanced at Ariel. Her head was cocked curiously, listening. "I see you've found out she's blind. We tried to make it real, but none of us could touch her. It's amazing to watch; we couldn't even hit her with arrows. I ended up using a spell, a simple one, really, but the result's the same."

I launched myself at him, swinging Fred. He spoke a short syllable and my fingers went lax. The sword dropped to the carpet. I tried to move my fingers but the muscles wouldn't respond.

He shook his head. "You shouldn't be so predictable. You tried that last time you were here. All I have to do is say something that enrages you, and you react." He turned to Ariel, who was silent and still, head turned to the side as she listened. "She's weak now," he said. "I don't need to wait for her to die to get her horn. She can't defend herself anymore." He stepped forward until his face almost touched mine. "You had your chance. We could have arranged for me to take the horn and let the two of you go on your way. It's your own fault. Now I'm going to take it anyway, and you're going to watch."

I strained to move. He sneered and turned back to Ariel.

Her head had lowered, horn brushing the carpet. It rose as the necromancer spoke a harsh, two-syllable word. His hands wove an invisible cat's cradle. Something began to form between them. It was visible only because it disturbed the air around it, seemed to bend and compress it into a grid. A cage, the length of Ariel's horn. It shimmered and hummed between his palms, not quite touching them.

Ariel's head cocked to the other side as the hum grew louder. The necromancer stepped forward. Ariel shifted back, keeping her weight off her right foreleg.

He brought the thing up until it was parallel with her horn. Between his hand the length of air sparkled. He spoke another word in a guttural tongue and the shaft grew brighter. Internal harmonies grew within the humming. The cage thing glowed white-hot. Ariel backed up another pace as he advanced, carefully extending his hands toward her.

If I could move—

Another pace and she was against the wall. Another word, long and ugly with clicking sounds, and she shivered. Her head lowered unwillingly until the point was level with the floor. The necromancer brought the glowing space between his hands to her head. His body blocked my view as he stepped in front of her.

"No-o-o . . ." Her voice was fragile crystal.

There was a rending sound. As the necromancer's arms extended fully, his body jackknifed forward, bending at the waist, and a foot of spiral horn came out of his back. He gasped feebly. The glowing space disappeared from between his palms as his fingers curved into claws. He grabbed her head. She lifted her horn and he came up from the floor. His body slid further down the spiral length.

I fell to the floor as movement returned, stopping my fall with my hands. I stayed there, unable to take my eyes away. Ariel tossed her head from side to side. The necromancer flailed like a broken puppet. *"No-o-o-o-o!"* she screamed.

His eyes were clenched as he held the top of her mane. His mouth was drawn back and his teeth showed in a skull-like grin. She dipped her head and he slid from her horn. He landed on the carpet, half-rolled, and was still.

She raised her head and looked at me—*looked* at me—the spell of blindness broken. Red traced a glistening path down the bottom third of her horn. I seized my sword and stood.

The necromancer's men were as transfixed as I had been. Now they looked from his spread-eagled body to us. One of them raised his bow.

Walt ran into the room. He saw Ariel and stopped abruptly, looking from her to me and then to the necromancer's body. The bowman by the wall shifted his aim and let fly as Hank and Tom appeared through the door. The arrow struck Walt in the stomach. He clutched at it and doubled over. He hit face forward on the floor, and his weight pushed the arrow in all the way.

Hank had apparently picked up another bow from one of the bodies outside. He retraced the arrow's path, lifted his bow, drew, and released. The arrow struck the bowman in the right eye.

The rest of the enemy converged. Hank had only one arrow remaining in his thigh quiver. He fitted it swiftly and fired. Another man fell. He threw the bow at someone and drew his sword.

From outside the building came Shai-tan's screech. The rider was returning.

Tom swung his broadsword in wide, powerful arcs. I took out one man before he had a chance to attack. At the side of the room I saw Ariel limp forward. She worked her way to the door, batted two men aside with her bloody horn, and hobbled out the door. I yelled after her as I fought, but she seemed not to hear.

I stabbed one of Tom's opponents in the back and ran toward the door. One man saw me and intercepted my path, a delighted grin on his face. I stopped in front of him, twitched my blade toward his head, and cut him through the midsection as he went for the fake. He was still falling as I went around him and into the corridor after Ariel.

She wasn't there. Only bodies and blood.

I ran down the corridor yelling her name, leaving Tom and Hank battling in the room behind me.

I couldn't find her on the floor. I poked my head recklessly into open doorways but there was no sign of her. Why had she run?

"Ariel!" I shouted, not caring that I was broadcasting my presence to all who might want to come after me.

Perhaps she needed to be free of this building as quickly as she could because her imprisonment was killing her. I headed for the stairwell.

"Hello there," he said mildly, rounding the corner and stopping between me and the stairwell door. "I was hoping I'd run into you." He swung his ornate broadsword casually, then brought it down so that the point rested against the floor. He leaned against it, resting the handle on his right buttock. He rubbed at the ruin of his left eye with an index finger.

Pausing to play his game might lose it for me. I rushed forward, swinging, not at him, but at the broadsword propping him up. If I knocked it away he wouldn't have a chance.

He kicked his right foot against the flat of the blade, knocking the point up, and jumped backward as it rose. I checked my low slash immediately; I'd have been an easy target on the follow through. "Malachi Lee always did know I was better," he said, taunting me with his blade. "No wonder he killed himself." He began circling to my left, his body deceptively casual, relaxed. He feinted a jab toward my chest. I started to block, stopped before my blade moved more than an inch. He smiled. "If I wanted to I could say three words, and your sword would go limp as a banana peel."

"But you won't."

His smile broadened. "No, I won't. There's a certain eloquence to a blade." He jabbed and I dodged. "And I like the feeling you get," he said, "when you beat a man at his own game."

I struck. He blocked it easily, retreating a step as he did. I struck again, and again, crosscutting, jabbing, feinting, using every trick I could. He blocked it all with equal ease, countering only when my desperate attacks left me wide open. Each time he blocked, he retreated a step, and we fought our way down the length of the hall.

He was playing with me. He wasn't breathing hard, wasn't even sweating. The bemused smile stayed on his face the whole time, changing only when he counterattacked. Then his upper lip would slide up, baring his teeth, and a greedy look flashed into his eye.

His eye. . . . He had a huge blind spot on his left. If I swung broadly, it might not even register with him. It would also open my front up to attack as my blade swung way out to the side.

I tried it. He took two rapid steps backward but didn't block. My sword cut air across the level of his neck.

Had that been intentional? Or did he freeze up when something ran in on his blind side?

I tried it again to find out, and this time he was waiting for it. He met the swing solidly, twisted his arms to bat it aside, and came in over the top. I leaned back. The point grazed my chin, the barest razor's cut. Blood dripped onto my forearm. I had a flash of memory, picturing myself staring at the point of his sword when we'd been captured, mesmerized by it as it poised before my eyes.

I sprang forward and renewed my efforts, pounding at him with one technique after another, backing him up as he blocked each one. And still I felt that he hadn't even begun to exert himself.

I pressed on, letting rage direct my blade. You killed Russ. You tried to take Ariel, you motherfucker; you gloated while Malachi Lee committed suicide in front of you. . . . It built and built until raw sounds tore from my throat with every strike. I'll back you up, all right, you bastard. I'll back you until you're against a wall and can't back up any more, and then we'll see where you go when you have to block.

He backed into an open doorway and I forced him inside. He retreated well out of range and lowered his blade, waiting for me. I recognized the room, as he no doubt wanted me to. Behind him I saw half of the round wooden table with the pentagram, the picture window looking out on the East River at the far end of the room. I'd been played along.

Then let it end here, I thought, heart pounding, head throbbing. Let it all come together here, as it had before.

I lowered Fred until the point was aimed at his throat, and I rushed in. As I came through the doorway a foot shot up from the right side, hitting me just below the right wrist. Fred flew from my grip, and as I turned toward my hidden assailant I was struck from behind and wrestled to the floor.

The rider just shook his head contemptuously as I struggled beneath the two men holding me down. He set his broadsword on the desk top and leaned against the edge. "You know," he said conversationally, "you really aren't very smart."

The two men let me stand up, but still held my arms pinned behind me. It was only the two of them and the griffin rider, but they'd been enough. I'd fallen for it, hook, line, and sinker. "'I like the feeling you get,'" I said bitterly, "'when you beat a man at his own game.'"

He laughed. "But I wasn't playing your game. You were playing mine. And in my game there aren't any rules. Except to use whatever counts." He reached behind him and picked up the broadsword. "Shai-tan hasn't had fresh meat in quite some time," he said.

I stopped struggling. He drew the edge of his sword across one finger and raised it to his right eye to examine the blood.

Struggling harder would do no good. The one holding my arms was at least six-two and all muscle. The other one stood to my left, spear readied.

The rider walked to me with his broadsword aimed at my stomach. He wiped his finger across my cheek. I tried to work up spit but my mouth was dry. "Your master's dead," I said. "Ariel killed him."

He snorted and turned away. Walking behind the desk, he gestured expansively at the room, taking in the arcane talismans, the incongruous office trappings. "You think I care? He wasn't my master; I worked for him. You think I want all this? A group of loners who don't take orders very well, a useless building, an office?" He stepped behind the desk. I tried to keep my eyes on his face. "Take him to the observation deck," he ordered. "Get some help if you need it." He pulled the swivel chair back from the desk, smiling. "Shai-tan's waiting."

I returned his smile. "'Whatever counts,'" I said as he sat down in the well-padded swivel chair—

—and kept going.

"What did you do?" I asked Malachi Lee.

"I made a nasty. Come look. . . ."

Take a piece of pipe. Cut it at a sharp angle. It now has a point: a funnel knife.

A swivel chair turns on a three-inch-wide pipe. Remove the hard bottom of the seat, but leave the stuffing in, so that the chair rests on the pipe, waiting. . . .

He took a long, wheezing breath as his own weight pushed the pointed length of metal pipe into his bowels, spearing organs as it slid deep inside him. His mouth stretched open grotesquely. His eyes bulged.

A screech from outside filled the air as he died. I turned my head aside as the griffin burst in through the huge picture window. Glass fragments exploded inward. Something stung the back of my neck and left shoulder. My arms were freed as the man holding me pressed his hands to his bleeding face. The other writhed on the floor, a shard of glass in his chest and blood streaming from one ear.

The griffin screamed. It hurled the desk aside with a sweep of its huge talon. It struck the wall and splintered. Shai-tan looked at the body of its master, impaled as it reclined horribly in the office chair. It turned to me with those glowing gold eyes, and the hot brass smell of its screech warmed the room. I backed up as it lashed out at me and it struck the man hunched on the floor with his hands over his face, blood dripping from between his fingers. He slammed into the wall and fell to the floor broken and dead.

I picked up my fallen blade as the enraged beast advanced on me, hissing from far back in its throat.

I turned and ran from the room. The griffin's screams dwindled as I fled.

twenty–three

So we'll go no more a-roving,
So late into the night,
Though the heart be still as loving,
And the moon be still as bright.

For the sword outwears its sheath,
And the soul wears out the breast,
And the heart must pause to breathe,
And love itself must rest.

Though the night was made for loving,
And the day returns too soon,
Yet we'll go no more a-roving
By the light of the moon.

—Lord Byron,
"So We'll Go No More A-Roving"

A long time later I felt somebody tapping me gingerly on the shoulder. I looked up to see Shaughnessy, Tom Pert standing beside her, and I realized that there were other people from the Washington group hurrying about, barely glancing at me where I sat leaning against a wall in the corridor. She was talking to me. I stared blankly. Night had begun to fall and the corridor was dim. Tom gently moved her aside, leaned down, and asked me things, but I only stared. They pulled the glass slivers from my shoulder and checked me all over to be seriously injured. I felt none of it. There was only the burning of exhaustion, the refusal of muscles to coordinate themselves.

I heard Ariel's name mentioned and looked at Shaughnessy as if just realizing she was there. "What? What did you say?"

Concern softened her eyes. Her hair, I noted abstractly, is matted. It's blood. "I said, a lot of people saw Ariel heading down. They said she was trying to hurry down the stairs, but one of her legs looked broken. Some of them tried to touch her, but they couldn't—"

"No," I interrupted. "They couldn't."

She finished dressing my shoulder. "They just stood aside and watched her pass. Most of them tried to stop her, though, Pete. They know about you and—"

I shrugged her off and stood. I mumbled something and picked up my sword.

"Pete, you can't go, not now. You're too weak to—"

"Let him go." Tom's voice. Firm.

She turned to him angrily. "Look at him—he's exhausted. He's in no shape to—"

"Let him go," he repeated, voice milder than before.

I sheathed my sword and looked at him. He nodded. I turned without a word and walked down the body-strewn corridor to the stairwell. Shaughnessy followed.

It grew darker as we descended, footsteps echoing. I ignored her all the way down.

We came out on the ground floor. It was worse than the top had been. More bodies, ours and theirs. I picked my way around them and walked out onto Fifth Avenue. Shaughnessy stayed behind me, not daring to speak. I searched up and down the streets of the dark, empty city, stopping only when I dropped in my tracks from sheer exhaustion. I slept on the sidewalk until daybreak. Shaughnessy was beside me when I woke up. I got up and began walking again. She heard me and hurried after me.

I looked all that day and didn't find her. How could I tell which way she'd gone? A unicorn leaves no trail, no tracks, no hint of its passing, except for the impression it leaves on those few who see it pass.

Shaughnessy trailed after me as I walked the streets calling Ariel's name. In the afternoon I heard the sound of Shai-tan's shrill screeching. I tightened my face and thrust an extended middle finger in the direction it had come from. With the rider dead, the griffin would die, also, over a matter of days.

Toward evening I found a man on the street who said he'd seen her. My belligerence got me nowhere, so Shaughnessy questioned him while I waited impatiently. He glanced at me nervously as she explained that the unicorn was my Familiar and that I only wanted to know where she was.

"All I can tell you is she went that way." He pointed north.

I turned on my heel and walked in the direction he pointed.

We searched for her for five days. I slept only when I couldn't go on, ate only when forced to by the need to replenish my strength. Shaughnessy stayed with me and helped me as much as she could. For the most part I ignored her, needing the help yet wanting to do it alone. Whatever she thought of me, she kept it to herself.

On the fourth night, as I was sullenly eating the rabbit I'd snared, she began to talk. She went on about the battle and how it had all been so much easier than they'd expected it to be, that the necromancer's forces had been disorganized and unprepared—

I waved her to silence. "I don't care," was all I said. After I finished eating, I lay on the ground, facing away from her so she couldn't see me crying, and I pretended to sleep.

Next day we found somebody who said he'd seen her. He was a fat man and spoke to us eagerly, arm around a fatter woman.

"Yeah, most gorgeous thing I ever saw," he said, bobbing his round head. "Moved quieter than a cat. Leg was broken, though, poor thing."

We left him and searched the surrounding countryside. New York had become a rolling green place as we traveled north.

We found no sign of her.

That night Shaughnessy heard the sobs that wracked me as I lay on the grass, turned away from where she slept a few yards distant. I tried to keep them to myself, but they wouldn't stay contained and they flowed over the edge of my restraint. I felt tired, so very goddamned tired.

"Pete?" Her voice behind me, a whisper over the cricket sound.

My throat was too blocked to answer. She moved until she

was beside me. I tried to hide my face. She touched my neck.

"Pete, we'll find her."

It opened up then; whatever control I'd had burst at the seams. I shuddered with the force of my crying and she hugged me and stroked my hair. I wanted to bury myself in her breast, feeling like a baby in a rocking chair with its mother.

"We'll find her, Pete," she repeated, cradling my head. I needed to wipe my nose, but I didn't want to move. "We'll find her, you know we will. She wouldn't leave you. She's just confused, like you're confused, and she'll come back." She talked almost as if to herself, holding me tightly with one arm, stroking my hair with the other. I pressed my head against her. Her shirt was wet where my tears had fallen.

I lay there long after my tears had subsided and her stroking became less urgent. The wind blew across the cheek that faced up. I shivered.

She pressed closer to me, huddling me into her warmth, her face next to mine. She stroked my back. I opened my eyes, expecting to see her watching me, but her own eyes were closed.

I remembered the night we had kissed on board the *Lady Woof*. It had felt right then. Impulsively I reached out and stroked her cheek. She opened her eyes as it slid softly beneath my fingertips.

I kissed her. A brief kiss, and I pulled my head back and looked at her. There was no expression in her eyes, none that I could read. She bent her head to me. We kissed again. I felt her mouth opening and, after a moment's hesitation, mine followed. I felt an uncomfortable pressure somewhere deep inside. My breathing grew harsher, and I had to pull my lips back a fraction because my nose could not take in air fast enough. She pressed me hard against her. She kissed my cheek gently, kissed me again on the lips. I tasted salt from my dried tears on her tongue. She brought one hand up and turned my head to one side. She shifted forward a bit. Warm breath rushed into my ear, amplified, tingling. Her tongue traced the outside curves, working its spiraling way inward until it darted rapidly in and out of the center of my ear. I grabbed her arm, hard. I turned my head until my tongue was sliding against hers again, and this time the taste was the faintly bitter one of ear wax. We rolled until I was on top of her. She brought both hands to my head and tugged gently back until I was looking straight ahead, and she licked my throat. I did the same for her, feeling hurried, impatient. She moved beneath me. Her hair was fanned out on the grass, framing her face. Her eyes were closed and her mouth formed a small O, face tilted away as I flicked my tongue along the smooth contours of her neck. Her nails dug into my back. I reached her ear. Her hands clenched, bunching up my shirt. She began working it up, and I pulled my head from her as she brought it over my shoulders, my head, down my arms, and onto the grass by her head. I brought my mouth back to hers, and she clutched at me. Her right hand grabbed my shoulder where the slivers of glass had bit in. I sucked in a pained breath which hissed through clenched teeth.

"Sorry," she breathed, and kissed me.

My hips ground against her, a movement I did not consciously control. She brought her hands to my chest and pushed me away gently, sliding down beneath me and bringing her mouth to my chest. I gasped as her tongue lapped at my left nipple, and my breath was ragged as I expelled it. She brought her mouth to the other nipple. A small brightness exploded in the pit of my stomach, like fear, but not fear. It spread through me.

I pushed her back to the grass and roughly brought my mouth to hers. I worked my way down until the fabric of her shirt collar slid against my lips.

My hands trembled as I unbuttoned her shirt.

She sat up after the last button was undone, after I had slowly pulled it from where it had been tucked into her pants to get to it, and I drew it over her shoulders and down her arms.

Her bra was frosty white in the moonlight, contrasting with the dark of her. I kissed her shoulder and lay her back down. She arched her back as it touched the cold grass. I kissed her again, feeling the rough fabric of her brassiere tickling my chest, sliding against the skin. She helped me remove it because I didn't know how.

The fear hit me then. I looked into her eyes. She didn't smile, I think because she knew I might interpret it as amusement. Instead her hand found mine, and she brought it up to her breast. She urged me with gentle pressures and stroked the top of my hand when I continued. Her nipple grew taut beneath my palm. She moaned, and the sound of it made my heart beat faster. I brought my lips down to it, not quite sure what to do.

I brushed back and forth, and then sucked like an infant.

The fear hit me again, and I took my mouth from her and lay my head against her chest, feeling it rise and fall. She made a noise in her throat and turned me over until she was on top. Her hair tickled my nose and I brushed it aside. She was breathing hard and her breasts pressed into me. I shivered as she slid down until her mouth again covered my nipple. It gave way to trembling as her hands found my belt, slid it through the buckle, pulled it, unsnapped my pants, and fumbled with the tab of my zipper. I held onto her head, pushing it tightly into me, and shook all over. I could not think. There were things here that had always been here, lying half-submerged. There was a low rasp as she tugged down my zipper, and her fingers slid beneath the elastic band of my underwear. I clenched my eyes. My thigh muscles knotted up.

And then she was pulling down my pants and underwear simultaneously, making me arch my back to pull them over my buttocks, and they were sliding down my thighs, over my knees, my shins, my feet. She tossed them aside and stood up. I opened my eyes. Her breasts rose and fell as she breathed. I tried to swallow and couldn't. The night air moved, causing a prickling sensation in my scrotum as it whispered across my pubic hair. She took off her own pants and panties at the same time, impatiently, stepping out with one foot and then the other, tossing them aside, kneeling back down beside me. She passed her head back and forth. Her hair brushed against me from chest to stomach. She stopped at one end of the rhythmic swinging. Her warm breath, the wet-slick sliding of her tongue up and down the shaft of my penis, and then the soft ring of warmth, descending and ascending. She brought her mouth away and I looked at her through half-closed eyes as she straddled me. The insides of her thighs were warm against the tops of my own, a contrast to the night air moving across the rest of me. She leaned forward and kissed me, and began moving back and forth, so slowly.

"Don't be afraid," she whispered.

"Shaughnessy—"

"Shhh."

I felt that she was wet, rubbing against me, coating the underside of my hard penis. There was a faint ringing in my ears, and through it I heard the soft, coarse sound of her pubic hair brushing against mine. She lifted a little and reached down with one hand to lift me and guide me into her.

"Shaughn—"

She pressed down. A little hiss escaped between her teeth.

And then she was pounding and it was warm and I was grabbing her hips and there was nothing but moving, wet moving, and my own hips bucked uncontrollably, and she arched her back and turned her face up toward the moon, biting her bottom lip, and the expression she wore was pain but not pain and it was happening so frighteningly fast and then something began creeping stealthily into my head on nightbird wings, and then it was there and it was light and light pulsing, spreading, and I could feel the hot gushing into her, and it rose, and rose, and then slowed into rocking movement that gradually stopped.

She fell against me, and she was crying, and our tears mingled together.

twenty-four

"I was looking for my people," the unicorn said. "Have you seen them, magician? They are wild and sea-white, like me."

Schmendrick shook his head gravely. "I have never seen anyone like you, not while I was awake. There were supposed to be a few unicorns left when I was a boy, but I knew only one man who had ever seen one. They are surely gone, lady, all but you. When you walk, you make an echo where they used to be."

—Peter S. Beagle,
The Last Unicorn

I awoke at the sound of something crashing through the brush. It was midmorning. Shaughnessy's naked form was curled beside me. Something was coming toward us, something big, from the sound. Conscious of my nakedness, I picked up Fred and waited as the trampling neared.

The bushes parted and Ariel emerged.

She stopped when she saw me. Her head came up as though she were sniffing the air. She stepped toward me and stopped suddenly after a few paces. Her head was cocked questioningly, the way it had when she'd been blind.

There was a rust-colored smear on her neck where I'd hugged her in the Empire State Building. The dried blood on her horn had begun to flake off. Her hair was matted and tangled. Gone were the glossy rainbow ripples that used to spread across her in the sunlight as she moved. For the first time in her life, her coat was dirty. She looked like a wild thing, a thing that had never before seen a human being.

The first time I had ever seen her I had waded cautiously from a lake. I hadn't been ashamed of my nakedness then.

She blinked. She'd begun to put weight on her right front leg as she walked, and that was good. It would heal now. The pain was gone, New York but a memory. A bad memory, one with scars, but one that would also heal, with time and love.

She looked thin.

A stirring beside me as Shaughnessy moved in her sleep. I looked at her nude body and remembered.

"Ariel," I whispered. She couldn't have heard.

I stepped toward her. She didn't move. Stepped again, until I stood before her. I reached out and she backed away. I was close enough to see the outline of my naked form in her dark eyes.

Not this. Please, not this.

But as I stepped toward her again with both hands outstretched, she snorted and turned her head aside. A pool formed at the bottom of each dark eye, and a single tear flowed down her muzzle, crystalline.

"Ariel," I said again.

We looked at each other. I have walked the road with you, my beloved creature of purity. We've laughed and cried and traveled and fought, and now it's come to this. I felt cold inside.

"I can't," I said. "I can't, I can't." A spasm took me, a wave that made me twitch once and then was gone. The side of her muzzle glistened from her tears. I stepped closer to her. "Please—"

And she stepped back.

My sword had fallen from my hand, unnoticed until now. I looked at it and lowered myself to my knees before her. I looked up at her, then at the sword. She stepped forward and placed her horn between my hand and the blade. Gently, she nudged the sword away. I looked into her eyes and the pride was still there, now a part of the wildness. I tried once more to touch her, and she gave the barest shake of her head.

Tears brimmed and I shut my eyes. I brought my clenched fists to them and rubbed hard, as if it would scour me clean somehow, and when I opened them again she was gone.

I stared at the space where she had been for a long time and something broke inside me.

It feels as though a lot of time has passed since then, though only a year has gone by. We like to think our lives stop at these climactic spots, that all else will be superfluous, but of course that isn't so. The cliché holds true: life goes on.

Shaughnessy and I set ourselves up in a house in North Carolina. The place was in pretty good shape but required some repairs, and for a few months I lost myself in work. When that didn't satisfy me I hunted alone for days.

Even when I surfaced from my fugues I was cold to Shaughnessy, treating her more as a roommate than as the friend she wanted to be, or even the lover she was. Sometimes at night, when she lay breathing deeply beside me, I would lie awake in bed and, if I strained hard enough, just at the threshold of hearing, I felt I could hear the sound of wind chimes tinkling, the sound of silver hooves. I didn't, of course—life goes on, yes, and our capacity for self-deception accompanies it. It must have been hard for Shaughnessy to live in a shadow.

We went on like this, living our separate lives together, until the middle of winter when I was tracking a deer and thought I saw a unicorn. I couldn't be sure; it may have just been a trick of the snow. Somehow the incident pried me open and made me see what I had kept inside for half a year.

I spent that night crying in Shaughnessy's arms. I had been numb too long. The house, the work, our relationship. The façade.

But no more charades. We talked, Shaughnessy and I, and it surfaced that there *was* something between us, something I had too long denied, something we both thought worth saving. But the foundation of our relationship couldn't lie in the past, and I could no longer be content with the stagnancy of the present. Rolling stones and moss, I guess.

Before I could reconcile moving on, however, I felt the need to cauterize old wounds, and so this account was written. I will leave it behind when we go. It was intended as a cathartic, but if you wish I suppose you may read it as a sort of subjective history of the first years of these odd times.

Shaughnessy and I are taking only what we need to get by as we wander the land. It is less safe than domestic tranquility, perhaps, but I would rather live the life of a dolphin than that of a clam.

Besides—the world is a different place now, and I haven't even begun to scratch its surface.

ABOUT THE AUTHOR

Steven R. Boyett was born in Atlanta in 1960 and grew up in Miami. He attended the University of Tampa on a writing scholarship for two years, quit before it could become fatal, and wrote his first novel. You've just read it. He has studied Tae Kwon Do for ten years. Together with Lisa Simonne Pianka and two quirky dogs, Mr. Boyett lives in Gainesville, where he works as a word-processor operator at the University of Florida.